Dear Reader,

I'm delighted to welcome you to a very special Bestselling Author Collection for 2024! In celebration of Harlequin's 75 years in publishing, this collection features fan-favorite stories from some of our readers' most cherished authors. Each book also includes a free full-length story by an exciting writer from one of our current programs.

Our company has grown and changed since its inception 75 years ago. Today, Harlequin publishes more than 100 titles a month in 30 countries and 15 languages, with stories for a diverse readership across a range of genres and formats, including hardcover, trade paperback, mass-market paperback, ebook and audiobook.

But our commitment to you, our romance reader, remains the same: in every Harlequin romance, a guaranteed happily-ever-after!

Thank you for coming on this journey with us. And happy reading as we embark on the next 75 years of bringing joy to readers around the world!

Dianne Moggy

Vice-President, Editorial

Harlequin

Debbie Macomber is a #1 *New York Times* bestselling author and a leading voice in women's fiction worldwide. Her work has appeared on every major bestseller list, with more than a hundred and seventy million copies in print, and she is a multiple-award winner. The Hallmark Channel based a television series on Debbie's popular Cedar Cove books. For more information, visit her website, debbiemacomber.com.

Lee Tobin McClain is the *New York Times* bestselling author of emotional small-town romances featuring flawed characters who find healing through friendship, faith and family. Lee grew up in Ohio and now lives in Western Pennsylvania, where she enjoys hiking with her goofy goldendoodle, visiting writer friends and admiring her daughter's mastery of the latest TikTok dances. Learn more about her books at leetobinmcclain.com.

RAINY DAY KISSES

#1 *NEW YORK TIMES* BESTSELLING AUTHOR
DEBBIE MACOMBER

BESTSELLING AUTHOR COLLECTION

BESTSELLING AUTHOR COLLECTION

Recycling programs for this product may not exist in your area.

ISBN-13: 978-1-335-46620-4

Rainy Day Kisses
First published in 1990. This edition published in 2024.
Copyright © 1990 by Debbie Macomber

A Friend to Trust
First published in 2023. This edition published in 2024.
Copyright © 2023 by Lee Tobin McClain

For questions and comments about the quality of this book, please contact us at CustomerService@Harlequin.com.

TM and ® are trademarks of Harlequin Enterprises ULC.

 Harlequin Enterprises ULC
22 Adelaide St. West, 41st Floor
Toronto, Ontario M5H 4E3, Canada
www.Harlequin.com

Printed in U.S.A.

CONTENTS

RAINY DAY KISSES

Debbie Macomber

Prologue

"Is it true, Michelle?" Jolyn Johnson rolled her chair from her cubicle across the aisle and nearly caught the wheel on a drooping length of plastic holly. The marketing department had won the Christmas decoration contest for the third year in a row.

Michelle Davidson glanced away from her computer screen and immediately noticed her neighbor's inquisitive expression. It certainly hadn't taken long for the rumors to start. She realized, of course, that it was unusual for a high school senior to be accepted as an intern at a major company like Windy Day Toys, one of the most prestigious toy manufacturers in the country. She'd be working here during the Christmas and summer breaks—and she'd actually be getting paid!

Michelle had connections—*good* connections. She'd been a bit naive, perhaps, to assume she could keep her relationship to Uncle Nate under wraps. Still, she'd hoped that with the Christmas season in full swing, her fellow workers would be too preoccupied with the holidays to pay any attention to her. Apparently that wasn't the case.

"Whatever you heard is probably true," she answered, doing her best to look busy.

"Then you *are* related to Mr. Townsend?" Jolyn's eyes grew large.

"I'm his niece."

"Really?" the other girl said in awe. "Wow."

"I'm the one who introduced my aunt Susannah to my uncle Nate." If the fact that Michelle was related to the company owner and CEO impressed Jolyn, then this piece of information should send her over the moon.

"You've got to be kidding! When was that? I thought the Townsends have been married for years and years. I heard they have three children!"

"Tessa, Junior and Emma Jane." When she left the office this afternoon, Michelle would be heading over to her aunt and uncle's home on Lake Washington to babysit. She didn't think it would be good form to mention that, however. She figured interns for Windy Day Toys didn't usually babysit on the side.

"*You* were responsible for introducing your aunt and uncle?" Jolyn repeated, sounding even more incredulous. "When?" she asked again.

"I was young at the time," Michelle answered evasively.

"You must have been."

Michelle grinned and gave in to Jolyn's obvious curiosity. Might as well tell the truth, which was bound to emerge anyway. "I think that might be why Uncle Nate agreed to let me intern here." He loved to tease her about her—admittedly inadvertent—role as matchmaker, but Michelle knew he was grateful. So was her aunt Susannah.

Michelle planned to major in marketing when she enrolled in college next September, and doing an internship this winter and during the summer holidays was the perfect opportunity to find out whether she liked the job. It was only her second day, but already Michelle could see that she was going to love it.

A couple of the other workers had apparently been listening in on the conversation and rolled their chairs toward her cubicle, as well. "You can't stop the story there," Karen said.

Originally Michelle had hoped to avoid this kind of attention, but she accepted that it was inevitable. "When my aunt was almost thirty, she was absolutely sure she'd never marry or have a family."

"Susannah Townsend?"

This news astonished the small gathering, as Michelle had guessed it would. Besides working with Nate, her mother and aunt had started their own company, Motherhood, Inc., about ten years ago and they'd done incredibly well. It seemed that everything the Townsend name touched turned to gold.

"I know it sounds crazy, considering everything that's happened since."

"Exactly," Jolyn murmured.

"Aunt Susannah's a great mother. But," Michelle added, "at one time, she couldn't even figure out how to change a diaper." Little did the others know that the diaper Susannah had such difficulty changing had been Michelle's.

"This is a joke, right?"

"I swear it's true. Hardly anyone knows the whole story."

"What really happened?" the third woman, whom Michelle didn't know, asked.

Michelle shrugged. "Actually, I happened."

"What do you mean?"

"My mother was desperate for a babysitter and asked her sister, my aunt Susannah, to look after me."

"How old were you?"

"About nine months," she admitted.

"So how did everything turn out the way it did?" Jolyn asked.

"I'd love to hear, too," Karen said, and the third woman nodded vigorously.

Michelle leaned back in her chair. "Make yourselves comfortable, my friends, because I have a story to tell," she began dramatically. "A story in which I play a crucial part."

The three women scooted their chairs closer.

"It all started seventeen years ago…"

One

Susannah Simmons blamed her sister, Emily, for this. As far as she was concerned, her weekend was going to be the nightmare on Western Avenue. Emily, a nineties version of the "earth mother," had asked Susannah, the dedicated career woman, to babysit nine-month-old Michelle.

"Emily, I don't think so." Susannah had balked when her sister first phoned. What did she, a twenty-eight-year-old business executive, know about babies? The answer was simple—not much.

"I'm desperate."

Her sister must have been to ask her. Everyone knew what Susannah was like around babies—not only Michelle, but infants in general. She just wasn't the motherly type. Interest rates, negotiations, troubleshooting, staff motivation, these were her strong points. Not formula, teething and diapers.

It was nothing short of astonishing that the same two parents could have produced such completely different daughters. Emily baked her own oat-bran muffins, subscribed to *Organic Gardening* and hung her wash to dry on a clothesline—even in winter.

Susannah, on the other hand, wasn't the least bit domestic and had no intention of ever cultivating the trait. She was too busy with her career to let such tedious tasks disrupt her corporate lifestyle. She was currently a director in charge of marketing for H&J Lima, the nation's largest sporting goods company. The position occupied almost every minute of her time.

Susannah Simmons was a woman on the rise. Her name appeared regularly in trade journals as an up-and-coming achiever. None of that mattered to Emily, however, who needed a babysitter.

"You know I wouldn't ask you if it wasn't an emergency," Emily had pleaded.

Susannah felt herself weakening. Emily was, after all, her younger sister. "Surely, there's got to be someone better qualified."

Emily had hesitated, then tearfully blurted, "I don't know what I'll do if you won't take Michelle." She began to sob pitifully. "Robert's left me."

"What?" If Emily hadn't gained her full attention earlier, she did now. If her sister was an earth mother, then her brother-in-law, Robert Davidson, was Abraham Lincoln, as solid and upright as a thirty-foot oak. "I don't believe it."

"It's true," Emily wailed. "He…he claims I give Michelle all my attention and that I never have enough energy left to be a decent wife." She paused to draw in a quavery breath. "I know he's right…but being a good mother demands so much time and effort."

"I thought Robert wanted six children."

"He does…or did." Emily's sobbing began anew.

"Oh, Emily, it can't be that bad," Susannah had murmured in a soothing voice, thinking as fast as she could.

"I'm sure you misunderstood Robert. He loves you and Michelle, and I'm positive he has no intention of leaving you."

"He does," Emily went on to explain between hiccuping sobs. "He asked me to find someone to look after Michelle for a while. He says we have to have some time to ourselves, or our marriage is dead."

That sounded pretty drastic to Susannah.

"I swear to you, Susannah, I've called everyone who's ever babysat Michelle before, but no one's available. No one—not even for one night. When I told Robert I hadn't found a sitter, he got so angry...and that's not like Robert."

Susannah agreed. The man was the salt of the earth. Not once in the five years she'd known him could she recall him even raising his voice.

"He told me that if I didn't take this weekend trip to San Francisco with him he was going alone. I *tried* to find someone to watch Michelle," Emily said. "I honestly tried, but there's no one else, and now Robert's home and he's loading up the car and, Susannah, he's serious. He's going to leave without me and from the amount of luggage he's taking, I don't think he plans to come back."

The tale of woe barely skimmed the surface of Susannah's mind. The key word that planted itself in fertile ground was *weekend*. "I thought you said you only needed me for one night?" she asked.

At that point, Susannah should've realized she wasn't much brighter than a brainless mouse, innocently nibbling away at the cheese in a steel trap.

Emily sniffled once more, probably for effect, Susannah mused darkly.

"We'll be flying back to Seattle early Sunday afternoon. Robert's got some business in San Francisco Saturday morning, but the rest of the weekend is free... and it's been such a long time since we've been alone."

"Two days and two nights," Susannah said slowly, mentally tabulating the hours.

"Oh, please, Susannah, my whole marriage is at stake. You've always been such a good big sister. I know I don't deserve anyone as good as you."

Silently Susannah agreed.

"Somehow I'll find a way to repay you," Emily continued.

Susannah closed her eyes. Her sister's idea of repaying her was usually freshly baked zucchini bread shortly after Susannah announced she was watching her weight.

"Susannah, please!"

It was then that Susannah had caved in to the pressure. "All right. Go ahead and bring Michelle over."

Somewhere in the distance, she could've sworn she heard the echo of a mousetrap slamming shut.

By the time Emily and Robert had deposited their offspring at Susannah's condominium, her head was swimming with instructions. After planting a kiss on her daughter's rosy cheek, Emily handed the clinging Michelle to a reluctant Susannah.

That was when the nightmare began in earnest.

As soon as her sister left, Susannah could feel herself tense up. Even as a teenager, she hadn't done a lot of babysitting; it wasn't that she didn't like children, but kids didn't seem to take to her.

Holding the squalling infant on her hip, Susannah paced while her mind buzzed with everything she was supposed to remember. She knew what to do in case of diaper rash, colic and several other minor emergencies, but Emily hadn't said one word about how to keep Michelle from crying.

"Shhh," Susannah cooed, jiggling her niece against her hip. She swore the child had a cry that could've been heard a block away.

After the first five minutes, her calm cool composure began to crack under the pressure. She could be in real trouble here. The tenant agreement she'd signed specifically stated "no children."

"Hello, Michelle, remember me?" Susannah asked, doing everything she could think of to quiet the baby. Didn't the kid need to breathe? "I'm your auntie Susannah, the business executive."

Her niece wasn't impressed. Pausing only a few seconds to gulp for air, Michelle increased her volume and glared at the door as if she expected her mother to miraculously appear if she cried long and hard enough.

"Trust me, kid, if I knew a magic trick that'd bring your mother back, I'd use it now."

Ten minutes. Emily had been gone a total of ten minutes. Susannah was seriously considering giving the state Children's Protective Services a call and claiming that a stranger had abandoned a baby on her doorstep.

"Mommy will be home soon," Susannah murmured wistfully.

Michelle screamed louder. Susannah started to worry about her stemware. The kid's voice could shatter glass.

More tortured minutes passed, each one an eternity. Susannah was desperate enough to sing. Not knowing any appropriate lullabies, she began with a couple of ditties from her childhood, but quickly exhausted those. Michelle didn't seem to appreciate them anyway. Since

Susannah didn't keep up with the current top twenty, the best she could do was an old Christmas favorite. Somehow singing "Jingle Bells" in the middle of September didn't feel right.

"Michelle," Susannah pleaded, willing to stand on her head if it would keep the baby from wailing, "your mommy will be back, I assure you."

Michelle apparently didn't believe her.

"How about if I buy municipal bonds and put them in your name?" Susannah tried next. "Tax-free bonds, Michelle! This is an offer you shouldn't refuse. All you need to do is stop crying. Oh, please stop crying."

Michelle wasn't interested.

"All right," Susannah cried, growing desperate. "I'll sign over my Microsoft stock. That's my final offer, so you'd better grab it while I'm in a generous mood."

Michelle answered by gripping Susannah's collar with both of her chubby fists and burying her wet face in a once spotless white silk blouse.

"You're a tough nut to crack, Michelle Margaret Davidson," Susannah muttered, gently patting her niece's back as she paced. "You want blood, don't you, kid? You aren't going to be satisfied with anything less."

A half hour after Emily had left, Susannah was ready to resort to tears herself. She'd started singing again, returning to her repertoire of Christmas songs. "You'd better watch out,/you'd better not cry,/ Aunt Susannah's here telling you why...."

She was just getting into the lyrics when someone knocked heavily on her door.

Like a thief caught in the act, Susannah whirled around, fully expecting the caller to be the building superintendent. No doubt there'd been complaints and he'd come to confront her.

Expelling a weary sigh, Susannah realized she was defenseless. The only option she had was to throw herself on his mercy. She squared her shoulders and walked across the lush carpet, prepared to do exactly that.

Only it wasn't necessary. The building superintendent wasn't the person standing on the other side of her door. It was her new neighbor, wearing a baseball cap and a faded T-shirt, and looking more than a little disgruntled.

"The crying and the baby I can take," he said, crossing his arms and relaxing against the door frame, "but your singing has got to go."

"Very funny," she grumbled.

"The kid's obviously distressed."

Susannah glared at him. "Nothing gets past you, does it?"

"Do something."

"I'm trying." Apparently Michelle didn't like this stranger any more than Susannah did because she buried her face in Susannah's collar and rubbed it vigorously back and forth. That at least helped muffle her cries, but there was no telling what it would do to white silk. "I offered her my Microsoft stock and it didn't do any good," Susannah explained. "I was even willing to throw in my municipal bonds."

"You offered her stocks and bonds, but did you suggest dinner?"

"Dinner?" Susannah echoed. She hadn't thought of that. Emily claimed she'd fed Michelle, but Susannah vaguely remembered something about a bottle.

"The poor thing's probably starving."

"I think she's supposed to have a bottle," Susannah

said. She turned and glanced at the assorted bags Emily and Robert had deposited in her condominium, along with the necessary baby furniture. From the number of things stacked on the floor, it must seem as if she'd been granted permanent guardianship. "There's got to be one in all this paraphernalia."

"I'll find it—you keep the kid quiet."

Susannah nearly laughed out loud. If she was able to keep Michelle quiet, he wouldn't be here in the first place. She imagined she could convince CIA agents to hand over top-secret documents more easily than she could silence one distressed nine-month-old infant.

Without waiting for an invitation, her neighbor moved into the living room. He picked up one of the three overnight bags and rooted through that. He hesitated when he pulled out a stack of freshly laundered diapers, and glanced at Susannah. "I didn't know anyone used cloth diapers anymore."

"My sister doesn't believe in anything disposable."

"Smart woman."

Susannah made no comment, and within a few seconds noted that he'd come across a plastic bottle. He removed the protective cap and handed the bottle to Susannah, who looked at it and blinked. "Shouldn't the milk be heated?"

"It's room temperature, and frankly, at this point I don't think the kid's going to care."

He was right. The instant Susannah placed the rubber nipple in her niece's mouth, Michelle grasped the bottle with both hands and sucked at it greedily.

For the first time since her mother had left, Michelle stopped crying. The silence was pure bliss. Susannah's tension eased, and she released a sigh that went all the way through her body.

"You might want to sit down," he suggested next.

Susannah did, and with Michelle cradled awkwardly in her arms, leaned against the back of the sofa, trying not to jostle her charge.

"That's better, isn't it?" Her neighbor pushed the baseball cap farther back on his head, looking pleased with himself.

"Much better." Susannah smiled shyly up at him. They hadn't actually met, but she'd certainly noticed her new neighbor. As far as looks went, he was downright handsome. She supposed most women would find his mischievous blue eyes and dark good looks appealing. He was tanned, but she'd have wagered a month's pay that his bronzed features weren't the result of any machine. He obviously spent a great deal of time outdoors, which led her to the conclusion that he didn't work. At least not in an office. And frankly, she doubted he was employed outside of one, either. The clothes he wore and the sporadic hours he kept had led her to speculate about him earlier. If he had money, which apparently he did or else he wouldn't be living in this complex, then he'd inherited it.

"I think it's time I introduced myself," he said conversationally, sitting on the ottoman across from her. "I'm Nate Townsend."

"Susannah Simmons," she said. "I apologize for all the racket. My niece and I are just getting acquainted and—oh, boy—it's going to be a long weekend, so bear with us."

"You're babysitting for the weekend?"

"Two days and two nights." It sounded like a whole

lifetime to Susannah. "My sister and her husband are off on a second honeymoon. Normally my parents would watch Michelle and love doing it, but they're visiting friends in Florida."

"It was kind of you to offer."

Susannah thought it best to correct this impression. "Trust me, I didn't volunteer. In case you hadn't noticed, I'm not very maternal."

"You've got to support her back a little more," he said, watching Michelle.

Susannah tried, but it felt awkward to hold on to her niece *and* the bottle.

"You're doing fine."

"Sure," Susannah muttered. She felt like someone with two left feet who'd been unexpectedly ushered onto center stage and told to perform the lead in *Swan Lake*.

"Relax, will you?" Nate encouraged.

"I told you already I'm not into this motherhood business," she snapped. "If you think you can do better, you feed her."

"You're doing great. Don't worry about it."

She wasn't doing great at all, and she knew it, but this was as good as she got.

"When's the last time you had anything to eat?" he asked.

"I beg your pardon?"

"You sound hungry to me."

"Well, I'm not," Susannah said irritably.

"I think you are, but don't worry, I'll take care of that." He walked boldly into her kitchen and paused in front of the refrigerator. "Your mood will improve once you have something in your stomach."

Shifting Michelle higher, Susannah stood and followed him. "You can't just walk in here and—"

"I'll say I can't," he murmured, his head inside her fridge. "Do you realize there's nothing in here except an open box of baking soda and a jar full of pickle juice?"

"I eat out a lot," Susannah said defensively.

"I can see that."

Michelle had finished the bottle and made a slurping sound that prompted Susannah to remove the nipple from her mouth. The baby's eyes were closed. Little wonder, Susannah thought. She was probably exhausted. Certainly Susannah was, and it was barely seven on Friday evening. The weekend was just beginning.

Setting the empty bottle on the kitchen counter, Susannah awkwardly lifted Michelle onto her shoulder and patted her back until she produced a tiny burp. Feeling a real sense of accomplishment, Susannah smiled proudly.

Nate chuckled and when Susannah glanced in his direction, she discovered him watching her, his grin warm and appraising. "You're going to be fine."

Flustered, Susannah lowered her gaze. She always disliked it when a man looked at her that way, examining her features and forming a judgment about her by the size of her nose, or the direction in which her eyebrows grew. Most men seemed to believe they'd been granted a rare gift of insight and could determine a woman's entire character just by looking at her face. Unfortunately, Susannah's was too austere by conventional standards to be classified as beautiful. Her eyes were deep-set and dark, her cheekbones high. Her nose came almost straight from her forehead and together with her full mouth made her look like a classic Greek sculpture. Not pretty, she thought. Interesting perhaps.

It was during Susannah's beleaguered self-evaluation that Michelle stirred and started jabbering cheerfully, reaching one hand toward a strand of Susannah's dark hair.

Without her realizing it, her chignon had come undone. Michelle had somehow managed to loosen the pins and now the long dark tresses fell haphazardly over Susannah's shoulder. If there was one thing Susannah was meticulous about, and actually there were several, it was her appearance. She must look a rare sight, in an expensive business suit with a stained white blouse and her hair tumbling over her shoulder.

"Actually I've been waiting for an opportunity to introduce myself," Nate said, leaning against the counter. "But after the first couple of times we saw each other, our paths didn't seem to cross again."

"I've been working a lot of overtime lately." If the truth be known, Susannah almost always put in extra hours. Often she brought work home with her. She was dedicated, committed and hardworking. Her neighbor, however, didn't seem to possess any of those qualities. She strongly suspected that everything in life had come much too easily for Nate Townsend. She'd never seen him without his baseball cap or his T-shirt. Somehow she doubted he even owned a suit. And if he did, it probably wouldn't look right on him. Nate Townsend was definitely a football-jersey type of guy.

He seemed likable—friendly and outgoing—but from what she'd seen, he lacked ambition. Apparently there'd never been anything he'd wanted badly enough to really strive for.

"I'm glad we had the chance to introduce ourselves," Susannah added, walking back into the living room and toward her front door. "I appreciate the help, but as you said, Michelle and I are going to be fine."

"It didn't sound that way when I arrived."

"I was just getting my feet wet," she returned, defending herself, "and why are you arguing with me? You're the one who said I was doing all right."

"I lied."

"Why would you do that?"

Nate shrugged nonchalantly. "I thought a little self-confidence would do you good, so I offered it."

Susannah glared at him, resenting his attitude. So much for the nice-guy-who-lives-next-door image she'd had of him. "I don't need any favors from you."

"You may not," he agreed, "but unfortunately Michelle does. The poor kid was starving and you didn't so much as suspect."

"I would've figured it out."

Nate gave her a look that seemed to cast doubt on her intelligence, and Susannah frowned right back. She opened the door with far more force than necessary and flipped her hair over her shoulder with flair a Paris model would have envied. "Thanks for stopping in," she said stiffly, "but as you can see everything's under control."

"If you say so." He grinned at her and without another word was gone.

Susannah banged the door shut with her hip, feeling a rush of satisfaction as she did so. She knew this was petty, but her neighbor had annoyed her in more ways than one.

Soon afterward Susannah heard the soft strains of an Italian opera drifting from Nate's condominium. At least she thought it was Italian, which was unfortunate because that made her think of spaghetti and how hungry she actually was.

"Okay, Michelle," she said, smiling down on her niece. "It's time to feed your auntie." Without too much trouble, Susannah assembled the high chair and set her niece in that while she scanned the contents of her freezer.

The best she could come up with was a frozen Mexican entrée. She gazed at the picture on the front of the package, shook her head and tossed it back inside the freezer.

Michelle seemed to approve and vigorously slapped the tray on her high chair.

Crossing her arms and leaning against the freezer door, Susannah paused. "Did you hear what he said?" she asked, still irate. "I guess he was right, but he didn't have to be so superior about it."

Michelle slapped her hands in approval once again. The music was muted by the thick walls, and wanting to hear a little more, Susannah cracked open the sliding glass door to her balcony, which was separated from Nate's by a concrete partition. It bestowed privacy, but didn't muffle the beautiful voices raised in triumphant song.

Susannah opened the glass door completely and stepped outside. The evening was cool, but pleasantly so. The sun had just started to set and had cast a wash of golden shadows over the picturesque waterfront.

"Michelle," she muttered when she came back in, "he's cooking something that smells like lasagna or spaghetti." Her stomach growled and she returned to the freezer, taking out the same Mexican entrée she'd rejected earlier. It didn't seem any more appetizing than it had the first time.

A faint scent of garlic wafted into her kitchen. Susannah turned her classic Greek nose in that direction, then followed the aroma to the open door like a puppet drawn there by a string. She sniffed loudly and turned eagerly back to her niece. "It's definitely Italian, and it smells divine."

Michelle pounded the tray again.

"It's garlic bread," Susannah announced and whirled around to face her niece, who clearly wasn't impressed. But then, thought Susannah, she wouldn't be. She'd eaten.

Under normal conditions, Susannah would've reached for her jacket and headed to Mama Mataloni's, a fabulous Italian restaurant within easy walking distance. Unfortunately Mama Mataloni's didn't deliver.

Against her better judgment, Susannah stuck the frozen entrée into her microwave and set the timer. When there was another knock on her door, she stiffened and looked at Michelle as if the nine-month-old would sit up and tell Susannah who'd come by *this* time.

It was Nate again, holding a plate of spaghetti and a glass of red wine. "Did you fix yourself something to eat?" he asked.

For the life of her Susannah couldn't tear her gaze away from the oversize plate, heaped high with steaming pasta smothered in a thick red sauce. Nothing had ever looked—or smelled—more appetizing. The fresh Parmesan cheese he'd grated over the top had melted onto the rich sauce. A generous slice of garlic bread was balanced on the side.

"I, ah, was just heating up a…microwave dinner." She pointed behind her toward the kitchen as if that would explain what she was trying to say. Her tongue seemed to be stuck to the roof of her mouth.

"I shouldn't have acted like such a know-it-all earlier," he said, pushing the plate toward her. "I'm bringing you a peace offering."

"This…is for me?" She raised her eyes from the plate,

wondering if he knew how hungry she felt and was toying with her.

He handed her the meal and the wine. "The sauce has been simmering most of the afternoon. I like to pretend I'm a bit of a gourmet chef. Every once in a while I get creative in the kitchen."

"How...nice." She conjured up a picture of Nate standing in his kitchen stirring sauce while the rest of the world struggled to make a living. Her attitude wasn't at all gracious and she mentally apologized. Without further ado, she marched into her kitchen, reached for a fork and plopped herself down at the table. She might as well eat this feast while it was hot!

One sample told her everything she needed to know. "This is great." She took another bite, pointed her fork in his direction and rolled her eyes. "Marvelous. Wonderful."

Nate pulled a bread stick out of his shirt pocket and gave it to Michelle. "Here's looking at you, kid."

As Michelle chewed contentedly on the bread stick, Nate pulled out a chair and sat across from Susannah, who was too busy enjoying her dinner to notice anything out of the ordinary until Nate's eyes narrowed.

"What's wrong?" Susannah asked. She wiped her mouth with a napkin and sampled the wine.

"I smell something."

Judging by his expression, whatever it was apparently wasn't pleasant. "It might be the microwave dinner," she suggested hopefully, already knowing better.

"I'm afraid not."

Susannah carefully set the fork beside her plate as uneasiness settled over her.

"It seems," Nate said, covering his nose with one hand, "that someone needs to change Michelle's diaper."

Two

Holding a freshly diapered Michelle on her hip, Susannah rushed out of the bathroom into the narrow hallway and gasped for breath.

"Are you all right?" Nate asked, his brow creased with a concerned frown.

She nodded and sagged against the wall, feeling light-headed. Once she'd dragged several clean breaths through her lungs, she straightened and even managed a weak smile.

"That wasn't so bad now, was it?"

Susannah glared at him. "I should've been wearing an oxygen mask."

Nate's responding chuckle did little to improve her mood.

"In light of what I just experienced," she muttered, "I can't understand why the population continues to grow." To be on the safe side, she opened the hall linen closet and took out a large can of disinfectant spray. Sticking her arm inside the bathroom, she gave a generous squirt.

"While you were busy I assembled the crib," Nate told her, still revealing far too much amusement to suit Susannah. "Where would you like me to put it?"

"The living room will be fine." His action had been thoughtful, but Susannah wasn't accustomed to depending on others, so when she thanked him, the words were forced.

Susannah followed him into the living room and found the bed ready. She laid Michelle down on her stomach and covered her with a hand-knit blanket. The baby settled down immediately, without fussing.

Nate walked toward the door. "You're sure everything's okay?" he said softly.

"Positive." Susannah wasn't, but Michelle was her niece and their problems weren't his. Nate had done more than enough already. "Thanks for dinner."

"Anytime." He paused at the door and turned back. "I left my phone number on the kitchen counter. Call if you need me."

"Thanks."

He favored her with a grin on his way out the door, and Susannah stood a few moments after he'd left the apartment, thinking about him. Her feelings were decidedly mixed.

She began sorting through the various bags her sister had brought, depositing the jars of baby food in the cupboard and putting the bottles of formula in the fridge. As Nate had pointed out, there was plenty of room—all she had to do was scoot the empty pickle jar aside.

She supposed she should toss the jar in the garbage, but one of the guys from the office had talked about making pickled eggs. It sounded so simple—all she had to do was peel a few hard-boiled eggs and keep them refrigerated in the jar for a week or so. Susannah had been meaning to try it ever since. But she was afraid that when the mood struck her, she wouldn't have any pickle juice around, so she'd decided to keep it on hand.

Once she'd finished in the kitchen, Susannah soaked in a hot bath, leaving the door ajar in case Michelle woke and needed her. She felt far more relaxed afterward.

Walking back into the living room on the tips of her toes, she brought out her briefcase and removed a file. She glanced down at her sleeping niece and gently patted her back. The little girl looked so angelic, so content.

Suddenly a powerful yearning stirred within Susannah. She felt real affection for Michelle, but the feeling was more than that. This time alone with her niece had evoked a longing buried deep in Susannah's heart, a longing she'd never taken the time to fully examine. And with it came an aching restless sensation that she promptly submerged.

When Susannah had chosen a career in business, she'd realized she was giving up the part of herself that hungered for a husband and children. There was nothing that said she couldn't marry, couldn't raise a child, but she knew herself too well. From the time she was in high school it had been painfully apparent that she was completely inadequate in the domestic arena. Especially when she compared herself to Emily, who seemed to have been born with a dust rag in one hand and a cookbook in the other.

Susannah had never regretted the decision she'd made to dedicate herself to her career, but then she was more fortunate than some. She had Emily, who was determined to supply her with numerous nieces and nephews. For Susannah, Michelle and the little ones who were sure to follow would have to be enough.

Reminding herself that she was comfortable with her choices, Susannah quietly stepped away from the crib. For the next hour, she sat on her bed reading the details of the proposed marketing program the department had sent her. The full presentation was scheduled for Monday morning and she wanted to be informed and prepared.

When she finished reading the report, she tiptoed back to her desk, situated in the far corner of the living room, and replaced the file in her briefcase.

Once more she paused to check on her niece. Feeling just a little cocky, she returned to the bedroom convinced this babysitting business wasn't going to be so bad after all.

Susannah changed her mind at one-thirty when a piercing wail startled her out of a sound sleep. Not knowing how long Michelle had been at it, Susannah nearly fell out of bed in her rush to reach her niece.

"Michelle," she cried, stumbling blindly across the floor, her arms stretched out in front of her. "I'm coming.... There's no need to panic."

Michelle disagreed vehemently.

Turning on a light only made matters worse. Squinting to protect her eyes from the glare, Susannah groped her way to the crib, then let out a cry herself when she stubbed her toe on the leg of the coffee table.

Michelle was standing, holding on to the bars and looking as if she didn't have a friend in the world.

"What's the matter, sweetheart?" Susannah asked softly, lifting the baby into her arms.

A wet bottom told part of the story. And the poor kid had probably woken and, finding herself in a strange place, felt scared. Susannah couldn't blame her.

"All right, we'll try this diapering business again."

Susannah spread a thick towel on the bathroom counter, then gently placed Michelle on it. She was halfway through the changing process when the phone rang. Straightening, Susannah glanced around her, wondering what she should do. She couldn't leave Michelle, and picking her up and carrying her into the kitchen would be difficult. Whoever was calling at this time of night should know better! If it was important they could leave a message on her answering machine.

But after three rings, the phone stopped, followed almost immediately by a firm knock at her door.

Hauling Michelle, newly diapered, Susannah squinted and checked the peephole to discover a disgruntled Nate on the other side.

"Nate," she said in surprise as she opened the door. She couldn't even guess what he wanted. And she wasn't too keen about letting him into her apartment at this hour.

He stood just inside the condo, barefoot and dressed in a red plaid housecoat. His hair was mussed, which made Susannah wonder about her own disheveled appearance. She suspected she looked like someone who'd walked out of a swamp.

"Is Michelle all right?" he barked, despite the evidence before him. Not waiting for a reply, he continued in an accusing tone, "You didn't answer the phone."

"I couldn't. I was changing her diaper."

Nate hesitated, then studied her closely. "In that case, are *you* all right?"

She nodded and managed to raise one hand. It was difficult when her arms were occupied with a baby. "I lived to tell about it."

"Good. What happened? Why was Michelle crying?"

"I'm not sure. Maybe when she woke up and didn't recognize her surroundings, she suffered an anxiety attack."

"And, from the look of us, caused a couple more."

Susannah would rather he hadn't mentioned that. Her long, tangled hair spilled over her shoulders and she, too, was barefoot. She'd been so anxious to get to Michelle that she hadn't bothered to reach for her slippers or her robe.

Michelle, it seemed, was pleased with all the unexpected attention, and when she leaned toward Nate, arms outstretched, Susannah marveled at how fickle an infant could be. After all, she was the one who'd fed and diapered her. Not Nate.

"It's my male charm," he explained delightedly.

"More likely, it's your red housecoat."

Whatever it was, Michelle went into his arms as if he were a long-lost friend. Susannah excused herself to retrieve her robe from the foot of her bed. By the time she got back, Nate was sitting on the sofa with his feet stretched out, supported by Susannah's mahogany coffee table.

"Make yourself at home," she muttered. Her mood wasn't always the best when she'd been abruptly wakened from a sound sleep.

He glanced up at her and grinned. "No need to be testy."

"Yes, there is," she said, but destroyed what remained of her argument by yawning loudly. Covering her mouth with the back of her hand, she slumped down on the chair across from him and flipped her hair away from her face.

His gaze followed the action. "You should wear your hair down more often."

She glared at him. "I always wear my hair up."

"I noticed. And frankly, it's much more flattering down."

"Oh, for heaven's sake," she cried, "are you going to tell me how to dress next?"

"I might."

He said it with such a charming smile that any sting there might have been in his statement was diluted.

"You don't have to stick with business suits every day, do you? Try jeans sometime. With a T-shirt."

She opened her mouth to argue with him, then decided not to bother. The arrogance he displayed seemed to be characteristic of handsome men in general, she'd noted. Because a man happened to possess lean good looks and could smile beguilingly, he figured he had the right to say anything he pleased to a woman—to comment on how she styled her hair, how she chose to dress or anything else. These were things he wouldn't dream of discussing if he were talking to another man.

"You aren't going to argue?"

"No," she said, and for emphasis shook her head.

That stopped him short. He paused and blinked, then sent her another of his captivating smiles. "I find that refreshing."

"I'm gratified to hear there's something about me you approve of." There were probably plenty of other things that didn't please him. Given any encouragement, he'd probably be glad to list them for her.

Sweet little traitor that she was, Michelle had curled up in Nate's arms, utterly content just to sit there and study his handsome face, which no doubt had fascinated numerous other females before her. The least Michelle could do was show some signs of going back to sleep so Susannah could return her to the crib and usher Nate out the door.

"I shouldn't have said what I did about your hair and clothes."

"Hey," she returned flippantly, "you don't need to worry about hurting my feelings. I'm strong. I've got a lot of emotional fortitude."

"Strong," he repeated. "You make yourself sound like an all-weather tire."

"I've had to be tougher than that."

His face relaxed into a look of sympathy. "Why?"

"I work with men just like you every day."

"Men just like me?"

"It's true. For the past seven years, I've found myself up against the old double standard, but I've learned to keep my cool."

He frowned as if he didn't understand what she was talking about. Susannah felt it was her obligation to tell him. Apparently Nate had never been involved in office politics. "Let me give you a few examples. If a male coworker has a cluttered desk, then everyone assumes he's a hard worker. If my desk is a mess, it's a sign of disorganization."

Nate looked as if he wanted to argue with her, but Susannah was just warming to her subject and she forged ahead before he had a chance to speak. "If a man in an office marries, it's good for the company because he'll settle down and become a more productive employee. If a woman marries, it's almost the kiss of death because management figures she'll get pregnant and quit. If a man leaves because he's been offered a better job, everyone's pleased for him because he's taking advantage of an excellent career opportunity. But if the same position is offered to a woman and she takes it, then upper management shrugs and claims women aren't dependable."

When she'd finished there was a short pause. "You have very definite feelings on the subject," he said at last.

"If you were a woman, you would, too."

His nod of agreement was a long time coming. "You're right, I probably would."

Michelle seemed to find the toes of her sleeper fascinating and was examining them closely. Personally, Susannah didn't know how anyone could be so wide-awake at this ungodly hour.

"If you turn down the lights, she might get the hint," Nate said, doing a poor job of smothering a yawn.

"You're beat," said Susannah. "There's no need for you to stay. I'll take her." She held out her arms to Michelle, who whimpered and clung all the more tightly to Nate. Susannah's feelings of inadequacy were reinforced.

"Don't worry about me. I'm comfortable like this," Nate told her.

"But…" She could feel the warmth invading her cheeks. She lowered her eyes, regretting her outburst of a few minutes ago. She'd been standing on her soapbox again. "Listen, I'm sorry about what I said. What goes on at the office has nothing to do with our being neighbors."

"Then we're even."

"Even?"

"I shouldn't have commented on your hair and

clothes." He hesitated long enough to envelop her in his smile. "Friends?"

Despite the intolerable hour, Susannah found herself smiling back. "Friends."

Michelle seemed to concur because she cooed loudly, kicking her feet.

Susannah stood and turned the lamp down to its lowest setting, then reached for Michelle's blanket, covering the baby. Feeling slightly chilled herself, she fetched the brightly colored afghan at the foot of the sofa, which Emily had crocheted for her last Christmas.

The muted light created an intimate atmosphere, and suddenly self-conscious, Susannah suggested, "Maybe I'll sing to her. That should help her go to sleep."

"If anyone sings, it'll be me," he said much too quickly.

Susannah's pride was a little dented, but remembering her limited repertoire of songs, she gestured toward him and said, "All right, Frank Sinatra, have a go."

To Susannah's surprise, Nate's singing voice was soothing and melodious. Even more surprisingly, he knew exactly the right kind of songs. Not lullabies, but easy-listening songs, the kind she'd heard for years on the radio. She felt her own eyes drifting closed and battled to stay awake. His voice dropped to a mere whisper that felt like a warm caress. Much too warm. And cozy, as if the three of them belonged together, which was ridiculous since she'd only just met Nate. He was her neighbor and nothing more. There hadn't been time for them to get to know each other, and Michelle was her *niece,* not her daughter.

But the domestic fantasy continued, no matter how hard she tried to dispel it. She couldn't stop thinking about what it would be like to share her life with a husband and children—and she could barely manage to keep her eyes open for more than a second or two. Perhaps if she rested them for a moment...

The next thing Susannah knew, her neck ached. She reached up to secure her pillow, then realized she didn't have one. Instead of being in bed, she was curled up in the chair, her head resting uncomfortably against the arm. Slowly, reluctantly, she opened her eyes and discovered Nate across from her, head tilted back, sleeping soundly. Michelle was resting peacefully in his arms.

It took Susannah a minute or so to orient herself. When she saw the sun breaking across the sky and spilling through her large windows, she closed her eyes again. It was morning. Morning! Nate had spent the night at her place.

Flustered, Susannah twisted her body into an upright position and rubbed the sleep from her face, wondering what she should do. Waking Nate was probably not the best idea. He was bound to be as unnerved as she was to discover he'd fallen asleep in her living room. To complicate matters, the afghan she'd covered herself with had somehow become twisted around her hips and legs. Muttering under her breath, Susannah yanked it about in an effort to stand.

Her activity disturbed Nate's restful slumber. He stirred, glanced in her direction and froze for what seemed the longest moment of Susannah's life. Then he blinked several times and glared at her as though he hoped she'd vanish into thin air.

Standing now, Susannah did her best to appear dignified, which was nearly impossible with the comforter still twisted around her.

"Where am I?" Nate asked dazedly.

"Ah…my place."

His eyes drifted shut. "I was afraid of that." The mournful look that came over Nate's face would have been comical under other circumstances. Only neither of them was laughing.

"I, ah, must've fallen asleep," she said, breaking the embarrassed silence. She took pains to fold the afghan, and held it against her stomach like a shield.

"Me, too, apparently," Nate muttered.

Michelle woke and struggled into a sitting position. She looked around her and evidently didn't like what she saw, either. Her lower lip started to tremble.

"Michelle, it's okay," Susannah said quickly, hoping to ward off the screams he feared was coming. "You're staying with Auntie Susannah this weekend, remember?"

"I think she might be wet," Nate offered when Michelle began to whimper softly. He let out a muffled curse and hastily lifted the nine-month-old from his lap. "I'm positive she's wet. Here, take her."

Susannah reached for her niece and a dry diaper in one smooth movement, but it didn't help. Michelle was intent on letting them both know, in no uncertain terms, that she didn't like her schedule altered. Nor did she appreciate waking up in a stranger's arms. She conveyed her displeasure in loud boisterous cries.

"I think she might be hungry, too," Nate suggested, trying to brush the dampness from his housecoat.

"Brilliant observation," Susannah said sarcastically on her way to the bathroom, Michelle in her arms.

"My, my, you certainly get testy in the mornings," he said.

"I need coffee."

"Fine. I'll make us both a cup while I'm heating a bottle for Michelle."

"She's supposed to eat her cereal first," Susannah shouted. At least that was what Emily had insisted when she'd outlined her daughter's schedule.

"I'm sure she doesn't care. She's hungry."

"All right, all right," Susannah yelled from the bathroom. "Heat her bottle first if you want."

Yelling was a mistake, she soon discovered. Michelle clearly wasn't any keener on mornings than Susannah was. Punching the air with her stubby legs, her niece made diapering a nearly impossible task. Susannah grew more frustrated by the minute. Finally her hair, falling forward over her shoulders, caught Michelle's attention. She grasped it, pausing to gulp in a huge breath.

"Do you want me to get that?" she heard Nate shout.

"Get what?"

Apparently it wasn't important because he didn't answer her. But a moment later he was standing at the bathroom door.

"It's for you," he said.

"What's for me?"

"The phone."

The word bounced around in her mind like a ricocheting bullet. "Did...did they say who it was?" she asked, her voice high-pitched and wobbly. No doubt it was someone from the office and she'd be the subject of gossip for months.

"Someone named Emily."

"Emily," she repeated. That was even worse. Her sister was sure to be full of awkward questions.

"Hi," Susannah said as casually as possible into the receiver.

"Who answered the phone?" her sister demanded without preamble.

"My neighbor. Nate Townsend. He, ah, lives next door." That awkward explanation astonished even her. Worse, Susannah had been ready to blurt out that Nate had spent the night, but she'd stopped herself just in time.

"I haven't met him, have I?"

"My neighbor? No, you haven't."

"He sounds cute."

"Listen, if you're phoning about Michelle," Susannah hurried to add, anxious to end the conversation, "there's no need for concern. Everything's under control." That was a slight exaggeration, but what Emily didn't know couldn't worry her.

"Is that Michelle I hear crying in the background?" Emily asked.

"Yes. She just woke up and she's a little hungry." Nate was holding the baby and pacing the kitchen, waiting impatiently for Susannah to get off the phone.

"My poor baby," Emily moaned. "Tell me when you met your neighbor. I don't remember you ever mentioning anyone named Nate."

"He's been helping me out," Susannah said quickly. Wanting to change the subject, she asked, "How are you and Robert?"

Her sister sighed audibly. "Robert was so right. We needed this weekend alone. I feel a thousand times better and so does he. Every married couple should get away for a few days like this—but then everyone doesn't have a sister as generous as you to fill in on such short notice."

"Good, good," Susannah said, hardly aware of what she was supposed to think was so fantastic. "Uh-oh," she said, growing desperate. "The bottle's warm. I hate to cut you off, but I've got to take care of Michelle. I'm sure you understand."

"Of course."

"I'll see you tomorrow afternoon, then. What time's your flight landing?"

"One-fifteen. We'll drive straight to your place and pick up Michelle."

"Okay, I'll expect you sometime around two." Another day with Michelle. She could manage for another twenty-four hours, couldn't she? What could possibly go wrong in that small amount of time?

Losing patience, Nate took the bottle and Michelle and returned to the living room. Susannah watched through the doorway as he turned on her television and plopped himself down as if he'd been doing it for years. His concentration moved from the TV long enough to place the rubber nipple in Michelle's eager mouth.

Her niece began greedily sucking, too hungry to care who was feeding her. Good heavens, Susannah thought, Michelle had spent the night in his arms. A little thing like letting this man feed her paled in comparison.

Emily was still chatting, telling her sister how romantic her first night in San Francisco had been. But Susannah barely heard. Her gaze settled on Nate, who looked rumpled, crumpled and utterly content, sitting in her living room, holding an infant in his arms.

That sight affected Susannah as few ever had, and she was powerless to explain its impact on her senses.

She'd dated a reasonable number of men—debonair, rich, sophisticated ones. But the feeling she had now, this attraction, had taken her completely by surprise. Over the years, Susannah had always been careful to guard her heart. It hadn't been difficult, since she'd never met anyone who truly appealed to her. Yet this disheveled, disgruntled male, who sat in her living room feeding her infant niece with enviable expertise, attracted her more profoundly than anyone she'd ever met. It wasn't the least bit logical. Nothing could ever develop between them—they were as different as…as gelatin and concrete. The last thing she wanted was to become involved in a serious relationship. With some effort, she forced her eyes away from the homey scene.

When at last she was able to hang up the phone, Susannah moved into the living room, feeling weary. She brushed the tangled curls from her face, wondering if she should take Michelle from Nate so he could return to his own apartment. No doubt her niece would resist and humiliate her once more.

"Your sister isn't flying with Puget Air, is she?" he asked, frowning. His gaze remained on the television screen.

"Yes, why?"

Nate's mouth thinned. "You…we're in trouble here. Big trouble. According to the news, maintenance workers for Puget Air are going on strike. By six tonight, every plane they own will be grounded."

Three

"If this is a joke," Susannah told him angrily, "it's in poor taste."

"Would I kid about this?" Nate asked mildly.

Susannah slumped down on the edge of the sofa and gave a ragged sigh. This couldn't be happening, it just couldn't. "I'd better call Emily." She assumed her sister was blissfully unaware of the strike.

Susannah was back a few minutes later.

"Well?" Nate demanded. "What did she say?"

"Oh, she knew all along," Susannah replied disparagingly, "but she didn't want to say anything because she was afraid I'd worry."

"How exactly does she intend to get home?"

"Apparently they booked seats on another airline on the off chance something like this might happen."

"That was smart."

"My brother-in-law's like that. I'm not to give the matter another thought," she said, quoting Emily. "My sister will be back Sunday afternoon as promised." If the Fates so decreed—and Susannah said a fervent prayer that they would.

But the Fates had other plans.

* * *

Sunday morning, there were bags under Susannah's eyes. She was mentally and physically exhausted, and convinced anew that motherhood was definitely not for her. Two nights into the ordeal, Susannah had noticed that the emotional stirring for a husband and children came to her only when Michelle was sleeping or eating. And with good reason.

Nate arrived around nine bearing gifts. He brought freshly baked cinnamon rolls still warm from the oven. He stood in her doorway, tall and lean, with a smile bright enough to dazzle the most dedicated career woman. Once more, Susannah was shocked by her overwhelming reaction to him. Her heart leaped to her throat, and she immediately wished she'd taken time to dress in something better than her faded housecoat.

"You look terrible."

"Thanks," she said, bouncing Michelle on her hip.

"I take it you had a bad night."

"Michelle was fussing. She didn't seem the least bit interested in sleeping." She wiped a hand over her face.

"I wish you'd called me," Nate said, taking her by the elbow and leading her into the kitchen. He actually looked guilty because he'd had a peaceful night's rest. Ridiculous, Susannah thought.

"Call you? Whatever for?" she asked. "So you could have paced with her, too?" As it was, Nate had spent a good part of Saturday in and out of her apartment helping her. Spending a second night with them was above and beyond the call of duty. "Did I tell you," Susannah said, yawning, "Michelle's got a new tooth coming in—I felt it myself." Deposited in the high chair, Michelle was content for the moment.

Nate nodded and glanced at his watch. "When does your sister's flight get in?"

"One-fifteen." No sooner had the words left her lips than the phone rang. Susannah's and Nate's eyes met, and as it rang a second time she wondered how a telephone could sound so much like a death knell. Even before she answered it, Susannah knew it would be what she most dreaded hearing.

"Well?" Nate asked when she'd finished the call.

Covering her face with both hands, Susannah sagged against the wall.

"Say something."

Slowly she lowered her hands. "Help."

"Help?"

"Yes," she cried, struggling to keep her voice from cracking. "All Puget Air flights are grounded just the way the news reported, and the other airline Robert and Emily made reservations with is overbooked. The earliest flight they can get is tomorrow morning."

"I see."

"Obviously you don't!" she cried. "Tomorrow is Monday and I've got to be at work!"

"Call in sick."

"I can't do that," she snapped, angry with him for even suggesting such a thing. "My marketing group is giving their presentation and I've got to be there."

"Why?"

She frowned at him. It was futile to expect someone like Nate to understand something as important as a sales presentation. Nate didn't seem to have a job; he didn't worry about a career. For that matter, he couldn't possibly grasp that a woman holding a management position had to strive twice as hard to prove herself.

"I'm not trying to be cute, Susannah," he said with infuriating calm. "I honestly want to know why that meeting is so important."

"Because it is. I don't expect you to appreciate this, so just accept the fact that I *have* to be there."

Nate cocked his head and idly rubbed the side of his jaw. "First, answer me something. Five years from now, will this meeting make a difference in your life?"

"I don't know." She pressed two fingers to the bridge of her nose. She'd had less than three hours' sleep, and Nate was asking impossible questions. Michelle, bless her devilish little heart, had fallen asleep in her high chair. Why shouldn't she? Susannah reasoned. She'd spent the entire night fussing, and was exhausted now. By the time Susannah had discovered the new tooth, she felt as if she'd grown it herself.

"If I were you, I wouldn't sweat it," Nate said with that same nonchalant attitude. "If you aren't there to hear their presentation, your marketing group will give it Tuesday morning."

"In other words," she muttered, "you're saying I don't have a thing to worry about."

"Exactly."

Nate Townsend knew next to nothing about surviving in the corporate world, and he'd obviously been protected from life's harsher realities. It was all too obvious to Susannah that he was a man with a baseball-cap mentality. He couldn't be expected to fully comprehend her dilemma.

"So," he said now, "what are you going to do?"

Susannah wasn't sure. Briefly, she closed her eyes in an effort to concentrate. *Impose discipline,* she said to herself. *Stay calm.* That was crucial. *Think slowly and analyze your objectives.* For every problem there was a solution.

"Susannah?"

She glanced at him; she'd almost forgotten he was there. "I'll cancel my early-morning appointments and go in for the presentation," she stated matter-of-factly.

"What about Michelle? Are you going to hire a sitter?"

A babysitter hired by the babysitter. A novel thought, perhaps even viable, but Susannah didn't know anyone who sat with babies.

Then she made her decision. She would take Michelle to work with her.

And that was exactly what she did.

As she knew it would, Susannah's arrival at H&J Lima caused quite a stir. At precisely ten the following morning, she stepped off the elevator. Her black leather briefcase was clutched in one hand and Michelle was pressed against her hip with the other. Head held high, Susannah marched across the hardwood floor, past the long rows of doorless cubicles and shelves of foot-thick file binders. Several employees moved away from their desks to view her progress. A low rumble of hushed whispers followed her.

"Good morning, Ms. Brooks," Susannah said crisply as she walked into her office, the diaper bag draped over her shoulder like an ammunition pouch.

"Ms. Simmons."

Susannah noted that her assistant—to her credit—didn't so much as bat an eye. The woman was well trained; to all outward appearances, Susannah regularly arrived at the office with a nine-month-old infant attached to her hip.

Depositing the diaper bag on the floor, Susannah took her place behind a six-foot-wide walnut desk. Content for the moment, Michelle sat on her lap, gleefully viewing her aunt's domain.

"Would you like some coffee?" Ms. Brooks asked.

"Yes, please."

Her assistant paused. "Will your, ah…"

"This is my niece, Michelle, Ms. Brooks."

The woman nodded. "Will Michelle require anything to drink?"

"No, but thanks anyway. Is there anything urgent in the mail?"

"Nothing that can't wait. I canceled your eight-and nine-o'clock appointments," her assistant went on to explain. "When I spoke to Mr. Adams, he asked if you could join him for drinks tomorrow night at six."

"That'll be fine." The old lecher would love to do all their business outside the office. On this occasion, she'd agree to his terms, since she'd been the one to cancel their appointment, but she wouldn't be so willing a second time. She'd never much cared for Andrew Adams, who was overweight, balding and a general nuisance.

"Will you be needing me for anything else?" Ms. Brooks asked when she delivered the coffee.

"Nothing. Thank you."

As she should have predicted, the meeting was an unmitigated disaster. The presentation took twenty-two minutes, and in that brief time Michelle managed to dismantle Susannah's Cross pen, unfasten her blouse and pull her hair free from her carefully styled French twist. The baby clapped her hands at various inappropriate points and made loud noises. At the low point of the meeting, Susannah had been forced to leave her seat and dive under the conference table to retrieve her niece, who was cheerfully crawling over everyone's feet.

By the time she got home, Susannah felt like climbing back into bed and staying there. It was the type of day that made her crave something chocolate and excessively sweet. But there weren't enough chocolate chip cookies in the world to see her through another morning like that one.

To Susannah's surprise, Nate met her in the foyer outside the elevator. She took one look at him and resisted the urge to burst into tears.

"I take it things didn't go well."

"How'd you guess?" she asked sarcastically.

"It might be the fact you're wearing your hair down when I specifically remember you left wearing it up. Or it could be that your blouse is buttoned wrong and there's a gaping hole in the middle." His smile was mischievous. "I wondered if you were the type to wear a lacy bra. Now I know."

Susannah groaned and slapped a hand over her front. He could have spared her that comment.

"Here, kiddo," he said, taking Michelle out of Susannah's arms. "It looks like we need to give your poor aunt a break."

Turning her back, Susannah refastened her blouse and then brought out her key. Her once orderly, immaculate apartment looked as if a cyclone had gone through it. Blankets and baby toys were scattered from one end of the living room to the other. She'd slept on the couch in order to be close to Michelle, and her pillow and blankets were still there, along with her blue suit jacket, which she'd been forced to change when Michelle had tossed a spoonful of plums on the sleeve.

"What happened here?" Nate asked, looking in astonishment at the scene before him.

"Three days and three nights with Michelle and you need to ask?"

"Sit down," he said gently. "I'll get you a cup of coffee." Susannah did as he suggested, too grateful to argue with him.

Nate stopped just inside the kitchen. "What's this purple stuff all over the walls?"

"Plums," Susannah informed him. "I discovered the hard way that Michelle hates plums."

The scene in the kitchen was a good example of how her morning had gone. It had taken Susannah the better part of three hours to get herself and Michelle ready for the excursion to the office. And that was just the beginning.

"What I need is a double martini," she told Nate when he carried in two cups of coffee.

"It's not even noon."

"I know," she said, slowly lowering herself to the sofa. "Can you imagine what I'd need if it was two o'clock?"

Chuckling, Nate handed her the steaming cup. Michelle was sitting on the carpet, content to play with the very toys she'd vehemently rejected that morning.

Nate unexpectedly sat down next to her and looped his arm over her shoulder. She tensed, but if he noticed, he chose to ignore it. He stretched his legs out on the coffee table and relaxed.

Susannah felt her tension mount. The memory of the meeting with marketing was enough to elevate her blood pressure, but when she analyzed the reasons for this anxiety, she discovered it came from being so close to Nate. It wasn't that Susannah objected to his touch; in reality, quite the opposite was true. They'd spent three days in close quarters, and contrary to everything she'd theorized about her neighbor, she'd come to appreciate his happy-go-lucky approach to life. But it was diametrically opposed to her own, and the fact that she could be so attracted to him was something of a shock.

"Do you want to talk about marketing's presentation?"

She released her breath. "No, I think this morning is best forgotten by everyone involved. You were right, I should have postponed the meeting."

Nate sipped his coffee and said, "It's one of those live-and-learn situations."

Pulling herself to a standing position at the coffee table, Michelle cheerfully edged her way around until she was stopped by Nate's outstretched legs. Then she surprised them both by reaching out one arm and granting him a smile that would have melted concrete.

"Oh, look," Susannah said proudly, "you can see her new tooth!"

"Where?" Lifting the baby onto his lap, Nate peered inside her mouth. Susannah was trying to show him where to look when someone, presumably her sister, rang impatiently from the lobby.

Susannah opened her door a minute later, and Emily flew in as if she'd sprouted wings. "My baby!" she cried. "Mommy missed you so-o-o much."

Not half as much as I missed you, Emily, she mused, watching the happy reunion.

Robert followed on his wife's heels, obviously pleased.

The weekend away had apparently done them both good. Never mind that it had nearly destroyed Susannah's peace of mind *and* her career.

"You must be Nate," Emily said, claiming the seat beside Susannah's neighbor. "My sister couldn't say enough about you."

"Coffee anyone?" Susannah piped up eagerly, rubbing her palms together. The last thing she needed was her sister applying her matchmaking techniques to her and Nate. Emily strongly believed it was unnatural for Susannah to live the way she did. A career was fine, but choosing to forgo the personal satisfaction of a husband and family was beyond her sister's comprehension. Being fulfilled in that role herself, Emily assumed that Susannah was missing an essential part of life.

"Nothing for me," Robert answered.

"I'll bet you're eager to pack everything up and head home," Susannah said hopefully. Her eye happened to catch Nate's, and it was obvious that he was struggling not to laugh at her less-than-subtle attempt to usher her sister and family on their way.

"Susannah's right," Robert announced, glancing around the room. It was clear he'd never seen his orderly, efficient sister-in-law's home in such a state of disarray.

"But I've hardly had a chance to talk to Nate," Emily protested. "And I was looking forward to getting to know him better."

"I'll be around," Nate said lightly.

His gaze settled on Susannah, and the look he gave her made her insides quiver. For the first time she realized how much she wanted this man to kiss her. Susannah wasn't the type of person who looked at a handsome male and wondered how his mouth would feel on hers. She was convinced this current phenomenon had a lot to do with sheer exhaustion, but whatever the cause she found her eyes riveted to his.

Emily suddenly noticed what was happening. "Yes, I think you may be right, Robert," she said, and her voice contained more than a hint of amusement. "I'll pack Michelle's things."

Susannah's cheeks were pink with embarrassment by the time she tore her gaze away from Nate's. "By the way, did you know Michelle has an aversion to plums?"

"I can't say I did," Emily said, busily throwing her daughter's things together.

Nate helped disassemble the crib and the high chair, and it seemed no more than a few minutes had passed before Susannah's condo was once more her own. She stood in the middle of the living room savoring the silence. It was pure bliss.

"They're off," she said when she saw that Nate had stayed behind.

"Like a herd of turtles."

Susannah had heard that saying from the time she was a kid. She didn't find it particularly funny anymore, but she shared a smile with him.

"I have my life back now," she sighed. It would probably take her a month to recover, though.

"Your life is your own," Nate agreed, watching her closely.

Susannah would've liked to attribute the tears that flooded her eyes to his close scrutiny, but she knew better. With her arms cradling her middle, she walked over to the window, which looked out over Elliott Bay. A green-and-white ferry glided peacefully over the darker green waters. Rain tapped gently against the window, and the sky, a deep oyster-gray, promised drizzle for most of the afternoon.

Hoping Nate wouldn't notice, she wiped the tears from her face and drew in a deep calming breath.

"Susannah?"

"I… I was just looking at the Sound. It's so lovely in the fall." She could hear him approach her from behind, and when he placed his hands on her shoulders it was all she could do to keep from leaning against him.

"You're crying."

She nodded, sniffling because it was impossible to hold it inside any longer.

"It's not like you to cry, is it? What's wrong?"

"I don't know…" she said and hiccuped on a sob. "I can't believe I'm doing this. I love that little kid…we were just beginning to understand each other…and… dear heaven, I'm glad Emily came back when…she did." Before Susannah could recognize how much she was missing without a husband and family.

Nate ran his hands down her arms in the softest of caresses.

He didn't say anything for a long time, and Susannah was convinced she was making an absolute idiot of herself. Nate was right; it wasn't like her to dissolve into tears. This unexpected outburst must've been a result of the trauma she'd experienced that morning in her office, or the fact that she hadn't had a decent night's sleep in what felt like a month and, yes, she'd admit it, of meeting Nate.

Without saying another word, Nate turned her around and lifted her chin with his finger, raising her eyes to his.

His look was so tender, so caring, that Susannah sniffled again. Her shoulders shook and she wiped her nose.

He brushed away the hair that clung to the sides of her damp face. His fingertips slid over each of her features as though he were a blind man trying to memorize her face. Susannah was mesmerized, unable to pull away. Slowly, as if denying himself the pleasure for as long as he could, he lowered his mouth.

When his lips settled on hers, Susannah released a barely audible sigh. She'd wondered earlier what it would be like when Nate kissed her. Now she knew. His kiss was soft and warm. Velvet smooth and infinitely gentle, and yet it was undeniably exciting.

As if one kiss wasn't enough, he kissed her again. This time it was Nate who sighed. Then he dropped his hands and stepped back.

Startled by his abrupt action, Susannah swayed slightly. Nate's arms righted her. Apparently he'd come to his senses at the same time she had. For a brief moment they'd decided to ignore their differences. The only thing they had in common was the fact that they lived in the same building, she reminded herself. Their values and expectations were worlds apart.

"Are you all right?" he asked, frowning.

She blinked, trying to find a way to disguise that she wasn't. Everything had happened much too fast; her heart was galloping like a runaway horse. She'd never been so attracted to a man in her life. "Of course I'm all right," she said with strained bravado. "Are you?"

He didn't answer for a moment. Instead, he shoved his hands in his pants pocket and moved away from her, looking annoyed.

"Nate?" she whispered.

He paused, scowling in her direction. Rubbing his hand across his brow, he twisted the ever-present baseball cap until it faced backward. "I think we should try that again."

Susannah wasn't sure what he meant until he reached for her. His first few kisses had been gentle, but this one was meant to take charge of her senses. His mouth slid over hers until she felt the starch go out of her knees. In an effort to maintain her balance, she gripped his shoulders, and although she fought it, she quickly surrendered to the swirling excitement. Nate's kiss was debilitating. She couldn't breathe, couldn't think, couldn't move.

Nate groaned, then his hands shifted to the back of her head. He slanted his mouth over hers. At length he released a jagged breath and buried his face in the soft curve of her neck. "What about now?"

"You're a good kisser."

"That's not what I meant, Susannah. You feel it, too, don't you? You must! There's enough electricity between us to light up a city block."

"No," she lied, and swallowed tightly. "It was nice as far as kisses go—"

"Nice!"

"Very nice," she amended, hoping to appease him, "but that's about it."

Nate didn't say anything for a long minute, a painfully long minute. Then, scowling at her again, he turned and walked out of the apartment.

Trembling, Susannah watched him go. His kiss had touched a chord within her, notes that had been long-silent, and now she feared the music would forever mark her soul. But she couldn't let him know that. They had nothing in common. They were too mismatched.

* * *

Now that she was seated in the plush cocktail lounge with her associate, Andrew Adams, Susannah regretted having agreed to meet him after hours. It was apparent from the moment she stepped into the dimly lit room that he had more on his mind than business. Despite the fact that Adams was balding and overweight, he would have been attractive enough if he hadn't seen himself as some kind of modern-day Adonis. Although Susannah struggled to maintain a businesslike calm, it was becoming increasingly difficult, and she wondered how much longer her good intentions would hold.

"There are some figures I meant to show you," Adams said, holding the stem of his martini glass with both hands and studying Susannah with undisguised admiration. "Unfortunately I left them at my apartment. Why don't we conclude our talk there?"

Susannah made a point of looking at her watch and frowning, hoping he'd get the hint. Something told her differently. "I'm afraid I won't have the time," she said. It was almost seven and she'd already spent an hour with him.

"My place is only a few blocks from here," he coaxed.

His look was much too suggestive, and Susannah was growing wearier by the minute. As far as she could see, this entire evening had been a waste of time.

The only thing that interested her was returning to her own place and talking to Nate. He'd been on her mind all day and she was eager to see him again. The truth was, she felt downright nervous after their last meeting, and wondered how they'd react to each other now. Nate had left her so abruptly, and she hadn't talked to him since.

"John Hammer and I are good friends," Adams claimed, pulling his chair closer to her own. "I don't know if you're aware of that."

He didn't even bother to veil his threat—or his bribe, whichever it was. Susannah worked directly under John Hammer, who would have the final say on the appointment of a new vice president. Susannah and two others were in the running for the position. And Susannah wanted it. Badly. She could achieve her five-year goal if she got it, and in the process make H&J Lima history—by being the first female vice president.

"If you're such good friends with Mr. Hammer," she said, "then I suggest you give those figures to him directly, since he'll need to review them anyway."

"No, that wouldn't work," he countered sharply. "If you come with me it'll only take a few minutes. We'd be in and out of my place in, say, half an hour at the most."

Susannah's immediate reaction to situations such as this was a healthy dose of outrage, but she managed to control her temper. "If your apartment is so convenient, then I'll wait here while you go back for those sheets." As she spoke, a couple walked past the tiny table where she was seated with Andrew Adams. Susannah didn't pay much attention to the man, who wore a gray suit, but the blonde with him was striking. Susannah followed the woman with her eyes and envied the graceful way she moved.

"It would be easier if you came with me, don't you think?"

"No," she answered bluntly, and lowered her gaze to her glass of white wine. It was then that she felt an odd sensation prickle down her spine. Someone was staring at her; she could feel it as surely as if she were being physically touched. Looking around, Susannah was astonished to discover Nate sitting two tables away. The striking blonde was seated next to him and obviously enjoying his company. She laughed softly and the sound was like a melody, light and breezy.

Susannah's breath caught in her chest, trapped there until the pain reminded her it was time to breathe again. When she did, she reached for her wineglass and succeeded in spilling some of the contents.

Nate's gaze centered on her and then moved to her companion. His mouth thinned and his eyes, which had been so warm and tender a day earlier, now looked hard. Almost scornful.

Susannah wasn't exactly thrilled herself. Nate was dating a beauty queen while she was stuck with Donald Duck.

Four

Susannah vented her anger by pacing the living room carpet. Men! Who needed them?

Not her. Definitely not her! Nate Townsend could take his rainy day kisses and stuff them in his baseball cap for all she cared. Only he hadn't been wearing it for Miss Universe. Oh no, with the other woman, he was dressed like someone out of *Gentlemen's Quarterly*. Susannah, on the other hand, rated worn football jerseys or faded T-shirts.

Susannah hadn't been home more than five minutes when there was a knock at her door. She whirled around. Checking the peephole, she discovered that her caller was Nate. She pulled back, wondering what she should do. He was the last person she wanted to see. He'd made a fool of her... Well, that wasn't strictly true. He'd only made her *feel* like a fool.

"Susannah," he said, knocking impatiently a second time. "I know you're in there."

"Go away."

Her shout was followed by a short pause. "Fine. Have it your way."

Changing her mind, she turned the lock and yanked open the door. She glared at him with all the fury she could muster—which just then was considerable.

Nate glared right back. "Who was that guy?" he asked with infuriating calm.

She was tempted to inform Nate that it wasn't any of his business. But she decided that would be churlish.

"Andrew Adams," she answered and quickly followed her response with a demand of her own. "Who was that woman?"

"Sylvia Potter."

For the longest moment, neither spoke.

"That was all I wanted to know," Nate finally said.

"Me, too," she returned stiffly.

Nate retreated two steps, and like precision clockwork Susannah shut the door. "Sylvia Potter," she echoed in a low-pitched voice filled with disdain. "Well, Sylvia Potter, you're welcome to him."

It took another fifteen minutes for the outrage to work its way through her system, but once she'd watched a portion of the evening news and read her mail, she was reasonably calm.

When Susannah really thought about it, what did she have to be so furious about? Nate Townsend didn't mean anything to her. How could he? Until a week ago, she hadn't even known his name.

Okay, so he'd kissed her a couple of times, and sure, there'd been electricity, but that was all. Electricity did not constitute a lifetime commitment. If Nate Townsend chose to date every voluptuous blonde between Seattle and New York it shouldn't matter to her.

But it did. And that infuriated Susannah more than anything. She didn't *want* to care about Nate. Her career goals were set. She had drive, determination and a positive mental attitude. But she didn't have Nate.

Jutting out her lower lip, she expelled her breath forcefully, ruffling the dark wisps of hair against her forehead. Maybe it was her hair color—perhaps Nate preferred blondes. He obviously did, otherwise he wouldn't be trying to impress Sylvia Potter.

Refusing to entertain any more thoughts of her neighbor, Susannah decided to fix herself dinner. An inspection of the freezer revealed a pitifully old chicken patty. Removing it from the cardboard box, Susannah took one look at it and promptly tossed it into the garbage.

Out of the corner of her eye she caught a movement on her balcony. She turned and saw a sleek Siamese cat walking casually along the railing as if he were strolling across a city park.

Although she remained outwardly calm, Susannah's heart lunged to her throat. Her condo was eight floors up. One wrong move and that cat would be history. Walking carefully to her sliding glass door, Susannah eased it open and called, "Here, kitty, kitty, kitty."

The cat accepted her invitation and jumped down from the railing. With his tail pointing skyward, he walked directly into her apartment and headed straight for the garbage pail, where he stopped.

"I bet you're hungry, aren't you?" she asked softly. She retrieved the chicken patty and stuck it in her microwave. While she stood waiting for it to cook, the cat, with his striking blue eyes and dark brown markings, wove around her legs, purring madly.

She'd just finished cutting the patty into bite-size pieces and putting it on a plate when someone pounded at her door. Wiping her fingers clean, she moved into the living room.

"Do you have my cat?" Nate demanded when she opened the door. He'd changed from his suit into jeans and a bright blue T-shirt.

"I don't know," she fibbed. "Describe it."

"Susannah, this isn't the time for silly games. Chocolate Chip is a valuable animal."

"Chocolate Chip," she repeated with a soft snicker, crossing her arms and leaning against the doorjamb. "Obviously you didn't read the fine print in the tenant's agreement, because it specifically states in section 12, paragraph 13, that no pets are allowed." Actually she didn't have a clue what section or what paragraph that clause was in, but she wanted him to think she did.

"If you don't tattle on me, then I won't tattle on you."

"I don't have any pets."

"No, you had a baby."

"But only for three days," she said. Talk about nitpicking people! He was flagrantly disregarding the rules and had the nerve to throw a minor infraction in her face.

"The cat belongs to my sister. He'll be with me for less than a week. Now, is Chocolate Chip here, or do I go into cardiac arrest?"

"He's here."

Nate visibly relaxed. "Thank God. My sister dotes on that silly feline. She flew up from San Francisco and left him with me before she left for Hawaii." As if he'd heard his name mentioned, Chocolate Chip casually strolled across the carpet and paused at Nate's feet.

Nate bent down to retrieve his sister's cat, scolding him with a harsh look.

"I suggest you keep your balcony door closed," she told him, striving for a flippant air.

"Thanks, I will." Chocolate Chip was tucked under his arm as Nate's gaze casually caught Susannah's. "You might be interested to know that Sylvia Potter's my sister." He turned and walked out her door.

"'Sylvia Potter's my sister,'" Susannah mimicked. It wasn't until she'd closed and locked her door that she recognized the import of what he'd said. "His sister," she repeated. "Did he really say that?"

Susannah was at his door before she stopped to judge the wisdom of her actions. When Nate answered her furious knock, she stared up at him, her eyes confused. "What was that you just said?"

"I said Sylvia Potter's my sister."

"I was afraid of that." Her thoughts were tumbling over one another like marbles in a bag. She'd imagined... she'd assumed....

"Who's Andrew Adams?"

"My brother?" she offered, wondering if he'd believe her.

Nate shook his head. "Try again."

"An associate from H&J Lima," she said, then hurried to explain. "When I canceled my appointment with him Monday morning, he suggested we get together for a drink to discuss business this evening. It sounded innocent enough at the time, but I should've realized it was a mistake. Adams is a known sleazeball."

An appealing smile touched the edges of Nate's mouth. "I wish I'd had a camera when you first saw me in that cocktail lounge. I thought your eyes were going to fall out of your face."

"It was your sister—she intimidated me," Susannah admitted. "She's lovely."

"So are you."

The man had obviously been standing out in the sun too long, Susannah decided. Compared to Sylvia, who was tall, blonde and had curves in all the right places, Susannah felt about as pretty as a professional wrestler.

"I'm flattered that you think so." Susannah wasn't comfortable with praise. She was much too levelheaded to let flattery affect her. When men paid her compliments, she smiled and thanked them, but she treated their words like water running off a slick surface.

Except with Nate. Everything was different with him. She seemed to be accumulating a large stack of exceptions because of Nate. As far as Susannah could see, he had no ambition, and if she'd met him anyplace other than her building, she probably wouldn't have given him a second thought. Instead she couldn't stop thinking about him. She knew better than to allow her heart to be distracted this way, and yet she couldn't seem to stop herself.

"Do you want to come in?" Nate asked and stepped aside. A bleeping sound drew Susannah's attention to a five-foot-high television screen across the room. She'd apparently interrupted Nate in the middle of an action-packed video game. A video game!

"No," she answered quickly. "I wouldn't want to interrupt you. Besides I was…just about to make myself some dinner."

"You cook?"

His astonishment—no, shock—was unflattering, to say the least.

"Of course I do."

"I'm glad to hear it, because I seem to recall that you owe me a meal."

"I—"

"And since we seem to have gotten off on the wrong foot tonight, a nice quiet dinner in front of the fireplace sounds like exactly what we need."

Susannah's thoughts were zooming at the speed of light. Nate was inviting himself to dinner—one she was supposed to whip up herself! Why did she so glibly announce that she could cook? Everything she'd ever attempted in the kitchen had been a disaster. Other than toast. Toast was her specialty. Her mind whirled with all the different ways she could serve it. Buttered? With honey? Jam? Cheese? The list was endless.

"You fix dinner and I'll bring over the wine," Nate said in a low seductive voice. "It's time we sat down together and talked. Deal?"

"I, ah, I've got some papers I have to read over tonight."

"No problem. I'll make it a point to leave early so you can finish whatever you need to."

His eyes held hers for a long moment, and despite everything Susannah knew about Nate, she still wanted time alone with him. She had some papers to review and he had to get back to his video game. A relationship like theirs was not meant to be. However, before she was even aware of what she was doing, Susannah nodded.

"Good. I'll give you an hour. Is that enough time?"

Once more, like a remote-controlled robot, she nodded.

Nate smiled and leaned forward to lightly brush his lips over hers. "I'll see you in an hour then."

He put his hand at her lower back and guided her out

the door. For a few seconds she did nothing more than stand in the hallway, wondering how she was going to get herself out of this one. She reviewed her options and discovered there was only one.

The Western Avenue Deli.

Precisely an hour later, Susannah was ready. A tossed green salad rested in the middle of the table in a crystal bowl, which had been a gift when she graduated from college. Her aunt Gerty had given it to her. Susannah loved her aunt dearly, but the poor soul had her and Emily confused. Emily would have treasured the fancy bowl. As it happened, this was the first occasion Susannah had even used it and now that she looked at it, she thought the bowl might have been meant for punch. Maybe Nate wouldn't notice. The Stroganoff was simmering in a pan and the noodles were in a foil-covered dish, keeping warm in the oven.

Susannah drew in a deep breath, then frantically waved her hands over the simmering food to disperse the scent around the condo before she opened her door.

"Hi," Nate said. He held a bottle of wine.

His eyes were so blue, it was like looking into a clear, deep lake. When she spoke, her voice trembled slightly. "Hi. Dinner's just about ready."

He sniffed the air appreciatively. "Will red wine do?"

"It's perfect," she told him, stepping aside so he could come in.

"Shall I open it now?"

"Please." She led him into the kitchen.

He cocked an eyebrow. "It looks like you've been busy."

For good measure, Susannah had stacked a few pots and pans in the sink and set out an array of spices on the counter. In addition, she'd laid out several books. None of them had anything to do with cooking—she didn't own any cookbooks—but they looked impressive.

"I hope you like Stroganoff," she said cheerfully.

"It's one of my favorites."

Susannah swallowed and nodded. She'd never been very good at deception, but then she'd rarely put her pride on the line the way she had this evening.

While she dished up the Stroganoff, Nate expertly opened the wine and poured them each a glass. When everything was ready, they sat across the table from each other.

After one taste of the buttered noodles and the rich sauce, Nate said, "This is delicious."

Susannah kept her eyes lowered. "Thanks. My mother has a recipe that's been handed down for years." It was a half-truth that was stretched about as far it could go without snapping back and hitting her in the face. Yes, her mother did have a favorite family recipe, but it was for Christmas candies.

"The salad's excellent, too. What's in the dressing?"

This was the moment Susannah had dreaded. "Ah..." Her mind faltered before she could remember exactly what usually went into salad dressings. "Oil!" she cried, as if black gold had just been discovered in her living room.

"Vinegar?"

"Yes," she agreed eagerly. "Lots of that."

Planting his elbows on the table, he smiled at her. "Spices?"

"Oh, yes, those, too."

His mouth was quivering when he took a sip of wine. Subterfuge had never been Susannah's strong suit. If

Nate hadn't started asking her these difficult questions, she might've been able to pull off the ruse. But he obviously knew, and there wasn't any reason to continue it.

"Nate," she said, after fortifying herself with a sip of wine, "I... I didn't exactly cook this meal myself."

"The Western Avenue Deli?"

She nodded, feeling wretched.

"An excellent choice."

"H-how'd you know?" Something inside her demanded further abuse. Anyone else would have dropped the matter right then.

"You mean other than the fact that you've got enough pots and pans in your sink to have fed a small army? By the way, what could you possibly have used the broiler pan for?"

"I...was hoping you'd think I'd warmed the dinner rolls on it."

"I see." He was doing an admirable job of not laughing outright, and Susannah supposed she should be grateful for that much.

After taking a bite of his—unwarmed—roll, he asked, "Where'd you get all the spices?"

"They were a Christmas gift from Emily one year. She continues to hold out hope that a miracle will happen and I'll suddenly discover I've missed my calling in life and decide to chain myself to the stove."

Nate grinned. "For future reference, I can't see how you'd need poultry seasoning or curry powder for stroganoff."

"Oh." She should've quit when she was ahead. "So... you knew right from the first?"

Nate nodded. "I'm afraid so, but I'm flattered by all the trouble you went to."

"I suppose it won't do any more harm to admit that I'm a total loss in the kitchen. I'd rather analyze a profit-and-loss statement any day than attempt to bake a batch of cookies."

Nate reached for a second dinner roll. "If you ever do, my favorite are chocolate chip."

Perhaps he was the one who'd named his sister's cat, she mused. Or maybe chocolate chip cookies were popular with his whole family. "I'll remember that." An outlet for Rainy Day Cookies had recently opened on the waterfront and they were the best money could buy.

Nate helped her clear the table once they'd finished. While she rinsed the plates and put them in the dishwasher, Nate built a fire. He was seated on the floor in front of the fireplace waiting for her when she entered the room.

"More wine?" he asked, holding up the bottle.

"Please." Inching her straight skirt slightly higher, Susannah carefully lowered herself to the carpet beside him. Nate grinned and reached for the nearby lamp, turning it to the lowest setting. Shadows from the fire flickered across the opposite wall. The atmosphere was warm and cozy.

"All right," he said softly, close to her ear. "Ask away."

Susannah frowned, not sure what he meant.

"You've been dying of curiosity about me from the moment we met. I'm simply giving you the opportunity to ask me anything you want."

Susannah gulped her wine. If he could read her so easily, then she had no place in the business world. Yes, she was full of questions about him and had been trying to find a subtle way to bring some of them into the conversation.

"First, however," he said, "let me do this."

Before she knew what was happening, Nate had pressed her down onto the carpet and was kissing her. Kissing her deeply, drugging her senses with a mastery that was just short of arrogant. He'd caught her unprepared, and before she could raise any defenses, she was captured in a dizzying wave of sensation.

When he lifted his head, Susannah stared up at him, breathless and amazed at her own ready response. Before she could react, Nate slid one hand behind her. He unpinned her hair, then ran his fingers through it.

"I've been wanting to do that all night," he murmured.

Still she couldn't speak. He'd kissed and held her, but it didn't seem to affect his power of speech, while she felt completely flustered and perplexed.

"Yes, well," she managed to mutter, scrambling to a sitting position. "I...forget what we were talking about."

Nate moved behind her and pulled her against his chest, wrapping his arms around her and nibbling on the side of her neck. "I believe you were about to ask me something."

"Yes...you're right, I was... Nate, do you work?"

"No."

Delicious shivers were racing up and down her spine. His teeth found her earlobe and he sucked on it gently, causing her insides to quake in seismic proportions.

"Why not?" she asked, her voice trembling.

"I quit."

"But why?"

"I was working too hard. I wasn't enjoying myself anymore."

"Oh."

His mouth had progressed down the gentle slope of her neck to her shoulder, and she closed her eyes to the warring emotions churning inside her. Part of her longed to surrender to the thrill of his touch, yet she hungered to learn all she could about this unconventional man.

Nate altered his position so he was in front of her again. His mouth began exploring her face with soft kisses that fell like gentle raindrops over her eyes, nose, cheeks and lips.

"Anything else you want to know?" he asked, pausing.

Unable to do more than shake her head, Susannah sighed and reluctantly unwound her arms from around his neck.

"Do you want more wine?" he asked.

"No…thank you." It demanded all the fortitude she possessed not to ask him to keep kissing her.

"Okay," he said, making himself comfortable. He raised his knees and wrapped his arms around them. "My turn."

"Your turn?"

"Yes," he said with a lazy grin that did wicked things to her equilibrium. "I have a few questions for you."

Susannah found it difficult to center her attention on anything other than the fact that Nate was sitting a few inches away from her and could lean over and kiss her again at any moment.

"You don't object?"

"No," she said, gesturing with her hand.

"Okay, tell me about yourself."

Susannah shrugged. For the life of her, she couldn't think of a single thing that would impress him. She'd worked hard, climbing the corporate ladder, inching her way toward her long-range goals.

"I'm up for promotion," she began. "I started working for H&J Lima five years ago. I chose this company, although the pay was less than I'd been offered by two others."

"Why?"

"There's opportunity with them. I looked at the chain of command and saw room for steady advancement. Being a woman is both an asset and a detriment, if you know what I mean. I had to prove myself, but I was also aware of being the token woman on the staff."

"You mean you were hired because you were female?"

"Exactly. But I swallowed my pride and set about proving I could handle anything asked of me, and I have."

Nate looked proud of her.

"Five years ago, I decided I wanted to be the vice president in charge of marketing," she said, her voice gaining strength and conviction. "It was a significant goal, because I'd be the first woman to hold a position that high within the company."

"And?"

"And I'll find out in the next few weeks if I'm going to get it. I'll derive a great deal of satisfaction from knowing I earned it. I won't be their token female in upper management anymore."

"What's the competition like?"

Susannah slowly expelled her breath. "Stiff. Damn stiff. There are two men in the running, and both have been with the company as long as me, in one case longer. Both are older, bright and dedicated."

"You're bright and dedicated, too."

"That may not be enough," she murmured. Now that her dream was within reach, she yearned for it even more. She could feel Nate's eyes studying her.

"This promotion means a lot to you, doesn't it?"

"Yes. It's everything. From the moment I was hired, I've striven toward this very thing. And it's happening faster than I dared hope."

Nate was silent for a moment. He put another log on the fire, and although she hadn't asked for it, he replenished her wine.

"Have you ever stopped to think what would happen if you achieved your dreams and then discovered you weren't happy?"

"How could I not be happy?" she asked. She honestly didn't understand. For years she'd worked toward obtaining this vice presidency. Of course she was going to be happy! She'd be thrilled, elated, jubilant.

Nate's eyes narrowed. "Aren't you worried about there being a void in your life?"

Oh, no, he was beginning to sound like Emily. "No," she said flatly. "How could there be? Now before you start, I know what you're going to say, so please don't. Save your breath. Emily has argued with me about this from the time I graduated from college."

Nate looked genuinely puzzled. "Argued with you about what?"

"Getting married and having a family. But the roles of wife and mother just aren't for me. They never have been and they never will be."

"I see."

Susannah was convinced he didn't. "If I were a man, would everyone be pushing me to marry?"

Nate chuckled and his eyes rested on her for a tantalizing moment. "Trust me, Susannah, no one's going to mistake you for a man."

She grinned and lowered her gaze. "It's the nose, isn't it?"

"The nose?"

"Yes." She turned sideways and held her chin at a lofty angle so he could view her classic profile. "I think it's my best feature." The wine had obviously gone to her head. But that was all right because she felt warm and comfortable and Nate was sitting beside her. Rarely had she been more content.

"Actually I wasn't thinking about your nose at all. I was remembering that first night with Michelle."

"You mean when we both fell asleep in the living room?"

Nate nodded and reached for her shoulder, his eyes trapping hers. "It was the only time in my life I can remember having one woman in my arms and wanting another."

Five

"I've decided not to see him again," Susannah announced.

"I beg your pardon?" Ms. Brooks stopped in her tracks and looked at her boss.

Unnerved, Susannah made busywork at her desk. "I'm sorry, I didn't realize I'd spoken out loud."

Her assistant brought a cup of coffee to her desk and hesitated. "How late did you end up staying last night?"

"Not long," Susannah lied. It had, in fact, been past ten when she left the building.

"And the night before?" Ms. Brooks pressed.

"Not so late," Susannah fibbed again.

Eleanor Brooks walked quietly out of the room, but not before she gave Susannah a stern look that said she didn't believe her for one moment.

As soon as the door closed, Susannah pressed the tips of her fingers to her forehead and exhaled a slow steady breath. Dear heaven, Nate Townsend had her so twisted up inside she was talking to the walls.

Nate hadn't left her condo until almost eleven the night he'd come for dinner, and by that time he'd kissed her nearly senseless. Three days had passed and Susannah could still taste and feel his mouth on hers. The scent of his aftershave lingered in her living room to the point that she looked for him whenever she entered the room.

The man didn't even hold down a job. Oh, he'd had one, but he'd quit and it was obvious, to her at least, that he wasn't in any hurry to get another. He'd held her and kissed her and patiently listened to her dreams. But he hadn't shared any of his own. He had no ambition, and no urge to better himself.

And Susannah was falling head over heels for him.

Through the years, she had assumed she was immune to falling in love. She was too sensible for that, too practical, too career-oriented. Not once did she suspect she'd fall so hard for someone like Nate. Nate, with his no-need-to-rush attitude and tomorrow-will-take-care-of-itself lifestyle.

Aware of what was happening to her, Susannah had done the only thing she could—gone into hiding. For three days she'd managed to avoid Nate. He'd left a couple of messages on her answering machine, which she'd ignored. If he confronted her, she had a perfect excuse. She was working. And it was true: she spent much of her time holed up in the office. She headed out early in the morning and arrived home late at night. The extra hours she was putting in served two distinct purposes: they showed her employer that she was dedicated, and they kept her from having to deal with Nate.

Her intercom buzzed, pulling Susannah from her thoughts. She reached over and hit the speaker button. "Yes?"

"Mr. Townsend is on the phone."

Susannah squeezed her eyes shut and her throat muscles tightened. "Take a message, please," she said, her voice little more than a husky whisper.

"He insists on speaking to you."

"Tell him I'm in a meeting and...unavailable."

It wasn't like Susannah to lie, and Eleanor Brooks knew it. She finally asked, "Is this the man you plan never to see again?"

The abruptness of her question caught Susannah off guard. "Yes..."

"I assumed as much. I'll tell him you're not available."

"Thank you." Susannah's hand was trembling as she released the intercom button. She hadn't dreamed Nate would call her at the office.

By eleven, a feeling of normalcy had returned. Susannah was gathering her notes for an executive meeting with the finance committee when her assistant came in. "Mr. Franklin phoned and canceled his afternoon appointment."

Susannah glanced up. "Did he want to reschedule?"

"Friday at ten."

She nodded. "That'll be fine." It was on the tip of her tongue to ask how Nate had responded earlier when told she was unavailable, but she resisted the temptation.

"Mr. Townsend left a message. I wrote it out for you."

Her assistant knew her too well, it seemed. "Leave it on my desk."

"You might want to read it," the older woman urged.

"I will. Later."

Halfway through the meeting, Susannah wished she'd followed her assistant's advice. Impatience filled her. She wanted this finance meeting over so she could hurry back to her desk and read the message from Nate. Figures flew overhead—important ones with a bearing on the outcome of the marketing strategy she and her department had planned. Yet, again and again, Susannah found her thoughts drifting to Nate.

That wasn't typical for her. When the meeting ended, she was furious with herself. She walked briskly back to her office, her low heels making staccato taps against the polished hardwood floor.

"Ms. Brooks," she said, as she went into the outer office. "Could you—"

Susannah stopped dead in her tracks. The last person she'd expected to see was Nate. He was sitting on the corner of her assistant's desk, wearing a Mariners T-shirt, faded jeans and a baseball cap. He tossed a baseball in the air and deftly caught it in his mitt.

Eleanor Brooks looked both unsettled and inordinately pleased. No doubt Nate had used some of his considerable male charm on the gray-haired grandmother.

"It's about time," Nate said, grinning devilishly. He leaped off the desk. "I was afraid we were going to be late for the game."

"Game?" Susannah repeated. "What game?"

Nate held out his right hand to show her his baseball mitt and ball—just in case she hadn't noticed them. "The Mariners are playing, and I've got two of the best seats in the place reserved for you and me."

Susannah's heart sank to the pit of her stomach. It was just like Nate to assume she could take off in the middle of the day on some lark. He obviously had no understanding of what being a responsible employee meant. It was bad enough that he'd dominated her thoughts during an important meeting, but suggesting they escape for an afternoon was too much.

"You don't honestly expect me to leave, do you?"

"Yes."

"I can't. I won't."

"Why not?"

"I'm working," she said, deciding that was sufficient explanation.

"You've been at the office every night this week. You need a break. Come on, Susannah, let your hair down long enough to have a good time. It isn't going to hurt. I promise."

He was so casual about the whole thing, as if obligation and duty were of little significance. It proved more than anything that he didn't grasp the concept of hard work being its own reward.

"It *will* hurt," she insisted.

"Okay," he said forcefully. "What's so important this afternoon?" To answer his own question, he walked around her assistant's desk. Then he leaned forward and flipped open the pages of her appointment schedule.

"Mr. Franklin canceled his three-o'clock appointment," Ms. Brooks reminded her primly. "And you skipped lunch because of the finance meeting."

Susannah frowned at the older woman, wondering what exactly Nate had said or done that had turned her into a traitor on such short acquaintance.

"I have more important things to do," Susannah told them both stiffly.

"Not according to your appointment schedule," Nate said confidently. "As far as I can see, you haven't got an excuse in the world not to attend that baseball game with me."

Susannah wasn't going to stand there and argue with him. Instead she marched into her office and dutifully sat down at her desk.

To her chagrin both Nate and Ms. Brooks followed her inside. It was all Susannah could do not to bury her face in her hands and demand that they leave.

"Susannah," Nate coaxed gently, "you need a break. Tomorrow you'll come back rejuvenated and refreshed. If you spend too much time at the office, you'll begin to lose perspective. An afternoon away will do you good."

Her assistant seemed about to comment, but Susannah stopped her with a scalding look. Before she could say anything to Nate, someone else entered her office.

"Susannah, I was just checking over these figures and I—" John Hammer stopped midsentence when he noticed the other two people in her office.

If there'd been an open window handy, Susannah would gladly have hurled herself through it. The company director smiled benignly, however, looking slightly embarrassed at having interrupted her. Now, it seemed, he was awaiting an introduction.

"John, this is Nate Townsend...my neighbor."

Ever the gentleman, John stepped forward and extended his hand. If he thought it a bit odd to find a man in Susannah's office dressed in jeans and a T-shirt, he didn't show it.

"Nate Townsend," he repeated, pumping his hand. "It's a pleasure, a real pleasure."

"Thank you," Nate said. "I'm here to pick up Susannah. We're going to a Mariners game this afternoon."

John removed the glasses from the end of his nose, and nodded thoughtfully. "An excellent idea."

"No, I really don't think I'll go. I mean..." She stopped when it became obvious that no one was paying any attention to her protests.

"Nate's absolutely right," John said, setting the file

on her desk. "You've been putting in a lot of extra hours lately. Take the afternoon off. Enjoy yourself."

"But—"

"Susannah, are you actually going to argue with your boss?" Nate prompted.

Her jaw sagged. "I…guess not."

"Good. Good." John looked as pleased as if he'd made the suggestion himself. He was smiling at Nate and nodding as if the two were longtime friends.

Her expression more than a little smug, Eleanor Brooks returned to her own office.

Nate glanced at his watch. "We'd better go now or we'll miss the opening pitch."

With heavy reluctance, Susannah scooped up her purse. She'd done everything within her power to avoid Nate, yet through no fault of her own, she was spending the afternoon in his company. They didn't get a chance to speak until they reached the elevator, but once the door glided shut, Susannah tried again. "I can't go to a baseball game dressed like this."

"You look fine to me."

"But I've got a business suit on."

"Hey, don't sweat the small stuff." His hand clasped hers and when the elevator door opened on the bottom floor, he led her out of the building. Once outside, he quickened his pace as he headed toward the stadium.

"I want you to know I don't appreciate this one bit," she said, forced to half run to keep pace with his long-legged stride.

"If you're going to complain, wait until we're inside and settled. As I recall, you get testy on an empty stomach." His smile could have caused a nuclear meltdown, but she was determined not to let it influence her. Nate had a lot of nerve to come bursting into her office, and as soon as she could catch her breath, she'd tell him so.

"Don't worry, I'm going to feed you," he promised as they waited at a red light.

His words did nothing to reassure her. Heaven only knew what John Hammer thought—although she had to admit that her employer's reaction had baffled her. John was as hardworking and dedicated as Susannah herself. It wasn't like him to fall in with Nate's offbeat idea of attending a ball game in the middle of the afternoon. In fact, it almost seemed as if John knew Nate, or had heard of him. Hardly ever had she seen her employer show such enthusiasm when introduced to anyone.

The man at the gate took their tickets and Nate directed her to a pair of seats right behind home plate. Never having attended a professional baseball game before, Susannah didn't realize how good these seats were—until Nate pointed it out.

She'd no sooner sat down in her place than he leaped to his feet and raised his right hand, glove and all. Susannah slouched as low as she could in the uncomfortable seat. The next thing she knew, a bag of peanuts whizzed past her ear.

"Hey!" she cried, and jerked around.

"Don't panic," Nate said, chuckling. "I'm just playing catch with the vendor." Seconds after the words left his mouth he expertly caught another bag.

"Here." Nate handed her both bags. "The hot dog guy will be by in a minute."

Susannah had no intention of sitting still while food was being tossed about. "I'm getting out of here. If you want to play ball, go on the field."

Once more Nate laughed, the sound husky and rich.

"If you're going to balk at every little thing, I know a good way to settle you down."

"Do you think I'm a complete idiot? First you drag me away from my office, then you insist on throwing food around like some schoolboy. I can't even begin to guess what's going to happen next and—"

She didn't get any further, although her outrage was mounting with every breath she drew. Before she could guess his intention, Nate planted his hands on her shoulders, pulled her against him and gave her one of his dynamite-packed kisses.

Completely unnerved, she numbly lowered herself back into her seat and closed her eyes, her pulse roaring in her ears.

A little later, Nate was pressing a fat hot dog into her lifeless hands. "I had them put everything on it," he said.

A glance at the overstuffed bun informed her that "everything" included pickles, mustard, ketchup, onions and sauerkraut and one or two other items she wasn't sure she could identify.

"Now eat it before I'm obliged to kiss you again."

His warning was all the incentive she needed. Several minutes had passed since he'd last kissed her and she was still so bemused she could hardly think. On cue, she lifted the hot dog to her mouth, prepared for the worst. But to her surprise, it didn't taste half bad. In fact, it was downright palatable. When she'd polished it off, she started on the peanuts, which were still warm from the roaster. Warm and salty, and excellent.

Another vendor strolled past and Nate bought them each a cold drink.

The first inning was over by the time Susannah finished eating. Nate reached for her hand. "Feel better?" His eyes were fervent and completely focused on her.

One look certainly had an effect on Susannah. Whenever her eyes met his she felt as though she was caught in a whirlpool and about to be sucked under. She'd tried to resist the pull, but it had been impossible.

"Susannah?" he asked. "Are you okay?"

She managed to nod. After a moment she said, "I still feel kind of foolish...."

"Why?"

"Come on, Nate. I'm the only person here in a business suit."

"I can fix that."

"Oh?" Susannah had her doubts. What did he plan to do? Undress her?

He gave her another of his knowing smiles and casually excused himself. Puzzled, Susannah watched as he made his way toward the concession stand. Then he was back—with a Mariners T-shirt in one hand, a baseball cap in the other.

Removing her suit jacket, Susannah slipped the T-shirt over her head. When she'd done that, Nate set the baseball cap on her head, adjusting it so the bill dipped low over her forehead.

"There," he said, satisfied. "You look like one of the home team now."

"Thanks." She smoothed the T-shirt over her straight skirt and wondered how peculiar she looked. Funny, but it didn't seem to matter. She was having a good time with Nate, and it felt wonderful to laugh and enjoy life.

"You're welcome."

They both settled back in their seats to give their full

attention to the game. The Seattle Mariners were down by one run at the bottom of the fifth inning.

Susannah didn't know all that much about baseball, but the crowd was lending vociferous support to the home team and she loved the atmosphere, which crackled with excitement, as if everyone was waiting for something splendid to happen.

"You've been avoiding me," Nate said halfway through the sixth inning. "I want to know why."

She couldn't very well tell him the truth, but lying seemed equally unattractive. Pretending to concentrate on the game, Susannah shrugged, hoping he'd accept that as explanation enough.

"Susannah?"

She should've known he'd force the issue. "Because I don't like what happens when you kiss me," she blurted out.

"What happens?" he echoed. "The first time we kissed, you nearly dealt my ego a fatal blow. As I recall, you claimed it was a pleasant experience. I believe you described it as 'nice,' and said that was about it."

Susannah kicked at the litter on the cement floor with the toes of her pumps, her eyes downcast. "Yes, I do remember saying something along those lines."

"You lied?"

He didn't need to drill her to prove his point. "All right," she admitted, "I lied. But you knew that all along. You must have, otherwise..."

"Otherwise what?"

"You wouldn't be kissing me every time you want to coerce me into doing something I don't want to do."

Crow's-feet fanned out beside his eyes as he grinned, making him look naughty and angelic at once.

"You knew all along," she repeated, "so don't give me that injured-ego routine!"

"There's electricity between us, Susannah, and it's about time you recognized that. I did, from the very first."

"Sure. But there's a big difference between standing next to an electrical outlet and fooling around with a high-voltage wire. I prefer to play it safe."

"Not me." He ran a knuckle down the side of her face. Circling her chin, his finger rested on her lips, which parted softly. "No," he said in a hushed voice, studying her. "I always did prefer to live dangerously."

"I've noticed." Nerve endings tingled at his touch, and Susannah held her breath until he removed his hand. Only then did she breathe normally again.

The cheering crowd alerted her to the fact that something important had taken place on the field. Glad to have her attention diverted from Nate, she watched as a Mariner rounded the bases for a home run. Pleased, she clapped politely, her enthusiasm far more restrained than that of the spectators around her.

That changed, however, at the bottom of the ninth. The bases were loaded and Susannah sat on the edge of her seat as the designated hitter approached home plate.

The fans chanted, "Grand slam, grand slam!" and Susannah soon joined in. The pitcher tossed a fastball, and unable to watch, she squeezed her eyes shut. But the sound of the wood hitting the ball was unmistakable. Susannah opened her eyes and jumped to her feet as the ball flew into left field and over the wall. The crowd went wild, and after doing an impulsive jig, Susannah threw her arms around Nate's neck and hugged him.

Nate appeared equally excited, and when Susannah

had her feet back on the ground, he raised his fingers to his mouth and let loose a piercing whistle.

She was laughing and cheering and even went so far as to cup her hands over her mouth and boisterously yell her approval. It was then that she noticed Nate watching her. His eyes were wide with feigned shock, as if he couldn't believe the refined and businesslike Susannah Simmons would lower herself to such uninhibited behavior.

His apparent censure instantly cooled her reactions, and she returned to her seat and demurely folded her hands and crossed her ankles, embarrassed now by her response to something as mindless as a baseball game. When she dared to glance in Nate's direction, she discovered him watching her intently.

"Nate," she whispered, disconcerted by his attention. The game was over and the people around them had started to leave their seats. Susannah could feel the color in her cheeks. "Why are you looking at me like that?"

"You amaze me."

More likely, she'd disgraced herself in his eyes by her wild display. She was mortified.

"You're going to be all right, Susannah Simmons," he said cryptically. "We both are."

"Susannah, I didn't expect to find you home on a Saturday," Emily said as she stepped inside her sister's apartment. "Michelle and I are going to the Pike Place Market this morning and decided to drop by and see you first. You don't mind, do you?"

"No. Of course not. Come in." Susannah brushed the disheveled hair from her face. "What time is it anyway?"

"Eight-thirty."

"That late, huh?"

Emily chuckled. "I forgot. You like to sleep in on the weekends, don't you?"

"Don't worry about it," she said on the tail end of a yawn. "I'll put on a pot of coffee and be myself in no time."

Emily and Michelle followed her into the kitchen. Once the coffee was brewing, Susannah took the chair across from her sister. Michelle gleefully waved her arms, and despite the early hour, Susannah found herself smiling at her niece's enthusiasm for life. She held out her arms to the baby and was pleasantly surprised when Michelle came happily into them.

"She remembers you," Emily said.

"Of course she does," Susannah said as she nuzzled her niece's neck. "We had some great times, didn't we, kiddo? Especially when it came to feeding you plums."

Emily chuckled. "I don't think I'll ever be able to thank you enough for keeping Michelle that weekend. It was just what Robert and I needed."

"Don't mention it." Susannah dismissed Emily's appreciation with a weak gesture of her hand. She was the one who'd profited from that zany weekend. It might've been several more weeks before she met Nate if it hadn't been for Michelle.

Emily sighed. "I've been trying to get hold of you, but you're never home."

"Why didn't you leave a message?"

Emily shook her head and her long braid swung back and forth. "You know I hate doing that. I get all tongue-tied and I can't seem to talk. You might phone *me* sometime, you know."

Over the past couple of weeks, Susannah had considered it, but she'd been avoiding her sister because she knew that the minute she called, Emily was going to ply her with questions about Nate.

"Have you been working late every night?" Emily asked.

Susannah dropped her gaze. "Not exactly."

"Then you must've been out with Nate Townsend." Emily didn't give her time to respond, but immediately started jabbering away. "I don't mind telling you, Susannah, both Robert and I were impressed with your new neighbor. He was wonderful with Michelle, and from the way he was looking at you, I think he's interested. Now, please don't tell me to keep my nose out of this. You're twenty-eight, for heaven's sake, and that biological clock is ticking away. If you're ever going to settle down and get serious about a man, the time is now. And personally, I don't think you'll find anyone better than Nate. Why, he's…"

She paused to breathe, giving Susannah the chance she'd been waiting for. "Coffee?"

Emily blinked, then nodded. "You didn't listen to a word I said, did you?"

"I listened."

"But you didn't *hear* a single word."

"Sure I did," Susannah countered. "You're saying I'd be a fool not to put a ring through Nate Townsend's nose. You want me to marry him before I lose my last chance at motherhood."

"Exactly," Emily said, looking pleased that she'd conveyed her message so effectively.

Michelle squirmed and Susannah set her on the floor to crawl around and explore.

"Well?" Emily pressed. "What do you think?"

"About marrying Nate? It would never work," she said calmly, as though they were discussing something as mundane as stock options, "for more reasons than you realize. But to satisfy your curiosity I'll list a few. First and foremost I've got a career and he doesn't, and furthermore—"

"Nate's unemployed?" her sister gasped. "But how can he not work? I mean, this is an expensive complex. Didn't you tell me the condominium next to yours is nearly twice as large? How can he afford to live there if he doesn't have a job?"

"I have no idea."

Susannah forgot about Nate for the moment as her eyes followed Michelle, astonished by how much she'd missed her. She stood and got two cups from the cupboard.

"That's not decaffeinated, is it?" Emily asked.

"No."

"Then don't bother pouring me a cup. I gave up caffeine years ago."

"Right." Susannah should have remembered. Michelle crawled across the kitchen floor toward her and, using Susannah's nightgown for leverage, pulled herself into a standing position. She smiled proudly at her achievement.

"Listen," Susannah said impulsively, leaning over to pick up her niece. "Why don't you leave Michelle with me? We'll take this morning to become reacquainted and you can do your shopping without having to worry about her."

There was a shocked silence. "Susannah?" Emily said. "Did I hear you correctly? I thought I just heard you volunteer to babysit."

Six

The morning was bright and sunny, and unable to resist, Susannah opened the sliding glass door and let the salty breeze off Elliott Bay blow into her apartment. Sitting on the kitchen floor with a saucepan and a wooden spoon, Michelle proceeded to demonstrate her musical talents by pounding out a loud enthusiastic beat.

When the phone rang, Susannah knew it was Nate.

"Good morning," she said, pushing her hair behind her ears. She hadn't pinned it up when she got dressed, knowing Nate preferred it down, and she didn't try to fool herself with excuses for leaving it that way.

"Morning," he breathed into the phone. "Do you have a drummer visiting?"

"No, a special friend. I think she'd like to say hello. Wait a minute." Susannah put down the receiver and lifted Michelle from the floor. Holding the baby on her hip, she pressed the telephone receiver to the side of Michelle's face. Practically on cue, the child spouted an excited flow of gibberish.

"I think she said good-morning," Susannah explained.

"Michelle?"

"How many other babies would pay me a visit?"

"How many Simmons girls are there?"

"Only Emily and me," she answered with a soft laugh, "but trust me, the two of us were enough for any one set of parents to handle."

Nate's responding chuckle was warm and seductive. "Are you in the mood for more company?"

"Sure. If you bring the Danish, I'll provide the coffee."

"You've got yourself a deal."

It wasn't until several minutes had passed that Susannah realized how little resistance she'd been putting up lately when it came to Nate. Since the baseball game, she'd given up trying to avoid him; she simply didn't have the heart for it, although deep down, she knew anything beyond friendship was impossible. Yet despite her misgivings, after that one afternoon with him she'd come away feeling exhilarated. Being with Nate was like recapturing a part of her youth that had somehow escaped her. But even though seeing him was fun, it wasn't meant to last, and Susannah reminded herself of that every time they were together. Nate Townsend was like an unexpected burst of sunshine on an overcast day, but soon the rain would come, the way it always did. Susannah wasn't going to be fooled into believing there could ever be anything permanent between them.

When Nate arrived, the reunion was complete. He lifted Michelle high in the air and Susannah smiled at the little girl's squeals of delight.

"Where's Emily?" he wanted to know.

"Shopping. She won't be more than an hour or so."

With Michelle in one arm, Nate moved into the

kitchen, where Susannah was dishing up the pastries and pouring coffee. "She's grown, hasn't she?" she said.

"Is that another new tooth?" he asked, peering inside the baby's mouth.

"It might be," Susannah replied, taking a look herself.

Nate slipped his free arm around her shoulder and smiled at her. "Your hair's down," he murmured, his smile caressing her upturned face.

She nodded, not knowing how else to respond, although a dozen plausible excuses raced through her mind. But none of them would have been true.

"For me?"

Once more, she answered him with a slight nod.

"Thank you," he whispered, his face so close to her own that his words were like a kiss.

Susannah leaned into him, pressing herself against his solid length. When he kissed her, she could hardly stop herself from melting into his arms.

Michelle thought it was great fun to have two adults for company. She wove her fingers into Susannah's hair and yanked until Susannah was forced to pull away from Nate.

Smiling, Nate disengaged the baby's hand from her aunt's hair and kissed Susannah again. "Hmm," he said when he lifted his head. "You taste better than any sweet roll ever could."

Unnerved, and suddenly feeling shy, Susannah busied herself setting the pastries on the table.

"Do you have plans for today?" he asked, taking a chair, Michelle gurgling happily on his lap.

Michelle was content for now, but from experience

Susannah knew she'd want to be back on the floor soon. "I... I was planning to go to the office for an hour or so."

"I don't think so," Nate said flatly.

"You don't?"

"I'm taking you out." He surveyed her navy blue slacks and the winter-white sweater she wore. "I don't suppose you have any jeans."

Susannah nodded. She knew she did, somewhere, but it was years since she'd worn them. As long ago as college, and maybe even her last year of high school. "I don't know if they'll fit, though."

"Go try them on."

"Why? What are you planning? Knowing you, I could end up on top of Mount Rainier looking over a crevasse, with no idea how I got there."

"We're going to fly a kite today," he said casually, as if it was something they'd done several times.

Susannah thought she'd misunderstood him. Nate obviously loved this kind of surprise. First a baseball game in the middle of a workday, and now kites?

"You heard me right. Now go find your jeans."

"But...kites...that's for kids. Frankly, Nate," she said, her voice gaining conviction, "I don't happen to have one hidden away in a closet. Besides, isn't that something parents do with their children?"

"No, it's for everyone. Adults have been known to have fun, too. Don't worry about a thing. I built a huge one and it's ready for testing."

"A kite?" she repeated, holding in the desire to laugh outright. She'd been in grade school when she'd last attempted anything so...so juvenile.

By the time Susannah had rummaged in her closet and found an old pair of jeans, Emily had returned for

Michelle. Nate let her sister inside, but the bedroom door was cracked open, and Susannah could hear the conversation. She held her breath, first because her hips were a tiny bit wider than the last time she'd worn her jeans, and also because Susannah could never be sure what her sister was going to say. Or do.

It'd be just like Emily to start telling Nate how suitable Susannah would be as a wife. That thought was sobering and for a moment Susannah stopped wriggling into her pants.

"Nate," she heard her sister say, "it's so good of you to help with Michelle." In her excitement, her voice was a full octave higher than usual.

"No problem. Susannah will be out in a minute—she's putting on a pair of jeans. We're going to Gas Works Park to fly a kite."

There was a short pause. "Susannah wearing jeans and flying a kite? You mean she's actually going with you?"

"Of course I am. Don't look so shocked," Susannah said, walking into the room. "How did the shopping go?"

Emily couldn't seem to close her mouth. She stared at her sister to the point of embarrassment, then swung her gaze to Nate and back to Susannah again.

Susannah realized she must look different, wearing jeans and with her hair down, but it certainly didn't warrant this openmouthed gawking.

"Emily?" Susannah waved her hand in front of her sister's face in an effort to bring her back to earth.

"Oh...the shopping went just fine. I was able to get the fresh herbs I wanted. Basil and thyme and...some others." As though in a daze, Emily lifted the home-sewn bag draped over her arm as evidence of her successful trip to the market.

"Good," Susannah said enthusiastically, wanting to smooth over her sister's outrageous reaction. "Michelle wasn't a bit of trouble. If you need me to watch her again, just say so."

Her sister's eyes grew wider. She swallowed and nodded. "Thanks. I'll remember that."

The sky was as blue as Nate's eyes, Susannah thought, sitting with her knees tucked under her chin on the lush green grass of Gas Works Park. The wind whipped Nate's box kite back and forth as he scrambled from one hill to the next, letting the brisk breeze carry the multicolored crate in several directions. As it was late September, Susannah didn't expect many more glorious Indian summer days like this one.

She closed her eyes and soaked up the sun. Her spirits raced with the kites that abounded in the popular park. She felt like tossing back her head and laughing triumphantly, for no other reason than that it felt good to be alive.

"I'm beat," Nate said, dropping down on the grass beside her. He lay on his back, arms and legs spread-eagle.

"Where's the kite?"

"I gave it to one of the kids who didn't have one."

Susannah smiled. That sounded exactly like something Nate would do. He'd spent hours designing and constructing the box kite, and yet he'd impulsively given it away without a second thought.

"Actually I begged the kid to take it, before I keeled

over from exhaustion," he amended. "Don't let anyone tell you otherwise. Flying a kite is hard work."

Work was a subject Susannah stringently avoided with Nate. From the first he'd been completely open with her. Open and honest. She was confident that if she quizzed him about his profession or lack of one, he'd answer her truthfully.

Susannah had decided that what she didn't know about him couldn't upset her. Nate apparently had plenty of money. He certainly didn't seem troubled by financial difficulties. But it was his attitude that worried her. He seemed to see life as a grand adventure; he leaped from one interest to another without rhyme or reason. Nothing appeared to be more important or vital than the moment.

"You're frowning," he said. He slipped a hand around her neck and pulled her down until her face was within inches of his own. "Aren't you having fun?"

She nodded, unable to deny the obvious.

"Then what's the problem?"

"Nothing."

He hesitated and the edges of his mouth lifted sensuously. "It's a good thing you didn't become an attorney," he said with a roguish grin. "You'd never be able to fool a jury."

Susannah was astonished that Nate knew she'd once seriously considered going into law.

He grinned at her. "Emily told me you'd thought about entering law school."

Susannah blinked a couple of times, then smiled, too. She was determined not to ruin this magnificent afternoon with her concerns.

"Kiss me, Susannah," he whispered. The humor had left his face and his gaze searched hers.

Her breath caught. She lifted her eyes and quickly glanced around. The park was crowded and children were everywhere.

"No," he said, cradling the sides of her face. "No fair peeking. I want you to kiss me no matter how many spectators there are."

"But—"

"If you don't kiss me, I'll simply have to kiss you. And, honey, if I do, watch out because—"

Not allowing him to finish, she lowered her mouth and gently skimmed her lips over his. Even that small sample was enough to send the blood racing through her veins. Whatever magic quality this man had should be bottled and sold over the counter. Susannah knew she'd be the first one in line to buy it.

"Are you always this stingy?" he asked when she raised her head.

"In public, yes."

His eyes were smiling and Susannah swore she could have drowned in his look. He exhaled, then bounded to his feet with an energy she had to envy.

"I'm starved," he announced, reaching out for her. Susannah placed her hand in his and he pulled her to her feet. "But I hope you realize," he whispered close to her ear, wrapping his arm around her waist, "my appetite isn't for food. I'm crazy about you, Susannah Simmons. Eventually we're going to have to do something about that."

"I hope I'm not too early," Susannah said as she entered her sister's home on Capitol Hill. When Emily had called to invite her to Sunday dinner, she hadn't bothered to disguise her intentions. Emily was dying to grill Susannah about her budding relationship with Nate Townsend. A week ago, Susannah would've found an excuse to get out of tonight's dinner. But after spending an entire Saturday with Nate, she was so confused that she was willing to talk this out with her sister, who seemed so much more competent in dealing with male/female relationships.

"Your timing's perfect," Emily said, coming out of the kitchen to greet her. She wore a full-length skirt with a bib apron, and her long hair was woven into a single braid that fell halfway down her back.

"Here." Susannah handed her sister a bottle of chardonnay, hoping it was appropriate for the meal.

"How thoughtful," Emily murmured, leading her back into the kitchen. The house was an older one, built in the early forties, with a large family kitchen. The red linoleum countertop was crowded with freshly canned tomatoes. Boxes of jars were stacked on the floor, along with a wicker basket filled with sun-dried diapers. A rope of garlic dangled above the sink and a row of potted plants lined the windowsill.

"Whatever you're serving smells wonderful."

"It's lentil soup."

Emily opened the oven and pulled out the rack, wadding up the skirt of her apron to protect her fingers. "I made a fresh apple pie. Naturally I used organically grown apples so you don't need to worry."

"Oh, good." That hadn't been a major concern of Susannah's.

"Where's Michelle?" Father and daughter were conspicuously absent.

Emily turned around, looking mildly guilty, and Susannah realized that her sister had gone to some lengths to provide time alone with her. No doubt she was anxious to wring out as much information about Nate as possible. Not that Susannah had a lot to tell.

"How was your day in the park?"

Susannah took a seat on the stool and made herself comfortable for the coming inquisition. "Great. I really enjoyed it."

"You like Nate, don't you?"

Like was the understatement of the year. Contrary to every ounce of sense she possessed, Susannah was falling in love with her neighbor. It wasn't what she wanted, but she hadn't been able to stop herself.

"Yes, I like him," she answered after a significant pause.

Emily seemed thrilled by her admission. "I thought as much," she said, nodding profoundly. She pushed a stool next to Susannah and sat down. Emily's hands were rarely idle, and true to form, she reached for her crocheting.

"I'm waiting," Susannah said, growing impatient.

"For what?"

"For the lecture."

Emily cracked a knowing smile. "I was gathering my thoughts. You were always the one who could evaluate things so well. I always had trouble with that and you aced every paper."

"School reports have very little to do with real life," Susannah reminded her. How much simpler it would be if she could just look up everything she needed to know about dealing with Nate.

"I knew that, but I wasn't sure you did."

Perhaps Susannah hadn't until she'd met Nate. "Emily," she said, her stomach tightening, "I need to ask you something...important. How did you know you loved Robert? What was it that told you the two of you were meant to share your lives?" Susannah understood that she was practically laying her cards faceup on the table, but she was past the point of subtlety. She wanted hard facts.

Her sister smiled and tugged at her ball of yarn before she responded. "I don't think you're going to like my answer," she murmured, frowning slightly. "It was the first time Robert kissed me."

Susannah nearly toppled from her perch on the stool, remembering her experience with Nate. "What happened?"

"We'd gone for a nature walk in the rain forest over on the Olympic Peninsula and had stopped to rest. Robert helped me remove my backpack, then he looked into my eyes and leaned over and kissed me." She sighed softly at the memory. "I don't think he intended to do it because he looked so shocked afterward."

"Then what?"

"Robert took off his own backpack and asked if I minded that he'd kissed me. Naturally I told him I rather liked it, and he sat down next to me and did it again—only this time it wasn't a peck on the lips but a full-blown kiss." Emily's shoulders sagged a little in a sigh. "The moment his lips touched mine I couldn't think, I couldn't breathe, I couldn't even move. When he finished I was trembling so much I thought something might be physically wrong with me."

"So would you say you felt...electricity?"

"Exactly."

"And you never had that with any of the other men you dated?"

"Never."

Susannah wiped a hand down her face. "You're right," she whispered. "I don't like your answer."

Emily paused in her crocheting to glance at her. "Nate kissed you and you felt something?"

Susannah nodded. "I was nearly electrocuted."

"Oh, Susannah, you poor thing!" She patted her sister's hand. "You don't know what to do, do you?"

"No," she admitted, feeling wretched.

"You never expected to fall in love, did you?"

Slowly Susannah shook her head. And it couldn't be happening at a worse time. The promotion was going to be announced within the next week, and the entire direction of her life could be altered if she became involved with Nate. She didn't even know if that was what either of them wanted. Susannah felt mystified by everything going on in her life, which until a few short weeks ago had been so straightforward and uncluttered.

"Are you thinking of marriage?" Emily asked outright.

"Marriage," Susannah echoed weakly. It seemed the natural conclusion when two people were falling in love. She was willing to acknowledge her feelings, but she wasn't completely confident Nate felt the same things she did. Nor was she positive that he was ready to move into something as permanent as a lifelong commitment. She knew *she* wasn't, and the very thought of all this was enough to throw her into a tizzy.

"I don't…know about marriage," Susannah said. "We haven't discussed anything like that." The fact was, they hadn't even talked about dating regularly.

"Trust me, if you leave it to Nate the subject of marriage will never come up. Men never want to talk about getting married. The topic is left totally up to us women."

"Oh, come on—"

"No, it's true. From the time Eve slipped Adam the apple, we've been stuck with the burden of taming men, and it's never more difficult than when it comes to convincing one he should take a wife."

"But surely Robert wanted to get married?"

"Don't be silly. Robert's like every other man alive. I had to convince him this was what he wanted. Subtlety is the key, Susannah. In other words, I chased Robert until he caught me." She stopped working her crochet hook to laugh at her own wit.

From the first day she met her brother-in-law, Susannah had assumed he'd taken one look at her sister and dropped to his knees to propose. It had always seemed obvious to Susannah that they were meant for each other, far more obvious than it was that Nate was right for her.

"I don't know, Emily," she said with a deep sigh. "Everything's so confused in my mind. How could I possibly be so attracted to this man? It doesn't make any sense! Do you know what we did yesterday afternoon when we'd finished at the park?" She didn't wait for a response. "Nate brought over his Nintendo game and Super Mario Brothers cartridge, and we played video games. Me! I can't believe it even now. It was a pure waste of time."

"Did you have fun?"

That was a question Susannah wanted to avoid. She'd laughed until her stomach hurt. They'd challenged each other to see who could achieve the higher score, and then had done everything possible to sabotage each other.

Nate had discovered a sensitive area behind her ear and taken to kissing her there just when she was about to outscore him. Fair was fair, however, and Susannah soon discovered that Nate had his own area of vulnerability. Without a qualm, she'd used it against him, effectively disrupting his game. Soon they both forgot Nintendo and became far more interested in learning about each other.

"We had fun" was all Susannah was willing to admit.

"What about the kite flying?"

Her sister didn't know when to quit. "Then, too," she said reluctantly. "And at the baseball game Thursday, as well."

"He took you to a Mariners game...on Thursday? But they played in the middle of the afternoon. Did you actually leave the office?"

Susannah nodded, without explaining the details of how Nate had practically kidnapped her. "Back to you and Robert," she said, trying to change the subject.

"You want to know how I convinced him he wanted to get married? It wasn't really that difficult."

For Emily it wouldn't have been, but for Susannah it would be another story entirely. The biggest problem was that she wasn't sure she *wanted* Nate to be convinced. However, she should probably learn these things for future reference. She'd listen to what her sister had to say and make up her mind later.

"Remember that old adage—the way to a man's heart is through his stomach? It's true. Men equate food with comfort and love—that's a well-known fact."

"Then I'm in trouble," Susannah said flatly. Good

grief, she thought, Nate could cook far better than she could any day of the week. She couldn't attract him with her cooking. All she had in the way of looks was her classic profile. Painful as it was to accept, men simply weren't attracted to her.

"Now don't overreact. Just because you can't whip up a five-course meal doesn't mean your life is over before it even begins."

"My married life is. I can't put together soup and a sandwich and you know it."

"Susannah, I wish you'd stop demeaning yourself. You're bright and pretty, and Nate would be the luckiest man in the world if he were to marry you."

Now that they were actually discussing marriage, Susannah was having mixed feelings. "I...don't know if Nate's the marrying kind," she muttered. "For that matter, I don't know if I am."

Emily ignored that. "I'll start you out on something simple and we'll work our way up."

"I don't understand."

"Cookies," Emily explained. "There isn't a man alive who doesn't appreciate homemade cookies. There's something magical about them—really," she added when Susannah cast her a doubtful glance. "Cookies create an aura of domestic bliss—it sounds crazy, but it's true. A man can't resist a woman who bakes him cookies. They remind him of home and mother and a fire crackling in the fireplace." Emily paused and sighed. "Now, it's also true that men have been fighting this feeling since the beginning of time."

"What feeling?"

Emily rolled her eyes. "Domestic contentment. It's exactly what they need and want, but they fight it."

Susannah mulled over her sister's words. "Now that you mention it, Nate did say chocolate chip's his favorite."

"See what I mean?"

Susannah couldn't believe she was pursuing this subject with her sister. Okay, so she and Nate had shared some good times. But lots of people had good times together. She was also willing to admit there was a certain amount of chemistry between them. But that wasn't any reason to run to the nearest altar.

For the past few minutes, she'd been trying to sensibly discuss this situation between Nate and her with her sister, and before she even knew how it'd happened, Emily had her talking about weddings and chocolate chip cookies. At this rate Emily would have her married and pregnant by the end of the week.

"So how did dinner with your sister go?" Nate asked her later that same night. He'd been on the Seattle waterfront earlier in the day and had brought her back a polished glass paperweight made of ash from the Mount St. Helens volcano.

"Dinner was fine," she said quickly, perhaps too quickly. "Emily and I had a nice talk."

Nate put his arms around her, trapping her against the kitchen counter. "I missed you."

Swallowing tensely, she murmured, "I missed you, too."

He threaded his fingers through the length of her hair, pulling it away from her face and holding it there. "You wore it down again today," he whispered against her neck.

"Yes... Emily says she likes it better that way, too."

Talking shouldn't be this difficult, but every time Nate touched her it was. Susannah's knees had the consistency of pudding and her resolve was just as weak. After analyzing her talk with Emily, Susannah had decided to let the situation between her and Nate cool for a while. Things were happening much too quickly. She wasn't ready, and she doubted Nate was, either.

When he kissed her lightly at the hollow of her throat, it was all she could do to remain in an upright position. As she braced her hands against his chest, she began to push him gently away. But when his lips traveled up the side of her neck, blazing a trail of moist kisses, she was lost. His mouth grazed the line of her jaw, slowly edging its way toward her lips, prolonging the inevitable until Susannah thought she'd dissolve at his feet.

When he finally kissed her mouth, they both sighed, caught in a swelling tide of longing. His mouth moved hungrily over hers. Then he tugged at her lower lip with his teeth, creating a whole new wave of sensation.

By the time Nate went back to his own apartment, Susannah was shaking from the inside out. She'd walked all the way to the kitchen before she was conscious of her intent. She stared at the phone for a long moment. Calling Emily demanded every ounce of courage she had. With a deep calming breath, she punched out her sister's number.

"Emily," she said when her sister answered on the second ring, "do you have a recipe for chocolate chip cookies?"

Seven

The recipe for chocolate chip cookies was safely tucked away in a kitchen drawer. The impulse to bake them had passed quickly and reason had returned.

Monday morning, back at the office, Susannah realized how close she'd come to the edge of insanity. The vice presidency was almost within her grasp, and she'd worked too long and too hard to let this promotion slip through her fingers simply because she felt a little weak in the knees when Nate Townsend kissed her. To even contemplate anything beyond friendship was like...like amputating her right hand because she had a sliver in her index finger. She'd been overreacting, which was understandable, since she'd never experienced such a strong attraction to a man before.

"There's a call for you on line one," Ms. Brooks told her. She paused, then added dryly, "It sounds like that nice young man who stopped by last week."

Nate. Squaring her shoulders—and her resolve—Susannah picked up the phone. "This is Susannah Simmons."

"Good morning, beautiful."

"Hello, Nate," she said stiffly. "What can I do for you?"

He chuckled. "That's a leading question if there ever was one. Trust me, honey, you don't want to know."

"Nate," she breathed, briefly closing her eyes. "Please. I'm busy. What do you want?"

"Other than your body?"

Hot color leaped into her cheeks and she gave a distressed gasp. "We'd better put an end to this conversation—"

"All right, all right, I'm sorry. I just woke up and I was lying here thinking how nice it would be if we could escape for the day. Could I tempt you with a drive to the ocean? We could dig for clams, build a sand castle, and then make a fire and sing our favorite camp songs."

"As a matter of interest, I've been up for several hours. And since you've obviously forgotten, I do have a job—an important one. At least it's important to me. Now exactly what is the purpose of this call, other than to embarrass me?"

"Lunch."

"I can't today. I've got an appointment."

"Okay." He sighed, clearly frustrated. "How about dinner, just you and me?"

"I'm working late and was planning on sending out for something. Thanks, anyway."

"Susannah," he said in a burst of impatience, "are we going to go through this again? You should've figured out by now that avoiding me won't change anything."

Perhaps not, she reasoned, but it would certainly help. "Listen, Nate, I really am busy. Perhaps we should continue this conversation another time."

"Like next year—I know you. You'd be willing to bury your head in the sand for the next fifteen years if

I didn't come and prod you along. I swear, I've never met a more stubborn woman."

"Goodbye, Nate."

"Susannah," he persisted, "what about dinner? Come on, change your mind. We have a lot to talk about."

"No. I wasn't lying—I do have to work late. The fact is, I can't go outside and play today—or tonight."

"Ouch," Nate cried. "That hurt."

"Perhaps it hit too close to home."

A short silence followed. "Maybe it did," he murmured thoughtfully. "But before we hang up, I do want to know when I can see you again."

Susannah leaned forward and stretched her arm across the desk to her calendar, flipping the pages until she found a blank space. "How about lunch on Thursday?"

"All right," he said, "I'll see you Thursday at noon."

For a long moment after they'd hung up, Susannah kept her hand on the receiver. As crazy as it seemed, spending the afternoon with Nate at the beach sounded far too appealing. The way he made her think and feel was almost frightening. The man was putting her whole career in jeopardy. Something had to be done, only Susannah wasn't sure what.

An hour later, Ms. Brooks tapped on her door and walked inside, carrying a huge bouquet of red roses. "These just arrived."

"For me?" Surely there was some mistake. No one had ever sent her flowers. There'd never been any reason. There wasn't now.

"The card has your name on it," her assistant informed her. She handed the small white envelope to Susannah.

Not until Eleanor had left the room did Susannah read the card. The roses were from Nate, who wrote that he was sorry for having disturbed her earlier. She was right, he told her, now wasn't the time to go outside and play. He'd signed it with his love. Closing her eyes, Susannah held the card to her breast and fought down a swelling surge of emotion. The least he could do was stop being so damn wonderful. Then everything would be easier.

As it turned out, Susannah finished work relatively early that evening and returned home a little after seven. Her apartment was dark and empty—but it was that way every night and she didn't understand why it should matter to her now. Yet it did.

It was when she stood outside Nate's door and knocked that she realized how impulsive her behavior had become since she'd met him. She was doing everything in her power to avoid him, and yet she couldn't stay away.

"Susannah," he said when he opened the door. "This is a pleasant surprise."

She laced her fingers together. "I… I just wanted you to know how much I appreciated the roses. They're lovely and the gesture was so thoughtful."

"Come in," he said, stepping inside. "I'll put on some coffee."

"No, thanks. I've got to get back, but I wanted to thank you for the flowers…and to apologize if I sounded waspish on the phone. Monday mornings aren't exactly my best time."

Grinning, he leaned against the doorjamb and crossed his arms over his broad chest. "Actually, I'm the one who owed you an apology. I should never have phoned you this morning. I was being selfish. You do have an important job and these are anxious days for you. Didn't you tell me you'd hear about that promotion within the next week or two?"

Susannah nodded.

"You might find this hard to believe, but I don't want to say or do anything to take that away from you. You're a dedicated, hardworking employee and you deserve to be the first female vice president of H&J Lima."

His confidence in her was reassuring, but it confused her, too. From everything she'd witnessed about Nate, she could only conclude that he didn't appreciate hard work and its rewards.

"If I do get the promotion," she said, watching him closely, "things will change between you and me. I… I won't have a lot of free time for a while."

"Does that mean you won't be able to go outside and play as often?" he asked, his mouth curving into a sensuous smile. He was taunting her with the words she'd used earlier that day.

"Exactly."

"I can accept that. Just…" He hesitated.

"What?" Nate was frowning and that wasn't like him. He wore a saucy grin as often as he donned a baseball cap. "Tell me," she demanded.

"I want you to do everything possible to achieve your dreams, Susannah, but there are plenty of pitfalls along the way."

Now it was her turn to frown. She wasn't sure she understood what he was talking about.

"All I'm saying," he elaborated, "is that you shouldn't lose sight of who you are because this vice presidency means so much to you. And most important, count the cost." With that he stepped forward, gazed hungrily into her eyes and kissed her lightly on the lips. Then he stepped back reluctantly.

For a second Susannah teetered, then she moved forward into his arms as if that was the most natural place in the world for her to be. Even now, she didn't entirely understand what he meant, but she couldn't mistake the tenderness she heard in his voice. Once her head had cleared and she wasn't wrapped up in this incredible longing he created every time he touched her, she'd mull over his words.

Susannah woke around midnight, and rolling over, adjusted her pillow. The illuminated dial on her clock radio told her she'd only been sleeping for a couple of hours. She yawned, wondering what had woken her out of a sound peaceful slumber. Closing her eyes, she tucked the blankets more securely over her shoulders, determined to sleep. She tried visualizing herself accepting the promotion to vice president. Naturally, there'd be a nice write-up about her in the evening paper and possibly a short piece in a business journal or two.

Susannah's eyes drifted open as she recalled Nate's words reminding her not to forget who she was. Who *was* she? A list of possible replies skipped easily through her mind. She was Susannah Simmons, future vice president in charge of marketing for the largest sporting-goods store in the country. She was a daughter, a sister, an aunt… And then it hit her. *She was a woman.* That was what Nate had been trying to tell her. It was the same message Emily had tried to get across to her on Sunday. From the time Susannah had set her goals, she'd dedicated her life to her career and pushed aside every feminine part of herself. Now was the time for her to deal with that aspect of her life.

It was the following evening after work. Susannah was leaning against the kitchen counter, struggling to remove the heavy food mixer from its reinforced cardboard box. Emily's recipe for chocolate chip cookies made three dozen. After her trip to the grocery, plus a jaunt to the hardware store for the mixer, cookie sheets and measuring utensils, these cookies were costing her $4.72 apiece.

Price be damned. She was setting out to prove something important—although she wasn't sure exactly what. She would've preferred to dismiss all her sister's talk about cookies being equated with warmth and love as a philosophy left over from an earlier generation. Susannah didn't actually believe Emily's theory, but she wanted to give it a try. Susannah didn't know why she was doing this anymore. All she knew was that she had this urge to bake chocolate chip cookies.

Emily had eagerly given her the recipe, and Susannah had read it carefully. Just how difficult could baking cookies be?

Not very, she determined twenty minutes later when everything was laid out on her extended counter. Pushing up the sleeves of her shirt, she turned on the radio to keep her company. Next she tied the arms of an old shirt around her waist, using that as an apron. Emily always seemed to wear one when she worked in the kitchen and if her sister did, then it must be the thing to do.

The automatic mixer was blending the butter and white sugar nicely and, feeling extraordinarily proud of herself, Susannah cracked the eggs on the edge of the bowl with a decided flair.

"Damn," she cried when half the shell fell into the swirling blades. She glared at it a moment, watching helplessly as the beater broke the fragile shell into a thousand bits. Shrugging, she figured a little extra protein—or was it calcium?—wasn't going to hurt anyone. Finally she turned off the mixer and stirred in the flour, then the chocolate chips.

The oven was preheated exactly as the recipe required when Susannah slipped the shiny new cookie sheet inside. She closed the oven door with a swing of her hip and set the timer for twelve minutes.

Sampling a blob of dough from the end of her finger, she had to admit it was tasty. At least as good as Emily's. But Susannah considered it best not to let anyone know her secret ingredient was eggshell.

With a sense of genuine satisfaction, she poured herself a cup of coffee and sat down at the table with the evening paper.

A few minutes later she smelled smoke. Suspiciously sniffing the air, she set the paper aside. It couldn't possibly be her cookies—they'd been in the oven less than five minutes. To be on the safe side, however, she reached for a towel and opened the oven door.

She was immediately assaulted by billowing waves of smoke, followed by flames that licked out at her. Gasping in horror, she dropped the towel and gave a piercing scream. "Fire! Fire!"

The smoke alarm blared, and she thought she'd never heard anything louder in her life. Like a madwoman, Susannah raced for the door, throwing it open in an effort to allow the smoke to escape. Then she ran back to the table and hurled her coffee straight into the belly of the oven. Coughing hoarsely, she slammed the door shut.

"Susannah!" Breathless, Nate burst into her condominium.

"I started a fire," she shouted above the deafening din of the smoke alarm. Her voice still sounded raspy.

"Where?" Nate circled her table several times, looking frantically for the source of her panic.

"In the oven." Standing aside, she covered her face with her hands, not wanting to look.

A few minutes later, Nate took her in his arms. The smoke alarm was off. Two blackened sheets of charred cookies were angled into the sink. "Are you all right?"

Somehow she managed a nod.

"You didn't burn yourself?"

She didn't have so much as a blister and told him so.

Gently he brushed the hair away from her face, and expelled his breath, apparently to ease his tension. "Okay, how did the fire get started?"

"I don't know," she said dismally. "I… I did everything the recipe said, but when I put the cookies in the oven they…they caught on fire." Her voice quavered as she spoke.

"The cookies weren't responsible for the fire," he corrected her. "The cookie sheets were the culprits. They must've been new—it seems, ah, you forgot to remove the paper covering."

"Oh," she whispered. Her shoulders were shaking with the effort to repress her sobs.

"Susannah, there's no reason to cry. It was a reasonable mistake. Here, sit down." Gently he lowered her onto the kitchen chair and knelt in front of her, taking her hands in his and rubbing them. "It isn't the biggest disaster in the world."

"I know that," she wailed, unable to stop herself. "You don't understand. It was sort of a test...."

"A test?"

"Yes. Emily claims men love cookies...and I was baking them for you." She didn't go on to add that Emily also claimed that men loved the women who baked those cookies. "I can't cook... I started a fire...and I dropped part of the eggshell in the batter and...and left it.... I wasn't going to tell anyone."

Her confession must have shocked Nate because he stood up and left the room. Burying her face in her hands, Susannah endeavored to regain her composure and was doing an admirable job of it when Nate returned, holding a box of tissue.

Effortlessly lifting her into his arms, he pulled out the chair and sat down, holding her securely on his lap. "Okay, Betty Crocker, explain yourself."

She wiped her face dry with the tissue, feeling rather silly at the way she was reacting. So she'd burned a couple of cookie sheets and ruined a batch of chocolate chip cookies. Big deal, she told herself with as much bravado as she could muster. "Explain what?"

"The comment about men loving cookies. Were you trying to prove something to me?"

"Actually it was Emily I wanted to set straight," she whispered.

"You said you were baking them for my benefit."

"I was. Yesterday you said I shouldn't forget who I was, I should find myself, and... I think this sudden urge to bake was my response to that." Susannah suspected she wasn't making much sense. "Believe me, after today, I know I'm never going to be worth a damn in the kitchen."

"I don't remember suggesting you 'find yourself' in the kitchen," Nate said, looking confused.

"Actually that part was Emily's idea," she admitted. "She's the one who gave me the recipe. My sister seems to believe a woman can coerce a man into giving up his heart and soul if she can bake chocolate chip cookies."

"And you want my heart and soul?"

"Of course not! Don't be ridiculous."

He hesitated for a moment and seemed to be considering her words. "Would it come as a surprise if I said I wanted yours?"

Susannah barely heard him; she wasn't in the mood to talk about heart and soul right now. She'd just shown how worthless she was in the kitchen. Her lack in that area hadn't particularly troubled her—until now. She'd made a genuine effort and fallen flat on her face. Not only that, having Nate witness her defeat had badly dented her pride. "When I was born something must've been missing from my genes," she murmured thoughtfully. "Obviously. I can't cook, and I don't sew, and I can hardly tell one end of a knitting needle from the other. I can't do any of the things that…normal people associate with the female gender."

"Susannah." He said her name on a disgruntled sigh. "Did you hear what I just said?"

She shook her head. She understood the situation perfectly. Some women had it and others didn't. Unfortunately, she was in the latter group.

"I was telling you something important. But I can see you're going to force me to say it without words." Cupping her face, Nate directed her mouth to his. But he didn't only kiss her. The hot moist tip of his tongue traced the sensitive line of her lips until she shivered with a whole new realm of unexplored sensations. All her disheartened thoughts dissolved instantly. She forgot to think, to breathe, to do anything but tremble in his arms. The fire in her oven was nothing compared to the one Nate had started in her body. Without conscious volition, she wrapped her arms around his neck and slanted her mouth over his, surrendering to the hot currents of excitement he'd created. She opened herself to him, granting him anything he wanted. His tongue found hers, and Susannah whimpered at the shock of pleasure she received. Her response was innocent and abandoned, unskilled and unknowing, yet eager.

"There," he whispered, supporting his forehead against hers, while he drew in deep breaths. His husky voice was unsteady.

He seemed to think their kiss was enough to prove everything. Susannah slowly opened her eyes. She took a steadying breath herself, one that made her tremble all the way to her toes. If she was going to say anything, it would be to whisper his name repeatedly and ask why he was doing this and then plead with him never to stop.

He threaded his fingers through her hair and kissed her again with a mastery that caused her to cling to him as if he were a life raft in a stormy sea. Unable to keep still, Susannah ran her palms along his neck and onto his shoulders and down the length of his arms. He must have liked her touch because he groaned and deepened the kiss even more.

"Unfortunately I don't think you're ready to hear it yet," he said.

"Hear what?" she asked, when she could find her voice.

"What I was telling you."

She puckered her brow. "What was that?"

"Forget the cookies. You're more than enough woman for any man."

She blinked, not understanding him. She barely understood herself.

"I never meant for you to test who you are. All I suggested was that you take care not to lose sight of your own personality. Goals are all well and good, even necessary, but you should always calculate the cost."

"Oh." Her mind was still too hazy to properly assimilate his meaning.

"Are you going to be all right?" he asked, as he grazed her cheek with his fingertips. He kissed Susannah's eyelids, closing them.

All she could do was nod.

"John Hammer would like to see you right away," Ms. Brooks told Susannah when she walked into her office Thursday morning.

Susannah's heart flew into her throat and stayed there for an uncomfortable moment. This was it. The day for which she'd been waiting five long years.

"Did he say what he wanted?" she asked, making an effort to appear at least outwardly calm.

"No," Ms. Brooks replied. "He just asked me to tell you he wanted to talk to you at your convenience."

Susannah slumped into her high-backed office chair. She propped her elbows on the desk and hid her face in her hands, trying to put some order to her muddled thoughts. "At my convenience," she repeated in a ragged whisper. "I didn't get the promotion. I just know it."

"Susannah," her assistant said sternly, calling her by

her first name—something she rarely did. "I think you might be jumping to conclusions."

Susannah glared at her, annoyed by the woman's obtuseness. "If he planned to appoint me vice president, he would've called me into his office late in the afternoon. That's how it's done. Then he'd go through this long spiel about me being a loyal employee and what an asset I am to the company and all that stuff. Wanting to talk to me *now* means... Well, you know what it means."

"I can't say I do," Ms. Brooks said primly. "My suggestion is that you pull yourself together and get over to Mr. Hammer's office before he changes his mind."

Susannah got to her feet and stiffened her spine. But no matter how hard she tried she couldn't seem to stop shaking.

"I'll be waiting here when you get back," Ms. Brooks told her on her way out the door. She smiled then, an encouraging gesture that softened her austere features. "Break a leg, kid."

"I probably will, whatever happens," she muttered. If she didn't get this promotion, she was afraid she'd fall apart. Assuming a calm manner, she decided not to worry until she knew for sure.

John Hammer stood when she was announced. Susannah walked into his office, and the first thing she noticed was that the two men who were her competition hadn't been called. The company president smiled benignly and motioned toward a chair. Susannah sat on the edge of the cushion, doing her best to disguise how nervous she was.

A smile eased over her boss's face. "Good morning, Susannah..."

True to her word, Susannah's assistant was waiting for her when she strolled back to her office.

"Well?"

Eleanor Brooks followed her to her desk and watched as Susannah carefully sat down.

"What happened?" she demanded a second time. "Don't just sit there. Talk!"

Susannah's gaze slowly moved from the phone to her assistant. Then she started to chuckle. The laughter came from deep within her and she had to cover her mouth with her palms. When she could talk, she wiped the tears from the corners of her eyes.

"The first thing he did was ask me if I wanted to trade offices while mine was being repainted."

"What?"

Susannah thought Ms. Brooks's expression probably reflected her own when Mr. Hammer had asked that question. "That was my reaction, too," Susannah exclaimed. "I didn't understand what he meant. Then he said he was going to have my office redone, because he felt it was only right that the vice president in charge of marketing have a brand-new office."

"You got the promotion?" Eleanor Brooks clapped her hands in sheer delight, then pressed them over her lips.

"I got it," Susannah breathed, squeezing her eyes shut. "I actually got it."

"Congratulations."

"Thank you, thank you." Already she was reaching for the phone. She had to tell Nate. Only a few days before, he'd said she should go after her dreams, and now everything was neatly falling into place.

There was no answer at his apartment and, dejected,

she replaced the receiver. But the need to talk to him consumed her, and she tried again every half hour until she thought she'd go crazy.

At noon, she was absorbed in her work when Ms. Brooks announced that her luncheon date had arrived.

"Send him in," Susannah said automatically, irritated that her concentration had been broken.

Nate strolled casually into her office and plopped himself down in the chair opposite her desk.

"Nate," she cried, leaping to her feet. "I've been trying to get hold of you all morning. What are you doing here?"

"We're going out to lunch, remember?"

Eight

"Nate!" Susannah ran around her desk until she stood directly in front of him. "John Hammer called me into his office this morning," she explained breathlessly. "I got the promotion! You're looking at the vice president in charge of marketing for H&J Lima."

For a moment Nate said nothing. Then he slowly repeated, "You got the promotion?"

"Yes," she told him. "I got it." In her enthusiasm, Susannah nodded several times, with a vigor that almost dislocated her neck. She was smiling so hard, her face ached.

Throwing back his head, Nate let out a shout that must have shaken the ceiling tile. Then he locked his arms around her waist, picked her up and swung her around, all the while howling with delight.

Susannah laughed with him. She'd never experienced joy more profoundly. The promotion hadn't seemed real to her until she'd shared it with Nate. The first person she'd thought to tell had been him. He'd become the very center of her world, and it was time to admit she was in love with him.

Nate had stopped whirling her around, but he continued to clasp her middle so that her face was elevated above his own.

Breathless with happiness, Susannah smiled down on him and on impulse buried her fingers in his hair. She couldn't resist him, not now, when she was filled with such exhilaration. Her mouth was trembling when she kissed him. She made a soft throaty sound of discovery and pleasure. Her gaze fell to the sensual lines of his mouth, and she remembered how she'd felt when he'd held and reassured her after the cookie disaster. She lowered her lips once more, lightly rocking her head back and forth, creating a friction that was so hot, she thought she'd catch fire.

In an unhurried movement, Nate lowered her to the ground and slid his arms around her. "Susannah," he moaned, kissing the corner of her mouth with exquisite care.

With a shudder, she opened her mouth to him. She wanted him to kiss her the way he had in the past. Deep, slow, moist, kisses that made her forget to breathe. She yearned for the taste and scent of him. This was the happiest moment of her life, and only a small part of it could be attributed to the promotion. Everything else was Nate and the growing love she felt for him each time they were together.

Someone coughed nervously in the background, and Nate broke off the kiss and glanced past her to the open door.

"Ms. Simmons," her assistant said, smiling broadly.

"Yes?" Breaking away from Nate, Susannah smoothed the hair at the sides of her head and struggled to replace her business facade.

"I'll be leaving now. Ms. Andrews will be answering your calls."

"Thank you, Ms. Brooks," Nate muttered, but there was little appreciation in his tone.

Susannah chastised him with a look. "We'll... I'll be leaving directly for my lunch appointment."

"I'll tell Ms. Andrews."

"This afternoon, I'd like you to call a meeting of my staff," Susannah said, "and I'll announce the promotion."

Eleanor Brooks nodded, but her smiling eyes landed heavily on Nate. "I believe everyone's already guessed from the...commotion that came from here a few minutes ago."

"I see." Susannah couldn't help smiling, too.

"There isn't an employee here who isn't happy about your news."

"I can think of two," Susannah said under her breath, considering the men she'd been competing against. Nate squeezed her hand, and she knew he'd heard her sardonic remark.

Her assistant closed the door on her way out, and the minute she did, Nate reached for Susannah to bring her back into the shelter of his arms. "Where were we?"

"About to leave for lunch, as I recall."

Nate frowned. "That's not the way I remember it."

Susannah laughed and hugged him tightly. "We both forgot ourselves for a while there." She broke away again and reached for her purse, hooking the long strap over her shoulder. "Are you ready?"

"Anytime you are." But the eager look in his eyes told her he was talking about something other than lunch.

Susannah could feel the color working its way up

her neck and suffusing her face. "Nate," she whispered, "behave yourself. Please."

"I'm doing the best I can under the circumstances," he whispered back, his eyes filled with mischief. "In case you haven't figured it out yet, I'm crazy about you, woman."

"I... I'm pretty keen on you myself."

"Good." He tucked his arm around her waist and led her out of the office and down the long hallway to the elevator. Susannah was sure she could feel the stares of her staff, but for the first time, she didn't care what image she projected. Everything was right in her world, and she'd never been happier.

Nate chose the restaurant, Il Bistro, which was one of the best in town. The atmosphere was festive, and playing the role of gentleman to the hilt, Nate wouldn't allow her to even look at the menu, insisting that he'd order for her.

"Nate," she said once the waiter had left the table, "I want to pay for this. It's a business lunch."

His thick brows arched upward. "And how are you going to rationalize *that* when your boss questions you about it, my dear?" He wiggled his eyebrows suggestively.

"There's a reason I agreed to go to lunch with you— other than celebrating my promotion, which I didn't even know about until this morning." As she'd explained to Nate earlier, her life was going to change with this promotion. New responsibility would result in a further commitment of time and energy to the company, and could drastically alter her relationship with Nate. If anything, she wanted them to grow closer, not apart. This advancement had the potential to make or break them, and Susannah was looking for a way to keep them together. She thought she'd found it.

"A reason?" Nate questioned.

They were interrupted by the waiter as he produced a bottle of expensive French wine for their inspection. He removed the cork and poured a sample into Nate's glass to taste. When Nate nodded in approval, the waiter filled their glasses and discreetly retreated.

"Now, you were saying?" Nate continued, studying her. His mouth quirked up at the edges.

Gathering her resolve, Susannah reached across the table and took Nate's hand. "You've always been open and honest with me. I want you to know how much I value that. When I asked you if you had a job, you told me you'd had one until recently and that you'd quit." She waited for him to elaborate on his circumstances, but he didn't, so she went on. "It's obvious you don't need the money, but there's something else that's obvious, too."

Nate removed his fingers from hers and twirled the stem of the wineglass between his open palms. "What's that?"

"You lack purpose."

His eyes rose to meet hers and his brow creased in query.

"You have no direction," she said. "Over the past several weeks, I've watched you flit from one interest to another. First it was baseball, then it was video games and kite flying, and tomorrow, no doubt, it'll be something completely different."

"Traveling," he concluded for her. "I was thinking of doing some serious sightseeing. I have a hankering to stroll the byways of Hong Kong."

"Hong Kong," she repeated, gesturing with one hand.

"That's exactly what I mean." Her heart slowed to a sluggish beat at the thought of his being gone for any length of time. She'd become accustomed to having Nate nearby, to sharing bits and pieces of her day with him. Not only had she fallen in love with Nate Townsend, he'd quickly become her best friend.

"Do you think traveling is wrong?" he asked.

"Not wrong," she returned swiftly. "But what are you going to do once you've run out of ways to entertain yourself and places to travel? What are you going to do when you've spent all your money?"

"I'll face that when the time comes."

"I see." She lowered her gaze, wondering if she was only making matters worse. There wasn't much she could say to counter his don't-worry attitude.

"Susannah, you make it sound like the end of the world. Trust me, wealth isn't all that great. If I run out of money, fine. If I don't, that's all right, too."

"I see," she murmured miserably.

"Why are you so worried?" he asked in a gentle voice.

"It's because I care about you, I guess." She paused to take a deep breath. "We may live in the same building, but our worlds are totally opposite. My future is charted, right down to the day I retire. I know what I want and how to get there."

"I thought I did once, too, but then I learned how unimportant it all was."

"It doesn't have to be like that," she told him, her voice filled with determination. "Listen, there's something important I'm going to propose, but I don't want you to answer me now. I want you to give yourself time to think about it. Promise me you'll at least do that."

"Are you suggesting we get married?" he teased.

"No." Flustered, she smoothed out the linen napkin in her lap, her fingers lingering there to disguise her nervousness. "I'm offering you a job."

"You're doing what?" He half rose out of his seat.

Embarrassed, Susannah glanced nervously around and noted that several people had stopped eating and were gazing in their direction. "Don't look so aghast. A job would make a lot of difference in your attitude toward life."

"And exactly what position are you offering me?" Now that the surprise had worn off, he appeared amused.

"I don't know yet. We'd have to figure something out. But I'm sure there'd be a position that would fit your qualifications."

The humor drained from his eyes, and for a long moment Nate said nothing. "You think a job would give me purpose?"

"I believe so." In her view, it would help him look beyond today and toward the future. Employment would give Nate a reason to get out of bed in the morning, instead of sleeping in until nine or ten every day.

"Susannah—"

"Before you say anything," she interrupted, holding up her hand, "I want you to think it over seriously. Don't say anything until you've had a chance to consider my offer."

His eyes were more serious than she could ever remember seeing them—other than just before he kissed her. His look was almost brooding.

Their meal arrived, and the lamb was as delicious as Nate had promised. He was unusually quiet during the remainder of the meal, but that didn't alarm her. He was reflecting on her job offer, which was exactly what she wanted. She hoped he'd come to the right decision. Loving him the way she did, she longed to make his world as right as her own.

Despite Nate's protests, Susannah paid for their lunch. He walked her back to her office, standing with her on the sidewalk while they exchanged a few words of farewell. Susannah kissed him on the cheek and asked once more that he consider her offer.

"I will," he promised, running his finger lightly down the side of her face.

He left her then, and Susannah watched as he walked away, letting her gaze linger on him for several minutes.

"Any messages?" she asked Dorothy Andrews, who was sitting in her assistant's place.

"One," Dorothy said, without looking up. "Emily— she didn't leave her full name. She said she'd catch you later."

"Thanks." Susannah went into her office and, sitting down at her desk, punched out her sister's telephone number.

"Emily, this is Susannah. You phoned?"

"I know I probably shouldn't have called you at the office, but you never seem to be home and I had something important to ask you," her sister said, talking so fast she ran her words together.

"What's that?" Already Susannah was reaching for a file, intending to read while her sister spoke. It sometimes took Emily several minutes to get around to the reason for any call.

Her sister hesitated. "I've got a bunch of zucchini left from my garden, and I was wondering if you wanted some."

"About as much as I want a migraine headache."

After her disaster with the chocolate chip cookies, Susannah planned to never so much as read a recipe again.

"The zucchini are excellent," Emily prompted, as if that would be enough to induce Susannah into agreeing to take a truckload.

Her sister hadn't phoned her to ask about zucchini; Susannah would have staked her promotion on it. That was merely a lead-in for some other request, and no doubt Susannah would have to play a guessing game. Mentally, she scanned a list of possible favors and decided to jump in with both feet.

"Zucchini are out, but I wouldn't mind looking after Michelle again, if you need me to."

"Oh, Susannah, would you? I mean, it'd work out so well if you could take her two weeks from this Saturday."

"All night?" As much as she loved her niece, another overnight stretch was more than Susannah wanted to contemplate. Still, Nate would probably be more than willing to lend a hand. No doubt she'd need it.

"Oh, no, not for the night, just for dinner. Robert's boss is taking us out to eat, and it wouldn't be appropriate if we brought Michelle along. Robert got a big promotion."

"Congratulate him for me, okay?"

"I'm so proud of him," Emily said. "I think he must be the best accountant in Seattle."

Susannah toyed with the idea of letting her sister in on her own big news, but she didn't want to take anything away from her brother-in-law. She could tell them both in two weeks when they dropped off Michelle.

"I'll be happy to keep Michelle for you," Susannah said, and discovered, as she marked the date on her calendar, how much she actually meant that. She might be a disaster waiting to happen in the kitchen, but she didn't do half badly with her niece. The time might yet come when she'd consider having a child of her own—not now, of course, but sometime in the future. "All right, I've got you down for the seventeenth."

"Susannah, I can't tell you how much this means to me," Emily said.

When Susannah arrived home that evening she was tipsy. The staff meeting that afternoon had gone wonderfully well. After five, she'd been taken out for a drink by her two top aides, to celebrate. Several others from her section had unexpectedly dropped by the cocktail lounge and insisted on buying her drinks, too. By seven, Susannah was flushed and excited, and from experience, she knew it was time to call it quits and phone for a taxi.

Dinner probably would have cut the effects of the alcohol, but she was more interested in getting home. After a nice hot bath, she'd fix herself some toast and be done with it.

She hadn't been back more than half an hour when her phone rang. Dressed in her robe and sipping tea in the kitchen, she grabbed the receiver.

"Susannah, it's Nate. Can I come over?"

Glancing down at her robe and fuzzy slippers, she decided it wouldn't take her long to change.

"Give me five minutes."

"All right."

Dressed in slacks and a sweater, she opened the door at his knock. "Hi," she said cheerfully, aware that her mouth had probably formed a crooked grin despite her efforts to smile naturally.

Nate barely looked at her. His hands were thrust deep in his pockets, and his expression was disgruntled as he marched into her apartment. He didn't take a seat but paced the carpet in front of her fireplace. Obviously something was going on.

She sat on the edge of the sofa, watching him, feeling more than a little reckless and exhilarated from her promotion and the celebration afterward. She was amused, too, at Nate's peculiar agitation.

"I suppose you want to talk to me about the job offer," she said, surprised by how controlled her voice sounded.

He paused, splayed his fingers through his thick hair and nodded. "That's exactly what I want to talk about."

"Don't," she said, smiling up at him.

His forehead puckered in a frown. "Why not?"

"Because I'd like you to give long and careful consideration to the proposal."

"I need to explain something to you first."

Susannah wasn't listening. There were far more important things she had to tell him. "You're personable, bright and attractive," she began enthusiastically. "You could be anything you wanted, Nate. Anything."

"Susannah…"

She waved a finger at him and shook her head. "There's something else you should know."

"What?" he demanded.

"I'm in love with you." Her glorious confession was followed by a loud yawn. Unnerved, she covered her mouth with the tips of her fingers. "Oops, sorry."

Nate's eyes narrowed suspiciously. "Have you been drinking?"

She pressed her thumb and index finger together and

held them up for his inspection. "Just a little, but I'm more happy than anything else."

"Susannah!" He dragged her name out into the sigh. "I can't believe you."

"Why not? Do you want me to shout it to all of Seattle? Because I will. Watch!" She waltzed into the kitchen and jerked open the sliding glass door.

Actually, some of the alcohol had worn off, but she experienced this irrepressible urge to tell Nate how much she'd come to care for him. They'd skirted around the subject long enough. He didn't seem to want to admit it, but she did, especially now, fortified as she was with her good fortune. This day had been one of the most fantastic of her life. After years of hard work, everything was falling into place, and she'd found the most wonderful man in the world to love—even if he *was* misguided.

The wind whipped against her on the balcony, and the multicolored lights from the waterfront below resembled those on a Christmas tree. Standing at the railing, she cupped her hands around her mouth and shouted, "I love Nate Townsend!" Satisfied, she whirled to face him and opened her arms as wide as she could. "See? I announced it to the world."

He joined her outside and slid his arms around her and closed his eyes. Susannah had expected him to show at least *some* emotion.

"You don't look very happy about it," she challenged.

"You're not yourself," he said as he released her.

"Then who am I?" Fists digging into her hips, she glared up at him, her eyes defiant. "I feel like me. I bet you think I'm drunk, but I'm not."

He didn't reply. Instead he threw an arm over her

shoulder and urged her into the kitchen. Then, quickly and efficiently, he started to make coffee.

"I gave up caffeine," she muttered.

"When was this? You had regular coffee today at lunch," he said.

"Just now." She giggled. "Come on, Nate," she cried, bending forward and snapping her fingers. "Loosen up."

"I'm more concerned about sobering *you* up."

"You could kiss me."

"I could," he agreed, "but I'm not going to."

"Why not?" She pouted, disappointed by his refusal.

"Because if I do, I may not be able to stop."

Sighing, she closed her eyes. "That's the most romantic thing you've ever said to me."

Nate rubbed his face and leaned against the kitchen counter. "Have you had anything to eat since lunch?"

"One stuffed mushroom, a water chestnut wrapped in a slice of bacon and a piece of celery filled with cheese."

"But no dinner?"

"I was going to make myself some toast, but I wasn't hungry."

"After a stuffed mushroom, a celery stick and a water chestnut? I can see why not."

"Are you trying to be cute with me? Oh, just a minute, there was something I was supposed to ask you." She pulled herself up short and covered one eye, while she tugged at her memory for the date her sister had mentioned. "Are you doing anything on the seventeenth?"

"The seventeenth? Why?"

"Michelle's coming over to visit her auntie Susannah and I know she'll want to see you, too."

Nate looked even more disturbed, but he hadn't

seemed particularly pleased about anything from the moment he'd arrived.

"I've got something else that night."

"Oh, well, I'll make do. I have before." She stopped abruptly. "No, I guess I haven't, but Michelle and I'll be just fine, I think…"

The coffee had finished dripping into the glass pot. Nate poured a cup and, scowling, handed it to her.

"Oh, Nate, what's wrong with you? You've been cranky since you got here. We should be kissing by now and all you seem to do is ignore me."

"Drink your coffee."

He stood over her until she'd taken the first sip. She grimaced at the heat. "You know what I drank tonight? I've never had them before and they tasted so good. Shanghai Slungs."

"They're called Singapore Slings."

"Oh." Maybe she was more confused than she thought.

"Come on, drink up, Tokyo Rose."

Obediently Susannah did as he said. The whole time she was sipping her coffee, she was watching Nate, who moved restlessly about her kitchen, as if unable to stand still. He was disturbed about something, and she wished she knew what.

"Done," she announced when she'd finished her coffee, pleased with herself and this minor accomplishment. "Nate," she said, growing concerned, "do you love me?"

He turned around to face her, his eyes serious. "So much I can't believe it myself."

"Oh, good," she said with an expressive sigh. "I was beginning to wonder."

"Where are your aspirin?" He was searching through

her cupboards, opening and closing the ones closest to the sink.

"My aspirin? Did telling me how you feel give you a headache?"

"No." He answered her with a gentle smile. "I want to have it ready for you in the morning because you're going to need it."

Her love for him increased tenfold. "You are so thoughtful!"

"Take two tablets when you wake up. That should help." He crouched in front of her and took both her hands in his. "I'm leaving tomorrow and I won't be back for a couple of days. I'll call you, all right?"

"You're going away to think about my job offer, aren't you? That's a good idea—when you come back you can tell me your decision." She was forced to stop in order to yawn, a huge jaw-breaking yawn that depleted her strength. "I think I should go to bed, don't you?"

The next thing Susannah knew, her alarm was buzzing angrily. With the noise came a piercing pain that shot straight through her temple. She groped for the clock, turned it off and sighed with relief. Sitting up in bed proved to be equally overwhelming and she groaned.

When she'd managed to maneuver herself into the kitchen, she saw the aspirin bottle and remembered that Nate had insisted on setting it out the night before.

"Bless that man," she said aloud and winced at the sound of her own voice.

By the time she arrived at the office, she was operating on only three cylinders. Eleanor Brooks didn't seem to be any better off than Susannah was. They took one look at each other and smiled knowingly.

"Your coffee's ready," her assistant informed her.

"Did you have a cup yourself?"

"Yes."

"Anything in the mail?"

"Nothing that can't wait. Mr. Hammer was in earlier. He told me to give you this magazine and said you'd be as impressed as he was." Susannah glanced at the six-year-old issue of *Business Monthly,* a trade magazine that was highly respected in the industry.

"It's several years old," Susannah noted, wondering why her employer would want her to read it now.

"Mr. Hammer said there was a special feature in there about your friend."

"My friend?" Susannah didn't understand.

"Your friend," Eleanor Brooks repeated. "The one with the sexy eyes—Nathaniel Townsend."

Nine

Susannah waited until Eleanor had left the office before opening the magazine. The article on Nathaniel Townsend was the lead feature. The picture showed a much younger Nate standing in front of a shopping-mall outlet for Rainy Day Cookies, the most successful cookie chain in the country. He was holding a huge chocolate chip cookie.

Rainy Day Cookies were Susannah's absolute favorite. There were several varieties, but the chocolate chip ones were fantastic.

Two paragraphs into the article, Susannah thought she was going to be physically ill. She stopped reading and closed her eyes to the waves of nausea that lapped against her. Pressing a hand to her stomach, she resolutely focused her attention on the article, storing away the details of Nate's phenomenal success in her numb mind.

He had started his cookie company in his mother's kitchen while still in college. His specialty was chocolate chip cookies, and they were so popular, he soon found himself caught up in a roller-coaster ride that had led him straight to the top of the corporate world. By age twenty-eight, Nate Townsend was a multimillionaire.

Now that she thought about it, an article she'd read six or seven months ago in the same publication had said the company was recently sold for an undisclosed sum, which several experts had estimated to be a figure so staggering Susannah had gasped out loud.

Bracing her elbows on the desk, Susannah took several calming breaths. She'd made a complete idiot of herself over Nate, and worse, he had let her. She suspected this humiliation would stay with her for the rest of her life.

To think she'd baked the cookie king of the world chocolate chip cookies, and in the process nearly set her kitchen on fire. But that degradation couldn't compare to yesterday's little pep talk when she'd spoken to him about drive, ambition and purpose, before—dear heaven, it was too much—she'd offered him a job. How he must have laughed at that.

Eleanor Brooks brought in the mail and laid it on the corner of Susannah's desk. Susannah looked up at her and knew then and there that she wasn't going to be able to cope with the business of the day.

"I'm going home."

"I beg your pardon?"

"If anyone needs me, tell them I'm home sick."

"But…"

Susannah knew she'd shocked her assistant. In all the years she'd been employed by H&J Lima, Susannah had never used a single day of her sick leave. There'd been a couple of times she probably *should* have stayed home, but she'd insisted on working anyway.

"I'll see you Monday morning," she said on her way out the door.

"I hope you're feeling better then."

"I'm sure I will be." She needed some time alone to lick her wounds and gather the scattered pieces of her pride. To think that only a few hours earlier she'd drunkenly declared her undying love to Nate Townsend!

That was the worst of it.

When Susannah walked into her apartment she felt as if she was stumbling into a bomb shelter. For the moment she was hidden from the world outside. Eventually she'd have to go back and face it, but for now she was safe.

She picked up the afghan her sister had crocheted for her, wrapped it around her shoulders and sat staring sightlessly into space.

What an idiot she'd been! What a fool! Closing her eyes, she leaned her head against the back of the sofa and drew in several deep breaths, releasing the anger and hurt before it fermented into bitterness. She refused to dwell on the might-have-beens and the if-onlys, opting instead for a more positive approach. *Next time,* she would know enough not to involve her heart. *Next time,* she'd take care not to make such a fool of herself.

It astonished her when she awoke an hour later to realize she'd fallen asleep. Tucking the blanket more securely around her, she analyzed her situation.

Things weren't so bad. She'd achieved her primary goal and was vice president in charge of marketing. The first female in the company's long history to hold such a distinguished position, she reminded herself. Her life was good. If on occasion she felt the yearning for a family of her own, there was always Emily, who was more than willing to share. Heaving a sigh, Susannah told herself that she lacked for nothing. She was respected, hardworking and healthy. Yes, life was good.

Her head ached and her stomach didn't feel much better, but at noon, Susannah heated some chicken noodle soup and forced that down. She was putting the bowl in the dishwasher when the telephone rang. Ms. Brooks was the only one who knew she was home, and her assistant would call her only if it was important. Susannah answered the phone just as she would in her office.

"Susannah Simmons."

"Susannah, it's Nate."

She managed to swallow a gasp. "Hello, Nate," she said as evenly as possible. "What can I do for you."

"I called the office and your assistant said you'd gone home sick."

"Yes. I guess I had more to drink last night than I realized. I had one doozy of a hangover when I woke up this morning." But she didn't add how her malady had worsened once she read the article about him.

"Did you find the aspirin on the kitchen counter?"

"Yes. Now that I think about it, you were by last night, weren't you?" She was thinking fast, wanting to cover her tracks. "I suppose I made a fool of myself," she said, instilling a lightness in her tone. "I didn't say anything to embarrass you—or me, did I?"

He chuckled softly. "You don't remember?"

She did, but she wasn't going to admit it. "Some of it, but most of the evening's kind of fuzzy."

"Once I'm back in Seattle I'll help you recall every single word." His voice was low, seductive and filled with promise.

That was one guarantee, however, that Susannah had no intention of accepting.

"I...probably made a complete idiot of myself," she mumbled. "If I were you, I'd forget anything I said. Obviously, I can't be held responsible for it."

"Susannah, Susannah, Susannah," Nate said gently. "Let's take this one step at a time."

"I...think we should talk about it later, I really do... because it's all too obvious I wasn't myself." Tears pooled at the corners of her eyes. Furious at this display of emotion, she wiped them aside with the back of her hand.

"You're feeling okay now?"

"Yes...no. I was about to lie down."

"Then I'll let you," Nate said. "I'll be back Sunday. My flight should arrive early afternoon. I'd like us to have dinner together."

"Sure," she said, without thinking, willing to agree to just about anything in order to end this conversation. She was still too raw, still bleeding. By Sunday, she'd be able to handle the situation far more effectively. By Sunday, she could disguise her pain.

"I'll see you around five, then."

"Sunday," she echoed, feeling like a robot programmed to do exactly as its master requested. She had no intention of having dinner with Nate, none whatsoever. He'd find out why soon enough.

The only way Susannah made it through Saturday was by working. She went to her office and sorted through the mail Ms. Brooks had left on her desk. News of her promotion was to be announced in the Sunday business section of the *Seattle Times,* but apparently word had already leaked out, probably through her boss;

there was a speaking invitation in the mail, for a luncheon at a conference of local salespeople who had achieved a high level of success. The request was an honor and Susannah sent a note of acceptance to the organizer. She considered it high praise to have been asked. The date of the conference was the seventeenth, which was only two weeks away, so she spent a good part of the morning making notes for her speech.

On Sunday, Susannah woke feeling sluggish and out of sorts. She recognized the source of her discomfort almost instantly. This afternoon, she would confront Nate. For the past two days, she'd gone over in her mind exactly what she planned to say, how she'd act.

Nate arrived at four-thirty. She answered his knock, dressed in navy blue slacks and a cream shell-knit sweater. Her hair was neatly rolled into a chignon.

"Susannah." His gaze was hungry as he stepped across the threshold and reached for her.

It was too late to hide her reaction by the time she realized he intended to kiss her. He swept her into his arms and eagerly pressed his mouth over hers. Despite everything that he'd failed to tell her, Susannah felt an immediate excitement she couldn't disguise.

Nate slipped his fingers into her hair, removing the pins that held it in place, while he leisurely moved his mouth over hers.

"Two days have never seemed so long," he breathed, then nibbled on her lower lip.

Regaining her composure, she broke away, her shoulders heaving. "Would you like some coffee?"

"No. The only thing I want is you."

She started to walk away from him, but Nate caught her, hauling her back into the warm shelter of his arms.

He linked his hands at the small of her back and gazed down at her, his eyes soft and caressing. Gradually, his expression altered.

"Is everything all right?" he asked.

"Yes…and no," she admitted dryly. "I happened upon an article in an old issue of *Business Monthly*. Does that tell you anything?"

He hesitated, and for a moment Susannah wondered if he was going to say anything or not.

"So you know?"

"That you're the world's cookie king, or once were—yes, I know."

His eyes narrowed slightly. "Are you angry?"

She sighed. A good deal depended on her delivery, and although she'd practiced her response several times, it was more difficult than she'd expected. She was determined, however, to remain calm and casual.

"I'm more embarrassed than amused," she said. "I wish you'd said something before I made such a fool of myself."

"Susannah, you have every right to be upset." He let her go and rubbed the back of his neck as he began to walk back and forth between the living room and kitchen. "It isn't like it was a deep dark secret. I sold the business almost six months ago, and I was taking a sabbatical—hell, I needed one. I'd driven myself as far as I could. My doctor thinks I was on the verge of a complete physical collapse. When I met you, I was just coming out of it, learning how to enjoy life again. The last thing I wanted to do was sit down and talk about the past thirteen years. I'd put Rainy Day Cookies behind me, and I was trying to build a new life."

Susannah crossed her arms. "Did you ever intend to tell me?"

"Yes!" he said vehemently. "Thursday. You were so sweet to have offered me a job and I knew I had to say something then, but you were..."

"Tipsy," she finished for him.

"All right, tipsy. You have to understand why I didn't. The timing was all wrong."

"You must have got a good laugh from the cookie disaster," she said, surprised at how steady her voice remained. Her poise didn't even slip, and she was proud of herself.

The edges of his mouth quivered, and it was apparent that he was struggling not to laugh.

"Go ahead," she said, waving her hand dramatically. "I suppose those charred cookies and the smoldering cookie sheets were pretty comical. I don't blame you. I'd probably be in hysterics if the situation were reversed."

"It isn't that. The fact that you made those cookies was one of the sweetest things anyone's ever done for me. I want you to know I was deeply touched."

"I didn't do it for you," she said, struggling to keep the anger out of her voice. "It was a trial by fire—" Hearing what she'd said, Susannah closed her eyes.

"Susannah—"

"You must've got a real kick out of that little pep talk I gave you the other day, too. Imagine *me* talking to *you* about drive, motivation and goals."

"That touched me, too," he insisted.

"Right on the funny bone, I'll bet." She faked a laugh herself just to prove what a good sport she was. Still, she wasn't exactly keen on being the brunt of a joke.

Nate paused, then gestured at her. "I suppose it looks bad considered from your point of view."

"Looks bad," she echoed, with a short hysterical laugh. "That's one way of putting it!"

Nate strode from one end of the room to the other. If he didn't stop soon, he was going to wear a path in the carpet.

"Are you willing to put this misunderstanding behind us, Susannah, or are you going to hold it against me? Are you willing to ruin what we have over a mistake?"

"I don't know yet." Actually she did, but she didn't want him to accuse her of making snap decisions. It would be so easy for Nate to talk his way out of this. But Susannah had been humiliated. How could she possibly trust him now? He'd thought nothing of hiding an important portion of his life from her.

"How long will it be before you come to a conclusion about us?"

"I don't know that, either."

"I guess dinner is out?"

She nodded, her face muscles so tight, they ached.

"Okay, think everything through. I trust you to be completely fair and unbiased. All I want you to do is ask yourself one thing. If the situation were reversed, how would you have handled it?"

"All right." She'd grant him that much, although she already knew what she would have done—and it wasn't keep up a charade the way he had.

"There's something else I want you to think about," he said when she held open the door for him.

"What?" Susannah was frantic to get him out of her home. The longer he stayed, the more difficult it was to remain angry with him.

"This." He kissed her then and it was the type of kiss that drove to the very depths of her soul. His mouth on hers was hot, the kiss deep and moist and so filled with longing that her knees almost buckled. Tiny sounds interrupted the moment, and Susannah realized she was the one making them.

When Nate released her, she backed away and nearly stumbled. Breathing hard, she leaned against the door frame and heaved in giant gulps of oxygen.

Satisfied, Nate smiled infuriatingly. "Admit it, Susannah," he whispered and ran his index finger over her collarbone. "We were meant for each other."

"I... I'm not willing to admit anything."

His expression looked forlorn. It was no doubt calculated to evoke sympathy, but it wouldn't work. Susannah wouldn't be fooled a second time.

"You'll phone me?" he pressed.

"Yes." When the moon was in the seventh house, which should be somewhere around the time the government balanced the budget. Perhaps a decade from now.

For two days, Susannah's life returned to a more normal routine. She went in to the office early and worked late, doing everything she could to avoid Nate, although she was sure he'd wait patiently for some signal from her. After all, he, too, had his pride; she was counting on that.

When she arrived home on Wednesday, there was a folded note taped to her door. Susannah stared at it for several thundering heartbeats, then finally reached for it.

She waited until she'd put her dinner in the microwave before she read it. Her heart was pounding painfully hard as she opened the sheet and saw three words: "Call me. Please."

Susannah gave a short hysterical laugh. Ha! Nate Townsend could tumble into a vat of melted chocolate chips before she'd call him again. Guaranteed he'd say or do something that would remind her of what a fool she'd been! And yet... Damn, but it was hard to stay angry with him!

When the phone rang she was still ambivalent. Jumping back, she glared at it before answering.

"Hello," she said cautiously, quaveringly.

"Susannah? Is that you?"

"Oh, hi, Emily."

"Good grief, you scared me. I thought you were sick. You sounded so weak."

"No. No, I'm fine."

"I hadn't talked to you in a while and I was wondering how you were doing."

"Fine," she repeated.

"Susannah!" Her sister's tone made her name sound like a warning. "I know you well enough to realize something's wrong. I also know it probably has to do with Nate. You haven't mentioned him the last few times we've talked, but before you seemed to be overflowing with things you wanted to say about him."

"I'm not seeing much of Nate these days."

"Why not?"

"Well, being a multimillionaire keeps him busy."

Emily paused to gulp in a breath, then gasped, "I think there must be a problem with the phone. I thought you just said—"

"Ever been to Rainy Day Cookies?"

"Of course. Hasn't everyone?"

"Have you made the connection yet?"

"You mean Nate…"

"…is Mr. Chocolate Chip himself."

"But that's marvelous! That's wonderful. Why, he's famous… I mean his cookies are. To think that the man who developed Rainy Day Cookies actually helped Robert carry out Michelle's crib. I can't wait until he hears this."

"Personally, I wasn't all that impressed." It was difficult to act indifferent when her sister was bubbling over with such enthusiasm. Emily usually only got excited about something organic.

"When did you find out?" Emily asked, her voice almost accusing, as if Susannah had been holding out on her.

"Last Friday. John Hammer gave me a magazine that had an article about Nate in it. The issue was a few years old, but the article told me everything Nate should have."

A brief sound of exclamation followed. "So you just found out?"

"Right."

"And you're angry with him?"

"Good heavens, no. Why should I be?" Susannah was afraid Emily wouldn't appreciate the sarcasm.

"He probably planned on telling you," Emily argued, defending Nate. "I don't know him all that well, but he seemed straightforward enough to me. I'm sure he intended to explain the situation when the time was right."

"Perhaps," Susannah said, but as far as she was concerned, that consolation was too little, too late. "Listen, I've got something in the microwave, so I've got to scoot." The excuse was feeble, but Susannah didn't want to continue discussing Nate. "Oh, before I forget," she added quickly. "I've got a speaking engagement on the seventeenth, but I'll be finished before five-thirty so you can count on me watching Michelle."

"Great. Listen, if you want to talk, I'm always here. I mean that. What are sisters for if not to talk?"

"Thanks, I'll remember that."

Once she replaced the receiver, Susannah was left to deal, once more, with Nate's three-word note. By all rights, she should crumple it up and toss it in the garbage. She did, feeling a small—very small—sense of satisfaction.

Out of sight, out of mind, or so the old adage went. Only this time it wasn't working. Whenever she turned around, the sight of the telephone seemed to pull at her.

Her dinner was ready, but as she gazed down at the unappetizing entrée, she considered throwing it out and going to the Western Avenue Deli for a pastrami on rye instead. That would serve two purposes; first, it would take her away from the phone, which seemed to be luring her to its side; and second, she'd at least have a decent meal.

Having made her decision, she was already in the living room when there was a knock at the door. Susannah groaned, knowing even before she answered it that her visitor had to be Nate.

"You didn't call," he snapped the minute she opened the door.

He stormed inside without waiting for an invitation, looking irritated but in control. "Just how long were you planning to keep me waiting? It's obvious you're going to make me pay for the error of my ways, which to a certain point I can understand. But we've gone well past that point. So what are you waiting for? An apology? Okay—I'm sorry."

"Ah—"

"You have every reason to be upset, but what do you want? Blood? Enough is enough. I'm crazy about you, Susannah, and you feel the same about me, so don't try to fool me with this indifference routine, because I can see right through it. Let's put this foolishness behind us and get back on track."

"Why?" she demanded.

"Why what?"

"Why did you wait to tell me? Why couldn't you have said something sooner?"

He gave her a frown that suggested they were rehashing old news, then started his usual pacing. "Because I wanted to put Rainy Day Cookies out of my mind. I'd made the business my entire world." He stopped and whirled to face her. "I recognized a kindred spirit in you. Your entire life is wrapped up in some sporting-goods company—"

"Not just *some* sporting-goods company," she returned, indignant. "H&J Lima is the largest in the country."

"Forgive me, Susannah, but that doesn't really impress me. What about your *life?* Your whole world revolves around how far you can climb up the corporate ladder. Let me tell you that once you're at the top, the view isn't all that great. You forget what it means to appreciate the simple things in life. I did."

"Are you telling me to stop and smell the flowers? Well, I've got news for you, Nate Townsend. I like my life just the way it is. I consider it insulting that you think you can casually walk into my world and my career and tell me I'm headed down the road to destruction, because I'll tell you right now—" she paused to take a deep breath "—I don't appreciate it."

Nate's expression tightened. "I'm not talking about flowers, Susannah. I want you to look out this window at Puget Sound and see the lovely view with ferryboats and snowcapped mountains. Life, abundant life, is more than that. It's meaningful relationships. Connecting with other people. Friends. Fun. We'd both lost sight of that. It happened to me first, and I can see you going in the same direction."

"That's fine for you, but I—"

"You need the same things I do. We need each other."

"Correction," she said heatedly. "As I told you, I like my life just the way it is, thank you. And why shouldn't I? My five-year goals have been achieved, and there are more in the making. I can go straight to the top with this company, and that's exactly what I want. As for needing relationships, you're wrong about that, too. I got along fine before I met you, and the same will be true when you're out of my life."

The room went so still that for a second Susannah was convinced Nate had stopped breathing.

"*When* I'm out of your life," he echoed. "I see. So you've made your decision."

"Yes," she said, holding her head high. "It was fun while it lasted, but if I had to choose between you and the vice presidency, the decision wouldn't be difficult at all. I'm sure you'll encounter some other young woman who needs to be saved from herself and her goals. As far as I can see, from your perspective our relationship was more of a rescue mission. Now that you know how the cookie crumbles—the pun's intended—perhaps you'll leave me to my sorry lot."

"Susannah, would you listen to me?"

"No." She held up her hand for effect. "I'll try to be happy," she said, a heavy note of mockery in her voice.

For a moment, Nate said nothing. "You're making a mistake, but that's something you're going to have to learn on your own."

"I suppose you're planning on being around to pick up the pieces when I fall apart?"

His blue eyes bored into hers. "I might be, but then again, I might not."

"Well, you needn't worry, because either way, you've got a long wait."

Ten

"Ms. Simmons, Mr. Hammer, it's an honor to meet you."

"Thank you," Susannah said, smiling politely at the young man who'd been sent to greet her and her boss. The Seattle Convention Center was filled to capacity. The moment Susannah realized her audience was going to be so large, her stomach was attacked by a bad case of nerves. Not the most pleasant conditions under which to be eating lunch.

"If you'll come this way, I'll show you to the head table."

Susannah and John Hammer followed the young executive toward the front of the crowded room. There were several other people already seated on the stage. Susannah recognized the mayor and a couple of city councillors, along with the King County executive and two prominent local businessmen.

She was assigned the chair to the right of the podium. John was assigned the place beside her. After shaking hands with the conference coordinator, she greeted the others and took her seat. Almost immediately, the caterers started serving lunch, which consisted of an elegantly prepared salad tossed with a raspberry vinaigrette, wild rice and broiled fresh salmon with a teriyaki glaze.

She didn't think she could manage even a bite while sitting in front of so many people. Glancing out over the sea of unfamiliar faces, she forced herself to remain calm and collected. She was, after all, one of the featured speakers for the afternoon, and she'd come well prepared.

There was a slight commotion to her right, but the podium blocked her view.

"Hi, gorgeous. No one told me you were going to be here."

Nate. Susannah nearly swallowed her forkful of salmon whole. It stuck in her throat and she would've choked had she not reached for her water and hurriedly gulped some down.

Twisting around in her chair, she came eye to eye with him. "Hello, Nate," she said as nonchalantly as she could. Her smile was firmly in place.

"I thought Nate Townsend might be here," John whispered, looking pleased with himself.

"I see you've taken to following me around now," Nate taunted as he took his seat, two chairs down from John's.

Susannah ignored his comment and both men, studiously returning to her salmon, hoping to suggest that her meal was far more appealing than their conversation.

"Have you missed me?"

It was ten agonizing days since she'd last seen Nate. Avoiding him hadn't been easy. He'd made sure of that. The first night she'd come home to an Italian opera played just loud enough to be heard through her kitchen wall. The sound of the music was accompanied by the tangy scent of his homemade spaghetti sauce. The aroma of simmering tomatoes and herbs mingled with the pungent scent of hot garlic and butter.

Evidently Nate assumed the way to *her* heart was through her stomach. She'd nearly succumbed then, but her conviction was strong and she'd hurried to a favorite Italian restaurant to alleviate her sudden craving for pasta.

By the weekend, Susannah could've sworn Nate had whipped up every recipe in an entire cookbook, each one more enticing than the last. Susannah had never eaten as many restaurant meals as she had in the past week.

When Nate realized she couldn't be bought so easily with fine food, wine and song, he'd tried another tactic, this one less subtle.

A single red rose was waiting outside her door when she arrived home from the office. There wasn't any note with it, just a perfect fresh flower. She picked it up and against her better judgment took it inside with her, inhaling the delicate scent. The only person who could have left it was Nate. Then, in a flurry of righteousness, she'd taken the rose and put it back where she found it. Five minutes later, she jerked open her door and to her dismay discovered the flower was still there, looking forlorn and dejected.

Deciding to send him her own less than subtle message, Susannah dropped the rose outside Nate's door. She hoped he'd understand once and for all that she refused to be bought!

Nate, however, wasn't dissuaded. The rose was followed the next evening by a small box of luscious chocolates. This time Susannah didn't even bring them inside, but marched them directly to Nate's door.

"No," she said now, forcing her thoughts back to the present and the conference. She surveyed the crowded, noisy room. "I haven't missed you in the least."

"You haven't?" He looked dashed. "But I thought you were trying to make it up to me. Why else would you leave those gifts outside my door?"

For just a second her heart thumped wildly. Then she gave him a fiery glare and diligently resumed her meal, making sure she downed every bite. If she didn't, Nate would think she was lovesick for want of him.

Her boss tilted his head toward her, obviously pleased with himself. "I thought it would be a nice surprise for you to be speaking with Nate. Fact is, I arranged it myself."

"How thoughtful," Susannah murmured.

"You have missed me, haven't you?" Nate asked again, balancing on two legs of his chair in an effort to see her.

Okay, she was willing to admit she'd been a bit lonely, but that was to be expected. For several weeks, Nate had filled every spare moment of her time with silliness like baseball games and kite flying. But she'd lived a perfectly fine life before she met him, and now she'd gone back to that same serene lifestyle without a qualm. Her world was wonderful. Complete. She didn't need him to make her a whole person. Nate was going to a lot of trouble to force her to admit she was miserable without him. She wasn't about to do that.

"I miss you," he said, batting his baby blues at her.

"The least you could do is concede that you're as lonely and miserable as me."

"But I'm not," she answered sweetly, silently acknowledging the lie. "I have a fantastic job and a promising career. What else could I want?"

"Children?"

She leaned forward and spoke across the people between them. "Michelle and I have loads of fun together, and when we get bored with each other, she goes home to her mother. In my opinion that's the perfect way to enjoy a child."

The first speaker approached the podium, and Susannah's attention was diverted to him. He was five minutes into his greeting when Susannah felt something hit her arm. She darted a glance at Nate, who was holding up a white linen napkin. *"What about a husband?"* was inked across the polished cloth.

Groaning, Susannah prayed no one else had seen his note, especially her boss. She rolled her eyes and emphatically shook her head. It was then that she noticed how everyone was applauding and looking in her direction. She blinked, not understanding, until she realized that she'd just been introduced and they were waiting for her to stand up and give her talk.

Scraping back her chair, she stood abruptly and approached the podium, not daring to look at Nate. The man was infuriating! A lesser woman would have dumped the contents of her water glass over his smug head. Instead of venting her irritation, she drew in a deep calming breath and gazed out over her audience. That was a mistake. There were so many faces, and they all had their eyes trained on her.

Her talk had been carefully planned and memorized.

But to be on the safe side, she'd brought the typed sheets with her. She had three key points she intended to share, and had illustrated each one with several anecdotes. Suddenly her mind was blank. It took all her courage not to bolt and run from the stage.

"Go get 'em, Susannah," Nate mouthed, smiling up at her.

His eyes were so full of encouragement and faith that the paralysis started to leave her. Although she'd memorized her speech, she stared down at the written version. The instant she read the first sentence she knew she was going to be fine.

For the next twenty minutes she spoke about the importance of indelibly marking a goal on one's mind and how to minimize difficulties and maximize strengths. She closed by explaining the significance of building a mental ladder to one's dreams. She talked about using determination, discipline, dedication and demeanor as the rungs of this ladder to success.

Despite Nate's earlier efforts to undermine her dignity and poise, she was pleased by the way her speech was received. Many of her listeners nodded at key points in her talk, and Susannah knew she was reaching them. When she came to the end, she felt good, satisfied with her speech and with herself.

As she turned to go back to her seat, her gaze caught Nate's. He was smiling as he applauded, and the gleam in his eyes was unmistakably one of respect and admiration. The warm, caressing look he sent her nearly tripped her heart into overdrive. Yet he'd maddened her with his senseless questions, distracted her, teased and taunted her with his craziness and then written a note on a napkin. But when she finished her speech, the first

person she'd looked at, whether consciously or uncon-
sciously, was Nate.

Once Susannah was seated, she saw that her hands
were trembling. But she couldn't be sure if it was a release from the tension that had gripped her when she
first started to speak, or the result of Nate's tender look.

Nate was introduced next, and he walked casually to
the podium. It would serve him right, Susannah thought,
if she started writing messages on her napkin and holding them up for him to read while he gave his talk.
She was immediately shocked by the childishness of
the idea. Five minutes with Nate seemed to reduce her
mentality to that of a ten-year-old.

With a great deal of ceremony, or so it seemed to
Susannah, Nate retrieved his notes from inside his suit
jacket. It was all she could do to keep from laughing
out loud when she saw that everything he planned to
say had been jotted on the back of a single index card.
So this was how seriously he'd taken that afternoon's
address. It looked as if he'd scribbled a couple of notes
while she was delivering her speech. He hadn't given
his lecture a second thought until five minutes before
he was supposed to stand at the podium.

But Nate proved her wrong, as seemed to be his
habit. The minute he opened his mouth, he had the audience in the palm of his hand. Rarely had she heard a
more dynamic speaker. His strong voice carried to the
farthest corners of the huge hall, and although he used
the microphone, Susannah doubted he really needed it.

Nate told of his own beginnings, of how his father
had died the year he was to enter college, so that the
funds he'd expected to further his education were no
longer available. It was the lowest point of his life and

out of it had come his biggest success. Then he explained that his mother's chocolate chip cookies had always been everyone's favorite. Because of his father's untimely death, she'd taken a job in a local factory, and Nate, eager to find a way to attend university in the fall, had started baking the cookies and selling them to tourists for fifty cents each.

Halfway through the summer he'd made more than enough money to see him through his first year of school. Soon a handful of local delis had contacted him, wanting to include his cookies as part of their menus. These requests were followed by others from restaurants and hotels.

Nate went to school that first year and took every business course available to him. By the end of the following summer, he had set up a kitchen with his mother's help and opened his own business, which thrived despite his mistakes. The rest was history. By the time he graduated from college, Nate was already a millionaire and his mother was able to retire comfortably. To his credit, he'd resisted the temptation to abandon his education. It had served him well since, and he was glad he'd stuck with it, even though everyone around him seemed to be saying he knew more, from personal experience, than most of the authors of the textbooks did. A fact he was quick to dispute.

Susannah was enthralled. She'd assumed Nate would be telling this audience what he'd been beating her over the head with from the moment they'd met—that the drive to succeed was all well and good, but worthless if in the process one forgot to enjoy life. However, if that thought was on Nate's mind, he didn't voice it. Susannah suspected he'd reserved that philosophy for her and her alone.

When he returned to his seat, the applause was thunderous. The first thing he did was look at Susannah, who smiled softly, as touched by his story as the rest of the audience was. Not once had he patted himself on the back, or taken credit for the phenomenal success of Rainy Day Cookies. Susannah would almost have preferred it if his talk had been a boring rambling account of his prosperous career. She didn't want to feel so much admiration for him. It would be easier to get Nate out of her life and her mind if she didn't.

The luncheon ended a few minutes later. Gathering up her things, Susannah hoped to make a speedy escape. She should've known Nate wouldn't allow that. Several people had hurried up to the podium to talk to him, but he excused himself and moved to her side.

"Susannah, could we talk for a minute?"

She made a show of glancing at her watch, then at her boss. "I have another appointment," she said stiffly. She secured the strap of her purse over her shoulder and offered him what she hoped was a regretful smile.

"Your speech was wonderful."

"Thank you. So was yours," she said, then mentioned the one thing that had troubled her. "You never told me about your father's death."

"I've never told you I love you, either, but I do."

His words, so casual, so calm and serene, were like a blow to her solar plexus. Susannah felt the tears form in her eyes and tried to blink them back. "I… I wish you hadn't said that."

"The way I feel about you isn't going to change."

"I…really have to go," she said, turning anxiously

toward John Hammer. All she wanted to do was escape with her heart intact.

"Mr. Townsend," a woman bellowed from the audience. "You're going to be at the auction tonight, aren't you?"

Nate's gaze slid reluctantly from Susannah to the well-dressed woman on the floor. "I'll be there," he called back.

"I'll be looking for you," she said and laughed girlishly.

Susannah decided the other woman's laugh resembled the sound an unwell rooster would make. She was tempted to ask Nate exactly what kind of auction he planned to attend where he expected to run into someone who yelled questions across a crowded room. But she ignored the urge, which was just as well.

"Goodbye, Nate," she said, moving away.

"Goodbye, my love." It wasn't until she was walking out of the Convention Center that Susannah realized how final his farewell had sounded.

It was what she wanted, wasn't it? As far as she was concerned, Nate had proved he wasn't trustworthy; he had an infuriating habit of keeping secrets. So now that he wasn't going to see her again, there was absolutely no reason for her to complain. At least that was what Susannah told herself as she headed home, making a short side trip to the Seattle waterfront.

Within a couple of hours, Emily and Robert would be dropping off Michelle before they went to dinner with Robert's employer. Once the baby was with her, Susannah reminded herself, she wouldn't have a chance to worry about Nate or anyone else.

By the time Emily arrived with her family, Susannah was in a rare mood. She felt light-headed and witty, as though she'd downed something alcoholic, but the strongest thing she'd had all day was coffee.

"Hi," she said cheerfully, opening the door. Michelle looked at her with large round eyes and grabbed for her mother's collar.

"Sweetheart, this is your auntie Susannah, remember?"

"Emily, the only thing she remembers is that every time you bring her here, you leave," Robert said, carrying in the diaper bag and a sack full of blankets and toys.

"Hello, Robert," Susannah murmured, kissing him on the cheek. The action surprised her as much as it did her brother-in-law. "I understand congratulations are in order."

"For you, too."

"Yes, well, it wasn't that big a deal," she said, playing down her own success.

"Not according to the article in the paper."

"Oh," Emily said, whirling around. "Speaking of the paper, I read Nate's name today."

"Yes…we were both speakers at a conference this afternoon."

Emily seemed impressed, but Susannah couldn't be sure if it was because of her or Nate.

"That wasn't what I read about him," Emily continued, focusing her attention on removing the jacket from Michelle's arms. The child wasn't being cooperative. "Nate's involved in the auction."

"Da-da!" Michelle cried once her arms were free.

Robert looked on proudly. "She finally learned my name. Michelle's first and only word," he added, beaming. "Da-da loves his baby, yes, he does."

It was so unusual to hear Robert using baby talk that for an instant, Susannah didn't catch what her sister was saying. "What was that?"

"I'm trying to tell you about the auction," Emily said again, as if that should explain everything. At Susannah's puzzled look, she added, "His name was in an article about the auction to benefit the Children's Home Society."

The lightbulb that clicked on inside Susannah's head was powerful enough to search the night sky. "Not the *bachelor* auction?" Her question was little more than a husky murmur. No wonder the woman who'd shouted to Nate at the luncheon had been so brazen! She was going to bid on him.

Slowly, hardly conscious of what she was doing, Susannah lowered herself onto the sofa next to her sister.

"He didn't tell you?"

"No, but then why should he? We're nothing more than neighbors."

"Susannah!"

Her sister had the annoying ability to turn Susannah's name into an entire statement just by the way she said it.

"Honey," Robert said, studying his watch, "it's quarter to seven. We'd better leave now if we're going to be at the restaurant on time. I don't want to keep my boss waiting."

Emily's glance at Susannah promised a long talk later. At least Susannah had several hours during which to come up with a way of warding off her sister's questions.

"Have a good time, you two," Susannah said lightheartedly, guiding them toward the door, "and don't worry about a thing."

"Bye, Michelle," Emily said as she waved from the doorway.

"Tell Mommy goodbye." Since the baby didn't seem too inclined to do so, Susannah held up the chubby hand and waved it for her.

As soon as Emily and Robert had left, Michelle started whimpering softly. Susannah took one look at her niece and her spirits plummeted. Who was she trying to fool? Herself? She'd been miserable and lonely from the moment she'd rejected Nate. Michelle sniffled, and Susannah felt like crying right along with her.

So the notorious Nate Townsend had done it again—he hadn't even bothered to mention the bachelor auction. Obviously he'd agreed to this event weeks in advance and it had never even occurred to him to tell her. Oh, sure, he swore undying love to her, but he was willing to let some strange woman buy him. Men, she was quickly learning, were not to be trusted.

The more Susannah thought back to their previous conversations, the angrier she became. When she'd asked Nate about helping her out with Michelle, he'd casually said he had "something else" this evening. He sure did. Auctioning off his body to the highest bidder!

"I told him I didn't want to see him again," Susannah announced to her niece, her fervor causing her to raise her voice. "That man was trouble from the night we met. You were with me at the time, remember? Don't we wish we'd known then what we know now?"

Michelle's shoulders began to shake, with the effort to either cry or keep from crying. Susannah didn't know which.

"He has this habit of hiding things from me—important information. But I'm telling you right now that

I'm completely over that man. Any woman who wants him tonight can have him, because I'm not interested."

Michelle buried her face against Susannah's neck.

"I know exactly how you feel, kid," she said, stalking the carpet in front of the large picture window. She stared out at the lights and sounds of the city at night. "It's like you've lost your best friend, right?"

"Da-da."

"He's with your mommy. I thought Nate was my friend once," she said sadly to the baby. "But I learned the hard way what he really is—nothing earth-shattering, don't misunderstand me. But he let me make a complete idiot of myself. And…and he doesn't trust me enough to tell me anything important."

Michelle looked at Susannah wide-eyed, apparently enthralled with her speech. In an effort to keep the baby appeased, she continued chattering. "I hope he feels like a fool on the auction block tonight," she said as she imagined him standing in front of an auditorium full of screaming women. She slowly released a sigh, knowing that with his good looks, Nate would probably bring in top money. In past auctions, several of the men had gone for thousands of dollars. All for an evening in the company of one of Seattle's eligible bachelors.

"So much for love and devotion," she muttered. Michelle watched her solemnly, and Susannah felt it was her duty as the baby's aunt to give her some free advice. "Men aren't all they're cracked up to be. You'd be wise to figure that out now."

Michelle gurgled cheerfully, obviously in full agreement.

"I for one don't need a man. I'm totally happy living on my own. I've got a job, a really good job, and a few close friends—mostly people I work with—and of course your mother." Michelle raised her hand to Susannah's face and rubbed her cheek where a tear had streaked a moist trail.

"I know what you're thinking," Susannah added, although it was unnecessary to explain all that to anyone so young. "If I'm so happy, then why am I crying? Darned if I know. The problem is I can't help loving him and that's what makes this so difficult. Then he had to go and write that note on a napkin." She brought her fingers to her mouth, trying to calm herself. "He asked me if I was willing to live my life without a husband… on a napkin he asked me that. Can you imagine what the caterers are going to think when they read it? And we were sitting at the head table, no less."

"Da-da."

"He asked about that, too," Susannah said, sniffling as she spoke. She was silent a moment and when she began again her voice trembled slightly. "I never thought I'd want children, but then I didn't realize how much I could love a little one like you." Holding the baby against her breast, Susannah closed her eyes to the pain that clawed at her. "I'm so mad at that man."

Fascinated by Susannah's hair, Michelle reached up and tugged it free from the confining pins.

"I wore it up this afternoon to be contrary—and to prove to myself that I'm my own woman. Then he was there and the whole time I was speaking I wished I'd left it down—just because Nate prefers it that way. Oh, honestly, Michelle, I think I may be ready to go off the deep end here. Any advice you'd care to give me?"

"Da-da."

"That's what I thought you'd say." Forcing in a deep

breath, Susannah tried to control the tears that sprang to her eyes. She hadn't expected to cry.

"I really believed that once I was promoted to vice president everything would be so wonderful and, well, it *has* been good, but I feel…empty inside. Oh, Michelle, I don't know if I can explain it. The nights are so long and there are only so many hours I can work without thinking about getting home and the possibility of seeing Nate. I… I seem to have lost my drive. Here I was talking to all these people today about determination and drive and discipline, and none of it seemed real. Then…then on the way home I was walking along the waterfront and I saw an old college friend. She's married and has a baby a little older than you and she looked so happy." She paused long enough to rub the back of her hand under her nose. "I told her all about my big promotion and Sally seemed genuinely happy for me, but I felt this giant hole inside."

"Da-da."

"Michelle, can't you learn another word? Please. How about Auntie? It's not so difficult. Say it after me. Auntie."

"Da-da."

"Nate's probably going to meet some gorgeous blonde and fall madly in love with her. She'll bid thousands of dollars for him and he'll be so impressed he won't even mind when she—" Susannah stopped, her mind whirling. "You won't believe what I was thinking," she said to Michelle, who was studying her curiously. "It's completely crazy, but…perhaps not."

Michelle waved her arms and actually seemed interested in hearing about this insane idea that had popped into Susannah's head. It was impossible. Absurd. But then she'd made a fool of herself over Nate so many times that once more certainly wasn't going to hurt.

It took several minutes to get Michelle back into her coat. Susannah would've sworn the thing had more arms than an octopus.

After glancing at the balance in her checkbook, she grabbed her savings-account records and, carrying Michelle, headed to the parking garage. She'd been saving up to pay cash for a new car, but bidding for Nate was more important.

The parking lot outside the theater where the bachelor auction was being held was full, and Susannah had a terrible time finding a place to leave her car. Once she was inside the main entrance, the doorman was hesitant to let her into the auditorium, since Michelle was with her and neither one of them had a ticket.

"Ma'am, I'm sorry, I can't let you in there without a ticket and a bidding number—besides I don't think married women are allowed."

"I'll buy one and this is my niece. Now, either you let me in there or...or you'll... I'll... I don't know what I'll do. Please," she begged. "This is a matter of life and death." Okay, so that was a slight exaggeration.

While the doorman conferred with his supervisor, Susannah looked through the swinging doors that led into the theater. She watched as several women raised their hands, and leaped enthusiastically to their feet to show their numbers. A television crew was there taping the proceedings, as well.

Susannah was impatiently bouncing Michelle on her hip when the doorman returned.

"Ma'am, I'm sorry, but my supervisor says the tickets are sold out."

Susannah was about to argue with him when she heard the master of ceremonies call out Nate's name. A fervent murmur rose from the crowd.

Desperate times demanded desperate measures, and instead of demurely going back outside, Susannah rushed to the swinging doors, shoved them open and hurried down the narrow aisle.

As soon as the doorman saw what she'd done, he ran after her, shouting, "Stop that woman!"

The master of ceremonies ceased speaking, and a hush fell over the room as every head in the place turned toward Susannah, who was clutching Michelle protectively to her chest. She'd made it halfway down the center aisle before the doorman caught up with her. Susannah cast a wretched pleading glance at Nate, who had shielded his eyes from the glare of the lights and was staring at her.

Michelle cooed and with her pudgy hand, pointed toward Nate.

"Da-da! Da-da!" she cried, and her voice echoed loudly in the auditorium.

Eleven

An immediate uproar rose from the theater full of women. Nothing Susannah did could distract Michelle from pointing toward Nate and calling him Da-da. For his part, Nate appeared to be taking all the commotion in his stride. He walked over to the master of ceremonies, whom Susannah recognized as Cliff Dolittle, a local television personality, and whispered something in his ear.

"What seems to be the problem?" Cliff asked the doorman.

"This lady doesn't have a ticket or a bidding number," he shouted back. He clutched Susannah's upper arm and didn't look any too pleased with this unexpected turn of events.

"I may not have a number, but I've got $6,010.12 I'd like to bid for this man," she shouted.

Her announcement was again followed by a hubbub of whispering voices, which rolled over the theater like a wave crashing onto the shore. That six thousand was the balance in Susannah's savings account, plus all the cash she had with her.

A noise from the back of the room distracted her, and that was when she realized the television crew had the cameras rolling. Every single detail of this debacle was being documented.

"I have a bid of $6,010.12," Cliff Dolittle announced, sounding a little shocked. "Going once, going twice—" he paused and scanned the female audience "—sold to the lady who gate-crashed this auction. The one with the baby in her arms."

The doorman released Susannah and reluctantly directed her to where she was supposed to pay. It seemed that everyone was watching her and whispering. Several of the women were bold enough to shout bits of advice to her.

A man with a camera balanced on his shoulder hurried toward her. Loving the attention, Michelle pointed her finger at the lens and cried "Da-da" once more for all the people who would soon be viewing this disaster at home.

"Susannah, what are you doing here?" Nate whispered, joining her when she'd reached the teller's booth.

"You know what really irritates me about this?" she said, her face bright with embarrassment. "I probably could've had you for three thousand, only I panicked and offered every penny I have. Me, the marketing wizard. I'll never be able to hold my head up again."

"You're not making any sense."

"And you are? One moment you're saying you love me and the next you're on the auction block, parading around for a bunch of women."

"That comes to $6,025.12," the white-haired woman in the teller's booth told her.

"I only bid $6,010.12," Susannah protested.

"The extra money is the price of the ticket. You weren't supposed to bid without one."

"I see."

Unzipping her purse and withdrawing her checkbook while balancing Michelle on her hip proved to be difficult.

"Here, I'll take her." Nate reached for Michelle, who surprised them both by protesting loudly.

"What have you been telling her about me?" Nate teased.

"The truth." With considerable ceremony, Susannah wrote out the check and ripped it from her book. Reluctantly she slid it across the counter to the woman collecting the fees.

"I'll write you a receipt."

"Thank you," Susannah said absently. "By the way, what exactly am I getting for my hard-earned money?"

"One evening with this young man."

"One evening," Susannah repeated grimly. "If we go out to dinner does he pay or do I?"

"I do," Nate answered for her.

"It's a good thing, because I don't have any money left."

"Have you eaten?"

"No, and I'm starved."

"Me, too," he told her, smiling sheepishly, but the look in his eyes said he wasn't talking about snacking on crêpes suzette. "I can't believe you did this."

"I can't, either," she said, shaking her head in wonder. "I'm still reeling with the shock." Later, she'd probably start trembling and not be able to stop. Never in her life had she done anything so bold. Love apparently did things like that to a woman. Before she met Nate she'd been a sound, logical, dedicated businesswoman. Six weeks later, she was smelling orange blossoms and thinking about weddings and babies—all because she was head over heels in love!

"Come on, let's get out of here," Nate said, tucking his arm around her waist and leading her toward the theater doors.

Susannah nodded. The doorman seemed relieved that she was leaving his domain.

"Susannah," Nate said, once they were in the parking lot. He turned and placed his hands on her shoulders, then closed his eyes as if gathering his thoughts. "You were the last person I expected to see tonight."

"Obviously," she returned stiffly. "When we're married, I'm going to have to insist that you keep me informed of your schedule."

Nate's head snapped up. "When we're married?"

"You don't honestly believe I just spent six thousand dollars for one dinner in some fancy restaurant, did you?"

"But—"

"And there'll be children, as well. I figure that two are about all I can handle, but we'll play that by ear."

For the first time since she'd met him, Nate Townsend seemed speechless. His mouth made several movements in an attempt to talk, but nothing came out.

"I suppose you're wondering how I plan to manage my career," she said, before he could ask the question. "I'm not sure what I'm going to do yet. Since I'm looking at the good side of thirty, I suppose we could delay having children for a few more years."

"I'm thirty-three. I want a family soon."

Nate's voice didn't sound at all like it normally did,

and Susannah peered at him carefully, wondering if the shock had been too much for him. It had been for her! And she was going to end up on the eleven-o'clock news. "Fine, we'll plan on starting our family right away," she agreed. "But before we do any more talking about babies, I need to ask you something important. Are you willing to change messy diapers?"

A smile played at the edges of his mouth as he nodded.

"Good." Susannah looked at Michelle, who'd laid her head against her aunt's shoulder and closed her eyes. Apparently the events of the evening had tired her out.

"What about dinner?" Nate asked, tenderly brushing the silky hair from the baby's brow. "I don't think Michelle's going to last much longer."

"Don't worry about it. I'll buy something on the way home." She paused, then gestured weakly with her hand. "Forget that. I… I don't have any money left."

Nate grinned widely. "I'll pick up some takeout and meet you back at your place in half an hour."

Susannah smiled her appreciation. "Thanks."

"No," Nate whispered, his eyes locked with hers. "Thank *you*."

He kissed her then, slipping his hand behind her neck and tilting her face up to meet his. His touch was so potent Susannah thought her heart would beat itself right out of her chest.

"Nate." Her eyes remained shut when his name parted her lips.

"Hmm?"

"I really do love you."

"Yes, I know. I love you, too. I knew it the night you bought the Stroganoff from the Western Avenue

Deli and tried to make me think you'd whipped it up yourself."

She opened her eyes and raised them to his. "But I didn't even realize it then. We barely knew each other."

He kissed the tip of her nose. "I was aware from the first time we met that my life was never going to be the same."

His romantic words stirred her heart and she wiped a tear from the corner of her eye. "I... I'd better take Michelle home," she said, and sniffled.

Nate's thumb stroked the moisture from her cheek before he kissed her again. "I won't be long," he promised.

He wasn't. Susannah had no sooner got Michelle home and into her sleeper when there was a light knock at the door.

Hurriedly, she tiptoed across the carpet and opened it. She brought her finger to her lips as she let Nate inside.

"I got Chinese."

She nodded. "Great."

She paused on her way into the kitchen and showed him Michelle, who was sleeping soundly on the end of the sofa. Susannah had taken the opposite cushion and braced it against the side so there wasn't any chance she could fall off.

"You're going to be a good mother," he whispered, kissing her forehead.

It was silly to get all misty-eyed over Nate's saying that, but she did. She succeeded in disguising her emotion by walking into the kitchen and getting two plates from the cupboard. Opening the silverware drawer, she took out forks.

Nate set the large white sack on the table and lifted

out five wire-handled boxes. "Garlic chicken, panfried noodles, ginger beef and two large egg rolls. Do you think that'll be enough?"

"Were you planning on feeding the Seventh Infantry?" she teased.

"You said you were hungry." He opened all the boxes but one.

Susannah filled her plate and sat next to Nate, propping her feet on the chair opposite hers. The food was delicious, and after the first few mouthfuls she decided if Nate could eat with chopsticks she should try it, too. Her efforts had a humbling effect on her.

Watching her artless movements, Nate laughed, then leaned over and kissed the corner of her mouth.

"What's in there?" she asked pointing a chopstick at the fifth box.

He shrugged. "I forget."

Curious, Susannah picked up the container and opened it. Her breath lodged in her throat as she raised her eyes to Nate's. "It's a black velvet box."

"Oh, yes, now that you mention it I remember the chef saying something about black velvet being the special of the month." He went on expertly delivering food to his mouth with the chopsticks.

Susannah continued to stare at the velvet box as if it would leap out and open itself. It was the size of a ring box.

Nate waved a chopstick in her direction. "You might as well take it out and see what's inside."

Wordlessly she did as he suggested. Once the box was free, she set the carton aside and lifted the lid. She gasped when she saw the size of the diamond. For one wild moment she couldn't breathe.

"I picked it up when I was in San Francisco," Nate told her, with no more emotion than if he'd been discussing the weather.

The solitary diamond held her gaze as effectively as a magnet. "It's the most beautiful ring I've ever seen."

"Me, too. I took one look at it and told the jeweler to wrap it up."

He acted so casual, seeming far more interested in eating his ginger beef and noodles than talking about anything as mundane as an engagement ring.

"I suppose I should tell you that while I was in San Francisco, I made an offer for the Cougars. They're a professional baseball team, in case you don't know."

"The baseball team? You're going to own a professional baseball team?" Any news he hit her with, it seemed, was going to be big.

He nodded. "I haven't heard back yet, but if that doesn't work out, I might be able to interest the owner of the New York Wolves in selling."

He made it all sound as if he were buying a car instead of something that cost millions of dollars.

"But whatever happens, we'll make Seattle our home."

Susannah nodded, although she wasn't sure why.

"Here." He set his plate aside and took the ring box from her limp hand. "I suppose the thing to do would be to place this on your finger."

Once again, Susannah nodded. Her meal was sitting like a ton of lead in the pit of her stomach. From habit, she held out her right hand. He grinned and reached for her left one.

"I had to guess the size," he said, deftly removing the diamond from its lush bed. "I had the jeweler make it a size five, because your fingers are dainty." The ring slipped on easily, the fit perfect.

Susannah couldn't stop staring at it. Never in all her life had she dreamed she'd ever have anything so beautiful. "I…don't dare go near the water with this," she whispered, looking down at her hand. Lowering her eyes helped cover her sudden welling up of tears. The catch in her voice was telltale enough.

"Not go near the water…why?"

"If I accidentally fell in," she said, managing a light laugh, "I'd sink from the weight of the diamond."

"Is it too big?"

Quickly she shook her head. "It's perfect."

Catching her unawares, Nate pressed his mouth to her trembling lips, kissing what breath she had completely away. "I planned to ask you to marry me the night I came back from the trip. We were going out for dinner, remember?"

Susannah nodded. That had been shortly after she'd read the article in *Business Monthly* about Nate. The day it felt as though her whole world was rocking beneath her feet.

"I know we talked briefly about your career, but I have something else I need to tell you."

Susannah nodded, because commenting at this point was becoming increasingly impossible.

"What would it take to lure you away from H&J Lima?"

The diamond on her ring finger seemed incentive enough, but she wasn't going to let him know that quite yet. "Why?"

"Because I'm starting a kite company. Actually, it's going to be a nationwide franchise. I've got plans to open ten stores in strategic cities around the country to see how it flies." He stopped to laugh at his pun. "But from the testing we're doing, this is going to be big. However—" he drew in a deep breath "—I'm lacking one important member of my team. I need a marketing expert, and was wondering if you'd like to apply for the job."

"I suppose," she said, deciding to play his game. "But I'd want top salary, generous bonuses, a four-day week, a health and retirement plan and adequate maternity leave."

"The job's yours."

"I don't know, Nate, there could be problems," she said, cocking her head to one side, implying that she was already having second thoughts. "People are going to talk."

"Why?"

"Because I intend to sleep with the boss. And some old fuddy-duddy's bound to think that's how I got the job."

"Let them." He laughed, reaching for her and pulling her into his lap. "Have I told you I'm crazy about you?"

Smiling into his eyes, she nodded. "There's one thing I want cleared up before we go any further, Nate Townsend. No more secrets. Understand?"

"I promise." He spit on the end of his fingertips and used the same fingers to cross his heart. "I used to do that when I was a kid. It meant I was serious."

"Well," Susannah murmured, "since you seem to be in a pledging mood, there are a few other items I'd like to have you swear to."

"Such as?"

"Such as…" she whispered, and lowered her mouth

to a scant inch above his. Whatever thoughts had been in her mind scattered like autumn leaves in a brisk wind. Her tongue outlined his lips, teasing and taunting him as he'd taught her to do.

"Susannah…"

Whatever he meant to say was interrupted by the door. Susannah lifted her head. It took a moment to clear her muddled thoughts before she realized it must be her sister and brother-in-law returning from their celebration dinner with Robert's boss.

She tried to move from Nate's lap, but he groaned in protest and tightened his arms around her. "Whoever it is will go away," he said close to her ear.

"Nate—"

"Go back to doing what you were just doing and forget whoever's at the door."

"It's Emily and Robert."

Nate moaned and released her.

Susannah had no sooner unlocked the door than Emily flew in as though she were being pursued by a banshee. She marched into the living room and stopped suddenly. Robert followed her, looking nearly as frenzied as his wife. Sane sensible Robert!

"What's wrong?" Susannah asked, her heart leaping with concern.

"You're asking *us* that?" Robert flared.

"Now, Robert," Emily said, gently placing her hand on her husband's forearm. "There's no need to be so angry. Stay calm."

"Me? Angry?" he cried, facing his wife. "In the middle of our after-dinner drink you let out a shriek that scared me out of ten years of my life and now you're telling me not to be angry?"

"Emily," Susannah tried again, "what's wrong?"

"Where's Nate?" Robert shouted. One corner of her brother-in-law's mouth curved down in a snarl. He raised his clenched fist. "I'd like ten minutes alone with that man. Give me ten minutes."

"Robert!" Emily and Susannah cried simultaneously.

"Did someone say my name?" Nate asked, as he strolled out of the kitchen.

Emily threw herself in front of her husband, patting his heaving chest with her hands. "Now, honey, settle down. There's no need to get so upset."

Susannah was completely confused. She'd never heard her brother-in-law raise his voice before. Whatever had happened had clearly unsettled him to the point of violence.

"He's not getting away with this," Robert shouted, straining against his wife's restricting hands.

"Away with what?" Nate said with a calm that seemed to inflame Robert even more.

"Taking my daughter away from me!"

"What?" Susannah cried. It astonished her that Michelle could be sleeping through all this commotion. But fortunately the baby seemed oblivious to what was happening.

"You'd better start at the beginning," Susannah said, leading everyone into the kitchen. "There's obviously been some kind of misunderstanding. Now sit down and I'll put on some decaffeinated coffee and we can sort this out in a reasonable manner."

Her brother-in-law pulled out a chair and put his elbows on the table, supporting his head in his hands.

"Why don't you start?" Susannah said, looking at her sister.

"Well," Emily began, taking in a deep breath, "as I told you, we were having dinner with Robert's boss and—"

"They know all that," Robert interrupted. "Tell them about the part when we were having a drink in the cocktail lounge."

"Yes," Emily said, heaving a great sigh. "That does seem to be where the problem started, doesn't it?"

Susannah shared a look with Nate, wondering if he was as lost as she was. Neither Emily nor Robert was making any sense.

"Go on," Susannah encouraged.

"As I explained, we were all sitting in the cocktail lounge having a drink. There was a television set in the corner of the room. I hadn't been paying much attention to it, but I looked up and I saw you and Michelle on the screen."

"Then she gave a scream that was loud enough to curdle a Bloody Mary," Robert explained. "I got everyone to be quiet while the announcer came on. He said you'd taken *my daughter* to this…this bachelor auction. They showed Michelle pointing her finger at Nate and calling him Da-da."

"That was when Robert let out a fierce yell," Emily said.

"Oh, no." Susannah slumped into a chair, wanting to find a hole to crawl into and hibernate for the next ten years. Maybe by then Seattle would have forgotten how she'd disgraced herself.

"Did they say anything else?" Nate wanted to know, doing a poor job of disguising his amusement.

"Only that the details would follow at eleven."

"I demand an explanation!" Robert said, frowning at Nate.

"It's all very simple," Susannah rushed to explain. "See... Nate's wearing a suit that's very similar to yours. Same shade of brown. From the distance, Michelle obviously mistook him for you."

"She did?" Robert muttered.

"Of course," Susannah went on. "Besides, Da-da is the only word she can say...." Her voice trailed off.

"Michelle knows who her daddy is," Nate said matter-of-factly. "You don't need to worry that—"

"Susannah," Emily broke in, "when did you get that diamond? It looks like an engagement ring."

"It is," Nate said, reaching to the middle of the table for the last egg roll. He looked at Susannah. "You don't mind, do you?"

"No. Go ahead."

"What channel was it?" Nate asked between bites. Emily told him.

"Must be a slow news day," Susannah mumbled.

"Gee, Susannah," said Emily, "I always thought if you were going to make the television news it would be because of some big business deal. I never dreamed it would be over a man. Are you going to tell me what happened?"

"Someday," she said, expelling her breath. She'd never dreamed it would be over a man, either, but this one was special. More than special.

"Well, since we're going to be brothers-in-law I guess I can forget about this unfortunate incident," Robert said generously, having regained his composure.

"Good. I'd like to be friends," Nate said, holding out his hand for Robert to shake.

"You're going to be married?" Emily asked her sister.

Susannah exchanged a happy smile with Nate and nodded.

"When?"

"Soon," Nate answered for her. His eyes told her the sooner the better.

She felt the heat crawl into her face, but she was as eager as Nate to get to the altar.

"Not only has Susannah agreed to be my wife, she's also decided to take on the position of marketing director for Windy Day Kites."

"You're leaving H&J Lima?" Robert asked, as if he couldn't believe his ears.

"Had to," she said. She moved to Nate's side, wrapped her arms around his waist and smiled up at him. "The owner made me an offer I couldn't refuse."

Nate's smile felt like a summer's day. Susannah closed her eyes, basking in the warmth of this man who'd taught her about love and laughter and rainy day kisses.

Epilogue

Michelle Davidson arrived at her aunt and uncle's waterfront home just before six. Although she'd been to the house countless times, its beauty never failed to impress her. The place was even lovelier at Christmas, illuminated by string upon string of sparkling lights. The figures on the lawn—the reindeer and St. Nick and everything else—were downright magical.

Michelle's favorite was the young boy running with his kite flying high above his head. Her uncle's kites were what had launched Windy Day Toys all those years ago. Michelle didn't have any memory of those early days, of course. She'd been much too young.

Her aunt Susannah had worked with Uncle Nate for seven years. In that time, the company had gone from one successful venture to another. The first major success had been with kites, and then there was a series of outdoor games, geared toward getting kids outside instead of sitting in front of a TV or a computer screen. Buried Treasure came next and then a game called Bugs that caught national attention.

In the meantime Aunt Susannah had three children

in quick succession and became a stay-at-home mother for a while. Despite her initial doubts, she'd loved it. Michelle's own mother had three children in addition to her, all born within a few months of their Townsend cousins. When her youngest sibling, Glory, entered kindergarten, Michelle's mother and Aunt Susannah had formed Motherhood, Inc.

The two sisters had introduced a series of baby products that were environmentally friendly, starting with cloth diapers and organic baby food. They'd recognized the desire of young mothers all across the country for alternatives to disposable diapers and ways to feed their babies wholesome food.

"Michelle! Michelle!"

Ten-year-old Junior was out the door and racing toward her even before Michelle had made it up the driveway. Eight-year-old Emma Jane was directly behind him. Tessa, who was twelve, was far too aloof, too cool, to show any excitement over Michelle's visit. That was all right, because Michelle knew exactly how Tessa felt. Michelle had hated it when her parents had insisted on hiring a sitter, so she couldn't very well blame Tessa now.

"Michelle." Aunt Susannah waited for her by the entrance. "I really appreciate your doing this," she said. Two large evergreen wreaths decorated the front doors, and a fifteen-foot-high Christmas tree dominated the entry, with gifts stacked all around.

Her aunt finished fastening an earring. "How'd it go at the office today?"

"People heard that we're related," Michelle confessed.

Junior and Emma Jane sat down beneath the massive

Christmas tree and began sorting through the gifts—
obviously an activity they indulged in often.

"I suppose everyone was likely to find out sooner or
later," Aunt Susannah said, turning toward the stairs.
"Nate, hurry up or we're going to be late for dinner."

"I ended up telling everyone that it was because of
me that you met Uncle Nate."

At that, Tessa came out of the library. "You were?"

"It's true," Michelle said, accustomed to looks of astonishment after her coworkers' reactions earlier in the
day.

"How come no one's ever mentioned *this* before?"
Tessa demanded.

Aunt Susannah glanced at Michelle, frowning slightly.
"It was a long time ago, sweetie."

"All you said was that you met Dad when you lived
in that condo building in downtown Seattle."

"That's how we did meet." Susannah called upstairs
again. "Nate!"

"I'll be right down," Nate shouted from the landing.

"Michelle?" Tessa asked, looking to her for the explanation that wasn't being offered by her mother.

"I'll tell you all about it," Michelle whispered.

"Us, too," Emma Jane said.

"Of course," Michelle promised.

Nate Townsend bounded down the stairs, looking
as handsome and debonair as always. He really was a
wonderful uncle—energetic, funny and a terrific cook.

"Honey, we need to leave right now."

"I know." He opened the hall closet and took out
Susannah's coat and his own. He helped Susannah on
with hers, then reached over to kiss each of the kids.

"Be good," he said. "And Michelle, if you're going

to tell them the story of your aunt and me, don't leave out the part about how you nearly ruined my reputation at the Seattle Bachelor Auction."

"Or the fact that I spent far too much money to buy you," Susannah muttered. "I could've got you for half of what I paid."

Nate chuckled. "That's what you think. And, hey, I was worth every penny."

"Honey, we—"

"Have fun," Michelle interrupted, steering her aunt and uncle toward the entrance. Once they were on their way, she closed the door—and found her three cousins watching her expectantly.

"Now, where were we?" she murmured.

"Tell us everything," Tessa insisted.

"Can we have dinner first?" Junior asked.

"No," Tessa answered.

"Can you tell us while we eat?" Emma Jane asked.

"I do believe I can," Michelle said and the three followed her into the kitchen. "This is one of the most romantic and wonderful love stories I've ever heard—and to think it all started because of me."

* * * * *

A FRIEND TO TRUST

Lee Tobin McClain

To Andrea, who suggested the
perfect finishing touch for my pastor hero.

There is therefore now no condemnation to them
which are in Christ Jesus, who walk not after
the flesh, but after the Spirit. For the law of the
Spirit of life in Christ Jesus hath made me
free from the law of sin and death.
—*Romans* 8:1–2

One

"Mom! You said Mr. Stan would be in charge here."

The boy's anxiety-laced words made Hayley Harris look up from the paperwork she was frantically trying to complete on each new camper at the Bright Tomorrows Residential Academy's summer camp.

Standing above her at the outdoor check-in table was the ninth teen boy in the group of twenty-eight campers. All young teenagers, and all somehow at risk. The one in front of her appeared to be about thirteen, tall and lanky, and he was looking worriedly at his frowning mother.

Hayley pushed back her hair. Why hadn't she brought a ponytail holder? It was hot in the afternoon sunshine.

She took a deep breath, then another, and managed a sympathetic smile. *She* had expected Stan Davidson to be in charge here, too. His absence meant she was winging it, getting all the campers registered while appearing to be a calm, confident leader.

That shouldn't be a problem. She'd run the school cafeteria for three years and was used to hectic situations. Stan knew her and her qualifications well, and he'd hired her for the camp position almost as soon as she'd applied.

But there was a lot riding on this job. If she hoped to get the recommendations she needed for her fast-track teacher-training program, she needed to shine as a camp co-director. Even if things weren't going according to plan. Even if Stan, her far more experienced partner, had gone AWOL.

The air smelled of the large ponderosa pines that surrounded the school grounds. Behind the mother-son pair, the Colorado Rocky Mountains loomed, gorgeous, still snowcapped even in mid-June. God had created the mountains, and the worried boy, and the Bright Tomorrows Academy where the camp was being held. He knew everything that was going to happen today, and He had it under control.

Calmed by the natural beauty and her understanding of where it came from, she felt her shoulders loosen. Everything would be okay.

Unfortunately, the environment wasn't having the same effect on the mother and son in front of her.

"The brochure indicated that Stan Davidson was in charge," the mother said to the boy then frowned at Hayley as if she'd outright lied or else kidnapped her co-director. "I spoke to him just yesterday, and he didn't mention a word about not being here."

Nothing was going as planned today, but Haley mustered up a smile. She *had* to make this work. Had to help these boys have breakthroughs this summer. To Hayley, it was personal. And this summer job was her big chance. "Stan is running behind today, but I'm sure he'll be here any minute. Meanwhile, your name?"

"He's Jeremy Ruffles, and he needs a male influence." The boy's mother stepped closer.

"He'll get plenty of that." Hayley tried to make eye contact with the boy and failed because he was staring down at his feet, chewing on his lower lip. Poor kid. She scanned the group of counselors standing near the dorm building behind her. There was Markus, a kind college-aged intern, and she beckoned to him. "Could you take Jeremy to room..." She checked her list. "To room 302, and help him get settled?" Using the residential school as a camp meant the boys got to stay in a dormitory, not tents or cabins.

"Sure thing. Come on this way."

Only as Jeremy and his mother turned and started walking away did Hayley see the dog beside the boy. A gorgeous, fluffy-white Samoyed, wearing a red vest that identified it as a working dog. The dog trotted beside Jeremy, bumping against his leg, so striking that people stopped their conversations to stare at it and smile.

The dog must have been sitting quietly at the boy's feet while she'd checked him in, but even so, she should have noticed. Shouldn't be so frazzled. She had to pull it together.

Quickly, Hayley scanned her paperwork. How had she missed that there was a service or emotional support dog coming to camp? Maybe he was the mother's dog. But no, he was in harness, sticking close to the boy, who was holding his leash.

Before Hayley could figure out what to ask, the mother turned back. "I'm not happy with the organization here. We waited in line for twenty minutes!" She stomped off after her son.

"I'm sorry about that, ma'am," Hayley said to her retreating back. No, now wasn't the time to dig into the service dog issue. Not that it was an issue, or not an insurmountable one. It was just that if Jeremy's roommate was allergic to animals or had a fear of them, they'd have to make a last-minute change. The dog was gorgeous, but with that amount of fur... Hayley made a mental note to tell the cleaning staff they'd need to take extra care in Jeremy's room.

Surreptitiously, Haley checked the time again. Where was Stan? Her sixtysomething partner in this endeavor had years of experience running the camp. Maybe he'd know what was up with Jeremy and his dog.

Maybe he'd know how to smooth Mom's ruffled feathers.

A thread of worry wound itself around her heart. Stan was never late. What if something had happened to him?

Nothing's wrong. Just prove you can do this.

It was an unorthodox way to transition from her current school-year job, directing food service at Bright Tomorrows, to working directly with the boys. The fast-track teaching certification program, the only one she could afford, would accept the camp director job as education experience, but only if she got two positive recommendations and no complaints about her work.

She beckoned to the next family in the check-in line. "Hi, I'm Hayley, one half of the director team. And you are...?"

She continued checking campers in, trying to project warmth and friendliness and reassurance. Even though the boys, every one of them, presented a tough image, Hayley knew from other kids she'd worked with that images didn't reflect reality. A lot of these boys were probably scared inside.

There were twenty-eight of them, all in the summer before eighth grade. All at risk in one way or another.

If they had a wonderful time here, they might return and spend their high school years at Bright Tomorrows Residential Academy. That would be a boon for the school, always struggling to boost its enrollment.

Just as she finished with the last two boys and sent them along with one of the counselors to get set up in the dormitory, Nate Fisher walked in.

Or maybe *strode* was a better word. *Marched?*

Nate was a pastor, but he carried himself like the soldier he'd been.

At six feet tall with dark hair and eyes and a strong jaw, he was good-looking enough to draw the eye of every female in the room. The combination of nurturing pastor and tough veteran was irresistible.

Hayley, however, had so far managed to resist, despite the efforts of her friends to match them up.

She shoved her laptop aside, along with the confusing feelings Nate often evoked in her, and stood. "Pastor Nate. How come you're wearing a Bright Tomorrows shirt? We don't need you until Sunday." Nate had worked with the campers on spiritual development for the past two summers and was slated to do the same this year.

"Actually," Nate said, "you need me now. Stan's had a heart attack."

Haley gasped, clapping a hand over her mouth as her stomach plummeted. "Oh no! Is he okay?" She noticed that a couple of the families had overheard something in her voice and looked back in their direction. Not wanting to alarm them, she walked around the table to stand closer to Nate. Her heart twisted at the thought of fit, energetic, Stan Davidson having such a serious health crisis. "Please tell me he's doing okay."

"He's going to recover, but he's in the hospital and facing a lot more tests. They don't expect him to be able to work for three or four weeks."

Haley swallowed. "The camp program is only six weeks long." She glanced around at the milling counselors, the couple of families who'd come back into the area. What would they do without him? She'd expected to learn the ropes from Stan, not jump in and take his place.

"Uh—Hayley." Nate cleared his throat. "The board of directors asked me to fill in."

She must have misheard that. "They asked you to what?"

"Fill in. Take Stan's place leading the summer program. Co-leading it. With you."

"But…you know nothing about it." *And I really don't want to work with you that closely.* "I'm sure you have all kinds of important things to do for the church."

He looked at her sharply, as if to detect whether she'd been sarcastic. Had she been? She hardly knew herself. Nate was an excellent pastor, full of charm, a good speaker, always ready to reach out and lend a hand. He even did a lot of the maintenance at the church, saving the congregation from having to hire repair workers. In fact, he volunteered for everything that needed doing in the town of Little Mesa.

The woman who'd complained before, Jeremy's mom, came toward them. She was definitely marching and definitely displeased. "There are no towels or linens in the room." She propped her hands on her hips and scowled at Hayley.

"They were on the packing list," Hayley said gently. "Campers bring their own sheets and towels."

"I never received a list!"

Jeremy came out of the dorm then, chatting easily with the counselor who'd helped them, his dog trotting beside him.

The counselor stopped beside a couple of other boys, and it was clear he was introducing Jeremy. The dog sat beside him, eyes sparkling, ears attentive, mouth curved up in what seemed to be a smile.

"Girl or boy?" she heard one of the other boys ask.

"Girl," Jeremy answered. "Her name's Snowflake."

The dog was gorgeous, but how long would her fur stay so beautifully white in a camp environment?

The other boys seemed fascinated by the friendly, alert dog, one of them reaching out to pet it. The counselor deterred him, gently, pointing to the dog's red service vest. But Jeremy spoke and nodded, kneeling beside the dog. First one boy, then the other, reached out to pat the dog's snowy head.

The best thing was that Jeremy was smiling and talking to the other boys. Maybe when his mother left, the problems would resolve.

"I'm going to complain to the people in charge." Jeremy's mother lifted her chin and flared her nostrils. She didn't seem to notice that her son had come out of the dorm. That, or she just paid him no attention. "I'm shocked and unimpressed."

Hayley opened her mouth to speak and then shut it again, her stomach churning. Would this woman really complain? Any serious grievance would make a terrible impression on the teaching program's admissions committee.

Beside her, Nate cleared his throat and stuck out his right hand to the angry woman. "I'm Nate Fisher, and I'm going to help run the camp for the moment," he said, giving her the eye contact and smile that made him a popular pastor.

"But—"

"Although you were expected to bring your own linens and towels, I'm sure we can find some spares for your son." There was the tiniest touch of censure in Nate's voice, and the woman closed her mouth abruptly. "Would you like for me to walk you to your car," he went on, "and you can tell me what you're hoping your son will gain from the camp experience?"

Hayley had to turn away so that her smile didn't show. Nate had neatly turned things around, putting the woman in her place without ever being impolite.

When she looked back, the two of them were walking toward the parking lot, talking earnestly.

Nate had a ridiculous amount of charm, as well as leadership abilities he'd no doubt developed in the military and honed in his role as a church pastor. He would be a boon for the program. Maybe he could even prevent the cranky woman from reporting her dissatisfaction.

She should welcome his assistance, be grateful for it. He'd showed up like a rescuing superhero, and any sensible woman would embrace his support. But Hayley was wary of a man like Nate, who represented all she'd vowed to forgo.

Hayley started gathering up paperwork. She was worried about Stan, wanted to drop everything and go to the hospital to check on him, but she was responsible for the boys and the camp.

She thought through the rest of the day, trying to

plan for the new circumstances. The counselors were already dividing the boys into groups for an icebreaker activity and then they'd all have dinner together in the cafeteria. Dinner that Hayley would oversee, of course, since she ran food services at the school year-round.

Hopefully, at some point soon, she'd make the switch from food service to teaching, but for now, during this summer's camp, she'd do a little of both.

After dinner, the counselors would have hall meetings to make sure everyone understood the rules and complete more icebreakers to help the boys bond together.

Nate came back toward her. "I think she's calmed down," he said. "Tell me what I can do to help now, and when there's a free moment, we can talk about the change of co-directors and how we'll need to punt."

He sounded so calm and sure of himself, and his attitude convinced Hayley that it was really true. She'd be directing the camp with Nate all summer.

She needed him, the boys and the camp needed him. She should be welcoming and grateful. Should be eager to plan how to work together. That was what a true professional would feel and how a true professional would act.

But Hayley's background meant that confidence was hard to come by. And something about Nate's apparently endless self-assurance—as well as his good looks and charming smile—rubbed her the wrong way.

"There won't be a free moment anytime soon." Hayley glanced down at her tablet, which held her to-do list. "I guess just…look around for any other wandering parents and make sure there are no more complaints? And encourage them to say their goodbyes and go. I'll make sure the volunteers are set for now, and then I'll be cooking in the cafeteria. Training my temporary staff, as well, so maybe we can talk after lights out? Briefly?"

He was studying her, his head tilted to one side, his expression speculative. She forced herself to meet his eyes. *Calm, steady, professional.*

"Sure. After lights out." He turned and headed for a small group of parents emerging from the dorm building.

She tore her eyes away. Nate Fisher was attractive and appealing, and that was just what she needed to be cautious about.

If she really had to work with him, which seemed inevitable, she needed to keep him at a safe distance.

By ten o'clock, Nate was exhausted. Twenty-eight boys, all jostling for status, most homesick. Quite a handful.

He'd worked with new recruits during his time in the army, but they were *way* more disciplined than these boys. And he'd been the chaplain for the campers for the past two years, but he'd never known all that went on behind the scenes until today. Glancing over Stan's notes for half an hour had been the extent of his training before being thrown into the role.

It didn't help that his pretty co-director seemed to hate him.

That didn't make sense. He was doing her a favor, right? And he and Hayley were friends, kind of. At least, they hung out with the same group of people. She was an active member of his church.

Although, come to think of it, they hadn't spent much time one-on-one.

That was odd, because their friends were always sug-

gesting that he should ask her out. If he'd been interested in getting into a relationship, he would probably
have done it, because Hayley was pretty and smart and
caring.

Caring toward other people. Not so much toward him.

He walked out to the bench where they'd agreed to
meet. Hayley was already there, slumped, scrolling on
her phone. "Hey," he said softly so as not to startle her.

"Hey, Nate," she said and looked up at him. "Thank
you for stepping in today. You were a big help, but you
don't have to continue."

Yes, she definitely had an attitude toward him. "I'll
stay the course."

"But…how will you do it alongside your other full-
time job?"

That wasn't her problem, but in the interest of work-
place harmony, he sketched out the basics of his plan.
"Church programming slows down in the summer, and
the staff-parish relations committee is bringing in some
guest speakers." He would lose whatever recreational
time he had, but that was fine. Since his vast error of
judgment that had cost his twin brother's life, Nate had
made a vow: other people's needs came before his own.

There was a shout from the direction of the cottages.
Not a having-fun shout; an upset shout. "Uh-oh," Nate
said, and both he and Hayley started walking in that
direction.

Reggie, one of the younger counselors who stood
out because of the tattoos that covered both arms, ran
toward them. "We can't find the Margolis brothers," he
said breathlessly.

Nate's brain and heart snapped into emergency mode

as he called the sullen, almost-same-age boys to mind. "When did you see them last?"

"The campers went to wash up and then we were going to have hall meetings," he said. "Jeff Margolis wasn't there, and his roommate said he went to take a shower, but he never came back. We checked to see if he was with his brother, and it turns out Mark is missing, too."

Another counselor emerged from the dorms and came over. "They're not in the building. I checked everywhere."

"Where are the other boys?" Hayley asked.

"They're inside, doing hall meetings. We didn't want to freak everyone out, so we kept it between the two of us."

"Good decision," Nate said. "Let's split up. You two take the area in front of the school, and Hayley and I will search behind it." He quickly put their numbers into his phone.

The two counselors looked relieved to be told what to do. They hurried off toward the front of the residence hall.

"Text me if you find out anything," he called after them, only belatedly recognizing that he was using his drill sergeant voice.

Hayley looked up at him, frowning. "I get that this is an emergency, but you don't need to take over like that. We should work as a team."

"Sorry," Nate said automatically. Military personnel understood the importance of having one person in charge in a dangerous situation. Civilians sometimes didn't, and there was no time to explain. "Let's start doing circles around our section."

"You do that," Hayley said, still frowning. "I think I'll look over by the old shed."

"We need to stay together." He barked it out, a clear order. They needed to search, now.

She lifted an eyebrow, clearly unintimidated. "Then come with me. I have a hunch about this."

What good was a hunch when two kids were missing? On the other hand, Hayley worked here year-round and knew the lay of this land better than Nate did. He *wasn't* the officer in charge. She was. He nodded and fell into step behind her.

Minutes later, they crept up to the shed. Hayley raised her hand and put it to her ear, indicating that they should listen.

Sure enough, a low comment and a laugh, quickly stifled, came from inside. As did a vapory cloud of smoke.

The two of them glanced at each other then stepped forward together. Nate flung open one rickety wooden door and Hayley the other. They'd neither one thought to bring flashlights, but their phones did the job of revealing the two Margolis brothers inside, one sitting on an old tractor, the other leaning against the wall.

The one on the tractor, Mark, was smoking a cigarette while the other, Jeff, seemed to be using a vape pen. They didn't even try to hide what they were doing, and Nate saw red. "Do you know how dangerous smoking is?" he demanded. "Hand it over. Now." He held out his hand for the vape pen, looming over the kid.

He felt Hayley's hand on his sleeve. "Nate."

He was too angry to pay attention. "And you." He pointed at Mark. "Put that cigarette out, now. All the way out. In addition to the damage to your lungs, cigarettes cause fires. Lives lost and property damage in the millions."

"Nate." Hayley's hand tightened on his arm and she spoke quietly but emphatically. "Stand down. Let me handle the rest of this."

"They need to—"

"Nate." Her voice was a little sharper, and it brought him back to himself and the situation in front of him. The two boys looked scared, and young. Mark had ground out his cigarette and was stomping it, his shoulders hunched. Jeff had thrown his vape pen to the floor and backed into the corner of the shed like he was afraid Nate was going to hit him.

"Let's all go cool off outside." Hayley's glare said that she meant the words for Nate as she took the pack of cigarettes, picked up the vape pen and beckoned for both of the boys to follow her.

Nate still felt angry, but he knew he'd gone too far. Hayley beckoned to the boys, and it was clear that she had the situation under control.

He walked away from the shed and texted the two searching counselors that the boys had been found. Meanwhile, Hayley talked to the boys, sternly, in a low voice, and then walked them back to the entrance of the dorm, where the counselors had just arrived.

Hayley walked toward Nate and, before she could open her mouth, he held up a hand. "I know, I know. You think I came down too hard on them."

"You did. This is important to me, Nate. Really important. I want to do right by these boys."

And he didn't? "Sometimes tough love is the best way to reach kids."

She raised an eyebrow. "It's their first day. I don't want to start with a hardline approach."

"We need to start as we mean to go on. Stricter, even."

Rather than continue the argument, she crossed her arms over her chest and studied him thoughtfully. "What's really going on, Nate? I've known you awhile and I've seen you working with kids at church. I've never heard you get angry before."

Her words stopped him, made him realize, suddenly, why he'd gotten so mad. He banged his fists together, lightly, and shook his head. "My mom has COPD. Years of smoking means it's advancing fast. I can't stand to see kids smoking."

"Ouch." She bit her lip as she looked up at him. "That makes sense. I'm sorry about your mom."

The compassion in her voice touched a part of his heart he usually kept locked away. "Thanks."

"And," she said, "it's probably not a bad idea to put a little fear into those boys, try to set them on the right path." She turned. "I'm going to head for my cabin. It's been a long day."

"I'll walk you back."

"There's no need."

"I'm not letting you walk alone."

She shrugged. "Fine."

So they walked together down the road, the sky a dark, jewel-spattered bowl overhead, the air crisp. She was wearing a short-sleeved Bright Tomorrows T-shirt and jeans, and when she shivered, he felt a strange impulse to put an arm around her, barely stopping himself in time.

They didn't have that close and affectionate of a relationship. Not by a mile.

When they reached her door, Hayley unlocked it and stepped inside. "Thanks," she said. She flashed a smile that had him backing away fast to quell his own reaction. She had a *great* smile.

His phone buzzed, breaking the nighttime quiet. He glanced down to see a message from Stan.

We need to talk privately. ASAP. Something you need to know.

Two

On Tuesday morning, Nate tapped on the door of Stan's hospital room then walked in.

Stan was one of Nate's favorite parishioners, despite his occasional abrasive ways. Although he was over sixty, he was as active and energetic as many people half his age, spending his free time hiking, playing pickle-ball and interfering in the lives of his fellow teachers at Bright Tomorrows. For the past three summers, he'd directed the summer camp in addition to his teaching math during the school year.

Now, he lay back against his pillows, his normally ruddy face pale, an IV attached to his arm.

Nate sucked in a breath of air tinged with hospital disinfectant and greeted the man. "How are you feeling?"

Stan offered a weak smile. "Pull up a chair, pastor. It'll take a while to answer that question."

"I have time." That was only partially true. Normally, Nate was able to avoid rushing through hospital visits—a challenging but rewarding part of his job. There was nothing a clergyman could do to ease physical illness; but sometimes it was possible to help with spiritual pain. The hidden blessing of illness was that it caused people to slow down and focus on what was important.

Nate wished he could relax into a leisurely visit today, but now that he was working two jobs, he had a tight schedule. He and Hayley had agreed that he'd take the afternoons while she did mornings, and then they'd work together on the evening activities and compare notes. That meant he would be on duty at the Bright Tomorrows camp in two hours.

"Thanks for coming to visit," Stan said. "And more than that, for taking over my job at the camp. I sure appreciate your stepping in."

"Glad to do it. The important thing is your health. How are things going?"

Stan launched into a description of the heart attack symptoms and the tests and procedures he'd experienced at the hospital. "It was downright scary for a while. They wouldn't tell me anything. But they're getting some test results in and they've stopped frowning so much. Sounds like I'll pull through."

"It's got to stink being hooked up to all those machines."

"It does. But tell me, how's camp?"

"Hayley and I are figuring it out," Nate said. "Between us, we'll do fine."

"Good, because the camp is a recruitment tool and the board wants to make sure it's working. We want happy campers, literally."

"Understood."

They were silent for a moment and Nate glanced at the time on his phone. He was about to ask Stan if he wanted to pray together, a predeparture tradition, when he remembered what Stan's text had said.

"You mentioned you wanted to tell me something," he said.

Stan met his eyes for a moment and then looked away. "There's a mess," he said. "A mess I created, and I don't know what to do about it."

Nate was surprised to see the normally self-assured man looking so upset. He pocketed his phone and leaned forward. "It might help to talk."

Stan nodded. "We have confidentiality, right?"

This was a delicate question, but Nate had plenty of experience answering it. "I'll do my best to keep anything you tell me confidential. If you disclose something that's illegal or puts you or another person in harm's way, though, I have a moral obligation to protect you and others, and I may have to disclose what you tell me."

"Of course, of course." Stan waved a hand. "This is nothing illegal. It concerns the camp. One of the campers, actually."

Nate nodded but didn't speak. It was important to let Stan express his concerns at his own pace.

"Jeremy Ruffles. Have you met him?"

"The one with the support dog, right? I've met him, but I haven't gotten to know him."

"He's not easy to know. Kid struggles with anxiety. That's why he has the dog. Which… I agreed informally that Jeremy could bring the dog to camp. Figured I could smooth it over if there was a problem."

"The dog thing seems okay." If this was what Stan had texted about, it was a minor concern. "Jeremy's roommate likes dogs, and we don't have anyone with significant allergies."

"Good." Stan hesitated, then spoke again. "I was going to keep an eye on Jeremy. He's not the typical kid at the camp."

No point pretending he didn't know what Stan meant. Some kids were just sensitive, and it made them vulnerable. "He seems a little…gentler than some of the boys. I can watch out for him."

"That's not all. I'm…well, I'm dating his mother. Did you meet her?"

Nate nodded, his image of the difficult Arlene readjusting in his mind. "She seems a little high strung."

"She is, and she might not handle… Look, Jeremy is adopted."

Another readjustment. "I didn't know that." And he wasn't sure why Stan was telling him all of this. "Is it relevant, something I should know?"

"Normally, no, but this is a special case. He was adopted as an infant and it's not talked about much in his family. Look, we're definitely confidential, right?"

"Within the constraints I mentioned before, yes."

Stan's forehead creased and his callused hands clutched the bedsheet, crumpling and releasing it, over and over.

Nate's heart went out to Stan. He'd never have suspected the jovial math teacher of being a troubled man, but people were complicated, far more than they appeared on the surface.

Sometimes conversations about the deep stuff could be upsetting, even traumatic, though. And Stan was seriously ill. "We can talk when you're feeling better," Nate said. "I'm available anytime. For now, just focus on healing."

"No. I want someone to know, in case something happens to me."

Nate bit back the reassurances that wanted to rise to his lips. Stan was probably going to be fine, but there were no guarantees.

"So, Arlene…that's Jeremy's mom. She knows I'm good with computers, and she asked if I could locate Jeremy's birth mother."

Quiet conversations were audible from the hall outside, along with continuous beeping from one of Stan's monitors, and the occasional ping of an elevator. Despite the background sounds, Stan's room felt like a quiet cell set off from the rest of the world. "I'm surprised she didn't know the birth mother," Nate said. "Most adoptions are open these days."

"It was semiopen, which means she had some non-identifying information on the birth mother. Medical records, the like. So I had something to work with."

"Is there a problem with Jeremy?"

"No, but Arlene was concerned, moving back to the area where the adoption took place. She wanted to reassure herself that the birth mother wasn't some troubled person who was going to be coming around, trying to get in touch with Jeremy."

Nate winced. It was a harsh attitude toward the woman who'd given birth to Arlene's child, if Stan was right about Arlene's motivations.

Stan paused and took a sip of water. Tiny beads of sweat dotted his forehead.

"You're feeling okay? You can tell me the rest later."

"I'm fine. I… Look, I did find the birth mother."

"How did Arlene react?"

"I didn't tell her."

Nate drew his eyebrows together. Why would Stan do all the requested research, dig up a fact that had to have been hard to find, and then hide it from the woman who'd asked him to uncover the truth? The woman he presumably cared about?

Stan seemed to read the questions in Nate's eyes. "Honestly, I didn't think she could handle what I found out. Not now, anyway. But I want someone to know, in case something…happens to me, like I said. In case Jeremy needs to know. Arlene's great, but she's difficult. She's one of the reasons he struggles with anxiety."

"Okay." Nate nodded, unsurprised by Stan's assessment of Arlene. "If the adoption is closed, though, or somewhat closed, you should tread very carefully. The birth mother may not want to be found or may have a reason she kept it closed."

"I think she does want to keep it closed. I've known her awhile and she never mentioned having a child." Stan looked at Nate, then down at his hands, now folded in front of him. "Nate, it's Hayley."

An hour later, Nate was still reeling from Stan's revelation. So much so that, after parking at the school, he found an out-of-the-way bench and sat down, hoping for the chance to think about what he'd heard.

Stan had seemed at peace after telling Nate his story. Nate, though, was anything but.

Hayley had had a child and placed it for adoption? Twelve, thirteen years ago?

He'd known Hayley since she'd come to town to work at Bright Tomorrows two years ago. Had, in fact, been friendly enough with her to be aware of sparks between them for most of that time. Sparks on his side, at least. Though he had never followed up on the attraction—too busy trying to make amends for what had happened to his brother overseas—he'd always enjoyed her sunny nature and her ease with the boys.

He'd never have guessed she had such a difficult thing in her past.

It shouldn't be a problem for him. After six years working as a pastor, he knew that people had all kinds of issues in their past. And after the mistakes he'd made, he had no business judging Hayley.

Still, the whole idea gave him a knot in his stomach, and he was pretty sure he knew why. And he also knew that the reason didn't reflect well on him.

Even though he wasn't planning to build a relationship with Hayley, his inner caveman wanted her for his own.

That was ridiculous. He knew it. But as he often told people he counseled, feelings weren't right or wrong, they were just feelings. The important thing was how you handled them, and whether you did or didn't act on them.

Beyond his personal thoughts about what had happened, he now had practical issues to face. He was co-directing the camp with a woman who had no idea her biological son was a camper there. Jeremy didn't know Hayley was his birth mother, either. How was he supposed to deal with that? Stan had put him in an impossible situation.

He couldn't break Stan's confidence and tell her. No one was at risk here, not of bodily harm. And he wasn't sure whether revealing the truth would help or hurt either of the involved parties.

On the one hand, he felt that Hayley had the right to know that Jeremy was her son. She'd given birth to the child. If anyone had the right to the truth, it was Hayley.

And then there was Jeremy's side of things. How would he feel if it came out that he'd been at camp with his birth mother and hadn't even known it?

On the other hand, Stan's reason for keeping the secret, at least right now, had made sense. Arlene did seem unstable. To carelessly throw this information at the three of them could result in a dangerous explosion and could put one or more of them at risk.

He leaned forward and let his head sink into his hands. *Lord, I'll do my best, but please guide me.*

He heard talking and shouting and laughing, and boys started heading into the school cafeteria for lunch.

He spotted Hayley as she walked alongside Jeremy and his dog, chatting easily with him.

The sight made Nate's heart lurch. If the two of them got close without knowing their true relationship, there could be problems. Big problems.

Whatever happened, he had to try to protect Hayley and Jeremy from harm.

Hayley sank down into a folding chair near the campfire Tuesday night. She was exhausted but cautiously satisfied.

The boys were mostly talking and laughing and fooling around, several poking at the fire under the supervision of the counselors. Jeremy, she was glad to see, was talking with another quiet boy who lived on his hall. Between them, Snowflake lay staring into the fire like a dog in a Jack London novel. Both boys occasionally touched the calm, friendly canine.

Two days in and the campers were settling in fine. Even the two boys who'd shoved at each other upon first arrival were now one-upping one another with clever jokes, a rivalry she was much more comfortable with.

The moon shone in a crescent amid millions of stars. The air was cool, jacket weather, surprising the boys who weren't from around here. But June nights in the mountains were always cool if not downright cold.

Nate sat talking with one of the counselors and a couple of the boys. Everyone had been friendly to Nate, and he'd tried to pull his share of the weight today. Neither Nate nor Hayley knew exactly what they were doing, but with a few calls to Stan or consultations with one of the counselors who'd been at the camp last summer, they'd figured it out.

She was starting to make her peace with the fact that they'd be working together for the next few weeks. Stan was optimistic that he'd get out of the hospital and back to directing the camp soon, but a little research on Hayley's part suggested it wasn't likely. Recovering from a heart attack took time.

Reggie, another counselor, was playing a guitar, quietly strumming. Boys started to calm down and, once the counselors started singing a popular country song, several joined in. Hayley did, too.

This was going well. She was going to make a success of this.

"Hey! Stop touching me!" One of the boys who'd shoved another earlier, Mickey O'Henry, a big, red-headed kid, was now standing, leaning over another boy, getting in his face.

Booker Jackson, much smaller and sporting thick glasses, raised his two hands, palms out. "I didn't touch you," he said, his voice mild.

Unfortunately, he added an ugly name at the end, and suddenly the two were brawling way too close to the campfire.

She rushed over and grabbed Mickey. Nate grabbed Booker and, with Reggie's help, they got them apart.

"What were you two thinking?" she asked the pair. "You know our rules about fighting."

"He was buggin' me," Booker said.

Mickey made a face at the smaller boy, who lunged

toward him, requiring Nate and the other counselor to pull him back.

"We're going to talk over here," she said firmly, guiding Mickey to a picnic table out of the sightline of the other boys. "You need to promise me you'll control yourself and your body, even if someone does something that makes you mad."

He looked down at the ground. "Are you gonna kick me out?" In his slumped posture Hayley read a history of discouragement and setbacks and too-quick judgments.

She felt like giving him a hug but opted for a shoulder pat instead. "No, not this time. But I'll have no fighting at our camp. This is just a warning."

Mickey was still looking down, but she saw his shoulders straighten, barely.

"What are you going to do the next time someone makes you mad? Because it's going to happen. We're in close quarters here, and a bunch of strangers will probably annoy each other. Do you have any strategies?"

He nodded. "I'm supposed to take deep breaths and think about something I like."

"That's a great plan. What do you like?"

"My dog," he said, and there was a very slight scratch in his voice.

He missed his home. That was why he was acting out. "It must be hard to be away from your dog," she said.

He didn't answer, but swiped a fist under his eye.

"Have you met Jeremy yet? He's the one with the white dog."

Mickey shook his head, still looking down.

Jeremy had walked a little apart from the group, getting Snowflake some water. She called to him quietly. "Hey, Jeremy. Can you bring Snowflake over here a minute?"

He strode over, looking at Mickey warily. Mickey was one of the toughest boys in the group, while Jeremy seemed to be anything but.

Snowflake trotted beside him, head up, dark eyes watchful and eager.

Hayley smiled at the gorgeous dog then at Jeremy. "Is it okay if Mickey and I pet your pup, or is she working right now?"

"You can pet her," Jeremy said. "She's an ESA, not a service dog. You can really pet her anytime unless I tell you not to."

"What's an ESA?" Mickey didn't look at either of them but knelt on the ground at Snowflake's level. He touched the dog's fur and his face lit up. "She's soft!"

"I brush her every day," Jeremy said, kneeling. "An ESA is an Emotional Support Animal. Snowflake likes to have her ears rubbed."

Mickey obliged, and soon Snowflake had rolled over on the ground, pink tongue out, seeming to smile as Jeremy rubbed her stomach while Mickey rubbed her ears.

Hayley let out a breath she hadn't known she was holding. Snowflake was obviously therapeutic.

Mickey stiffened, and Hayley looked up to see Nate walking over with Booker beside him.

"Booker wants to apologize," Nate said.

"Sorry I got rough," Booker said. He knelt beside the dog.

"Me, too," Mickey said without prompting.

Apparently sensing an opportunity, Snowflake rolled over, stood and then bent in a play bow, front low and back end high. When none of the humans responded, she straightened, lifted her nose and howled a little, almost like singing.

"She wants to play," Jeremy said. He fumbled in his

pocket and pulled out a rope toy. He held it out to Mickey. "She likes to tug."

Amazingly, the boys took turns tugging with the dog, and when Jeremy determined she was tired of playing, all three of them walked back to the fire and sat together.

Nate stayed with Hayley, sitting beside her on the bench. "That's the power of a dog," he said.

"You're right." She watched the boys. "It's great to see Jeremy coming out of his shell. Snowflake really helps with that. I never anticipated Jeremy would connect with those particular boys."

Things were working out. If Jeremy became friends with the toughest boys, that might protect him from bullying. And his calmer manner might wear off on the other two.

Nate cleared his throat. "I wouldn't advise getting too close to any one camper," he said. It was a casual remark, but his tone didn't sound casual.

She raised an eyebrow. "I'm not close to anyone yet. But that Jeremy…he tugs at my heart."

"You'll learn to keep your distance," Nate said. "As for Jeremy, he needs to toughen up."

"He needs emotional support." She frowned. "Just because he's a boy, that doesn't mean he's not allowed to have feelings."

"I *have* worked with a lot of young people." Nate sounded either defensive or patronizing, she couldn't decide which.

Either way, it annoyed her. "So have I." Although it was mostly in the context of running a food service operation here at the Bright Tomorrows Academy, or studying about kids in her online classes, or volunteering at church.

They were glaring at each other. Nate's eyes glittered

in the firelight. His shoulders were broad, his stomach flat in the camp T-shirt.

Wow, handsome. Stray, distracting thought.

His eyes seemed to get darker. Their gazes tangled now in a different way.

"Okay, full disclosure." He glanced away for a few seconds then looked back and smiled a little. "I've never been in charge of a group of teens before."

"Nor have I," she admitted. "I thought the first two days went pretty well, but I'm still worried about how the rest of the camp session will go."

"We'll get through it together."

More tangled gazes.

He cleared his throat again and looked away. "How did you get into running the camp, anyway?"

"I want to teach." Admitting it to Nate made her shy. "I'm hoping to be admitted to a fast-track program that starts in the fall, and to do that, I have to have some background in teaching. They're letting me count this, as long as things go well."

"You're ambitious," he said, eyes crinkling at the corners as he nodded.

His approval warmed her. It also lit up some red lights in her head. *No men.*

It was a plan she'd made when she'd given up her baby. Filled with horrible guilt, she'd decided she wasn't going to get involved with a man again, didn't deserve to.

Nate was right. She shouldn't get too close to a camper. But a bigger danger just might be getting too close to her co-director.

Three

Late Friday morning, Nate headed down to the camp's indoor-outdoor pool.

Technically, he wasn't on duty until this afternoon, but one of the counselors was sick so he'd decided to come in early and see how he could assist. Although the first week of camp had gone well, he still felt like he needed to help Hayley troubleshoot any issues. Also, Ashley and Jason had said they might stop by. Since Ashley was the principal of the Bright Tomorrows Academy, Nate figured she would report to the board on how things were going.

He wanted everything to go well.

In that regard, he supposed, he was like Hayley. Once she'd explained her goal of joining a fast-track teaching program, her extreme dedication to the job had made sense. He admired it, and it made her a great co-director.

As for Nate, he wanted to excel at everything he did, which, according to his spiritual mentor, was sometimes a problem. Nate knew what the man meant. He knew he was trying to compensate for the role he'd played in his brother's death, and he also knew that no such compensation would ever make up for what had happened, nor bring his brother back. That didn't stop him from trying, continually, in everything he did.

Right now, his and Hayley's combined efforts seemed to be bearing fruit. They'd had a good first week. Since Tuesday evening's campfire, he and Hayley had worked together well. Kept it businesslike. Today would be more of the same.

Even before he reached the pool, the sounds of splashing, happy boys were audible. He rounded the corner of the building.

The large pool was indoors, but the pool enclosure had an entire wall that could be opened, giving the effect of an outdoor pool. At one end, a group of boys was having swim lessons. In the middle of the pool, about eight boys were playing and roughhousing, supervised, Nate was thankful to see, by a lifeguard. And on the other end, a group was learning—from Hayley—how to paddleboard.

Dressed in a completely modest swimsuit half covered by running shorts, she balanced easily on the board, talking and laughing with the boys, demonstrating how to balance and use the paddle. Her arms were shapely, no doubt due to her active lifestyle and hard work in the kitchens. Hayley was petite, but she wasn't a delicate flower. She was a strong woman.

Nate swallowed and looked away.

Scattered along the open deck were small clusters of boys, either waiting their turns or drying off, shivering in the cool breeze. Jeremy was among that group, and Snowflake lay at his side.

Nate approached the boys on the deck, determined to focus on them instead of Hayley. He mock-glared at the Margolis brothers, who were having words too close

to the pool's edge, and they backed off and went to opposite ends of the group. Nate couldn't be sorry they
were a little afraid of him. He knelt beside Jeremy. "Did
you get a chance to try paddle boarding?"

"Yeah, it was fun. Hayley said once I get good, I can
try bringing Snowflake on the board with me."

"That'll be cool!" Booker turned toward them and
scooted closer to pet Snowflake. "Can she swim?"

Nate moved on, glad that Jeremy continued to inter-
act with the other boys and make friends.

"You're not teaching?" The voice behind him belonged to Ashley, and he turned and smiled at his friend.
Technically, now his boss.

"No. I can swim, but not well, so teaching it's not in
my wheelhouse. I'll be plenty involved with the boys
when I'm on duty this afternoon."

"I didn't mean to criticize." Ashley patted his arm.
"You're already going above and beyond for us, and
we're grateful. Jason and I just stopped by to see how
things are going with your substitution for Stan. You're
able to keep up with everything?"

"Not a problem," Nate assured her.

Her husband, Jason, had stopped to chat with someone. Now he walked up beside her. He was a big man,
a combat veteran, and beside him was his service dog,
a huge mastiff named Titan. Jason had mobility issues
and nearly always had the dog with him. Ashley had
hired him last year, despite their complicated history
together, and they'd fallen in love and married. Now,
they were expecting their first child.

"Okay, lunchtime in fifteen for my group," Hayley
called from the end of the pool. She climbed out, answered questions and watched as the boys toweled off

and hurried toward the dorm to change for lunch. Then she wrapped a towel around her shoulders and made her way over to greet Nate, Jason and Ashley. Drops of water shone on her lightly tanned skin.

"No, don't hug me," she said to Ashley, laughing and waving her hands. "I don't want to get you wet." She squeezed her hair as she spoke, wringing water out of it.

Nate took slow breaths and looked away. His eyes landed on Jeremy, who had his arm around Snowflake. Both of them were watching Titan.

The big dog looked up at Jason, nudged his leg then looked again. Jason glanced down, surveyed the scene and seemed to read his dog's mind. "I know, buddy. You want to make a new friend." He walked over to Jeremy. "Nice dog. This is Titan."

"Can they play?" Jeremy asked.

"As long as your pup gets along with other dogs, sure." Jason undid Titan's harness and slapped the dog's haunch gently. "Go ahead."

After another inquiring look up at his master, Titan stepped closer to the Samoyed. Tails wagging, the two dogs greeted each other. Then Snowflake lowered her front end into a play bow and gave two sharp barks.

Titan shook his big head hard, causing drool to fly in all directions, and nudged back at Snowflake. The two trotted over to the grassy area beside the pool deck and bumped, rolled and sniffed together. Snowflake gave Titan's ears a playful nip, and Titan stood and head-butted her, knocking her down.

"Hey, they're fighting!" Mark Margolis yelled.

"No, they're not," Jason and Jeremy said at the same time. The big man and the much smaller boy looked at each other and laughed.

"Is this okay?" Ashley asked, looking at Hayley and Nate. "I don't want to throw you guys off schedule."

"It's fine," Hayley said. "We'll wait for the last group to finish and then get changed for lunch. The boys eat in two shifts on swim days."

They all watched the dogs playing. Snowflake flipped onto her back and up again, yipping at Titan. The bigger dog moved slowly, panting, seeming to smile back at Snowflake. He nudged the other dog gently with a large paw.

"I think he's being careful of her," Jeremy said, looking up at Jason. "'Cause he's bigger."

Jason nodded. "Titan does fine playing with even really small dogs. He has a friend in town who's a Chihuahua."

"No way!" Booker and Mark said at almost the same time.

Soon both dogs were trotting side by side around the area, sniffing, and a moment later the swim lesson boys finished up. "Everyone, go get ready for lunch," Hayley called. "You, too, Jeremy," she added, sounding a little regretful.

Jeremy called Snowflake and put her vest back on, then waved and followed the other boys to the dorm.

The adults followed slowly. "So, everything's really going okay at the camp?" Ashley asked. "Particularly with Jeremy Ruffles?"

"It is," Hayley said. "He's starting to make friends. The dog actually helps with that. Why?"

"It's the Captain," Ashley said, and Nate nearly groaned. The Captain, a retired marine, was the chairman of Bright Tomorrows' board of directors and Nate knew from various sources and encounters that the man could be hard to work with.

"What about the Captain, exactly?" Hayley's voice was wary.

Ashley sighed. "He heard something from Arlene Ruffles, Jeremy's mom," she said. "She's on the board, a brand-new member, and, apparently, she wasn't happy with how Jeremy's first day went."

"That much I knew," Hayley said. "We were a little disorganized. I was expecting Stan to show up any minute, but of course, he couldn't. She and Jeremy had to wait in line, and then there was a mix-up about whether she had to bring sheets. Fortunately, Nate helped calm her down."

Jason gave Nate a fist bump. "Good job, man."

"I thought Arlene and Jeremy just moved to the area," Hayley said. "How is she already on the board?"

"Because she's a donor," Ashley said. "Apparently, she has an interest in kids who face challenges. Her son is adopted and has had some problems related to that, and so she's gotten involved in some organizations for kids with issues."

Nate glanced quickly at Hayley's face. Would she put it together, that she'd placed a child who would now be Jeremy's age?

If she made the connection herself, then Nate could be off the hook.

But she just continued walking, seemingly unaware.

"Speaking of adoption..." Jason said, "It's looking better and better for Dev and Emily to adopt that sibling group."

As they talked about their friends, Nate again looked

for a reaction from Hayley. He didn't see one. Nothing obvious, anyway. Maybe a little wince.

After all, she must hear adoption mentioned on a regular basis, especially since she was good friends with Emily and solidly behind Emily and Dev's plans. She couldn't think about her own situation every time adoption was discussed.

"How are your folks?" Jason asked Nate, distracting him from his thoughts of Hayley.

"Doing okay." His throat tightened, just briefly. "Dad insists that he wants to care for Mom himself, and so far, with some help from me and my sisters, it's working."

The rapid progression of his mother's COPD had come as a shock. Nate still could barely believe the disease had laid his energetic, nurturing mother so low. Her prognosis wasn't good.

Nate's family had done so much for him. Now, it was time for him to do for them. Two years ago, when Mom was first diagnosed, he'd moved from Chicago, where he'd been doing urban ministry, to the small town next to theirs. He spent time with them as often as he could, doing yardwork and housework, praying and reading the Bible with Mom.

It didn't seem like enough.

Ashley and Hayley had gotten a little bit ahead on the path, chatting and laughing together.

"So, what about you and Hayley?" Jason asked bluntly as soon as the two women were out of earshot.

"What about us?" Nate asked, even though he had a pretty good guess of what Jason was talking about.

"Everyone thinks you two would be a good couple. Ever consider dating her?"

"Ah, no."

"Why? She's a great girl." Jason leaned on Titan as he navigated a rocky stretch of trail.

"She is, for sure. I just…" He thought about the secret he knew. Dating Hayley would make keeping the secret egregious. "It's not a priority for me right now."

"Because of your parents?"

"Partly," Nate said. He did want to focus on doing whatever Mom and Dad needed. Between that, Stan's secret, Nate's church job and now his camp directorship, there wasn't a lot of time for building a relationship.

And that was fine. His focus needed to be on others, not on his own needs. He'd taken the selfish route before and it had cost his brother his life.

"Maybe they'd like to see you settled," Jason said.

"Who? My parents?" He thought about them and smiled. "They would. Especially Mom. She's been matching me up with her friends' daughters and neighbors for years."

"There you go. Getting together with Hayley will solve all your problems."

Nate blew out a sigh, wishing it were that easy. "She's not interested," he said. "And there are…barriers."

Jason glanced over at him. "Maybe those barriers are mostly in your head. Ashley thinks you'd be a good couple, too." He said it as if his wife held definitive answers to the mysteries of life.

"Not this time." From up ahead, laughter rang out, a musical sound. Hayley. It made him think of sunny mornings and porch swings and lemonade.

Keeping the secret of what he knew about Hayley meant he couldn't hear that laughter on a regular basis. Couldn't ask Hayley out. Couldn't get to know her better.

Confidentiality was his duty as Stan's pastor. That

was fine, because Nate didn't deserve a fun, carefree, promising relationship. Not when his brother couldn't have the same.

Nate loved his work, but never before had the responsibility of the ministry hung so heavy on him, felt like such a sacrifice. And never had his guilty history filled him with so much regret.

Jason studied him, but didn't speak, thankfully, as they made their way toward the dining hall.

Nate was pretty sure the other man had seen past his words to the confusion he hadn't voiced.

Hayley couldn't quite figure out how she ended up going to dinner at Nate's parents' house on Sunday.

Very possibly, it had been orchestrated by Ashley and Jason. Probably in cahoots with Nate's mother, who'd called Hayley, explained who she was and issued a very friendly and very persistent invitation.

One thing was for sure: Nate hadn't initiated her visit to his family's home. He seemed as uncomfortable with it as she was.

Everyone—Nate's two sisters, their husbands and their kids, along with Nate's father—worked together to get dinner on the table, with Nate's mother directing the show from a chair in the big eat-in kitchen, her oxygen tank beside her. After a prayer, they passed roast beef and mashed potatoes, three kinds of vegetables, bread and a huge salad. Plates were loaded, and jokes and gibes exchanged. Nate was the youngest, and it was clear that his sisters and parents adored him.

It was also clear that they were watching Hayley and Nate. Nobody was thinking of her as some random guest. Instead, they spoke as if Nate and Hayley were a couple. Questions like, "What did you guys do yesterday?" and "How was your week?" were directed to both of them.

It made Hayley nervous. She didn't know how to clarify that they were just friends. Fortunately, Nate's sisters' kids—twin toddler boys and a pair of slightly older blonde girls, maybe four and six—kept everyone so busy that no one topic could be focused on for long.

The little dining room was full and echoed with warmth and caring, good smells and delectable comfort food, and it was exactly the type of Sunday dinner, the type of *family*, she'd always wanted.

All her life, Sundays had been lonely. When she was small, Sundays were the days her friends all gathered with their cousins and sisters and brothers, leaving no time for play dates with a neighbor girl. Some families in their neighborhood had gathered at church, but not Hayley's. Her parents, older than most others, and dedicated hippies, didn't believe in authoritarian institutions like church.

They'd spent Sundays partying. Hayley had learned young that being the only sober person in the room felt more lonesome than actually being alone.

When she'd gotten older and been sent to live with her grandmother, it was usually just the two of them for Sunday dinner. They'd gone to church, but it was an old church in the middle of a run-down part of Denver, and the small, mostly white-haired congregation had tended to rush home after services. She and Gram had usually picked up lunch from a local chicken-and-pizza joint on the way home from church and eaten it in front of the old movies Gram loved.

It hadn't been awful, but for a teen girl, it hadn't been quite engaging enough to keep her out of trouble.

No good going down that stretch of memory lane. Hayley refocused on the here and now.

Nate's mom didn't eat much, but she looked around the table in evident satisfaction as everyone else raved about the food and asked for seconds. She reached over and touched Nate's hand or arm at regular intervals. Hayley, on her other side, couldn't help but notice the affection, and it showed her another dimension of the pastor she'd known for the past two years.

He was clearly the favored child, but from the indulgent glances his sisters gave him, he was their pet, too. And wouldn't anyone favor him? He was so quick to help his mom with a heavy dish or go to the kitchen to refill drinks. He joked with his nieces and spontaneously hugged one of his sisters from behind.

He was central to this family, and Hayley couldn't help but feel glad she'd seen him in this role.

A pang twisted her heart. Was her child, the baby boy she'd placed for adoption, at a friendly family table like this?

Oh, she hoped so. She hoped so with all her heart. That would make up for all her hours of anguish about her decision.

"Now, tell me all about the camp," Nate's mother said in a soft voice.

Nate's sister put down the basket of rolls she'd been carrying in and patted her mother's shoulder, her expression proud. "Mom's one of the donors, you know."

Mrs. Fisher waved a hand. "Oh, well."

Hayley cocked her head, curious. "We're very grateful for that. How did you get into donating for the camp?" She wouldn't have thought Nate's mother would have a connection, not until her son started working there, which had only happened this week. The woman must have made her financial gift well before that.

Mrs. Fisher smiled, but not as widely as before. "Nate's brother had some of the kinds of issues your boys struggle with. ADHD, in particular. When he passed away, we wanted to do something concrete in his memory."

Hayley glanced at Nate, but he was staring down at the table.

"Tell us more about the camp and the campers," his other sister urged and, behind the request, Hayley heard a plea to get the conversation back onto cheerier ground. So she explained the summer program's three-year history, and most people at the table listened, appearing interested.

Nate chimed in, at first mechanically and then with more energy, and they soon had people laughing with stories of their first-week ups and downs.

After dinner, Hayley helped Nate's sisters with the dishes—and dodged their sly questions about her relationship with Nate—while the men watched football and the kids ran around underfoot. Just as they were finishing up, Nate leaned into the room. "I'm going to say 'bye to Mom," he said to Hayley, "and then I'll drive you home."

"Bring her in," came a faint voice from somewhere off the house's main hallway. "I want to say goodbye to Hayley, too."

Hayley dried her hands and followed Nate into a tiny bedroom. Nate's mother sat propped up in a hospital bed, leaning on thick pillows. An open window looked out onto six or seven bird feeders, where small birds fluttered and a Steller's jay scolded. Family pictures lined a small table at the foot of the bed, and the color scheme was soft purples and browns. It was a restful place, clearly designed with love.

Mrs. Fisher smiled and stretched out a hand to Hayley. "It was so nice to meet you, dear. You're welcome anytime."

"Thank you. I really enjoyed it." Hayley squeezed Mrs. Fisher's hand and then stepped back so Nate could move closer.

"Thanks for having us, Mom," he said, hugging her. "See you soon."

Mrs. Fisher clung to Nate a little, and when she released him and lay back, her eyes were filled with tears.

"What's wrong?" Nate asked immediately. "Was today too much?"

"I'm just so happy about the two of you," she said.

"Mom—"

"It's been my fondest dream, seeing you settled like your sisters," the older woman choked out. "Now, I'm at peace."

Hayley's throat tightened at the same time that her heart pounded hard. How could she disappoint the woman by correcting her?

And yet how could she let a misperception like this one stand?

The exact same puzzle was on Nate's face. He looked helplessly at Hayley.

She gave a tiny shrug, tacitly giving him permission to let it go.

So he simply hugged his mother again and they left.

Once outside, they stared at each other. How were they going to manage this new twist in their so-called relationship?

Four

When they reached their cars outside Nate's family's house, the sun had begun to sink behind the mountains, painting the snowy peaks in shades of pink and rose and gold. Peaceful, Hayley thought.

At least, the view was peaceful. Inside, she felt anything but.

Only when she'd seen Mrs. Fisher in bed, looking pale, an oxygen tank beside her, had Hayley realized how very sick the woman was.

It was what had stopped her from jumping in to correct the idea that Hayley and Nate were a couple. How could you destroy the happiness in a sick woman's life?

But she felt uncomfortable with the dishonesty. Uncomfortable, too, was the way the thought of being Nate's girlfriend made her heart beat as if she'd just been running a high-altitude race. That was wrong, and needed to be halted right away.

A better person would march right back into the house and explain to Mrs. Fisher that their relationship was strictly business. But the thought of putting out the light in the woman's eyes—and of giving up the warm family connections she'd always longed for—made Hayley sweat, unsure of what to do. "We need to talk about this," she said.

"Yes." Nate's voice was tight. "There's an ice cream stand about half a mile away. Let's walk and talk."

"Sure." The last thing Hayley wanted was more food, but she could see how upset Nate was. She wasn't going to quibble over their destination.

"Your mom's pretty sick," she said once they were strolling down the sidewalk, past modest frame houses and fenced yards, most with people doing yardwork or sitting on porch steps. "You mentioned that she has COPD?"

Nate nodded. "That's right. She's been struggling with it for a couple of years."

"But she's so young!"

"Yeah. She has something genetic that made it come on early." He glanced over at her then looked away. "We don't have a timeline, but she's gone downhill pretty fast. They're thinking months, not years, now."

She took his hand and squeezed it. "Oh, Nate, I'm sorry."

He squeezed back and was quiet for a minute, keeping hold of her hand. "There's always hope," he said finally, "but you can see why I didn't jump in and rain on her parade about us being a couple."

"I can," she said. "She's your mom, and you don't want to hurt her."

"Right. But I'll correct it. I'll get Dad to help, and do it carefully."

She thought of the kind woman at the center of the family, possibly nearing the end of her life. Thought of the family gathered around the table. "Or…"

He tightened his hold on her hand, lifting it to help her over a big crack in the sidewalk. "Or what?"

"Or…could we just let her think it?" Even as she said it, Hayley was scolding herself. There was no way. She couldn't hold up her end.

But you'd get to have a few more Sunday dinners with a wonderful extended family.

She glanced back in the direction of the house then looked at Nate. His forehead was wrinkled, his expression serious. He wasn't looking at her.

"I don't know if it's a good idea," he said.

Heat rushed to Hayley's face. "No, of course not. I wasn't thinking." Boy, he'd been quick to smash that notion. Maybe even the thought of being with her was repugnant to him.

As well it would be, if he knew the truth about her. Nate was a wonderful son, a good and moral man, a pastor. He needed a strong Christian woman by his side, not someone with a mess of a past, like Hayley.

"I just couldn't do that to you," Nate went on. "If it were just me, I'd jump on that idea in a minute. Anything for Mom. But I can't expect you, who's only met her once, to make a sacrifice like that."

"It wouldn't be a sacrifice," Hayley blurted and then felt her face heat again. Did she need to make it so pathetically obvious that she didn't have a life and would love to glom onto his for a little ride?

He stared at her and dropped her hand, and Hayley's heart sank to the sandy ground. She'd not only embarrassed herself, but she'd also embarrassed him.

And then she felt his arm around her shoulders, tugging her closer as their walk slowed almost to a standstill. "You, Hayley Harris, are an amazing person. I don't know if there's anything you wouldn't do to help others. I'm in awe."

She shook her head and laughed, and tried to ignore the absolutely wonderful feeling of his arm around her shoulders. Even more, of his warm approval.

"You'd really do that for my mom? For my family?"

Hayley thought about what it might mean. Not just pretending in front of his mom, but in front of his dad and his sisters. "We would need to let your family know it isn't true," she said.

Nate shook his head. "No. I can't do that. None of them need the burden of a secret. And they wouldn't be able to keep it."

They'd reached the ice cream stand. Hayley suddenly felt that she *could* maybe eat a small cone, if it were chocolate. She needed the comfort.

So, Nate waited at the window and bought them each cones, and Hayley watched him and thought it through.

She had the opportunity to make a dying woman happy.

As a side benefit, it would get her friends off her case, those who kept wanting her and Nate to join up. If they thought she and Nate had finally gotten together, they'd cut her a break when things ended.

There was danger, for sure, but it was mostly to her own heart.

She didn't want to cause pain to others; she wanted to relieve their pain. And for now, this deception wouldn't be difficult; in fact, it might be kind of wonderful to play at a relationship she wasn't destined to have in real life.

She would never be the happily engaged woman, would never be the bride welcomed as the newest relative.

The moment she'd handed her gorgeous, wrinkly-faced baby to a social worker to take away forever, she'd vowed to herself that she would never form another family.

It wouldn't be fair to this loved, and lost, child.

But maybe, just maybe, she could taste what it would be like. Her short, pretend relationship would be something to go on in the cold and lonely future, after Nate had moved on to find a good preacher's wife.

Hopefully, at that point, she would have moved on, too, becoming a teacher, fulfilling her dream of nurturing others another way.

Nate returned with two dripping ice cream cones. She took one, licked it. Cool and delicious.

He was watching her and there was a funny expression on his face. She couldn't interpret it.

"I made a decision," she said. "If you want to go forward with this, I'm game."

He leaned over and hugged her, coming dangerously close to smashing their ice cream cones between them. "Thank you." His hug felt strange, but good.

Maintaining a boundary between a fake and a real relationship might not be so easy to do.

Nate was mostly glad for the rafting field trip scheduled two days after he and Hayley had decided to pretend date for his mother's sake. He'd been struggling to focus on anything else. Driving one of the vans should get his mind off the challenges caused by their decision.

What had he been thinking? How, exactly, were they going to keep up the dating charade for his parents without throwing everyone else into the same misconception? And was he going to be able to put up a feasible front without losing his heart to Hayley, who obviously didn't want it?

A high-pitched sound from the back of the van he was driving made Nate brake hard. That had sounded like Snowflake's distinctive howl.

He pulled to the side of the road and looked over the twelve boys in the van.

"What was that?" From the seat beside him, Hayley twisted toward the back of the van, too.

He glared at Jeremy. "Did you bring Snowflake?"

Jeremy's face went bright red. "I…yeah, I brought Snowflake," he said. Apparently hearing her name, the dog jumped from the floor to the seat beside Jeremy. Her characteristic smile and bright eyes seemed to laugh at Nate.

Nate took a deep breath to calm his own annoyance. "You can't bring a dog on a raft."

"Well…actually, he probably can," Hayley countered. "But, Jeremy, you should have checked with us first so we could make plans. Now, we'll have to see if the rafting company has life vests for dogs."

"Life vests for *dogs*?" One of the Margolis boys, Mark, spoke with disgust. "Does that mean *we* have to wear life vests?"

"Absolutely," Hayley said.

As the boys groaned and bickered, Nate shook his head and pulled the van back onto the road. Being late for their scheduled rafting time wouldn't do any good.

His mind played out various scenarios, none of them good. What if something happened to Jeremy's dog? What if the dog distracted the other rafters and safety measures went out the window?

The whole thing was wrong. "I wish you hadn't told him it was okay," he huffed to Hayley as he drove.

"It *is* okay," she said, waving her phone. "I just looked it up. Service dogs can ride in all kinds of vehicles, including a raft."

"Okay, but first, he's an emotional support dog, not a service dog, so those rules may not apply," Nate said, keeping his voice low so the boys wouldn't hear them arguing. "And second, a raft isn't like other vehicles. Dogs can't hold on if things get rough. Think of all the bad things that could happen."

Hayley started tapping her phone again and, a moment later, she held it up. "According to this website, dogs are safe in up to class four rapids, and our max on this trip is class three."

"What else does it say?" he pressed. It couldn't be this easy to take an animal on a rafting trip.

She was reading the page and "Oh" came out of her mouth.

"What?"

"They say to introduce your dog to boating slowly," she said, and turned around. "Hey, Jeremy, has Snowflake ever been on a raft?"

"No. But he's been in a rowboat."

"Not the same," Nate said.

"No, but it should help." Hayley slid her phone back into her pocket. "Look, we'll talk to the people at the rafting company. If they think it's safe, we'll take her, and if not, then I, or Jeremy and I, can stay back with Snowflake while everyone else does the trip."

"It's not fair for you to miss rafting." He wasn't sure whether his displeasure at that notion had to do with her missing a fun trip or with him wanting her along.

He saw the sign for the rafting company and turned off the highway onto a dirt road. The van bounced and lurched along. Around them, pines, red rocks and glimpses of green water ahead soothed away some of Nate's annoyance.

They were here in God's beautiful world, sharing it with boys who hadn't, in most cases, had a lot of experience hanging out in nature. It was important to share the beauty, as well as the risky excitement of rafting, with all of the boys. Nate couldn't get hung up on a mistake one boy had made.

He was almost sure the rafting company would nix Snowflake's participation in the trip, which was disappointing in that Hayley would have to stay back. But maybe that was a good thing. Maybe they needed to keep their distance. Getting into a pretend relationship had made things strange between them. Given him feelings he didn't want to name.

He climbed out of the van, opened the doors and started directing boys to carry things to the put-in area. They'd brought coolers containing lunch and drinks, and backpacks with extra clothes and towels, and first-aid kits. Some of it they'd leave here for after the trip, but the first-aid kit and lunch coolers were going along.

He caught a glimpse of the white fur covering the van's dark seats where Snowflake had been sitting. Oh well. The van would need a good cleaning after a bunch of wet and muddy boys rode home in it, anyway.

Hayley was talking with the rafting company employees, gesturing toward Snowflake, who'd taken the opportunity to sniff around the sagebrush. Nate moved closer to hear the conversation.

"That dog's going to get pretty dirty," the young

guy said, "but sure, she can come if she's comfortable in a boat."

"Is there a place we could test her out?" Hayley asked. "Like, have her get in a raft and float a bit, and see how she likes it?"

"Not a problem," the employee said. He beckoned them toward the shoreline.

"Come on, Jeremy," Hayley said. "Bring Snowflake over here."

Jeremy ran over, Snowflake beside him. "It's okay if we don't go. I'm sorry I didn't ask. I can stay here."

Nate studied the boy, sudden suspicion nudging at him. Had Jeremy brought the dog so that he wouldn't have to join the trip?

Hayley glanced at Nate. She seemed to be thinking the same thing.

"Could one of us do a test ride with Jeremy and the dog?" she asked the rafting guide.

"I'll go," Nate volunteered. He'd spent a lot of time on the river and was confident of his abilities.

"Great, let me grab a dog life vest. You two, get your human vests from over there." The guide indicated a stack of them.

Nate helped Jeremy put on his lifejacket, noticing that the boy clung tightly to Snowflake's leash, not even wanting to release it to put his arm through the sleeve. "You can swim okay, right?" he asked. All the boys on the trip had at least minimal water skills, according to the paperwork.

"Kind of. Not well."

"The water here is low, but still, listen carefully to the safety instructions," he said. "And, seriously, if Snowflake is uncomfortable, you'll have to stay back. You should have consulted us before bringing her."

Jeremy nodded. "I'm sorry."

The kid was so cute and seemed genuinely contrite. Nate clapped him gently on the shoulder. "Come on. Let's see if Snowflake wants to be a water dog."

The guide tugged a raft to the beach area. Jeremy got in and then called Snowflake to him. Without hesitation, the snowy-white dog leapt into the raft and trotted confidently to the boy. She jumped onto the seat beside him and looked around.

Jeremy visibly relaxed. Snowflake was doing her job.

Several of the other boys had come to watch. Nate climbed in, and then the guide, and they went out into the gentle water.

Snowflake lifted her nose in the air and gave an excited bark, almost as if she were proud to be on the boat with her master.

Jeremy looked proud, too, when a couple of the other boys cheered.

"Looks like she's a natural," the guide said, and paddled the boat back to shore.

"I wanna ride with the dog," Jeff Margolis yelled, which prompted his brother to say, "I do, too." Several of the other boys chimed in, which made Jeremy look even more proud.

Emotional support took all kinds of different forms. Snowflake was great for Jeremy.

Hayley had a clipboard. "Sorry, boys. We made the boat assignments ahead." Amid groans, she began to direct campers to stand in little clusters before the rafts. One of the river guides launched into a safety talk while the others started handing out life vests and showing the boys how to fasten them.

Nate crossed his arms over his chest. Sure, the river was mild here, but he knew there were rapids below. If something happened to one of the boys or to Snowflake...

"What's wrong?" Hayley asked.

"Nerves," he admitted. "Rafting is risky."

"It is," she said, and he was glad she didn't mock his concerns. "Anything could happen to one of them at any time, though, and we can't exactly have them sit in a circle doing needlepoint."

"We have to do *needlepoint*?" Booker Jackson groaned.

Hayley joked with the boy before assuring him that, no, needlepoint wasn't on the agenda.

Nate admired that about her; her easy way with the boys. He admired the combination of fun and practicality she brought to the job. They were fortunate to have her at the Bright Tomorrows camp, as well as the school. She would be a fine teacher.

In her shorts and T-shirt, she looked young. Way younger than Nate. And he would have thought she *was* way younger, too, except for what he knew about her. In addition to her directing food service, which was critical to the school, she had borne a child. That wasn't something that you got over easily.

It had to have been a maturing experience, placing the child for adoption.

And that child was Jeremy. Nate blew out a breath. He was keeping a secret he shouldn't be keeping.

A smarter man would have already found a way to admit the truth, to confront Hayley with it and gently share it. A smarter man would never have allowed the confidence from Stan in the first place.

But he was a pastor first, and sometimes, what people needed desperately was to get their concerns off their chest. Part of the role of a minister was to carry the burdens of others. To make other people's yokes easy to bear, their burdens light, because you were willing to carry them yourself.

He'd done it before, many times. He wasn't sure why this case felt so different. Maybe because he was working so closely with Hayley, and now, pretend-dating her as well.

The Margolis boys were bickering again, in the amiable way of brothers, and Nate had a sudden acute flashback of bickering in a very similar way with his brother.

His heart ached with missing Tom. And never far away from that ache was the guilt.

He had so much to make up for. He had to make a success of this rafting trip, this job, this camping experience, for all the boys. He had to do it for his mother, who was involved in funding the camp.

"Let's go," said one of the guides, and the boys whooped, and Nate climbed into the last raft and pushed it off from shore.

Five

The river was calm as Hayley and her group of boys, along with a counselor and an experienced guide from the company, floated downstream. Their raft was at the front and she'd seen Nate and his group bring up the rear.

She wasn't going to think about him. She was here to help the boys have a safe and fun trip, not to moon over Nate.

She tried to focus on the clear blue sky above, the rocky slopes on either side of them, the scrubby vegetation jutting out from rock outcroppings. The boys talked excitedly, but when they started to roughhouse, both Haley and the guide, Carina, spoke up. Carina was operating the long oars at the back of the raft and there were two paddles up front that could be pulled out and used to help navigate through the rapids.

"When will we get to the whitewater?" Jeff Margolis asked. She'd made sure to assign him to a separate raft from his brother, knowing how the two loved to argue.

"You'll know it when you see it," Carina said. "Relax while you can, boys, because it'll be all hands on deck when we get to the whitewater."

Hayley had studied the outfitters' website enough to know that, in reality, this half-day trip was along one of the mildest stretches of river. But the boys didn't have to know that. To them, most of whom had never been rafting before, the excitement and fear would be real.

After they'd floated for a time, she looked and saw two of the other rafts coming up behind them. Nate's raft brought up the rear.

But something was wrong.

The boys in the middle two rafts were shouting at each other. The counselors made gestures that seemed meant to calm, but it was not effective. The boys seemed more agitated.

"Can we slow down any?" she asked Carina.

"Sure can." The woman leaned on the oars and the raft slowed. "At least some, but there's whitewater coming."

The boys' shouts weren't distinguishable now, over the roar of the water in front of them. But it was clear that there was some kind of confrontation between the boys on the two boats.

She could see Nate gesturing from way back behind the boys. So he was aware of the situation.

From the jumble of indistinguishable words, a repeated one was clear. "Snowflake." The dog was in the boat with Jeremy, her white fur gleaming in the sun. Was she okay?

It looked like she was, but the boys in the other boat were motioning toward her. One was waving something around.

A boy in Hayley's boat had a pair of binoculars and he zoomed in on the boats behind them. "He's got a package of hot dogs! He's trying to get Snowflake to swim over!"

"Those little..." Hayley stopped herself before calling the mischief-makers an unkind name. "That would be so dangerous."

"Water's getting a little too fast for dogs," Carina said. "But not to worry. We'll all pull off in that little cove and scout the rapids." She started rowing hard to the side of the river.

Hayley was relieved. Once everyone was together on land, they could straighten this out and she could put the fear of punishment into the boys.

The boats behind them were closer together now, and the hot dog boy was holding the package out toward the other boat, ignoring the shouts of his counselor.

"No!" Jeremy cried. He leaned precariously out of the raft.

Snowflake barked.

The other rafts were pulling up to them now, all headed toward shore, all fighting the increasingly fast water.

Jeremy started to lose his balance.

Automatically, Hayley jumped into the thigh-deep water to get him.

He didn't fall in. But she struggled against the water's strong pull. Her heart pounded with a mixture of adrenaline and fear. Could she be sucked down into the rapids?

Suddenly, strong arms wrapped around her, pulling her to shore. "You're okay." It was Nate's voice; low but clear over the noise of the rapids.

He held on to her until they were both out of the water. The other boats were there, and everyone was shouting. Shaky, Hayley staggered across the sandy bank and sank down, breathing hard.

From the safety of dry ground, she looked around until she located Jeremy. She beckoned him over. "You okay, kiddo?"

He nodded, shamefaced. "I should have known Snowflake wouldn't jump out of the boat."

"Snowflake grabbed him by the seat of his pants and pulled him back in," another boy said, laughing. "I got a picture!" The boys weren't allowed to have phones, but some had brought disposable cameras on the trip.

Hayley took a few deep breaths, looked around to double-check that everyone was okay and saw Nate, standing arms crossed, looking at her. A flash of awareness went through her.

When she tried to stand, she could barely make it. Her ankle hurt. She winced, hopped, and started to fall. And once again, Nate was there, easing her to the ground.

Carina must have noticed, because she hurried over. She knelt to examine Hayley's ankle. After a moment, she frowned. "I'd rather you didn't continue the trip with that ankle. It would be fine in the raft, but if something happened in the rapids and we capsized, you'd have a hard time bracing yourself to stay safe."

"We want to keep going!" The boys looked upset, even Jeremy.

Why had she been so impulsive as to jump out of the raft? Hayley groaned. "I don't want to ruin everyone's trip."

"We can send a truck to pick you up here. You can meet up with the boys at the takeout."

"That would be great. Thank you."

"I'll wait with you," Nate said. "You shouldn't be out here alone."

"You don't need to do that," she protested. But the guides were already reorganizing the boats, making sure that each still had a counselor from the camp as well as a guide. Nate lectured everyone about safety and horseplay and keeping each other safe.

And then she and Nate were alone, soaked and shivering, the river rushing beside them. "Come on," Nate said, "we need to be on the rocks in the sun. It's the warmest."

She let him help her over to them.

"That was a dangerous move you made," he said. "I warned you about getting too close to a camper."

"You don't think I would have jumped out of the boat for any kid at risk?"

He frowned, something crossing his face.

"What?"

He shook his head. "Nothing. I just don't think you should put yourself in danger."

"It's in the job description, although I'll admit I didn't think before I jumped," she said. Her teeth were chattering, and he put out his arm and pulled her next to him. "Body heat. It's the least I can share with my pretend girlfriend."

Oh right. She had a fake relationship with this man. This man who had rescued her. Who'd given up his own trip to wait with her.

His kindness was wreaking havoc with her emotions. Disaster.

Putting his arm around Hayley might be a mistake. She was soaked and shivering, and clearly needed

258 *Lee Tobin McClain*

Nate's warmth. But being this close to her made him want things he couldn't have.

He eased away and plucked a piece of river grass out of her hair. "Do you think you can make it up to that dark rock?" he asked. "It'll be even warmer than this one, and you can start to dry off."

There. He'd come up with a practical reason for her to move, one that made sense.

"Sure." She sounded as flustered as he felt. She looked at the narrow path to the high rock, hesitated then headed toward it, still shivering.

"Wait." Nate passed her and climbed halfway up, then held out a hand to help her. She grabbed it as she made her way up over the rocky, muddy ground.

Her hand was cold in his, her grip tight. Being able to steady and assist her warmed his heart.

He wanted to help Hayley. Wanted to support her.

He climbed the rest of the way, slowly, holding her hand and sometimes physically supporting her.

Of course, helping others always felt good. But would it feel so wonderful if it were anyone except Hayley?

Not quite.

Once she was atop the warm rock, soaking in the sunshine, he scrambled back down, got the cooler and brought it up. He grabbed a bottle of water for her and insisted that she drink some.

She took a long drink and then studied him. "You're almost as wet as I am. Thank you for pulling me out."

"Of course. I'd do it for anyone." Realizing that his words were insulting, he added, "But I'm especially glad to help you." Awkward, awkward.

She didn't seem to notice. "Is there any food in there?"

He dug through the cooler. "They left us two hoagies and some chips."

"I'm starving." She grabbed a hoagie and started unwrapping it, her teeth still chattering. "It's turkey. D-d-do you want it?"

He laughed at her. "No, I'll take the ham and cheese. It's fine."

They munched for several minutes, sharing a bag of potato chips as well. By the time they'd finished the sandwiches, she'd stopped shivering. Nate's clothes were drying quickly in the warm sun, too.

The immediate emergency was over, and Nate found himself enjoying the chance to spend time with her. A little too much. "Wonder how long it'll be until they pick us up?"

"In a hurry?" she asked.

"No, not exactly."

"I am. I'm worried about Jeremy and Snowflake."

He nodded. "I think they'll be fine, though. The other boys were sufficiently scolded. I don't think they'll do anything like that again." He mock-glared at her. "You were the one who was the most at risk in that scenario. You can't jump out of a boat! Especially near rapids!"

"I know. I was stupid, you don't have to rub it in." She said the words without rancor. "We're here on the rock for an hour, at least. I don't want to spend the whole time getting yelled at."

"You're right. Then what do we talk about?"

She shrugged. "Tell me about when you were a kid. Your family seems so great."

Nate went still. It was a normal question, but for him, it inevitably brought up his brother, and that required explanations he wasn't sure he wanted to make.

She tilted her head to one side. "Did I say something wrong?"

"No, no. Not really."

She leaned closer. "What, Nate? What is it?"

All of a sudden, he wasn't the rescuer but the one in pain. It was an uncomfortable feeling. How had it turned out that she was more together than he was? "It's just… when I was a kid, it was always me and my brother," he said.

Compassion crossed her face. "Your mom mentioned she'd become a donor in his memory. What happened?"

Nate pulled out his usual two-word explanation. "Battlefield casualty," he said. Then, because Hayley seemed to want to hear more, he added, "He was scouting ahead of his team, and he was in a climbing accident. He…he didn't make it."

"Oh, Nate, how awful."

"It was," he said, and prepared to change the subject. No need to drag her into the circumstances surrounding his brother's enlistment and service.

"Were you close?" she asked.

The question surprised him. "Yes, although we were pretty different."

"Older? Younger?"

"Twins," he said.

"Oh…" The word came out of her like a sigh and she grasped his hand. "I'm so sorry. I know I said that before. But…is it true what they say, that twins have a special bond?"

Was that true? He knew it was supposed to be, and yet he and his twin brother had been so different. "I… kind of." It was weak of him, but he hated to reveal his own inadequacy and guilt to someone he liked so well and wanted to impress. "Tell me something about *your* childhood," he said.

"Change of subject? I guess that's fair." She pulled her knees to her chest and wrapped her arms around them, staring off at the river below and the trees on the opposite bank. "I made a lot of mistakes growing up."

Nate winced inwardly. He knew more about her past than she knew he did. "Tell me about when you were little," he said, figuring that was safe.

She grinned. "For starters, my name wasn't actually Hayley for the first five years of my life. It was Hailstorm."

"That's unusual."

"Hippie parents," she explained. "When they left me with my grandma to raise, she changed it to Hayley. Said the other kids would tease me if I had a weird name. Which is probably true."

He studied her, realizing how much he didn't know about her. "You were raised by your grandma, then?"

She nodded. "My parents visited every now and then, but…" She spread her hands, palms up. "They lived in a commune for a while and in their VW bus awhile. My grandma had a lot steadier of a life."

"So, was she right? That you fit in better with a more traditional name?"

"No, not really." She started to say something else and then broke off, making a wry face.

"What happened?"

"It's the school I attended," she said. "It was an academy, only not like Bright Tomorrows. It was a school for wealthy girls. My grandma worked there, so I got free tuition, but I didn't exactly fit in."

"Were you bullied?"

She shrugged. "Nothing like the awful stuff you hear about nowadays, with social media, but yeah. I had a few tough years."

"How did you cope?"

She studied him for a few seconds. "I did a lot of drugs."

He almost laughed and then realized she wasn't joking. "I'm sorry, Hayley. That can be a hard place to get out of."

"It was." She gave him another wry grin. "On the bright side, it helped me connect better with my parents when they visited. They could relate to me better as a teen addict than they could as a needy little child."

"You were an *addict*?" It was hard to associate that word with competent, wholesome Hayley.

"For a time." She stood, stretched, and then put her hands on her hips and confronted him. "Do you hate me for that?"

"No, of course not!" He was shocked she'd asked. "Everyone makes mistakes. Look at how much you've done with your life in the years since." He was uncomfortably aware that he knew more than he was saying about her past.

His own words had also startled him, though. *Everyone makes mistakes.*

It was true, and he believed it about others, but he'd never been able to forgive himself for his mistakes with his brother. He felt the slightest brush of a feeling: maybe he, too, could be forgiven.

Hayley spun around, her clothes mostly dried, her hair wild. She grabbed a long stick and used it as a crutch. "It'll probably still be a while until we're rescued," she said. "Want to do something fun?"

He had to admire the way she could continue to have fun even though she'd covered some hard ground with him, had been dunked in icy water and sprained her ankle trying to rescue a kid today. "What did you have in mind?"

She beckoned for him to come to where she was standing, and when he did, she pointed. "Is that a rope swing?" she asked.

He shaded his eyes and looked in the direction she was pointing. Sure enough, there was a thick rope hanging down from a tree branch.

"Want to try it?" she asked, her eyes full of mischief.

"No, we're not trying it! We just got dried off."

"But our ride should be here in a little while," she said. "They'll have towels and our packs with dry clothes. We'll be fine."

He shook his head, looking at the rocks below. "It's too dangerous."

"It doesn't go into the current. If you swing out, you'll just land in that pool." She pointed at a calm-looking inlet and then started making her way sideways on the rocks, surprisingly nimble for someone with a sprained ankle.

"Hayley! Come back!" He climbed after her, rocks falling down the side of the embankment.

She just laughed and kept going.

Nate sped up and joined her just as she got to the rope and reached for it. He gripped her wrist and tugged, ignoring her protests. His adrenaline raced and he could barely even think or speak. He just knew he had to get her down, and fast.

Get her to safety.

Prevent a loss that would be as insurmountable as losing his brother.

"Stop it, Nate! I just want to swing."

"No. Absolutely not." He tugged and, finally, she gave in and let him help her to a nearby rock ledge.

He sat her down and faced her, breathing hard. "You're not going to run off and do something stupid again, are you?"

"Not if you're going to be such a jerk about it."

He sat, his knees wobbly. "I *am* going to be a jerk, meaning I'll stop you from taking a serious risk. You can get that idea out of your head."

She studied him and, slowly, her expression changed from annoyed to curious. "What's going on? Why did a rope swing make you so upset?"

He waved a hand. "It's nothing. Just being safe."

Realization dawned on her face. "It's your brother, isn't it? You said he died in a climbing accident."

There was no point in hiding it now. "That's right."

"Were you there?"

He shook his head. That was his biggest regret.

She scooted closer and put an arm around him, pulling him into a warm embrace. "Oh, Nate. I'm so sorry."

He let her hug him, even though he was supposed to be comforting her. He was the pastor and yet he was falling apart.

"That must have been so hard," she said. "Do you want to talk about it?"

"Not really," he said and then couldn't stop himself. "He was more of a risk-taker than I was. He served in a unit on the front, and scouting makes the risk even worse."

"Your mom mentioned ADHD," she said hesitantly.

"Was that a part of why he took risks? I mean I don't want to blame him, it sounds like he was a hero and someone has to do the dangerous things in wartime… Sorry, I'm babbling. I don't know what to say."

"It's fine." Her words were actually a little bit of a comfort. His brother *had* needed the stimulation of taking risks, though whether that was linked to his diagnosis, Nate wasn't sure.

There was the sound of a truck, and then a shout. "We're over here," Hayley called, which was fortunate, because he was having trouble speaking more than a few quiet words. The lump in his throat was nearly choking him.

He'd revealed way more than he had intended to and yet he hadn't revealed the worst.

Six

After the rafting trip, the rest of the week was much less eventful and, by Saturday morning, Hayley felt reassured enough to take her day off.

Hayley had paid special attention to Jeremy, and how he and the other boys were getting along, but the scare in the rafts had actually seemed to jolt the boys into treating each other a little better. Their roughhousing and joking seemed to have a friendlier tone. Snowflake was becoming just another creature on the boys' various adventures, leaving the dog free to support Jeremy as he needed. And that appeared, at least to Hayley, to be less and less.

Her thoughts about Nate were less reassuring. He was still doing wonderful work as a camp co-director, seeming to handle that and his pastoral duties with ease. But Hayley had glimpsed the troubled man behind the confident façade, and she couldn't stop thinking about their conversation.

She shouldn't have encouraged the openness, not if her intent was to keep Nate at a distance. What had she been thinking? But the truth was, she hadn't thought.

She'd simply allowed him to take care of her when she was cold and scared, and then returned the favor when he'd seemed to need some emotional caretaking.

He'd seemed so lost, talking about his brother. All she'd wanted to do was to help him, to let him be the person confessing for once, rather than the all-kind minister being confessed to.

But that had led to her reaching out to him, hugging him, comforting him. That had deepened her feelings. Made her want what she couldn't have.

She steered her car into the parking lot in Little Mesa's small shopping district. She was here to help her friend Emily, not to fret over herself, things she'd done, things that couldn't change.

And, thankfully, their next off-campus field trip wasn't until next week. Things should be calm at the camp for a few days, at least.

She got out of the car and spotted Emily and Ashley waiting in front of the small department store. They were talking excitedly, their voices—although not their words—audible even at this distance. And no wonder. Emily and her husband, Dev, had learned that they'd been approved to foster the sibling group they'd been working with. It was very likely they'd get to adopt the children. Their family was going to grow rapidly.

Their son, Landon, needed reassurance about his place in the family, and they also needed a lot of supplies.

So Dev and Landon had gone fishing, and Emily had called Ashley and Hayley to help her shop.

The three of them high-fived and then hugged. "I'm so excited for you," Hayley said, giving Emily an extra squeeze. "This is going to be great. You're already an amazing mom to Landon, and you'll be an amazing mom to these kids, too."

"I don't feel amazing," Emily said. "I feel terrified."

"How's Landon handling the news?" Ashley asked.

"He's excited to have new brothers and sisters. We've been working with him to make sure he understands he won't get quite as much attention from Dev and me, at least at first. I think he gets it, but we'll see."

Hayley watched her friend's emotions flash across her face. She envied Emily's certainty and happiness; wanted to find that love and sense of purpose for herself. And she would. In a different way from Emily, but she'd find it.

It had nothing to do with Nate Fisher. It couldn't.

They walked around the children's department, picking out warm jackets and sturdy sneakers for the two older children.

"Look at these!" Emily held up two bright purple all-weather coats. "The sizes are right and they're on sale!"

Hayley glanced at Ashley and saw the same horrified expression on her face, which gave her the courage to speak up. "Em, they might be on sale for a reason," she said.

"I don't think boys will want neon-purple coats," Ashley added.

"Oh. You're right." Emily looked crestfallen.

"And I doubt they'll want to match." Hayley took the jackets out of Emily's hands. "It's good you have us with you. Now, come on, there are more sale jackets over here, in more neutral colors."

"Guys, what if I screw up mothering the way I'm screwing up shopping?" Emily fretted as they walked across the department to the other rack of hoodies and jackets on sale.

"You won't," Ashley and Hayley said in unison then fist bumped.

"You'll be awesome," Ashley said. "It's just…" She surveyed Emily's lavender T-shirt and bright blue shorts. "You wear *really* bright colors. And kids of nine and ten usually want to fit in more than stand out."

"Fine." Emily pretended to pout. "I hope your baby turns out to love bright floral dresses."

"We don't even know if it's a boy or girl," Ashley said. "But whatever he or she wants to wear, that's what they'll wear."

After they'd picked out some bedding for the children's rooms and carried their stash to Emily's SUV, Emily and Ashley looked at each other and squealed. Literally squealed. "Now for the fun part," Ashley said.

"What's that?" Hayley hadn't been in on the itinerary for the trip.

"The *baby store*!" Emily raised her hands high. "Yes! I can get all the bright, colorful baby clothes I want, because our littlest foster, Ceci, is too young to know she doesn't like it!"

"I'm right there with you," Ashley said. "I can't pick out a ton of stuff, since I don't know the gender, but I want to look at everything."

The two women started down the street.

Hayley stood, biting her lip, looking after them.

The two of them looked over their shoulders then turned and came back to where she was standing.

"What's wrong?" Ashley asked.

"I just… I need a cup of coffee. I'll meet you guys after you hit the baby store."

"No, you have to come," Emily said. "We need your fashion advice. We'll get coffee after."

"I don't think so," Hayley said, and when Ashley opened her mouth to protest, she held up a hand. "I can't."

"You can't what?" Emily asked.

Hayley swallowed hard, looked at her two best friends, and risked honesty. "I don't do baby stores."

Her voice must have sounded strange because both women studied her. Then Emily took hold of one of her arms and Ashley grabbed the other.

"Change of plans," Emily said. "Let's get that coffee first."

Hayley let them guide her down the street. She forced a smile when Ashley pointed to a couple of hot-air balloons overhead, which she normally loved, and knelt to mechanically pet a pedestrian's friendly dog when Emily stopped and exclaimed over it. It was nice, the way her friends were trying to distract her. She knew that, intellectually.

They guided her toward a cute coffee shop, where she shrugged when they asked what she wanted, then waited at a table while they ordered for her, talking to each other in low voices.

She felt hollow inside. Like there was nothing where a heart was supposed to be.

She'd talked to a social worker a few times after placing her baby for adoption, and had been promised more counseling if she needed it. The birth center had been nothing but wonderful, with no judgment about her placing her baby for adoption or about her desire to make it a closed one.

She should be over what had happened to her thirteen years ago. Instead, she felt like the poor little girl in the folk tale, standing outside of someone's home in the cold, envying the warm fireplace and hearty meal and caring companionship of the family inside.

Hayley ought to feel unambivalently happy about her friends' joy in their growing families. And she did, most of the time. But she'd never had a strong, solid family, and she couldn't help envying theirs.

Ashley and Emily returned, carrying three frothy iced-coffee drinks. "Mocha or French Vanilla or Birthday Cake sprinkle," Ashley said. "You choose first."

"Then I want the Birthday Cake, of course," Hayley said, trying to smile.

The other two bickered over the remaining coffees and then settled down into chairs.

"We were insensitive," Emily said. "We weren't thinking about how we have kids or expect them and you don't yet."

"It can be hard to be the one who's left out when people are talking about their pregnancies or babies," Ashley said, her hand resting on her stomach. "Believe me, I know. I was there for a few years."

"We know you'll get there, if you want to," Emily said. "But that doesn't mean you have to go baby-clothes shopping with us."

Hayley took a too-big sip of the ultrasweet beverage and went into a coughing fit. Once she'd caught her breath, she held up her hands. "You're both kind," she said. And then, because she'd been feeling a little broken open and because these women were, after all, her closest friends, she continued. "It's a little more complicated."

They glanced at each other. "See?" Emily said.

"Tell us," Ashley said.

Both pairs of eyes looked at her with kindness, and

Hayley sucked in a breath. "I... A long time ago, I had a baby." She ignored their audible gasps, but when Emily reached out, Hayley clasped her hand. "And I placed it—him—for adoption."

Ashley clutched her other hand, tears in her eyes. "That must have been so hard to do."

"You're not in touch with him now?" Emily asked.

She shook her head.

"Did you get to bond with him at all?" Ashley's face drooped with sadness. She'd miscarried a baby after being in a car accident, Hayley remembered.

"I did. I... I nursed him for a couple of days."

Emily's eyes widened. She was the only one of the three who'd given birth, although she'd lost her baby in a tragic accident. "Wow. It must have been hard to give him up after that."

Hayley nodded and cleared her tight throat. "It was, but I wanted him to have the advantage of that early milk. Nobody wanted me to do it, but... I figured it was the last thing I could do for..." She couldn't finish the sentence. She just stared down at the table as tears plopped onto it.

Ashley handed her a couple of napkins and she wiped her eyes and nose. "Sorry to break down," she said. "I just... I just don't talk about this much. Ever," she amended.

"Anytime you want to talk, we're here to listen," Emily said firmly.

"You did a very courageous thing, going through with the pregnancy and then placing the baby," Ashley added. "How old were you?"

"Seventeen," she said. "That's why..." She cleared

her throat. "That's why I just have my GED, you might remember from my résumé."

Ashley nodded. "I do remember."

"And…if it's okay, I don't want to talk about it any more right now." Hayley felt like she'd been run over by a giant steamroller. Her emotions had never been so close to the surface. "You guys can go shop."

"No way," Emily said. "We can order stuff we need online. Let's just chat about something else and drink our coffee and then go home."

Hayley fanned her face and tried to smile. "Thanks."

"And," Emily continued, "I know just what we can talk about, but shut me up if this is too intrusive. Are you dating Pastor Nate?"

"You're really going there?" Hayley leaned back in her chair and looked from Emily's face to Ashley's, both equally curious, neither surprised. "And you both heard about it?"

"Uh-huh. His sisters are pretty vocal."

"Ohhhh." Hayley blew out a breath. As long as her friends knew the worst about her, she might as well go for broke. "Can you guys keep another secret?"

"Of course!" Ashley said.

"Pinky promise," Emily added, letting Hayley's hand go and hooking their pinky fingers together in a quick squeeze.

"Okay." Hayley sucked in a big breath, let it out and told them about the pretend relationship for Nate's mom's sake.

"Oh wow," Emily said. "Won't it be hard to keep that up?"

"I don't know." Hayley lifted her hands and shrugged.

"It was a split-second decision, and now I feel like I can't back out."

"Do you want to back out?" Emily's head was tilted to one side.

"Um, yes? I don't know?"

Ashley's brow creased. "You've been locking away a lot of your past already and adding more secrets... it's a lot."

"Secrets can backfire," Emily said.

Hayley nodded. "I know," she said. "But what can I do?"

Nate drove up the familiar road to Bright Tomorrows, but took a different-than-usual turn: to the cabins where many of the staff lived during the school year. And where some—like Hayley—lived year-round.

He'd made the arrangements by text. This was a quick dinner date to appease his family and also to discuss with Hayley how the whole situation would work.

After their rafting trip, where he'd revealed more about himself than he'd intended, he'd stuck to himself. Done his afternoon work with the campers and then left. Communicated with Hayley primarily by text.

But the upshot was that his sisters were bugging him. Why hadn't he taken Hayley out Friday night, if they were dating? Was he taking her out tonight?

That was when he'd decided, apologetically, to invite her to dinner tonight.

He pulled up to her cabin and there she was on her front step, talking to a couple of the counselors. When he got out of the car, the two counselors greeted him, waved to Hayley and headed off toward the dorms.

Hayley stood, waiting for him. Dressed in faded

jeans and a simple, flowing shirt—dark pink flowers on a lighter pink background—she looked like summer. Her hair hung loose over her shoulders.

She looked her usual self and yet she took his breath away.

He tried for composure, a casual approach. He had no intention of touching her. And then he noticed the shadows beneath her eyes, the faint wrinkles on her forehead.

"Everything okay?" he asked as he reached out a hand to her. The gesture was automatic and he intended a quick—what? Handshake? Touch of the arm?

But when she extended her hand to him, he took it and didn't let go. He looked closer into her troubled eyes. "What's been happening?"

She looked away, shrugged, withdrew her hand. "Everything's fine. Those two—" she gestured in the direction where the counselors had gone "—they just wanted to talk about the open house. It's coming up in a couple of weeks."

"It's a casual thing, right?"

She nodded. "Skits, popcorn, tours. Just a way to build connections with the community, but a few of the boys were planning a skit they didn't think was appropriate."

"Uh-oh. Did you nix it?"

She nodded. "No big deal. They're going to tell the boys tonight, and steer them in a different direction. I told them they could blame me."

"Good plan."

"Thanks." She offered a small smile that looked forced.

He could tell something was wrong, but she obviously didn't want to talk about it. That meant he needed to have the energy for both of them, needed to cheer her up. His idea of what they'd do tonight changed on the spot. "Are you ready to go? Comfortable shoes?"

She raised an eyebrow. "We're just going to dinner, right?"

"Well…" He hesitated. He *should* just take her to dinner, have a businesslike discussion as planned and then bring her home.

But that wasn't likely to remove the shadows from her eyes. "I thought we'd go to the street fair in Little Mesa," he said. "There are food trucks, so we can get dinner. But there are rides, and a couple of bands, and carnival games. It might be fun to check it out."

"Sure," she said without enthusiasm. "I'm ready to go. Just let me grab my purse."

Twenty minutes later, they'd parked on a side street. As they approached the festival, Hayley's face brightened. "I *love* country music! Is that Tres Hijos?"

"I think so." Nate didn't know the Latino country band well, but he'd read that they would be appearing at the street fair.

"I've been listening to their music ever since I started studying Spanish," she said. "I've never seen them in person. This is so cool!"

Nate just nodded, but inside he was cheering. He really liked putting that happy expression on her face. Would like to do it more often.

They listened to the band for a few songs and then ambled through the fair. It was crowded, as you'd expect on a beautiful July night. Couples strolled, families waited in line for the rides and teens clustered around the carnival games. The sun was still high, but the light had begun to glow golden, foreshadowing sunset.

"Any rides you'd like to try?" he asked, expecting her to say no.

"The Ferris wheel," she said promptly.

"All right then." He bought tickets and they got in line. Soon they were clicked into a seat and ascending slowly into the sky, with a stop at each passenger car for more people to get on.

They reached the top of the Ferris wheel and Hayley looked around. "Wow," she said. "Just gorgeous."

Nate had been too busy looking at her to notice the scenery. Now, he looked out over the mountains. Below them, the crowds still roamed, but up here, they were in their own world.

He could smell her light floral perfume, could feel the warmth from her leg and arm. He slid an arm across the back of the seat and then held his breath. Would she find him too forward? Cringe away?

But she just smiled and settled comfortably against him. "Guess we're showing the world that we're dating," she said with a wry smile.

"Is that okay?"

She shrugged. "I'm not sure it was our most brilliant move, letting your mom think that. I'm concerned about the deception."

"Me, too," he admitted. "But I saw her yesterday and she's so happy. She tends to worry about me."

She glanced over at him. "Because of your brother?"

"Yeah. That's one reason."

"There are others?"

"Well…" He hazarded a look at her. "She knows

I haven't dated much. She thinks a pastor should be married."

Hayley wrinkled her nose. "That sounds a little outdated."

"It is, but all the same, a lot of people tend to agree." He could add that he was lonely, that he longed for the close companionship and human touch that happened in good marriages, but he didn't want to sound pathetic. "Anyway, my dad's happy because he wants the family name to carry on, and I'm the only opportunity to do that now."

"Oh, so we're having babies already?" She grinned at him and then her face went serious. "I'm sorry. I didn't mean to laugh when you're thinking about the loss of your brother."

"I know." She was way too kind to make light of someone else's pain.

She twisted a strand of her hair over and over. "This situation we've gotten ourselves into is no joking matter. We did this for your mom, but it seems like your whole family is excited about it."

"They are." Nate looked up at the sky. "They'll be fine, though. It's Mom I worry about. Anything I can do to make her happy." He felt his throat close up. Mom was terminal, and he'd in some way accepted that, but he was having a hard time envisioning a world without his mother in it.

He thought of his family. His grandparents were all gone, and in this region, it was his parents, his sisters, and his nieces and nephews. And Mom was the glue that held them together. When she was gone, what would happen?

Hayley reached up and touched his hand, still resting on her shoulder. Having her next to him, feeling her sympathy and comfort, soothed something deep inside him.

Their romantic relationship wasn't real, but their friendship was. That mattered. A lot.

The Ferris wheel was done loading now and it started to speed up, and then they were both laughing and holding on to the bar in front of them. The sights and sounds of the carnival flew past: people's faces, neon lights just starting to glow, shrieks from another, faster-moving ride.

As they went over the top of the wheel's circuit at the fastest pace yet, Hayley let out a small shriek, a little scared, but mostly gleeful. He looked over at her laughing face.

He'd known her for more than two years, had seen her many times at church and social events. He'd even been attracted to her. But that had been child's play compared to his feelings now.

Had it started when they'd become co-directors? When they'd agreed to pretend date?

All he knew was that watching her laugh felt like standing outside in a warm spring rain, after a cold winter. Refreshment and happiness poured over him.

He didn't need for that to be happening. It wasn't good, because of the enormous secret in Hayley's past, the one she didn't know he knew.

But tonight was about helping Hayley feel better and enjoy herself.

He was definitely enjoying being in her company. And with that thought, he reached out and took Hayley's hand in his just as the Ferris wheel topped its cycle again.

Seven

They were still holding hands ten minutes later as they strolled toward the food trucks, and Hayley's insides skittered around like drops of water on a hot griddle.

Nate's grip was strong, his hand more callused than she'd have expected from a minister. She should have known he'd be that way, considering that she'd seen him plastering a wall in one of the Sunday School rooms and repairing the retaining wall outside the church.

He was a man who could preach the gospel or change a tire or laugh like a child on a Ferris wheel. He served people daily in his work and he'd served his country. He was the kind of man she'd have liked to marry, if things were different.

She sucked in a deep breath of air that smelled like funnel cakes and grilled sausage and fry bread, trying to ground herself in reality, but it was a hopeless effort. The moment Nate smiled over at her, she couldn't help smiling back and squeezing his hand for all the world as if they were a real couple on a real date.

They agreed on tacos but as they were approaching

the food truck painted in the red, white and green of Mexico's flag, Nate made a sound.

It wasn't loud, but it heralded something wrong.

She looked up, and there was Stan, on a bench.

Jeremy's mom was beside him. And they were both staring, frowning as if Hayley and Nate had committed a sin.

Heat rushed into Hayley's face and she dropped Nate's hand as if she'd been burned by a hot dish. What was she thinking, letting Nate hold her hand, letting herself pretend they were a couple on a date?

Was Stan dating Jeremy's mom? Should they approach the older couple or pretend they hadn't seen them?

She glanced over at Nate. His expression was inscrutable, and he'd allowed the hand drop, but now he put a hand on her lower back and gently guided her toward Stan and Arlene. "Hi, Arlene," he said. "Stan, it's good to see you out and about. Are you feeling better?"

He was probably right to approach them. But didn't he realize they were compromising their professional reputation by appearing to date?

Then again, they'd agreed to enact that fiction for Nate's parents. Why hadn't they discussed what would happen if work colleagues saw them playacting?

Had it *been* playacting? It hadn't felt like it.

Arlene seemed like the type who'd complain to anyone she knew if she thought something untoward was happening at the camp her son was attending.

Stan and Nate seemed to be exchanging meaningful glances. But when Stan finally spoke, what he said was noncontroversial. "I've been home for a week now. Stuck inside, so you probably didn't even know I was there. Anyway, I'm restless. I can't work, but Arlene agreed to bring me out for an hour to see people instead of my cabin's four walls."

"Good idea," Hayley managed to agree.

"Well," Nate said, "we were just heading over to grab some tacos. Did you two eat?"

Please say yes. Please don't eat with us.

"Yes, we did," Arlene said. She pursed her lips. "Shouldn't the two of you be at the camp, supervising the children?"

Her accusatory tone twisted Hayley's stomach. She opened her mouth to explain, but Stan waved a hand. "I told you, the directors can't be on duty twenty-four-seven," he said to Arlene. "There are counselors for that. We don't want our directors to get burned out."

"That's true," Nate said, "but all the same, we'll be getting back right after we've eaten."

"You live together on the property?" Arlene sounded scandalized, and Hayley felt her cheeks heat at the implication.

"No." Nate's cheeks flushed a little, too, although his tone remained calm. "I live in town, and Hayley lives in the faculty cabins at the school. Which means she's on call a lot more than I am." He looked at her. "Are you ready? We can get the tacos to go."

Just like that, there went their fun date. In its place was a knot of guilt.

Was she neglecting the campers in her care, going out to have fun? Was it wrong for her to be in Nate's company socially?

She longed to be a simpler woman who could be on a carefree date with a wonderful man. All around them, couples laughed together in the fading daylight, hold-

ing hands, or pushing strollers, or handing cotton candy
to their excited kids. Hayley wanted that. Longed for it
with the fierce energy of an unpopular middle schooler
watching the higher-status kids have fun.

That was silly. She had so much. She had friends,
and a place to live, and a good job. She had plans for
the future. She should be content with that.

But always, inside her, there was some aching rem-
nant of the seventeen-year-old she'd been, the one who'd
been willing to do anything just to get attention and
affection, to get someone to see her and hold her and
love her.

And look where that had gotten her.

Why was she out having fun instead of doing the
work God had given her to do? Why was she pretending she could be in a relationship when that could never,
ever, happen?

July third was a Monday and a lot of working people
had the day off. A long weekend would be welcome to
anyone, including most of the pastors Nate knew.

But most pastors didn't have two jobs.

At the sink outside the Bright Tomorrows maintenance shed, Nate washed his hands, greasy from a
morning of fixing the school bus in front of an audience of campers. Today was scheduled as an all-camp
workday, and he'd seized the opportunity to teach some
basic engine maintenance to the boys who hadn't gone
home for the holiday.

A truck pulled up in the parking lot. Jason and Dev
got out.

They'd promised to come help with the workday

when they could get free, and here they were. Nate's spirits lifted at the sight of his friends.

He looked at the small group of boys around him. "Okay, men. Who wants to skip lunch and paint the walls of the game room?"

"No way!"

"It's too hot in there!"

"I'm starving!"

He had his answer, and it didn't surprise him in the least. Jeremy was right in there groaning with the others, and Nate was glad to see it. Much of his anxiety seemed to be dissipating as his time went on at camp. Friendships, fresh air and a little independence seemed to be working wonders on the boy.

"We'll do it." Dev and Jason had approached during the conversation and, apparently, had heard Nate's request.

"Speak for yourself, man. I want a hot dog," Jason said. He was an enormous man, and had an enormous appetite. His service dog, Titan, panted beside him.

"We just got here," Dev pointed out, "and I'm guessing Ashley fixed you a lumberjack's breakfast, just like she does every morning."

"Busted," Jason said with a grin. "I'll work. But I'll text Hayley to save me half a dozen hot dogs."

"Ask her to save me a couple." Nate was hungry, too, but it was important to make progress on the school upkeep. Plus, he was self-aware enough to know that, on some level, he was punishing himself for getting caught with Hayley.

And he was trying to avoid her.

He led the other men into the building, where painting supplies had already been laid out. They made quick work of spreading drop cloths over the floor and the Ping-Pong tables, and then started taping off trim.

"How's your mom?" Dev was Nate's distant cousin and knew Nate's mother well, had lived with them for a short while in childhood.

"She's...okay." The last time he'd visited, she hadn't felt well enough to get out of bed. But he didn't want to talk about it and risk getting emotional. He swallowed the lump in his throat. "We're all getting together on the fifth, big family picnic."

Dev was pouring paint into a tray. "Is *Hayley* going?"

Nate looked quickly at him. "No. Or at least, I haven't invited her." Yet. He supposed he should, if he didn't want his mom and sisters to hassle him about it.

"How's that work," Jason asked, "when you're supposed to be dating her?" There was steel in his voice, and Titan, who'd plopped down on his side in the middle of the room, lifted his massive head and let out a quiet growl.

Nate looked from Jason to Dev. They'd both stopped working and were waiting for his response. They seemed to be double-teaming him.

Because he didn't know how to answer, he kept taping off trim, hoping that they'd move on to something else. He really should have turned on the TV, gotten a Rockies game on.

But he hadn't, and the silence grew behind him.

Finally, he looked over his shoulder to find them both still watching him. Jason's arms were crossed, making him look like the Jolly Green Giant, and Dev was glaring.

"You guys going to work or what?" he asked.

Dev lifted an eyebrow. "How about if you tell us what's going on first."

"What do you mean?" He was buying time to try to formulate a response.

"There are rumors flying, man. You should know that. You're the town minister."

"You were seen together at the fair," Jason added. He cleared his throat, his arms still crossed over his chest. "You better not hurt her, man."

If looks could kill, Nate would be knocking on the pearly gates just about now. He blew out a breath. "It's complicated."

Instantly, Dev started shaking his head. "No, man, that's not good enough. This is real life, not a dating app."

"And Hayley's our friend," Jason said with finality.

That was fair. Nate kept taping. "I have feelings," he said, "but there are issues."

"On your end or hers?" Dev asked.

"Mine, for sure." Nate grabbed a paint roller. "It's just doubtful it'll work out." As he said it, despair washed over him.

He was telling the truth: it wasn't likely to work out. But, more and more, he wished that wasn't so.

Maybe he could find a way to talk to her about the secret without breaking Stan's confidence. It seemed impossible, but he was motivated, maybe more motivated than he'd ever been in his life.

If he could talk to her about it, discuss the secret, was it possible that a relationship between them could work?

At the thought of having a real relationship with Hayley, cold, slick guilt washed over his body like an oil spill. How could he toss off his concerns and enter into the joyous life of love that his brother would never experience?

His dedication to making up for Tom's life meant that he could never allow himself happiness. He'd known it, but until getting closer with Hayley, he hadn't minded.

Maybe if being with Hayley would make his parents happy and continue the Fisher family name...

Or maybe he was just making excuses to let himself off the hook and get what he wanted.

He blew out a breath, unable to find an answer to the thorny issues tangling in his head.

Dev cleared his throat. "It's not really my place to say this to a pastor," he said, "but have you taken it to the Lord?"

Nate nodded. "I have. But...not as much as I should, maybe."

"Then you know what to do." Jason dipped a paintbrush in a can and started painting trim, his touch surprisingly deft for such a big man.

"Just bear in mind," Dev said as he ran a roller through the paint tray he'd poured, "if you hurt her, you'll have us to deal with."

"I will." As they went to work seriously on the painting job, Nate's dilemma seesawed through his mind.

He couldn't betray Stan's confidence. But he didn't feel right getting involved with Hayley while knowing this vast secret about her past.

Maybe he could talk to Hayley. If they took a hike together or had a picnic, something that gave them time to relax together—*alone* together, not with his interfering family or their interfering friends—maybe their pasts would come up naturally. Maybe she'd share the truth that she'd borne a child and placed him for adoption. That would be a start.

And maybe he'd sit down with Stan, now that the man was at least a little bit up and about. If he explained the situation, illustrated how awkward it was to know something so big and be unable to share it with the individuals most involved, maybe Stan would offer to either tell Hayley the story or to let Nate tell her.

Nate had spent too much time in the military to be free with his thoughts and words. The phrase "loose lips sink ships" was still followed pretty closely by the men he'd served with. Keeping things to yourself was the norm.

But in his ministerial training, he'd learned that being open worked better in the civilian, interpersonal world. It wasn't comfortable, but it needed to happen.

Sooner rather than later.

Eight

On the morning of July Fourth, Hayley submitted the last of her online assignments for the week—yet another effort to impress the admissions committee—checked her watch, and exhaled, feeling satisfied. It was almost time to meet with the counselors, and she'd managed to achieve her goal of working steadily without thinking—much—about Nate.

After their encounter with Arlene and Stan had cut short their date at the street fair, Hayley had decided it was time to refocus on her teaching goals and forget her silly romantic dreams about Nate.

She'd slogged steadily through her online course in the hours when she wasn't working with the campers and staff or doing the paperwork required by her administrative position as camp director. Now that she'd caught up with all of that, she'd stay busy with the counselors and campers.

It was a beautiful Rocky Mountain day, warm and clear, so she intercepted the five counselors as they headed into the meeting room. "Let's talk outside today," she said. "And I brought us a treat." She'd stayed up late last night baking a coffee cake, and now she handed out slices along with $10 gift cards for the independent bookseller the next town over.

It was a stretch, financially, but she wanted the counselors to know she appreciated them. Their job, being with the campers 24/7, wasn't an easy one, and they'd done tremendously well so far.

Judging from their smiles, the cake and gift cards were a success, and they got down to the business of the meeting in good spirits. She listened to their concerns and talked through some disciplinary techniques that might work well with these boys.

They were winding up when Nate approached. He sat on the outskirts of the group and, even though he didn't say anything, other than a quiet greeting to the counselors next to him, he raised an eyebrow at Hayley.

She could read it. Read his mind. She should have invited him.

She continued the meeting as best she could, but her focus faltered and her good feelings about her own leadership evaporated. She'd forgotten to include him. Or...had the idea of inviting him flashed into her mind? Maybe it had. If so, she'd set it aside and gotten busy with other things and it hadn't happened.

After the counselors left, she gathered her things and walked over to him.

"Look, I'm sorry—"

"You should have—" he said at the same time.

They both broke off and then Nate gestured for her to speak first.

"I'm sorry I didn't invite you to the staff meeting," she said quickly. "As soon as I saw you, I realized you might have wanted to be involved. I feel awful. I know how it is to be excluded—"

He held up a hand, stopping her flow of contrite words. "It's fine. You're forgiven."

She blinked. "Just like that?"

"Of course." He shrugged. "Everyone makes mistakes, and this one isn't even serious. I have plenty of meetings to attend. Just catch me up on what I missed."

His easy attitude shocked her. Forgiveness wasn't something she'd come by easily in her life. Ever since her grandmother had thrown her out for becoming pregnant—and then died—Hayley had realized that mistakes could be permanent.

As she explained the gist of the meeting, and offered Nate some conciliatory coffee cake, she felt warmed by his acceptance. Maybe it wouldn't mean much to others, but Hayley was a perfectionist and was used to people holding her to that standard. That Nate could relax about her flub spoke well of him, and also showed her she needed more people like that in her life.

Sunlight shone on his hair and highlighted his strong, tanned arms. She could look at him, could listen to his resonant preacher voice, forever.

That was exactly what she shouldn't be doing, of course, but she couldn't stop herself, not right away.

A shout from the dorm area distracted her. "Was that Jeremy?"

"Sounded like it," Nate said. "Let's go."

She and Nate headed toward the small group of boys now yelling at each other. A counselor was there, but he was lecturing one of the campers off to the side while the others continued arguing.

"What's going on here?" she asked as they approached.

There was a moment of red-faced silence. Then, "We just wanted to see if Snowflake is a good service dog or not," Mickey O'Henry said.

"Of course she is," Hayley said. "What did you do?"

One of the boys snorted out a laugh. "They were trying to act all upset and anxious to see if Snowflake would come help them, like she helps Jeremy."

"And she didn't," Mickey said. "She's not a good dog."

"Didn't even pay attention," Booker added.

"She's trained to help me, not you!" Jeremy knelt beside Snowflake, who was leaning against him, clearly doing her job right at this moment.

"That's not so hard! She should help anyone who's upset!" Booker crossed his arms.

"She does, but I'm her priority!"

The two boys looked ready to come to blows and the counselor was still talking to Mark Margolis, who must have been one of the instigators. "I'll help Jeremy, you take Mickey and Booker," she said to Nate.

He shook his head. "I'll talk with Jeremy. You take the others."

She opened her mouth to protest.

"I can give him some tips on how to deal with other boys," he said quietly. "He may need that more than sympathy."

Her jaw dropped. "I wasn't going to just offer…" She trailed off. Maybe she *had* been more likely to offer sympathy than anything else.

Without waiting for her consent, he turned and beckoned to Jeremy. "Come on over here," he said, gesturing toward a bench. "Bring Snowflake."

Hayley took the other boys aside and lectured them—about service dogs, about being sensitive to others. She kept an eye on Nate and Jeremy, worried Nate would be too hard on the boy. But, to her surprise, she soon saw Jeremy smiling and nodding, and then laughing.

After her lecture, the boys agreed to apologize to Jeremy. He waved it off. "No problem," he said. He tossed Snowflake a squeaky toy. Soon, the dog was alternately squeaking it and lifting her nose to howl along, making the other boys laugh.

Nate gave Jeremy a little nod of approval and the boy glowed.

Hayley glowed a little, too. Nate was really good with the campers.

And, she realized, she hadn't stopped thinking about him today. Despite her intentions, despite keeping herself as busy as she knew how, she was *still* way too attuned to the man.

As the sky darkened on the Fourth, Nate looked around the small group of campers clustered outside the Bright Tomorrows dormitory building, his feelings mixed.

They'd gathered the boys here to watch the fireworks being set off at a nearby ranch. The night was chilly and clear, and Nate was glad for his sweatshirt and jeans.

Getting them together tonight had been a last-minute decision. Hayley had noticed that some of the boys who hadn't gone home for the long weekend were homesick, and when she and Nate had talked about it, they'd realized they'd forgotten to arrange a special activity for the night of the Fourth.

Hayley had quickly searched around for local fireworks displays and found one that wouldn't require them to leave the grounds.

It was just another example of how well-organized and perceptive she was.

Hayley had been passing out red-, white- and blue-iced cookies, and now she came over to offer him what remained from her container. "Sorry," she said, "you get the broken ones. The boys loved these too much."

"I'm happy to eat the broken cookies," he said, taking a couple of halves. "Come sit. It's time to relax."

She looked at him quizzically for a minute and then nodded. "I'll have to run inside and get a blanket."

"Or you could share mine." The words were out before he could consider their wisdom. Hayley on a blanket beside him, on a dark Fourth of July night, seemed like a risky move.

It also seemed inevitable, as inevitable as the boys shoving at each other and joking around. You couldn't blame boys for being who they were.

You couldn't blame a man for being a man.

Maybe he should have settled himself right in the midst of the boys, eliminating the space for any adult interaction between him and Hayley. But as a pastor, he was well acquainted with how dampening his own presence could be. And the boys would feel quelled by having an adult, a camp director, in their midst.

At least, that was what he told himself as he took the container of cookie crumbs so Hayley could settle herself on the blanket beside him.

She wore jeans and a cream-colored knitted sweater, her hair loose around her shoulders. Maybe that hair was where the smell of flowers came from. She surveyed the boys, scattered nearby in groups of three and four, and then looked at Nate. "I hope the fireworks start soon. The boys are getting restless."

Just at that moment, there was a loud crack from the next-door ranch. A couple of fireworks screamed up into the sky then erupted in a fountain of red, white and blue. The boys exclaimed and cheered and, for the next few minutes, everyone was rapt with the colorful show.

Snowflake stood, walked to the end of her leash and returned to Jeremy, panting. "I wonder if she's seen fireworks before?" Nate said.

"I don't know." Hayley rose gracefully to her feet and trotted over to Jeremy's group. "Be sure to hold Snowflake tight," she said. "Some dogs are sensitive to loud noises."

"I *know* that," Jeremy said with a respectable amount of sass.

"Of course you do." Hayley didn't take offense, but patted Snowflake and then returned to Nate. When she got there and sat down again, her eyes widened. "Wait a minute. You're a combat vet. Are you sensitive to loud noises, too?"

Nate shook his head. "They do arouse a few memories," he said, "but I didn't get caught in the middle of firestorms all the time, like a lot of soldiers, so I dodged that." As he said it, a sick feeling twisted his stomach. He hadn't seen much conflict, but his brother had. Too much, as it turned out.

"What did you do overseas?" Hayley asked.

Nate pulled himself back from his funk. "I was a Religious Affairs specialist," he said. "Protecting army chaplains, since they don't bear arms themselves."

She tilted her head. "That's one of those jobs I never thought of, but it makes sense that it's needed," she said. "I'm sure having spiritual counselors nearby is super important to people in the armed services, and they'd of course need protection."

"Right." He didn't deny the validity of the job or the importance of the need. He just wished he hadn't taken it on himself when he could have been on the front lines, like his brother. Beside him, watching out for him.

"How'd you get into that?" she persisted.

"Honestly, there was a call for volunteers and nobody else offered," he said, remembering. "I think a lot of the guys didn't want to be around an older chaplain full-time. They were worried they'd get in trouble for swearing or be in for a lot of sermons."

"But you didn't feel that way?"

He shook his head. "I liked it. One of the chaplains became a real mentor to me and was a big part of why I ended up a clergyman."

"God has a plan," she said.

He didn't answer. Yes, God had a plan; he believed that with all his heart. "I just wish His plan had included keeping my brother alive." The moment he said it, his face heated. He was supposed to be the pastor, the one with the unquestioned faith. Hayley was a member of his flock. He couldn't be expressing that kind of wish, something opposite to trusting God.

To his surprise, she nodded. "It's hard to know what He has in mind sometimes." She put a hand over his and squeezed, briefly.

The touch felt like a balm of reassurance. He could let down his guard around her. He didn't have to be the perfect pastor.

It looked like she was winding up to ask another question, so he was glad when an especially spectacular firework erupted across the sky, causing everyone to ooh and aah.

Everyone, that is, except the group Jeremy was with.

They'd moved off to one side and were talking, laughing and bending together over something.

A moment later, there was a whoosh and a flash that had them all jumping back, hooting and high-fiving each other.

Nate was on his feet and marching over before the dust had settled. "What's going on?"

The boys looked abashed. "We, uh, we kinda made a bottle rocket," one of them said.

"I did it." Jeremy was confessing, but there was pride in his voice. "I figured it out in science class last year."

Nate's eyes narrowed. "Where did you get your supplies?" he asked, kneeling beside the heap of foil squares, wooden skewers and electrical tape in the center of the boys' circle.

"It's just household stuff," Jeremy said. "I borrowed it from the kitchen."

A couple of the boys giggled.

Nate frowned. What Jeremy had done was dangerous, but it was good to see him making friends.

Hayley came over then, and Nate was glad to have her approach so that he wouldn't have to deal with all of this alone. He couldn't figure out what an appropriate consequence would be, and Hayley tended to be great at that.

"Where's Snowflake?" she asked.

Nate looked around and didn't see her. "Did you put her inside?" he asked Jeremy.

"No." Jeremy's face was stricken. "She was right here. I... I must have let go of her leash. Snowflake! Come!" He let out a loud whistle.

No sign of the white dog. More whistles and yells didn't bring her running either.

Nate glanced at Hayley. "We'd better start hunting. You take one group of boys and I'll take the other."

"Oh no. Oh no." Jeremy's voice was tight, his face screwed up in an effort not to cry. "I let her go. I lost her. Snowflake!"

Nate glanced at Hayley. "Come on," he said to a group of four other boys. "We'll cover the area to the right. Hayley will take the left side with her crew." In this situation, with Jeremy so upset, he deemed it best to let Hayley deal with Jeremy. She'd probably manage his feelings better than Nate would.

Because she's his mother.

Nate winced and pushed the thought aside. He took his group over the hillside and they fanned out, staying in sight of one another at Nate's insistence.

Ten minutes later, they gathered back at the group area, where the grand finale from the firework display at the neighboring ranch was just going off.

"She'll be so scared of all the noise." Jeremy was openly sobbing now. "Why did I let her go?"

"Everyone makes mistakes," Nate reminded him.

"Nate, could you and Jeremy hunt inside while the rest of us go on looking out here?" Hayley gave him a meaningful gaze.

"Of course." She must want him to get Jeremy out of the public eye, since big meltdowns weren't something boys wanted other boys to see. But practicality compelled him to add, "Is there really a chance she could be inside, though?"

"People have been in and out of the dorm," Hayley said. "It's possible she ran in when one of them opened the door."

"When I went in to use the bathroom, the door was

propped open," Mark Margolis volunteered. "We're supposed to close the door but someone—" he glared at his brother "—left it open."

"Ah."

"I have a feeling," Hayley said. "I think you should look." She didn't say anything more about what the feeling was, but having experienced its power finding the boys who'd been smoking, Nate wasn't about to argue with Hayley's intuitions.

"Let's go," he said to Jeremy, and they headed inside.

The boy was still gasping and sobbing. "I shouldn't have let her go," he kept repeating.

Nate put a hand on Jeremy's shoulder. "No, you shouldn't have, and you shouldn't have made the bottle rockets either. But even if something happened to Snowflake, it doesn't mean you're a horrible person. Just that you screwed up, like we all do."

As he said it, he felt a little shiver, like a whisper from God.

Was the claim he'd just made true for him, too? Even if something had happened to his brother—which it had—it didn't mean Nate was a horrible person. Just that he'd screwed up.

He set that thought aside to deal with later. "Where would Snowflake have gone?" he asked.

Jeremy cleared his throat and wiped his face on his sleeve. "The lounge? There's usually some snacks in there."

"Let's go."

They hunted the lounges on each floor, but although Jeremy crawled around to look under every piece of furniture, the white dog was nowhere to be found.

"Do you have treats for her?" Nate asked. "Maybe

if she hears you shaking the box, she'll come out. If it doesn't work inside, we'll do it outside."

"They're in my room."

Nate followed the boy upstairs and winced at the dirty socks, empty potato chip bags and drawing supplies that covered the floor. Jeremy dug through a pile of clothes in the closet and finally came up with a box of dog biscuits. "Here they are!"

"We'll walk around shaking them," Nate suggested.

Just then, a quiet whine sounded from the other side of the room.

Nate and Jeremy looked at each other. "Was that her?" Nate asked.

"Snowflake! Here, girl, where are you?"

The white dog eased herself out of the narrow space under Jeremy's bed and ran to him, tail wagging.

"Snowflake!" The boy knelt and buried his face in her fur. "You're here! You came back to the room! You're safe!" He was laughing and crying at the same time.

Snowflake plowed into Jeremy over and over, bumping him with her head, knocking him down, even lifting her muzzle to howl a little.

Their joy in being back together was a beautiful sight.

Nate had to force himself to stop taking it in long enough to pull out his phone and text Hayley.

Found Snowflake inside.

His phone buzzed immediately with an incoming call. "You found her? She's okay?"

"She's fine, and so is Jeremy. We're in his room."

"I'll herd the boys inside and meet you downstairs. I want to hear all about it."

Fireworks went off inside Nate's chest. She wanted

to meet up with him and talk to him. And he wanted nothing more than to tell her about it, to see her happiness, to be with her.

An hour later, the boys were settled down and in their rooms. Nate walked Hayley back to her cabin.

And then he found that he didn't want to leave.

They'd been chatting casually about what had happened with Snowflake, but that conversation had come to its natural end. Now, she turned and looked up at him, her expression suddenly cautious.

"Seems a shame to go home so early on the Fourth of July," he risked saying. "Would you want to sit outside and look at the stars?"

Great job, Fisher. Sounds like the worst pickup line ever.

She tilted her head to one side, studying him as if she could discern his intent that way.

"I really do mean just look at the stars," he said.

"In that case, have a seat." She gestured to the swing on her porch. "I'll bring us out some sodas."

The fact that she was letting him stay sent hope soaring through him, as high and wild as an eagle's flight. Probably the wrong thing to feel, considering she'd only said yes when he'd clarified that he wasn't looking for romance but just some stargazing.

She'd made it plain that she didn't want anything more, and a decent, good man would accept that and move on. But Nate wasn't really looking for romance either. Or rather, he wasn't looking for it purposefully, and he wouldn't follow through if he got the chance. His focus had to be on work and service, not the pleasures of a wife and family.

Still, when she came back out onto the porch with two

glasses of orange soda on ice—his favorite, which she must have noticed during group gatherings—she seemed to glow like a beautiful beacon of all he'd ever wanted.

She hesitated before sitting on the swing. Pressed as far away from him as she could be.

That was a clear signal, for sure. But they could still have a friendly conversation, right? "You told me a little about your childhood before, but I'd like to hear more, if you don't mind sharing."

He figured that knowing more about her might quell his desire to get closer. After all, he knew what she didn't know he knew: she'd had a baby and placed it for adoption. Maybe if she told him something about that, he'd realize she wasn't the woman for him, contrary to what his heart said.

She looked at him searchingly and then away, staring out into the darkness. Overhead, the stars were bright and plentiful, and far, far away. A gentle breeze brought the fragrance of sage and the ponderosa pines that dotted the Bright Tomorrows landscape.

"My past is bad," she said finally in a flat voice.

Maybe digging into her history wasn't a good idea. "You don't have to—"

"I mentioned that I got into drugs," she interrupted. "Got in with a bad crowd and went out of control."

"It happens. But that must have been tough." Even though he was vehemently antidrug and avoided alcohol, due to his upbringing and his time in street ministry, he found that he didn't feel put off by her past. He just felt more sympathetic. "How did you get past it?"

"I never did a twelve-step program or anything. I was kind of...jolted out of it."

"Do you want to talk about it?" Nate's heart was pounding. Was she going to reveal what had happened?

She was still staring out into the darkness. "My grandmother, who mostly raised me...well, some stuff happened, and she kicked me out. Which was totally justified, although I didn't see it that way at the time. And then..." She stopped speaking abruptly, her head bowing.

She'd stopped clinging to the edge of the swing while she'd talked, and now he reached out and put an arm around her shoulders. "It's okay. You don't have to talk about it."

"I need to," she said. "She...she died. Before I could apologize to her for the awful things I'd said and done. Before I could thank her for raising me when my parents bailed on the job." Her voice sounded tight, like she was forcing out the words.

He squeezed her shoulder a little and then let go. He wanted to comfort her, but the dynamic between them was different than it would be if she were a guy or an older parishioner or...well, anyone else.

He was too attracted to Hayley to be able to put his arm around her without thinking about possibilities that could never come true.

Couldn't they? Maybe?

"That must have been hard to deal with," he said quietly, keeping his hands at his sides and reaching for his professional counseling techniques. "I'm guessing she knew you loved her and that anything bad you said came from the drugs and from being an adolescent, not from your heart."

"I hope so," she said, her eyes shining with unshed tears. "We didn't have the perfect relationship, but I...

The older I get, the more I realize how much she sacrificed for me. I had no idea at the time. I just felt embarrassed that my grandma wore old-fashioned clothes and shoes and came to every single open house or teacher event when half the other parents had stopped showing up." Her voice thickened and one tear rolled down her cheek. "I didn't know enough to be thankful."

Why wasn't he the kind of guy who carried a handkerchief? "Let me run in and grab you some tissues, is that okay?"

She nodded and he dashed inside and located the bathroom, where he found a box of tissues. As he walked through her cabin on the way to the porch, he noticed the embroidered pillows on the couch and the teaching books piled up beside an armchair. When he saw the Bible open on the dining room table with what looked like a journal beside it, he turned away quickly, feeling like he'd invaded her privacy.

He was also ashamed of himself. He'd expected her to tell him about her pregnancy and had thought maybe that would turn him off from caring about her. But she was simply a struggling child of God, as he was. She'd made mistakes, as he had. And she'd suffered through pain and guilt that obviously still affected her. The right response was compassion, not judgment.

He brought the tissues outside and she wiped her eyes and then looked over at him with a sad attempt at a laugh. "Sorry. You weren't counting on a breakdown when you said you wanted to gaze at the stars."

He took her hand between his own, leaning forward, not looking at her. "I'm glad for the chance to know you better," he said. "And I'm sorry you went through that."

"Don't be sorry for me. I brought it on myself."

He shook his head. "I'm sure there's some of that. We all have free will. But I'm hearing about a girl whose parents let her down and whose childhood was lonely. That wasn't your fault."

Her smile was watery but real. "You're the type to see the best in other people, aren't you?"

He shrugged. "We're all flawed, present company included, but you have a lot of strengths," he said. "There's a lot to...to like about you, Hayley." He'd had to stop himself then because he'd almost said "love." And it was true, there was a lot to love about Hayley.

She hadn't told him about the pregnancy and adoption, though, and he certainly didn't have the right to push her into a confession like that. Especially not when she was emotional from the other truths she'd revealed.

She was looking at him. "Thank you for being kind," she said, and this time she didn't look away. Her hand still between his, she reached out with her other hand, squeezing his.

He couldn't look away. Could not. Even a raging forest fire wouldn't have been able to distract his attention from her warm eyes. They were gray, he knew that, but in the dimness, they shone almost silver.

He extricated one of his hands and reached up to touch her face, drawn almost irresistibly, like there was a magnet attracting him.

She sucked in an audible breath and then turned her face into his palm, letting him cup it.

He felt each pore of her skin, each breath she took. His whole being hummed at this new closeness between them.

It was Hayley who broke away first. She didn't lean away, but rather forward. "Look out there," she said.

With an effort, he did, and was rewarded with the

sight of a pair of mule deer, silvery in the starlight, nibbling on a low bush across the road from her cabin.

"Wow," he said.

"Yeah. They're out there most nights."

"The same pair?"

"Uh-huh. I'm pretty sure."

Nate watched the deer, or tried to, but his thoughts took the sight in a whole different direction. They were beautiful animals, but even sweeter was that they were together, buck and doe, bonded in the silvery starlight.

Nate wanted to be bonded, too. He hadn't been this close with a woman in…well, ever. Not really. He and Hayley had worked together and laughed together and prayed together. Now they'd cried together.

Longing rose in him, so intense that it nearly pressed him back in the swing. He wanted more than friendship with her; he wanted a relationship. To be a man and a woman together.

Of its own volition, or so it seemed, his arm slid around her shoulders and he tugged her a few inches closer. She made a tiny sound in her throat, ambiguous— was it protest or affirmation? He used his other hand to brush back her hair, trying to read her expression.

"Nate…" She was staring at him again, her eyes enormous.

"Is this too much?" *Please say no. Please.*

She stared at him for a moment longer. Then, slowly, she shook her head.

There were all kinds of reasons he should back away, but right now he couldn't think of any of them. Instead, he gave in to the emotions raging through his blood.

He pulled her into his arms and kissed her.

Nine

The tenderness of Nate's kiss melted Hayley, allowing her to relax into his arms.

This was *Nate*. A good man, one who wouldn't take advantage.

She was unused to kissing, just like she was unused to being with a man, but it must be like riding a bike: you never forgot how.

Or…no, that was wrong, because kissing Nate was completely different from the kisses of her teenage years. Even when his gentle touch intensified, making her insides sizzle, it wasn't like the other times. It was tender and respectful and *right*.

At least, it could have been right, if she hadn't screwed up her life too badly for any man to care for her. Too badly to have the right for a loving relationship.

And she was going to pull away. Soon. Very soon. Just as soon as she'd taken the opportunity to put her hands on his muscular shoulders, to bask in the strength of his arms.

He pulled her gently into his chest and rested his cheek on the top of her hand. "Hayley, Hayley. I didn't mean to do that, but I'm not sorry I did."

"I'm not either," she admitted. "I guess our fake relationship just got real."

"I guess it did." He let her out of his arms, seeming reluctant to do it, and then leaned back far enough to study her face. "We should probably talk about what this could mean."

It can't mean anything. The reality of her life and her decisions tried to seep back in around the edges of her joy. But she didn't want it here. Didn't want anything to take away from the sweet feeling she'd gotten from his embrace and his kiss. "Not tonight," she said. "Please, not tonight."

"Okay." He was studying her speculatively, and suddenly she felt vulnerable. Like he could read her, at least a little. But she also felt vulnerable because she was a woman alone with a man in a very tempting situation. Nate was a good man, more than good; he was a man of God.

But he was still a man.

"You should go," she said and stood. "And I should go inside."

He looked like he was going to argue. His brown eyes held emotions that ran deep and complicated. His eyes drew her, with their beauty and their kindness, but they also awakened her conscience. He shouldn't be toyed with if she could never take their relationship to any kind of conclusion.

She backed away from him, unable to stop looking. She wanted to freeze this moment in time. To remember his slightly mussed hair and his breathing, a little thicker than normal. To feel the burning effect of his gaze.

Just for tonight, she wanted to pretend that something between them could work. So she stepped forward and dropped a quick kiss on his stubbled cheek and then darted back out of the reach of his arms.

"Talk tomorrow," she said.

The next morning, the idea of talking about what it could all mean was even less appealing. Hayley hadn't slept well. She'd been wrestling with her feelings: joy with shame, guilt with excitement.

Before they'd kissed, she had been able to enjoy her attraction to Nate without naming it or worrying too much about its implications. It had been an innocent daydream, like that of a girl reading a princess story.

Now everything was different. Now she'd tasted what it felt like to be a woman with Nate, a grown-up woman with a grown-up man.

She'd liked it. Wanted it to continue. Longing she hadn't known was inside her had come unleashed, and she was having trouble scolding it back into its closed box.

It would have been easier to handle if they could have had some time apart, so she could bring her heart back under control. But that wasn't possible because today was the gathering with his family, and she'd agreed to go.

She wished like anything she hadn't. But they'd let the counselors know they'd be gone all day, and the counselors had embraced the opportunity to be in charge. It would almost be more trouble, and would definitely require too many awkward explanations, to back out now.

"You look tired," Nate said when she got in his truck.

"Thanks a lot," she said, deliberately grouchy. "Don't you know that's as much as saying I look awful?"

"I didn't mean…" He trailed off.

"I know what you meant," she snapped.

He winced. "Sorry," he said, raising both hands, palms out.

"It's fine." But it wasn't. She wanted to look good, not tired. She wanted to know whether he'd slept well, whether he'd dwelt on their kiss as she had.

As he pulled out and headed down the road from her cabin, she crossed her arms and studied her phone, not talking.

Unfortunately, she couldn't stop herself from thinking. About how handsome he was, about how he'd wrapped her in his arms, about how respectful he'd been, not pushing any boundaries with their kiss.

She wanted to forget, but that wasn't going to be easy.

After five minutes of silence, he cleared his throat. "Sometimes, when people are unsure how to handle a situation or relationship, they pick a fight," he said. "I wonder if that's what you're doing."

"Mr. Know-it-all," she grumbled.

"If you didn't want to come, you should have said so."

"Who's picking a fight now?" she asked.

"Sorry. You're right."

His easy acquiescence made Hayley feel guilty. "I'm sorry. I'm just…you're right, I *am* tired. And I *don't* know how to handle this situation."

"I don't either." He sighed. "I'm not going to lie. I loved kissing you. But it was a mistake."

His words made her heart leap and pound harder. She felt the same way, but there was a part of her that wished he was unambiguously happy about their kiss. "You're probably right," she said.

"We're still friends though, right?" He reached out and clasped her fingers, just briefly.

His touch had an impact that was definitely not just friend-like. "Yeah. Of course."

"So maybe we should just put thinking or talking about it on hold for today, or at least, for the length of time we're with my family. It's…" He sighed. "It's not going to be an easy day, aside from any difficulties between us."

That didn't sound good. "You were vague about what today's event even is." Beyond telling her to dress casually, he'd seemed to evade her questions.

"Uh, yeah." He turned down a small side road. "It's actually a birthday party."

"Oh, for whom?" Hayley was distressed. "I didn't get a present."

"It's, uh, for me." He turned again.

Now she really felt bad, not having known it was his birthday, not having gotten him a gift. But it did clear up her confusion about why the family was gathering on the day after the 4th, rather than on the holiday itself. She looked out the window as the car slowed.

White gravestones, dozens of them, beside a small country church. "Wait, we're going to a birthday party at a cemetery?"

He nodded.

"Why?"

He pulled into the gravel parking lot and glanced over. "It's my birthday, but also my brother's."

"Whoa." She wanted to question him more, but there were a couple of cars and an SUV up ahead, a cluster of people. Someone was helping Mrs. Fisher out of her car, unfolding a wheelchair for her. Someone else was spreading a picnic blanket.

As soon as Hayley got out of the car, Mrs. Fisher beckoned her over. "I'm sure our tradition must seem strange to you, dear," she said. "We've been doing it ever since Nate moved back and Tom...well, since he left us."

"It's fine, I just wish I'd known. I didn't even buy Nate a gift."

His mother studied her, eyes sharp, and Hayley felt self-conscious. She was a bad girlfriend. A bad pretend girlfriend.

Nate rescued her by asking her if she'd get everyone drinks from the cooler he'd brought. Soon they were all settling down to eat delicious sandwiches, fruit and cake. They talked about Nate's brother and prayed. Discussed how he was happier now with Jesus, because he'd been a Christian—not a conventional one, but he'd believed. They shared funny stories about him, each one prompting laughter and reminding someone of another anecdote to share.

What a strange world. This family, close and connected, and everything Hayley had ever wanted, spent their living son's birthday focused on the son they'd lost. Nate seemed to take it in stride, but Hayley watched his face and wondered.

The sun rose higher in the sky and Nate and his sisters and father went over to an adjoining field to play softball. Hayley offered to stay with Nate's mother, who looked pleased and agreed.

"So I have a question," Hayley said after the others were out of earshot. "Does Nate ever get a happier birthday party?"

"This isn't..." Nate's mother looked around a little. "This isn't actually unhappy to us, but I see what you mean. It's keeping his birthday tied to a sad occasion."

"It's probably sort of inevitable, them being twins, but maybe..." Hayley let her words fall away.

"Go ahead. You can say it."

"I just thought...maybe something more festive would be good for him."

"More festive than a cemetery?" Mrs. Fisher patted Hayley's hand. "I'm so glad you're together. We need an outside perspective. You're good for Nate."

Hayley's stomach twisted. She wanted to be good for Nate and was pleased his mother thought she was. At the same time, if his family knew everything about her...knew what kind of a person she'd been, what she'd done, they'd have an entirely different attitude.

When Nate and his sisters came back over to start gathering things up to load into the cars, Nate's mother grabbed two metal serving spoons and banged them together. "Okay, everyone, I have a couple of announcements," she said. "First off, I do *not* want you doing this for me when I'm gone. No cemetery parties."

There were murmurs and hugs, and someone said "You're going to be fine," but the woman's face settled into determined lines and she shook her head. "I'm *not* going to be fine. Whenever I pass on—and that timeline is in the Lord's hands—you're to bury me respectfully and then go on to have happy lives full of fun." Looking around, she must have seen the stricken expressions on so many faces. "I'll be celebrating, too," she said quietly. "Me and Tommy. We'll be with Jesus, and we'll see you all again."

There was lots of hugging then. But Mrs. Fisher

wasn't finished. "One more thing. We're having a fish fry for Nate's birthday tonight. A real party." She pointed at Nate and then at his father. "And I expect you two men to catch us some nice trout, understand?"

Nate glanced quickly at Hayley and she read his question and gave a quick nod.

She hadn't expected the event to go on all day, nor to spend time with Nate's family without Nate. But she was growing more and more fond of them, and she wanted to support his mother in her wishes.

As they were packing up the cars, Nate took her hand and tugged her aside. "Are you sure this is okay? I can run you home if you don't want to stay."

What she *wanted* was to stay with her hand in his, forever, feeling the strength of it, relishing the closeness. "I'll be fine," she said, her voice coming out husky. "I want to stay."

As Nate and his father made their way down to one of their favorite fishing streams, Nate's thoughts were a chaotic tangle.

Everything mingled in him. His guilt that he and his father hadn't fished here together for more than a year, due to Nate's being overly busy and his father not wanting anyone else to care for Mom. His sadness about his lost brother. His confusion over what to do about Hayley and their pretend relationship and the kiss they'd shared.

And most of all, his own feelings about her.

Every time he was close to her, he wanted more.

He wanted forever. Wanted to live with her in sickness and health, for richer or poorer, for the rest of their lives, like his parents. Wanted to raise children with her.

Wanted to see that sunny smile and hear that throaty chuckle every single day.

It wasn't going to happen. Couldn't. The reason was crystal-clear today of all days, when his brother was at the forefront of his mind. If not for Nate's negligence, Tom would still be alive. He'd be here laughing and teasing and celebrating the day.

Nate didn't deserve a good woman. Not only that, but he didn't know how to handle things with Hayley, given the secret he knew about her past and her biological child.

It couldn't happen, but that didn't stop the wanting.

He should never have kissed her, but at the same time, he couldn't regret it. It had been the best kiss, the best moment, of his life.

He paused at the stream, waiting for his father to catch up, ready to offer a hand if he slipped on the steep, rocky ground. Dad was strong, but Mom's illness had aged him. How old was he now…sixty-five? Old enough to wince when he got into or out of a kneeling position.

The sun shone hot on Nate's back, and the water ran sparkling clear at his feet. Cold, when he reached down to rinse his hand after baiting his hook. He and his father weren't fancy fly fishermen; they fished with live bait, for food. At this time of year, they didn't use waders, either, but wore old sneakers. Working class fishing, Dad called it, and it was the only kind Nate knew.

He watched Dad cast his line out into the stream, his movement easy and assured, the result of many years of practice. He reeled in his line slowly. Then more slowly, then he stopped.

The tip of his fishing pole wasn't moving, so it wasn't that he had a fish on. When Nate looked at his face, it was set in careworn lines, and his gaze had settled on the ponderosa pines on the ridge above.

"You okay, Dad?"

"Oh, fine." Dad started reeling in his line again.

"Are you really?" Nate set his own line drifting so he could focus on his father.

Dad reeled in his line the rest of the way and then cast again before answering. "I'm worried about your mother, just like all of us."

Nate nodded. "It's tough. As a pastor, I'm supposed to have words at the ready, but when it's my own family... I just don't."

Dad didn't look at him. "Not sure how I'm going to do this life without her." His voice choked up a little at the end.

His father would be mortified for Nate to see him cry, so Nate said, "I know," patted Dad's arm, and then focused his attention on his own fishing and on settling his own emotions. He didn't know how to do life without his mother, either.

Eventually, he pulled in a brook trout and, when he looked over, Dad was smiling. "Good job. Now we need about ten of those, or maybe a few rainbows."

"Hey, I did my part, it's your turn," he joked.

"Can't you see I'm sending all the big fish your way?" Then his face went serious. "I've been blessed. It's a wonderful love your mother and I have, and it's been a wonderful marriage."

"I know." Now it was Nate's voice that was choking up.

"I want the same for you." Dad cast again.

Nate pulled in an empty hook and baited it. "We're not talking about me, we're talking about you."

"I wonder," Dad said, "if we never talked about you enough. Tom was always out there, always needing something, getting into trouble. You were the easy twin. You're still trying to be perfect, but you don't have to be."

"Thanks. I… I appreciate that, but you didn't do anything wrong." Determined to get the focus off himself and the uncomfortable truths Dad was revealing, he said, "When something…something happens, to Mom, you know we'll always be here for you."

"I know." But his father's face remained sad. He didn't say what he was surely thinking: having kids wasn't the same as having a wife, a life partner.

His parents had had a love for the ages, and Nate wanted the same thing for himself, and he wasn't going to have it. That was a loss and a regret he'd always carry.

"Son," Dad said, "this is the last thing I'm going to say about it. I'm sorry we allowed it to be all about your brother. We'll do better next…next year." His voice had gone low at the last words, and Nate could easily figure out why.

Dad was wondering whether Mom would be there next year.

They fished a little longer, focused on it and pulled in several more brookies and four beautiful rainbow trout, two each. It was plenty for dinner, and it was a joyous experience to be fishing together. Mom was wise; she'd known what they'd both needed.

As they went to the car, the sun dipped behind the mountain peak, throwing the valley into a premature dusk. A Steller's jay cawed from a branch above him, answered by its mate in an adjoining tree.

Nate put an arm around his father. "Good trip. Thanks."

"We should do it more," Dad said in a sort of growl.

"We will." And Nate vowed to make it so.

He'd maybe done something to comfort his father—or maybe not—but his father had focused more on comforting him. That wasn't how it was supposed to be.

Nate vowed to himself that he'd do better, be a better son. Not perfect, like Dad had accused him of trying to be; that wasn't possible, and Nate knew it.

But he'd try to be a better son, better than he'd been as a brother.

Ten

Hayley went back to the house, riding with one of Nate's sisters and his mother. She sat and visited for a few minutes and then, while Nate's mom lay down, she played with his sister's kids. The older girl, Ava, raced around the yard in her pink motorized car, screeching to a halt just on the verge of hitting Hayley. That, since the child's speed was at most three miles per hour, wasn't scary. The younger one, Brenna, tried to follow along on her bicycle, and she actually *did* run into Hayley, causing her mother to rush out and scold her.

Hayley waved off the concern. "I love playing with them," she said truthfully. "I could hang out here with them for hours."

"Well, Mom's napping and I'm catching up on some work email, so if you're willing, I'll take you up on that. Not hours, but maybe half an hour more."

"Go. They're sweet and I'm glad to spend time with them."

She wasn't just being nice. Spending time around younger children gave Hayley a sharp, joyous pang.

She was getting her teaching degree so that she could

teach at Bright Tomorrows, and she knew she was suited to the older aged children, boys in particular. She had a knack with them. But that didn't mean she didn't love smaller kids. Being around these cuties—who were now digging a hole in the dirt, talking about treasure they might find—made her long for children of her own.

Made her long for her own son.

You made the right plan for him. She believed that. She'd been in no shape to be a mother. Although the pregnancy had jolted her into giving up drugs and alcohol for the time being, she hadn't had a job, and she hadn't been hanging around with the right crowd. Certainly, her baby's father had had no interest in taking care of him and couldn't support him.

She could have kept him with her and cared for him, and she knew she would have loved him, but she also knew he would have had a hard life. She'd had no extended family to help, and no confidence that she could find work. She'd feared she might go back to substance abuse again.

Feared she might be as bad a parent as her own parents had been.

Making an adoption plan had been the only way. She'd never prayed as hard as she had during that last trimester, when she'd been trying to decide what to do. Having no long-term, caring friends to rely on at that point in her life, she'd been thrown into relying on the people at the pregnancy support center, and on God.

She'd read so much about adopted children in the Bible. She'd learned that God considered all His people His adopted children. The frequency with which she'd turned to those verses in the Bible had steered her toward the course she'd chosen.

That didn't mean it had been easy, and it didn't mean she'd felt happy about herself for making the choice. Guilt and regret were feelings she'd lived with daily since handing her child over to the social worker.

She didn't even know his name. She'd felt that naming was a privilege reserved for the person who would actually raise him.

Hayley shook off the memories and focused on the two adorable kids in front of her, helping them finish digging their hole. When no treasure appeared, she suggested that they choose a selection of shiny rocks to bury for someone else to find.

They did that with the same vigor as they'd searched for treasure, focused fully on the moment.

That was what she needed to do. There was a lot to be learned from children.

After they'd all gone inside, Nate's mother came back into the kitchen, looking more rested. She pulled out a bag of potatoes and started to peel them. That made Hayley smack her forehead. "I forgot. I was planning to spend the afternoon making food for a couple of friends."

Mrs. Fisher laughed. "It's your day off! You shouldn't be cooking."

"I love it," Hayley said. "It's fun to make food on a smaller scale rather than for a big group of ravenous boys. Plus, I want to help out my friends."

"What are you making?"

"A couple of breakfast casseroles. You know, the ones with potatoes and sausage and eggs? For my friend Emily, since she and her husband have new foster kids who just arrived. This will get their days off to a good start."

"I know them," Mrs. Fisher said. "That's a kind gesture."

Hayley sat down at the table and pulled out her phone to tap in a list. "Then I'm doing one for Ashley—do you know her and Jason?"

"A little. From church."

"His mother isn't well, and I know they're spending tons of time on the road, back and forth to Denver. Plus, Ashley's pregnant. She doesn't need to spend her time cooking." She tapped her fingers on the table. "I'll put vegetables in Ashley's, since she's health conscious. For Emily and Dev and the kids, I'll leave them out. Veggies don't always go over well with kids."

"Cook it here," Nate's mom suggested. "I'd love the company."

"You're so sweet. But I doubt you have all the ingredients here, and I wouldn't want to—"

"You don't understand," Mrs. Fisher said. "Dan loves to shop at warehouse stores. Plus, he grew up poor and likes to have things stockpiled. Believe me, we could open a grocery store here."

"Well…" It *would* be nice to stay. Easier than stopping at the grocery store and then going home to bake. Not to mention bothering someone for a ride. She pulled up the recipe on her phone and Mrs. Fisher looked at it and nodded. "Eggs, check. Cheese. We have hot and mild sausage. You'll have to use real potatoes and make the dough, but I'm guessing that's not hard for you to do."

"Nope, I would do that anyway. And I'll send Nate over with replacements for everything I use."

"Don't worry about that." Mrs. Fisher grasped her hand. "I'm just glad you can stay."

Suddenly, Hayley was glad she was staying, too. She wanted to spend more time with this woman and she liked making her happy. "Tell me where I can grab stuff, and I'll get started. I'll make a casserole for you all, too, to have tomorrow."

"That would be lovely."

So, Hayley grated potatoes and put together dough while Mrs. Fisher made a salad and rice to go with the fish they were hoping the men would bring home.

"What was Nate like as a child?" Hayley asked as she mixed up flour and baking powder and salt. "Was he always a good boy?"

Mrs. Fisher burst out laughing. "Not by a long shot. He and his brother climbed a dresser and got into their father's shaving supplies when they were barely a year old. They'd egg each other on, see, and help each other." She smiled fondly. "Dan and I were a little older when we had the twins, and I suppose we weren't as tight with the discipline as we were with their big sisters. At any rate, both of them got into their share of scrapes, especially Tom."

Her face went sad for a moment and then she turned from the tomato she was chopping and pointed a knife at Hayley. "You're good at asking questions, but Dan and I realized lately that we don't know as much about you. Are your parents nearby?"

Hayley frowned. "That's a good question. We're in touch sporadically, and it's been a while."

Mrs. Fisher looked surprised. Obviously, her own children knew where she and her husband were at all times. Hayley waved a hand around the kitchen. "My family isn't like this," she said, and explained about her parents and her grandmother.

Mrs. Fisher moved closer and palmed Hayley's back. "I'm sorry, dear. That sounds hard to deal with."

"It was, I guess, though it was all I knew," Hayley said. "I've really been enjoying being a part of your family."

"We love having you here, and seeing you and Nate," Mrs. Fisher said. She hesitated. "Is it okay if I ask you a personal question?"

Hayley froze. "Okay," she said cautiously.

"Do you want to have children?"

Hayley's insides clamped together and she felt like crying. She *did* want to have children, of course, but she'd resigned herself to not doing it.

But wouldn't it be amazing if she could actually have kids, a family? "If I did," she said, "I'd want a family like yours."

"That's very sweet," she said. "I just wondered because…well, I think Nate would be such a good father."

The back door opened and Nate came in. He looked from one to the other. "What did I miss?"

"We were just talking about children and what a good father you'd be," his mother said smoothly.

Nate's eyebrows lifted as he looked at Hayley. "That's a little premature, Mom," he said. "Let's focus on one thing at a time. Hayley and I are still getting to know each other."

Thank you, Hayley mouthed to Nate. She busied herself sprinkling cheese on her casserole dishes.

At the same time, some aching, longing part of her wished he hadn't been quite so quick to dismiss the idea.

Mrs. Fisher smiled. "I guess the bigger question is, did you bring home enough fish, or are we going to have to eat Hayley's breakfast casseroles for dinner?"

"Oh ye of little faith." Nate's father came in carrying a cooler. "Four nice rainbows and six brookies. We could feed an army."

Hayley took deep breaths and tried to loosen her shoulders. Nate's mom hadn't meant anything by asking about children, hadn't known it would pain Hayley.

But what they were doing, deceiving this lovely family, had lots of potential to cause pain.

Hayley needed to think long and hard about that, and maybe talk to Nate about the possibility of changing course.

Nate had every intention of taking Hayley home quickly and then going home himself. Dinner had been loaded with all kinds of insinuations. "So, Hayley, you like to cook family-sized meals as well as for a crowd" and "It's great how much you love children" and finally, "Nate, she's a keeper."

It had been awkward, and the only saving grace had been the happy expression on his mother's face.

Of course, he'd had to show Hayley some affection, taking her hand and putting an arm around her. Far from being a hardship, it had been a pleasure. Too much of one. He'd liked being close to her way too much, had found himself pretending it could be real, could last forever.

That was why he needed to get away from her pronto. But instead, here he was sitting with her on Ashley and Jason's porch.

They'd already dropped off one casserole at Emily and Dev's newly chaotic home, had met the foster kids, praised Landon for how well he was doing as a new brother, and offered encouragement to Emily and Dev, who'd both looked shell-shocked but happy.

Ashley and Jason had been going out the door, headed down to Denver to check on Jason's mother, when Nate and Hayley had arrived with the food Hayley had made.

"Stay, enjoy the porch," Ashley said. "We get a great view of the sunset. And thanks for this." She took hold of the cooler containing the breakfast casserole. "We'll take it along and, this way, we won't have to grocery shop or cook right away."

Nate knew they shouldn't stay, but he couldn't make himself say it. It seemed like it would be mean to Hayley after she'd spent the day sacrificing her time and energy for his family. He waited for her to suggest leaving— surely she would—but after she hugged Ashley and Jason, and their truck's taillights disappeared, she came back onto the porch and settled into a rocking chair.

He sucked in a breath, let out a sigh and tried not to notice the way the golden light kissed Hayley's hair.

He had to do something to get his emotions in check, so he put on his pastor's hat. "I can tell you're a strong woman of faith now," he said, "but the other night—" He broke off, stricken. The other night, the night they'd *kissed...* He cleared his throat and pushed past the awkward feeling. "The other night, you talked about being into drugs and running with the wrong people. What happened to turn that around?"

She looked at him, assessing, then wrinkled her nose and looked away. It was as if she didn't think he really wanted to, or should, hear that story.

"It's not my business," he said quickly. "We can talk about something else. Or not talk."

She looked at him then. "I'm not sure it's something you want to hear."

Oh. She was going to tell him about her baby. And, against his better judgment, he *did* want to hear the story. "I'm a pastor," he said. "I've heard it all. And I care about you—"

"Nate."

"As a friend," he added quickly. "But it's your call."

The sun was sinking behind the mountains, tinting the few puffy clouds with gold. Birds trilled and peeped, seeming to want to share one last song.

Hayley was quiet for several minutes. Just as he thought she wasn't going to speak, she looked over at him. "Among that wrong crowd I was running with, there was this guy."

He slowed his breathing, nodded. He kind of didn't want to hear it, kind of did. He definitely didn't want her to feel judged. "Go on."

"It's not an uncommon story," she said. "We were at a friend's apartment, late at night. Everyone else had gone to bed. I guess he…he thought I was like some of the other girls, not caring who I slept with. I wasn't, but I was too high and drunk to make that clear."

He reached out and took her hand as gently as he could. "Did he assault you?"

"No. No, not really. I just… I guess I figured, oh well, it was bound to happen sometime. I didn't try to stop him." She swallowed hard. "When he realized it was my first time, he just left. I mean…" She cleared her throat. "Right afterward."

Nate's clasp stiffened. Inside, he wanted to beat the tar out of that guy, but he needed to stay calm for Hayley. "I'm sorry. That stinks."

"Yeah. I was pretty upset." She cleared her throat and pulled her hand away from his. "Especially when I realized I was pregnant."

"Wow." Nate blew out a breath. So that was how it had happened.

"I went to him and told him. He called me a liar, said it couldn't happen the first time."

"What did you do?"

She shrugged. "I had no one. No one who could deal with that big of an issue. Not that a pregnancy is just an issue, it's a baby, but…" She lifted her hands, palms up. "It was hard. I felt so alone. Finally, a friend told me about this crisis pregnancy center, and I went there, and they helped me." Her eyes shone with unshed tears. "They were wonderful. They helped me find cheap, safe housing, and a part-time job."

"I thank God for places like that."

"Yeah. I donate part of every paycheck to them. Anyway, they also had counseling, and they encouraged me to go to church, and the people there were kind, too. I figured out what I'd been missing." She gave him a brief, watery smile. "A long answer to your question."

"I'm glad you told me. And I'm glad you got help and support."

She nodded. "Aren't you going to ask what happened to the baby?"

Nate's heart started pounding. Was this the moment he should tell her what he knew…what Stan had told him?

But that was confidential. And in this moment, it might serve Hayley better to just be able to talk it through. "Tell me," he said.

"It was a boy. I nursed him for two days, for the nutrients he could get. And then I…" Her voice quivered and she stopped.

He scooted his chair closer so that he could put an arm around her. "It's okay. You don't have to talk about it."

"Might as well finish the story," she said with a high little laugh. "I placed him for adoption. Or rather, had him placed through an agency."

"That took so much courage."

She leaned forward until she was bent double, hands over her face. "It was awful," she choked out. "I miss him every day."

"Oh, Hayley." He knelt beside her and put his arms around her, and as the sky turned a deep purple, he held her as she cried.

His heart burned with compassion for her, for what she'd been through. At the same time, his mind raced with his double knowledge.

He knew, now, what had happened to cause Hayley to place her baby for adoption. Unbeknownst to her, he also knew who that baby was and where he was. Tomorrow, when they went back to work, they'd be with Jeremy every day.

It was impossible to tell her that. Impossible, too, not to tell her.

Impossible not to feel incredibly close to her after what she'd revealed.

He let his head rest against her back, his arms around her, and tried to figure out what to do.

Eleven

It was the day of the big field trip to the dinosaur fossil grounds. Hayley was excited, but also wary.

For one thing, several board members had said they might stop by the site, including the difficult Arlene. Stan would also be there for part of the day, as he was heading off to see a specialist in Denver. He'd desperately wanted to join this field trip because he'd planned it.

The other thing that was making her extremely nervous was yesterday. All of it had been emotionally intense. She'd realized how much she cared for Nate's family. She'd felt for them in their pain about Nate's brother and about Mrs. Fisher's illness.

But last night…wow. She'd spilled all the garbage from her past on Nate. And rather than judging her or turning away, he'd listened and held her.

He was so kind and so good. He embodied everything she would have wanted in a man, if she'd felt that she deserved a man.

She didn't. But a tiny sliver of light had shone into the dark areas of her heart last night.

Nate hadn't condemned her. He'd heard about the worst mistake of her life and he hadn't rejected her for it.

The bus bumped and jostled down the last dirt road and finally pulled into the dinosaur monument. It was a branch of one of the bigger fossil preserves, but it featured a small museum and a couple of areas where the public could make arrangements to come in and dig for fossils.

They got out, and summer heat hit as if an oven door had been opened. "Man, this stinks," groused one of the boys.

Another let out a swear word, quickly muffled, which Hayley chose to ignore. "We're not in the mountains anymore," she said. "This will make us appreciate how cool we usually have it at Bright Tomorrows."

Stan and Arlene arrived in a luxury BMW sedan that Hayley knew didn't belong to the math teacher. Sure enough, Arlene got out, grumbling about the dust and the bumpy road, and what it might have done to her vehicle.

"Now, Arlene, you wouldn't expect an active archaeological site on a well traveled main road," Stan said. He rubbed his hands together. "This is going to be great."

Stan's enthusiasm brightened Hayley's mood. "I'm so glad you could come," she said to Stan. "This was a great idea."

Arlene snorted under her breath.

The boys were milling around, some gravitating toward the fence that protected the dig site, others toward the museum, which Hayley hoped was air-conditioned.

Nate flashed a smile at her and followed the latter group of boys.

Hayley's stomach flipped as she watched him go.

When she'd gotten on the bus, he'd already boarded and was in the back, and she'd deliberately sat in front. She didn't want him to think that, just because she'd been a total dishrag last night, he was obligated to take care of her this morning, or act as her best friend.

His smile just now told her he wasn't holding last night against her, and joy sparked from her head to her toes.

Maybe this can work.

Stan came up beside her. "Let's put an emphasis on how there are career opportunities in fields like this if the boys are interested," he said.

He'd already sent her an email about this very subject, and it had been in the camp publicity, too, but she didn't complain. "Will do. Maybe you could talk to some of the boys about it as well."

"I'll do that. I'm just here for the first half of the day, but I intend to make the most of it."

A uniformed park employee had come out and was talking to Nate. They seemed to agree on something, because the man beckoned to the boys by the fence. "If you could all come inside, we'll watch a short film before putting you to work on the dig," he said.

They all trooped inside, cheered considerably by the air conditioning and the big tray of doughnuts set out for them.

Nate sat at the back of the room and, when Hayley glanced over, he patted the chair beside him. Her heart rate accelerated and her palms got sweaty.

This isn't a date! It's a science talk for teens!

Her self-scolding didn't slow down her breathing one whit. She sat beside him, grateful the room wasn't bright.

The ranger spoke for a few minutes, welcoming the boys and joking with them, clearly at ease and capturing their attention, which let Hayley and Nate off the hook for discipline duties. Even the counselors seemed engaged. Reggie, who was becoming Hayley's favorite, looked over and gave them a thumbs-up.

Jeremy, Snowflake at his side, was seated beside his mother, looking less than thrilled. She must have insisted he sit with her, and now, she raised her hand. "Jeremy has been interested in dinosaurs since he was a little tyke," she said proudly. "He used to be able to name more than a hundred species."

Jeremy's face flamed red. The poor kid. Didn't Arlene know that boys didn't like to be singled out, especially for an obscure interest like dinosaurs?

Fortunately, the speaker took it in stride. "We may call you to report out on them," he said easily, "but these days, we're finding that the number of dinosaur species is actually in flux. New fossils are being discovered all the time. Maybe some of you will discover one today! And dinos we thought were new species are actually part of another group. Did you know we've found a teenage T-Rex?"

He went on, keeping the boys' interest. Stan said something to Arlene, and she then whispered to Jeremy and both of the adults moved to another seat in the back, leaving Jeremy to move down and sit with the other boys. Good on Stan.

Snowflake moved beside him, still panting, and Hayley noticed that Jeremy kept his hand on her.

"This was a great idea," Nate said, keeping his voice low so as not to disturb the speaker.

"It was, and I can't take credit. Stan wants to stoke

their interest in STEM careers. If it's a hit, they may do more science-related field trips like this during the school year."

Soon, the ranger led them all outside.

"Hey, look!" Booker pointed to the sky.

A hot-air balloon was floating overhead. Hayley clapped her hands and stopped beside Booker to watch it. "So pretty."

"None of those back home." Booker stared upward then turned 360 degrees to survey the area. "Man, I love it here! Wish I could live in Colorado." He gave Hayley a spontaneous hug and then backed away quickly, his skin darkening with a blush. He looked around quickly as if hoping none of the other boys had seen.

They hadn't, so Hayley put an arm around him and gave him a quick squeeze. "I'm glad you're here." Moments like these, she knew teaching was the right career for her. She loved these kids and she loved making a difference in their lives.

The ranger called the boys down to a sandbox-type structure to show them how to dig without damaging anything. Hayley and Nate followed, more slowly.

It was now or never. "Look, I'm sorry about last night," she said. "I lost it, and you were so kind, but it won't happen again."

"It's okay if it does," he said, his voice a low rumble. "I liked being close to you."

She glanced over at him quickly and their eyes met. Held.

Suddenly, it was a little bit hard to breathe.

A throat cleared behind them. Stan. Hayley jumped away from Nate as if she'd been caught doing something wrong. "I'd better go on down and see what the boys are learning," she said breathlessly.

"I'll be right there," Nate said. "Stan, a moment?"

The two men walked off to the side and Hayley went toward the boys, her face burning. She needed to keep her distance from Nate, especially with Stan and Arlene here. She had to get that good recommendation from Stan and from a board member. Nothing could interfere with that.

After the brief lesson, the ranger led the boys over to the fossil field. Soon they were spread out and digging away, with the ranger circulating to make sure everyone was following instructions and being careful.

The sun baked down, even though it was barely 10:00 a.m. The ground was dusty and dry, and a smell of sagebrush perfumed the air.

Jeremy chose a spot near a small resource hut, but a couple of the other boys objected. "That's the only shady spot on the field," Mickey complained.

"Snowflake needs the shade," he said, and indeed, the fluffy dog plopped down beside him, panting.

"Is she okay?" Hayley walked over. She hadn't considered how hot it would be down here in the valley and how hard that might be on a dog bred for icier climates.

"I *think* so," Jeremy said. He looked over to his mom, then at Snowflake.

"Do you want me to ask your mom if she should stay outside in this heat?" Hayley offered quietly once the other boys had settled into their digging and weren't in listening distance.

"Yeah. I don't want anything to happen to her."

"I'll ask your mom what she thinks. And I'll get a bowl of water for Snowflake."

Jeremy looked stricken. "I forgot."

"It's okay." Hayley reflected on what a lot of responsibility an animal was for a boy. Jeremy was fairly mature for thirteen, but he was still a child.

"Remember," the ranger was telling the boys as Hayley walked away, "if you find a fossil, it may be a turtle, a crocodile or a fish, because Colorado was mostly under water at the time this layer of rock was at the surface."

Arlene was inside the building, so, after Hayley had filled a water dish for Snowflake, she went over to the woman. "Is it okay for Snowflake to be outside in this heat? Jeremy wanted me to ask you, although I don't think he wanted to call attention to needing something from his mom in front of the other boys."

"Some time outside is fine," Arlene said. "In half an hour, he can bring her inside to sit with me."

"Sounds good."

Arlene walked outside with her, and they found all the boys clustered around Booker, who was hovering over a small bone. "Looks like the tailbone of a something in the *fruitadens* family," the ranger said. "Good job." He smiled at Booker, and the boy glowed.

All of the campers went back to digging with renewed vigor. Hayley took the bowl of water to Snowflake, who still lay in the shade. Mickey had come over and was digging beside Jeremy.

She watched for a moment and then backed off to give them their space. She soon found herself standing beside Nate.

"It's great to see this," she said. "I think we'll do a program on scientific careers, maybe a movie, if I can find one. Do you think that's a good idea?"

"I do," he said. "I almost always like your ideas." He smiled at her and she felt her face flame. There was no reason for it, but she still felt embarrassed.

Or maybe there *was* a reason for it, because it seemed like his gaze flickered to her lips.

Did he want to kiss her again? Did she want him to?

"Hey, there's a fossil!" Mickey and Jeremy both grabbed for a bone, something they had been told not to do.

"I found it!"

"No, I found it!"

There was a sharp crack and both boys dropped the now-broken bone, looking horrified.

"You broke it!"

"No, you broke it!"

Arlene marched toward the two boys. "What's going on?"

The ranger hurried over, along with Reggie, the nearest counselor. "Okay, men, this is why we're careful with the bones." He knelt to study the bone. Then he looked up at them and gave a wry grin. "And this is why it's best to have everyone dig in their own area. I've seen adult men do the exact same thing you two just did."

"Which doesn't make it right," Reggie added.

"I'm really sorry," Jeremy said, looking miserable. "You can have the shady spot, Mick. Mom, can you take Snowflake inside?"

"I can." She turned to Hayley. "And then I'd like to talk to you inside. You, too," she added, looking at Nate.

Uh-oh. Arlene had seemed friendly when Hayley had spoken with her about Snowflake, but now she was back to being critical. Hayley had no clue what she'd done to change the woman's attitude.

If only she didn't care. If only she could let it roll off her.

But Arlene clearly had Stan's ear, and probably influenced the board as well. Hayley needed positive letters of recommendation from both to do the teaching program.

She looked up at the clear blue sky, then down at the field of fossils. God had created both on His infinite timeline. She needed to remember that her own problems were a grain of sand by comparison, and the outcome was in God's hands.

She shot up a prayer for perspective and then waited to make sure that all the boys were settled in again. The ranger was talking to Jeremy in a reassuring way, and the boy looked a little more cheerful. Good. Jeremy was smart, and interested in science, and having him make a positive association with this work was important. Mickey stood next to Jeremy, listening to the ranger, their dispute apparently resolved.

"I'm heading in," Nate called to Hayley, giving her an encouraging smile, and after another check of the area, she followed.

Arlene was sitting in a comfortable chair and Stan in another, leaving Nate and Hayley with no place to sit. Stan started to stand, but Hayley waved him back. "No, you sit. You're the convalescent."

Nate glanced around the room. "I'll get us a couple of folding chairs."

Once they were all seated, Arlene looked at Hayley severely then at Nate. "That mishap wouldn't have happened if the two of you had been paying attention," she said. "You were making eyes at one another and an important fossil was broken as a result."

"Now, honey," Stan said, "it's not as if the boys destroyed something important. The ranger said that particular bone was from a crow and was recent. No harm done."

"Maybe, but Jeremy was upset. And the point remains." She glared at Nate and Hayley again. "You two need to concentrate on the boys, not each other."

Hayley bit her lip. "I'm sorry if it seemed like we weren't paying attention…" she started.

"I know you two are involved, but you need to keep that out of the workday. It's inappropriate."

Both Nate and Stan spoke at once.

"We're *friends*," Nate said.

"I haven't seen anything inappropriate," Stan added.

Hayley felt chilled in the air-conditioning. She knew she needed to back away from Nate. Now her connection with him was jeopardizing her ability to get her recommendation and become a teacher. That was all-important. More important than anything.

Anything?

The nagging voice in her head stopped Hayley still as the others went on talking about other things.

For the past year and a half, she'd been focused on getting her degree and becoming a teacher. That was supposed to make up for what she couldn't have, the love of a good man, children.

But maybe love was more important. Maybe she *could* have that.

Was it possible she could have both?

She didn't deserve it. But there was that light, shining into her darkness, the door opening a little wider. Maybe the past *could* be forgiven. Someday.

Soon it was time to round up the boys for lunch,

which they'd brought in brown paper bags. They gathered in the auditorium to eat, the smell of peanut butter and the sound of excited boys filling the air.

Arlene and Stan left for his doctor's appointment, Arlene hugging Jeremy and frowning at Hayley and Nate, Stan giving both of them a thumbs-up.

"Let's sit together on the bus," Nate suggested as they started their afternoon activities. "We can talk."

She wanted to, but knew it wasn't wise. "That's just what we can't do," she said. "We're giving people the wrong impression."

"Later, then," he said. "I think we've created enough controversy that we need to hash it out."

"You're right, we do," Hayley said. "But in private." That sounded like she was suggesting more than a talk, and her face heated. "Somewhere neutral. Not our houses."

"I have work to catch up on at the church, once we get back," Nate said. "Why don't you come to my office?"

"Sounds good." But as they figured out a time, Hayley wondered, would hashing it out lead to more togetherness, or an end to what togetherness they had?

In his office that evening, Nate surveyed the numerous emails in need of answers, the notes from the part-time church secretary, and the stack of books and papers that represented his as-yet-unplanned sermon.

So much to do, and yet all that was on his mind was Hayley.

He'd loved being with her today, seeing her excitement about the fossils, watching her skill with the boys, noticing the way the sunshine turned her hair golden. She was more and more at the forefront of his mind.

She was coming to his office in just half an hour.

He'd pulled Stan aside this afternoon to discuss the possibility of telling Hayley the truth about Jeremy. Even though he'd laid out all the reasons it would be a good idea, and pointed out the risks of keeping such a secret, Stan had been emphatic. Nate *couldn't* tell Hayley. He'd promised. The truth would be too damaging to Arlene, who was in a bad place right now, and possibly to Jeremy.

Nate had argued but Stan had held firm and, finally, Nate had agreed to keep the confidence. What choice had he had? The best he'd been able to do was to warn Stan that he would revisit the issue at a later date.

Stan had insisted he wouldn't change his mind, that letting the secret out would be a disaster.

The older man's vehemence had cemented Nate's dilemma.

He couldn't tell Hayley the truth. That meant he couldn't get too close with her. The trouble was, his heart wanted closeness, and a lot of it.

Rather than sitting down and starting to answer emails, he turned to the small altar in the back corner of his office and sank to his knees.

The church was empty and, for a few minutes, he just listened to the silence and cleared his mind.

Then, as always, he started his prayers with his family. Meditating on his brother, now in Heaven. Asking that Mom's illness be cured or that she would continue to be given the strength and faith to handle what came. His father, his sisters, his nieces and nephews.

Hayley. His prayed for her to find peace of mind, well-being and strength. Prayed that she achieve the goal she'd set for herself, that of becoming a teacher.

Prayed for the two of them, that they settle into the right type of relationship, whatever the Lord's will.

A soft ringing sound indicated that someone had come into the church, so he offered his final thanks and rose to his feet. A few seconds later, there was a quiet tapping on his door.

"Come in," he said. His heart pounded like a marching band's bass drum.

She'd changed into a casual dress and her hair hung loose around her shoulders. Accustomed to seeing Hayley in shorts and T-shirts, hair in a ponytail, he was tongue-tied to see how pretty she looked.

Had she cleaned up and dressed up for him? His mouth went dry at the thought.

"Hi," she said, her voice hesitant. "Is this still an okay time?"

"Yes, of course, come in. Have a seat." He wanted to hug her, but he knew better than to go in that direction. "All recovered from today?"

She sank gracefully into the chair on the opposite side of his desk. "I'm a little tired," she admitted.

"Me, too." Nate didn't like sitting behind a desk to talk to people, so he came out from behind it and sat in the chair catty-corner from her. "It was a good trip, though. I think the boys really enjoyed it. Did they settle down?"

She nodded. "The counselors had a brilliant idea. They're showing *Jurassic Park* on the outdoor screen."

Nate laughed. "That's perfect."

They looked at each other steadily for a moment and then both started to speak at once.

"We need to figure out—" he began.

"What are we going to do about—" she said.

They both laughed, awkwardly. "You first," he said.

"Okay. We need to figure out what to do about…well, about how our relationship is perceived," she said. "Stan and Arlene seem to think we're involved."

He started to say *We are*, and then didn't. He needed to let her speak her piece and to see where she stood.

"We're not," she said, directly contradicting what Nate thought, "but we're pretending to be, to your family."

"It's a bit of a mess, isn't it?" Honesty compelled him to add, "My feelings have gotten involved, too."

Her cheeks went pink. "Because we kissed."

"Well," he said slowly, "I wanted to kiss you because my feelings have gotten involved. On my side, at least, the feelings came first."

"Mine, too," she said quietly and then stared at her knees. "But it can't happen."

Her words made his heart plummet, but he cleared his throat and kept going, doggedly. "You want to focus on your goal to become a teacher," he said. "Right?"

"Ye-e-es," she said slowly. "And also…"

"What?"

She bit her lip and then met his eyes. "You're a pastor, Nate. A good man, who deserves a good woman. That's not me."

"Whoa, whoa, whoa." He leaned forward and reached out to take her hand, then stopped himself. Touching Hayley was dangerous. "You're a good person, Hayley. You're kind, and caring, and you pretty much devote your life to helping others."

"Thanks." Now she was looking at him steadily. "But you know what I mean."

"I don't."

She blew out a sigh. "You're going to make me say it, aren't you? I had a *baby*, Nate. And rather than take care of him, I gave him up. I was hooked on drugs and alcohol. That's a whole world of not-goodness."

He opened his mouth to protest.

She waved a hand, silencing him. "You deserve a woman without that kind of a past. A pastor's wife who can be a good example to other women. Not someone people talk about."

He studied her troubled face. "You know you're forgiven by God for mistakes you made in the past, right? That's what Christ did for us. He took on our sins."

"I *know* it," she said, "but I don't *know* it. If that makes sense."

"You haven't taken it in."

"Right." She sighed. "It's something I have to work on, but in the meantime, yes, I'm focused on my goal of becoming a teacher. I can't be doing things that are going to make me look bad in front of people like Stan. Nate, I need him to write me a strong recommendation, and I need his help to get a board recommendation. Arlene's, too, most likely. Otherwise, I won't be able to start that fast-track teaching program in the fall."

"Okay." It was disappointing, but it made sense and, on a deep level, Nate could identify. "I want to make the camp a success, too. And you're right, we can't do anything that might jeopardize it. It's too important for the boys."

She nodded, looking relieved. And then she studied him. "I know why I'm dedicated," she said, "but why are you?"

Maybe it was the evening, or the day they'd had,

that pushed him to dig deep and be honest. "I feel like I have to do twice as much."

"Because…?" She waited.

He shrugged. "My brother."

"Ohhhh." She frowned. "Is that really logical? He died, so you have to take on his life burden yourself?"

"He could have done so much if I had stopped him from going to war."

"Nate." She leaned forward and touched his hand. "Really? You blame yourself for not stopping him? When, actually, it sounds like you only joined up because of him?"

When she put it like that, it sounded kind of ridiculous. It also made him feel defensive. "You didn't know him. He was wild, a hothead. I was the calm, reasonable twin, and I stopped him from getting into a lot of trouble. Just not enough."

"You didn't stop him from enlisting."

"Right."

"So you're to blame for his death and you have to live your life doing twice the work to make up for it?"

"It's not—"

"Did you ever talk to your sisters about this?" she interrupted.

The question surprised him. "No. Why would I?"

"Because maybe they feel similar," she said, "or maybe they'd have another insight into your family and your brother."

"They weren't as close to him as I was. They were older. I was the one who…" Suddenly, he was flooded with memories. Of him and Tom running through the woods, camping out at the quarry, fishing with their dad. He'd never been alone as a young boy; he'd always had Tom.

His chest felt hollow and he didn't trust himself to speak.

She took his hand in hers, gently. "Look, I'm no counselor. But I wonder if, by doing all this extra work, you're trying to avoid the pain of his loss?"

He looked into her thoughtful eyes and pulled his hand away. "No that's not it."

She shrugged. "Okay. It was just a thought."

"Thanks," he said. He had a feeling he'd come back to her idea and ponder it, especially since she wasn't pushing him to agree with her. For now, though, he wanted to put the past aside and focus on the present. Focus on Hayley.

He leaned forward and grasped both of her hands this time. "It would be nice to explore these feelings," he said. "Figure out if it's just...well, temporary attraction, or something more."

She nodded without looking at him.

"But that would jeopardize your goals," he said. *Plus, I know a huge secret about you.*

An image of the three of them together popped into his mind. Hayley, Jeremy and Arlene. So interconnected, and no one knew about it except him and Stan.

Knowing it and not telling her made him feel like a jerk.

"I feel like a jerk," she said, uncannily echoing his thoughts, "for fooling your family."

"Me, too," he said. "It was a bad idea. Unless..."

Their eyes met. He was still holding her hands.

Unless it's real.

She pulled her hands away and stood. "I should go,"

she said. "Can we just agree to keep a little more distance?"

"Around the boys?"

"Around everyone," she said. She sounded a little choked.

He wanted to pull her into his arms, but she whirled around and went out the door. He heard her sandals click rapidly down the hall.

He blew out a sigh and looked heavenward. This was out of his area of expertise. He had no idea what to do.

But she'd suggested something, and since it was his only idea, he decided to do it. He'd talk to his family, see if they had any insight into the past and his brother.

Meanwhile, he'd try to keep more distance between them. Which wouldn't be easy to do.

Twelve

The day after the field trip was that rare thing in Colorado: an all-day rain. Fortunately, Hayley had looked at the forecast and called in a favor. Jason, Ashley's husband, was the industrial arts teacher during the school year, and he'd agreed to spend the afternoon working with the boys, teaching them to make a simple birdhouse in the school's woodshop. The activity was optional—the boys were also permitted to take the afternoon as free time—but most had chosen to participate.

Hayley checked in to make sure it was all going well. Boys were measuring wood and drilling holes and taking turns with a circular saw, closely supervised by Jason and a couple of the counselors. Jason's service dog, Titan, lay at ease in the front of the room, clearly off duty. She thanked Jason for stepping in and watched the busy shop for a few minutes, glad the boys seemed to be both learning from and enjoying the project.

As she turned to go, intent on catching up on paperwork and cooking, Jeremy approached her, Snowflake at his side. "Can you help me, Miss Hayley?"

His sweetness disarmed her. "Of course, Jeremy. Come on out into the hall. How can I help?"

"It's Snowflake," he said as he followed her.

"Is something wrong?" Hayley's heart thumped. The dog was panting up at her, all smiles, but that didn't mean she was okay. Jeremy knew her best.

"Look." He knelt and parted a section of the dog's hair, and Hayley immediately saw the problem. Stickers and burrs coated the underside of Snowflake's body.

"Last night after the movie, we went on a night hike, and she got into the weeds," he said.

"Do you know what to do?"

He nodded. "I brush her every day—well, most days—but my mom usually helps me when she needs a bigger groom. Could you…?" He flushed.

He was at that awkward age where he wanted help, but wasn't sure it was right to ask for it. Wanted his mom, but didn't know if that was still okay.

Hayley had so much to get done. But she also knew sometimes a boy needed some one-on-one time and, truth to tell, she loved that, too.

Anyway, if she went off and worked by herself, she knew what she would think about. Nate. Nate. And more Nate.

She needed to put her confused feelings about the man out of her mind and simply be in the moment with a child. "Get your grooming kit and come over to the cafeteria," she told Jeremy. "You can help me get started on some cookies, and then we'll take Snowflake out onto the covered porch and groom her. I'm not the expert, though. You'll have to show me what to do."

"Thanks, Miss Hayley!" His happiness made it all worthwhile. She let Jason know that he wouldn't have

Jeremy in class that afternoon and then headed for the cafeteria.

Rain beat against the windows and low clouds obscured the mountains. Her emotions felt as wild and dark as the weather outside.

She shouldn't feel so itchy and churned up, not when she had so much. A wonderful job, good friends, a home in one of the most beautiful places on earth.

It was just that she knew there could have been more. She could have found a better way to handle her teenage angst than drugs and alcohol. Could have placed a higher value on staying chaste until marriage.

Or at least, she could have kept her baby.

Although she questioned that decision on a regular basis, she was pretty sure it had been the right one. An innocent baby shouldn't have to suffer while she figured out how to be a self-supporting, drug-free adult.

She walked into the Bright Tomorrows cafeteria, blowing out a sigh. God worked everything for good. Even though she regretted what she'd done, it had helped her have more empathy for young people who made bad decisions. That was what she'd written on her application for the teaching program: she wanted to work with at-risk kids because she understood their problems from the inside out.

It was a plan that had seemed perfect, and enough, until she'd met Nate. Just the thought of him made heat rise to her face.

He'd said, last night, that he had feelings for her. For *her*.

Her mind couldn't help but create images. She could picture walking down the street with Nate, her hand in his, free to move closer, entitled to be open with her af-

fection. She could imagine a candlelight dinner, looking at each other across the table and letting their gazes
linger until they forgot about the food.

She could picture walking down the aisle in a beautiful wedding dress, looking toward the front of the
church to where he stood, handsome in a tux, for once
not the preacher performing the service, but just a man.
The groom.

And, wow, she needed to get those images out of her
mind before she melted into a sappy, sentimental puddle
right there in the cafeteria.

Fortunately, Jeremy entered the dining hall and
headed toward her, Snowflake trotting at his side.

Deliberately, Hayley pushed her romantic thoughts
away. She gestured for him to come into the kitchen
and showed him the industrial-sized mixer. After he'd
washed his hands and settled Snowflake on the mat just
outside the kitchen door, she had him measure out flour
and sugar and baking powder while she softened butter. They took turns breaking eggs and, after mixing
the wet and dry ingredients together and sprinkling in
chocolate chips, the dough was ready.

"It looks kind of...plain," Jeremy said.

Hayley lifted an eyebrow. "Should we jazz it up?"

He nodded eagerly. "Mom puts in coconut sometimes, to make the cookies crunchier, but..." He wrinkled his nose. "Yuck."

"We could make them crunchy another way," Hayley said, warming to the idea. She loved getting creative with her cooking. "What about adding in cereal?"

"What kind?" he asked, looking skeptical.

"Let's go look at our options." They walked over to

the cereal bins. "Cornflakes would work," Hayley said, "or we could crush up the oat rounds."

"How about chocolate rice crisps?" he suggested. "They're everyone's favorites."

"Done," Hayley said.

"Yeah!"

So they measured out cereal, and Hayley added a little more liquid to compensate for the dryness. "Now the chocolate chips look kind of sparse, though."

Jeremy peeked into the bowl. "Do you have more?"

"Sure, but…what about M&Ms instead?"

"Yeah!" He hugged her spontaneously. "You're a fun cook, Miss Hayley."

Hayley's heart expanded three sizes, just like the Grinch, but she didn't want to gush and embarrass Jeremy. "We'll let the dough chill for a bit while we work on Snowflake," she said. "I think outdoors on the covered porch is best, don't you?"

He laughed. "Yes. Mom hates when I groom her inside, because fur flies everywhere. She has a double coat, don't you, girl?"

Snowflake gave a little half howl, half yip in response.

"She seems to talk to you," Hayley said as they headed to the porch.

"She does." Jeremy ordered Snowflake to lie down and then started opening the grooming kit he'd brought.

When the dog saw the kit, she got to her feet and trotted a few paces away, looking over her shoulder at Jeremy.

"No way, I'm not chasing you." He held out a flat hand. "Touch."

Slowly, Snowflake trudged over and tapped Jeremy's outstretched hand with her nose.

"Good girl. Now, down."

Snowflake locked eyes with the boy for a moment and then plopped down, first her front end, then her back end.

"You're really good with her," Hayley said, impressed.

He smiled, his cheeks going pink. He handed the dog a tiny treat and then ordered her to lie on her side. When she complied, he began brushing her, firmly, lifting up sections of her white coat to get at the fur underneath.

"It can take a long time," he said. "But I don't mind. I like doing it."

Hayley knelt beside him and picked out the burrs as his brushing revealed them. "Did you choose to get a Samoyed, or was she just what was offered?"

"She was offered, but we could've said no," he said as he moved to brush the area of fur over Snowflake's haunch. "Mom thought maybe we should wait for a Lab or a Golden, but as soon as I met Snowflake, I knew she was the dog for me."

"I can tell how much you love each other," Hayley said.

"I do. I had to promise to help with her grooming, and I stuck to it. It's my responsibility."

Snowflake lay quietly on her side, allowing Jeremy to continue brushing her.

Hayley ran in, made a couple big trays of cookies and put them in the oven. Then she returned and took a turn brushing Snowflake before rushing back inside to take out the cookies.

In between, they chatted. Jeremy didn't really seem to need help with the dog brushing, and Hayley realized that what the sensitive boy had really needed was a little time with an adult, a mother figure. She was glad to fulfill that role.

She loved kids, loved helping kids, loved this one-on-one stuff. She wanted that. Yes, she could get a lot of satisfaction out of teaching, but if only she could have children of her own, too…well, that would be the most wonderful thing in the world.

Could she have that with Nate?

Again, she shook off the mental images of what could probably never happen and focused on Jeremy. "Tell me about how you and your mom ended up in Colorado."

"Sure. I was born in Colorado, but after I was adopted, we moved to Indiana. I lived there most of my life until now," he said.

"Wait, you're adopted? I don't think I knew that." There was no reason she should; it wasn't a category on the intake forms.

She wanted desperately to ask him how he felt about being placed for adoption. But it seemed too intrusive.

He answered without her asking. "Sometimes I wonder about my birth mom," he said.

"You're not in touch with her?" Hayley's heart was pounding.

He shook his head. "It was a closed adoption," he said. His expression was a little bit sad.

Hayley felt that to her gut. Was her own son out there somewhere, wondering about her, wishing his adoption hadn't been closed?

Her son would be about Jeremy's age. She looked at him, and a strange feeling washed over her. Could *he* be her son?

She'd had that thought about a few kids over the

years, though, and it had always turned out to be wishful thinking. Still, Jeremy's coloring was right, and he'd said he'd been born in Colorado. It was possible...

She wanted to know Jeremy's birth date, but asking him might arouse his suspicions, or worse, his hopes.

She'd never know.

Or, wait...she *could* find out his birth date. It was right in his records.

Tonight, she'd look at the records and see. Even though it would be a ridiculous, huge coincidence, she had to find out the truth. Had to know. Her heart demanded it.

On Friday, after his shift at the camp, Nate decided to head for the church to catch up on the stack of work that awaited him. When he saw the turnoff to his parents' place, though, he impulsively headed in that direction.

There had been something funny in his mother's voice when he'd spoken with her this morning. Something told him to check in.

When he got there, she was pulling out of the driveway, which surprised him. Lately, she hadn't been feeling well enough to drive. He tooted his horn, pulled halfway in and lowered his window. "Where are you headed?"

"To the yarn shop over in Fallsville," she said. "They're open late on Fridays."

Nate squinted. Were her eyes red?

He had way too much to do and zero desire to go to a yarn shop. "Want some company?"

Her face broke into a smile. "I would love that. Could you drive?"

Good. He hadn't wanted to suggest it, but he really

didn't want her driving, especially if she was upset. He got out and helped her into the passenger seat of his truck.

Hayley had implied that he should ask his sisters their impressions of how things had been when he and his brother were younger. But his mom was more insightful than anyone else in the family. Maybe this visit, in addition to giving them some good time together, would help him understand the issues that plagued him about his brother.

Maybe it had been a nudge from above that made him come to visit his parents today. And not just to help his mom out, but to get some answers.

They'd no sooner gotten to the end of the street than she spoke up. "There's something on your mind, isn't there?"

He glanced over, raising an eyebrow. "I could say the same to you."

"You go first," she said firmly.

He drove around the corner and headed for the highway. Fallsville was only twenty minutes away, a pretty drive over mountain roads. "I *have* been wondering something," he said.

"Is it related to Hayley?"

He blinked. "How do you know everything?"

"Mothers know." She sounded smug. "What are you wondering about?"

He kept his eyes on the road. "It's really more about Tom," he said. "His decision to enlist. I've always felt guilty that I didn't talk him out of that, and lately it's been making me feel bad about moving on with life."

She stared at him; he could feel it, even though he

didn't look over. "Oh, honey, it's not your fault he en-listed. Nor that he died."

"I could have talked him out of it. I talked him out of so many dangerous things he wanted to do."

She laughed a little and then tapped his hand. "I know you did. You were my responsible kiddo. But..." She paused, a little out of breath.

Concern for her overrode his desire to hear what she had to say. He slowed the car. "Are you sure you're up for this trip?"

"I am absolutely sure. Keep driving." She waited until he'd sped back up. "Nate, your father and I wanted to talk both of you out of enlisting, but that seemed self-ish. You boys felt called to serve your country. How could we interfere with that?"

A mule deer stopped nibbling a green plant to stare at them as they drove by.

But Nate didn't quite buy it. "I feel like Tom enlisted for other reasons than to serve," he said.

"I'm sure he did, like a lot of other young men," Mom said, surprising Nate. "But the upshot was, he served. He gave his life for his country. I hate so much that it happened, but I'm proud of him. Proud of you, too."

"I wish..." Nate trailed off.

"You wish you could have saved him from himself, but you couldn't. He was always a risk-taker. I'm sure he requested the riskiest assignments on purpose. That's who he was."

"And I wasn't." Nate had gotten into some dangerous situations in his position protecting chaplains. He re-membered rushing a priest to a dying man's side while shooting flared around them and an army jeep burned close by. Remembered covering a rabbi with his body when a bomb blast had surprised them on a trip they'd expected to be routine.

But those kinds of occasions were the exception. He'd also had the opportunity to spend a lot of time reading. And he'd gotten some great mentoring from a couple of the men he'd protected. "I got so many benefits from the military, way more than I expected. Whereas Tom—"

"We can't know what God had in mind," she said quietly. "We never do. But He's in control, Nate, so you don't have to be."

He knew that was true. He just hadn't applied it to his own situation. A weight seemed to lift off his shoulders.

He grasped her hand, squeezed it. "Thanks, Mom."

"You're welcome to my motherly wisdom anytime you want it. Even sometimes when you don't."

He felt a sudden urgency to learn everything he could from Mom, who was indeed wise. There was no telling how much time she'd be with them.

"Look, there's A Great Yarn, the one with the red-and-pink sign."

He pulled in and then walked into the store with her, thinking more about what she'd said. He guessed it had been self-absorbed of him to think he could have stopped Tom, or that he even should have. It was true, Tom had died the death of a hero, serving his country. Maybe Nate needed to focus on that.

Maybe he didn't have to beat himself up quite so much for Tom's death.

The yarn store was a completely alien world, full of women: several sitting around a table knitting, others browsing, a couple of workers talking to them with loud animation. One greeted his mother fondly and they went immediately toward a rack of pastel yarn. Not knowing what else to do, Nate trailed along.

"I'm in the market for a *lot* of baby yarn," Mom said, her voice cheerful. "I'm going to be laid up for a while, and I need something to do."

"We can help with that," the woman said, putting an arm around Mom and giving her shoulders a gentle squeeze. Obviously, she knew Mom's health wasn't the best.

After they'd selected what seemed like a huge amount of yarn and his mother had purchased it, spending an amount of money that made Nate wince, the clerk offered to ball the yarn, whatever that meant. "Just have a seat, and we'll be done in half an hour," the woman said.

As soon as they were settled, Nate turned to her. "Why are you going to be laid up?"

The corners of her mouth turned down. "I didn't mean for you to hear that. But since you did…well. There's a new drug regimen I'm going to be starting, and apparently there are some side effects. Extreme fatigue is one of them."

"Do you have to?" Mom was already weak.

"It's the only option, and your father and I agreed I need to give this a try."

His heart ached for her, and for Dad, and for himself. For all of the family. "I'll be with you every step of the way," he said.

"You're a good son." She looked around the yarn store. "I want to be able to make your sister a baby afghan. I've made them for all the kids, and she just let me know—" Mom clapped a hand over her mouth. "I probably wasn't supposed to tell you. Gina is expecting again."

"That's great news." He looked toward the counter at the stack of yarn the clerk was processing. "That'll make a big baby blanket."

She smiled, her eyes a little watery. "I plan to make a couple for your kids, too. And there's no time like the present to get started."

Nate's heart stuttered. Beneath her words was a clear message: she might not be there by the time he had kids.

He wanted to argue with her, but he knew from his experience doing pastoral counseling that being overly positive could be painful to seriously ill people. So he just swallowed hard. "Thank you. I'll treasure them." His throat closed up.

She put an arm around him. "We know we'll all be together again one day."

"I know." And he'd said those words to numerous people who were grieving, or worried about, a loss. They helped, but they didn't take away the sadness. When his mother passed away, Nate was going to miss her terribly.

"Until then," Mom went on, "don't forget that life is short. Don't spend your time—waste your time—blaming yourself for something that was never really under your control."

"I'll try," he croaked.

"And seize love while you can," she said. "I cherish every minute I've had with your father and with you kids."

Nate wanted to be that way, too. To cherish the moments.

To *have* the moments, moments and, hopefully, years of love with a family of his own.

Before that could happen, though, he had something to set right. Before he could move forward with Hayley, he needed to talk to Stan and explain the new, real reason why he had to reveal the truth about Jeremy's parentage.

So he could try to move ahead in his relationship with Hayley.

That was what he wanted. It was clearer and clearer to him. He'd meet with Stan tomorrow, or this weekend at the latest. He'd *make* Stan see his point of view.

Nate watched his mother make her way over to the table of women to chat, saw her greet everyone, ask about people's kids and grandkids and jobs. The women exclaimed over her and made a place for her to sit down, and soon she was smiling and talking with them.

Nate hadn't even known she had friends in Fallsville, but one thing he'd learned about his mother: she made friends everywhere she went. It was because she was always concerned about others and rarely spent time thinking or worrying about her own problems.

Mom was an amazing person. The world would be worse off when she was gone, whenever that might be. He closed his eyes and prayed her new treatment would be successful, would give them more time together.

Meanwhile, he'd take her wisdom to heart, because she was right: life was too short to waste it on regrets.

Thirteen

Hayley had asked Nate to do their evening meetup in the school office, now serving as a camp office. Now she waited, trembling, for him to arrive.

She'd been on pins and needles since considering the wild possibility that Jeremy could be her biological son. It seemed ridiculous that he would be here, now, the needle in the haystack. But maybe it was a God thing.

Twenty times in the hours since this afternoon, when Jeremy had talked about being born in this area, she'd walked into the office determined to check his birth date. But she had never had the courage to open his file.

Partly, it was because she wanted so much for it to be true. Partly, she was terrified that it *was* true.

And the person she wanted beside her when she learned the truth was Nate.

That thought gave her pause. She'd gotten so close with him, had come to trust him. He was a wise man, even though he wasn't much older than she was. He had the spiritual depth from his training, but he also had courage from his time in the war, and sympathy from all he'd gone through, losing his brother and facing his mother's serious illness.

Oh, he was everything she wanted in a man. Wants that were newly minted because she'd never allowed herself to want a relationship before. She didn't deserve it. Except…maybe she'd been wrong about that.

The weight of the guilt she'd carried for all this time had become too heavy to bear and she was now starting to think that maybe, just maybe, it was misplaced. Maybe she'd been foolish and self-absorbed all this time to focus on her own sins and failings. After all, one of the biggest tenets of the Christian faith was that nobody deserved good things, but through Christ, God gave them out anyway.

Maybe she *didn't* have to be alone. Maybe she had something to give a husband and a family.

Maybe Jeremy is my son.

If it were true… The very thought took her breath away.

It didn't mean she would try to change anything about his life. Wherever her son was, he'd settled in with his family and she had no right to try to make any changes.

But if it was true…if it was Jeremy…

She reached for the computer. Why not access the files right now?

Except that she didn't want to get her hopes dashed alone.

"Hey! Sorry I'm late." Nate came in at a fast pace and plopped down into a chair.

"Busy day?"

He nodded. "I ended up spending a few hours with Mom after my shift."

"Everything okay?"

"Fine." He must not want to talk about his mom, because he was studying her attentively. "You look nice."

"I do?" She glanced down at her plain red T-shirt and denim shorts.

"You look nice every day," he said. "I just don't always tell you." His voice was soft and warm.

Heat rose to her face. Outside her office, she could hear the cafeteria assistants banging pans as they finished up for the evening. The lingering smell of the pasta with meat sauce they'd had for dinner permeated the air. She gripped the smooth wooden edge of her chair.

Her goal tonight was to find out the truth and deal with it, and she wanted Nate to be there. She needed his support.

But she put her quest on pause for another minute so she could just look at him. His dark, attentive eyes seemed to draw her, to reveal the soul beneath the surface. His broad shoulders denoted reliability and strength.

And he hadn't stopped looking into her eyes. Flustered, she turned back to the computer. "I... I have to look something up," she said.

"That's fine. I have this week's paperwork to finish up." He went to the file cabinet and pulled out a sheath of forms.

Hayley took a deep breath and then clicked on Jeremy's file.

There, near the top, was his birth date.

She gasped and collapsed back against the chair. The room seemed to spin around her. As if from a distance, she heard Nate's concerned voice.

"Hayley! Are you okay? What's wrong?"

She couldn't answer.

Jeremy was her son.

Her *son*.

Just this afternoon, they'd baked cookies and groomed Snowflake together. Now it turned out that she'd been hanging with her biological son.

Her heart was so full that her feelings seemed ready to detonate, filling the air with fireworks.

This could only be God's doing. God, who'd pulled apart two souls and then brought them back together. Gratitude filled her, and love for her child.

Maybe it wasn't her right to feel that. Maybe a stronger person would just set the love aside, because her son was with the mother who'd raised him, just where he should be.

But she'd loved her baby from the moment she'd held him. She'd thought about him every day since.

And now she knew almost for certain that Jeremy was the child she'd been thinking of and praying for. Jeremy was her son.

He was such a good kid, so smart, kind, good with other kids and even with dogs. He was tall—tall like his biological father, but with a slightly darker version of her own hair color, her own grey eyes.

But he was anxious, a tense kid. Was that her fault, for placing him for adoption?

"You're scaring me. Hayley, what's wrong?" Nate's words, coming from above her, his warm hands on her shoulders, brought her back to the here and now.

She was too moved to speak. Instead, she pointed at the computer screen and he leaned over her shoulder to see.

"What's that, Jeremy's admission file?"

She turned to face him, slowly. Reached up and

gripped his hand. "You know how I told you I had a baby and placed him for adoption?"

He nodded.

"Jeremy was born on the same day my son was born."

"Same year?"

She nodded slowly. "Nate, I think he's my son." Even saying the words was terrifying. She searched his face, waiting for him to tell her she must be delusional.

The surprise she'd expected didn't appear on his face. "Ah, Hayley. I wish…"

Why wasn't he surprised? But she couldn't think about that. Her mind was racing with her discovery. "I don't understand why he showed up at the camp the very year I started working here. Is it a God thing? He said he was curious about his biological mom. Could Arlene know?"

Nate's expression was…something strange. Almost resigned. Almost as if…

Her heart was pounding impossibly hard. "I just can't believe it! I mean, of course it's possible there could be two boys born on that day and placed for adoption." She flipped through the electronic file. "Could his birth certificate be here? Some of the boys use that for ID, but others use a passport or some other form of ID. And since he's adopted… No, no birth certificate. Man." She searched the application form. "I wonder if there's any other way to tell? I mean…" She was breathing hard, almost panicking. "Isn't this amazing?"

Nate wasn't saying anything and, all of a sudden, his silence seemed loud.

When she looked at him, his expression was peculiar. Set. Again, resigned.

A huge contrast to her own shock and emotion. Why?

A horrible suspicion grew in her. "You're not surprised."

Slowly, he shook his head back and forth.

"You knew."

He drew in a breath and let it out slowly, his eyes never leaving hers. "I was informed in a confidential setting—"

"You *knew*." She stood quickly, paced the office, her breathing rapid. "How could you know and not tell me? We worked with Jeremy together. You saw us getting closer. Why didn't you tell me?"

"Confidentiality is part of my job," he said.

"So if you knew...then it's true? For sure?"

He looked at her for a long moment and then nodded.

She flopped back in her chair, limp as a rag doll. So it was true. The child she'd borne in such pain and suffering had become a part of her daily life.

Unbeknownst to her, and yet known to Nate.

She thought of them sitting together with Jeremy, hanging out with him. Thought of brushing Snowflake with him. "Jeremy doesn't know."

Nate shook his head. "I don't believe so."

She stared at Nate and thought of the time they'd spent together. Talking over everything. Sharing stories from their past. Planning and playacting their pretend relationship, which had started to feel real.

Trusting him. *Kissing* him.

And all that time, he'd known something life-changing and hadn't told her. He must have been hiding it every single time they were together. Her anger about that was a lot more clear-cut than the soup of emotions around Jeremy.

"You knew, and didn't tell me. How can I ever trust you again?"

* * *

Hayley couldn't relax. Even though it was after eleven and she had to be up early, she paced her cabin restlessly.

What was she to do with the information she'd discovered, information Nate, the jerk, had confirmed?

How had he learned about it? Did Arlene know, and had she told him? But why would she have? She didn't go to Nate's church. And, supposedly, the adoption was to remain closed forever. The agency had had a few facts on file about Hayley, mostly medical information, but Hayley had never received any information about the adoptive family.

Now that she knew, how was she to act around Jeremy, who—her heart twisted painfully—was starting to question his situation and to want information about his birth parents?

Her longing to see him, to talk to him and to hug him was as powerful as the pain she'd felt when she'd placed him for adoption. It was as if this new information had opened up a floodgate of worries and settled them all on Jeremy, this young boy she'd just gotten to know.

If she found a way to tell him the truth, if Arlene would even allow that, would that be the best thing for him? Or too much of a shock?

She picked up her Bible and flipped it open then put it down. She was too agitated to read anything, even God's words. Too agitated to think.

She would normally have turned to Nate with a moral question like that. But Nate had known all along and had withheld the information. How could she ever trust him again? As her pastor, her friend, her potential boyfriend?

She wasn't sure what to do about Jeremy, but she did

know what to do about Nate: stay as far away from him as possible for as long as possible.

On Sunday evening, Nate tried hard to make the outdoor worship service the best it could be.

Nature had cooperated with warm, clear weather. The sky was darkening, and every time he looked heavenward, he saw more stars. Within an hour, they would coat the sky as if someone had spilled diamonds there.

The boys were used to the weekly routine now, and most sat quietly. But Nate's heart wasn't in performing the service. His message was basic, probably too basic even for a group of young teens. Even so, he stumbled over his words. His reading of the New Testament passage was lackluster.

Fortunately, Reggie led the boys in some praise songs that were catchy enough to get the majority of the boys involved.

When Snowflake started to howl along, everyone broke out laughing, and afterward, they all clustered around Jeremy and the panting white dog.

Nate joined in, wanting to check on Jeremy's state of mind. Ever since the terrible discussion with Hayley on Friday, when she'd learned the identity of the son she'd placed for adoption, he'd been worried that Jeremy would somehow find out the truth in a way that hurt him.

Of course, Hayley was a good person and was not likely to blurt anything out to Jeremy. She wasn't selfish and she'd figure out the best way to do it. Nonetheless, he wanted to check for himself.

Jeremy was talking and laughing, animated. One thing was for sure: camp was good for him. He looked worlds different from the anxious boy who'd arrived at Bright Tomorrows Camp just a few weeks ago.

Reassured about that problem, Nate decided he needed to go knock on Hayley's door.

He'd spent a lot of time praying about the situation, and he'd sent her text messages and tried calling, too, but she was ignoring him. Every nonanswer flattened him and that, more than anything, told him that he cared about her, a lot, and that he had to make this up. Had to fix it.

His heart rate accelerated as he approached her front door, and sweat dripped down his back even in the cool evening air. He could hear music playing inside.

He knocked then rang the doorbell. Saw her peek out through the door's high glass.

But she didn't come out. The volume of the music increased.

After five minutes, he realized she wasn't going to come out.

He sucked in a breath, let it out in a sigh and trudged away.

He was halfway to the parking area when he saw Stan, walking. The older man usually moved fast, but after his health troubles, he was walking more tentatively. It was easy for Nate to catch up, but first, he had to dispel the surge of anger that rose in him.

Because of Stan, his relationship with Hayley was ruined. His chance of being with this woman he'd come to care for so much...gone. Just gone.

He approached Stan from behind and greeted him. "It's good to see you out and about," he said, going automatically into pastor mode.

The older man looked at him sharply. "I'm fine, but how are you?"

"Okay. Why?"

"You don't seem okay. Your sermon was off."

Nate's eyes narrowed. Great. The man who'd caused all his problems was now judging him.

The moment he had that thought, he scolded himself. Stan had revealed something important and he'd needed to do it. That was what a pastor was for.

"So what is it, Nate?"

He looked over at the man, whose sharp blue eyes seemed to pin him. Then he glanced around to make sure they had their privacy. In the distance, the boys' laughter was audible. The golden remains of the sunset revealed no one else on the dirt road except the two of them.

He'd intended to talk to Stan about this anyway. No time like the present. "Hayley found out that Jeremy's her son," he said.

Stan stopped walking. "What? How?"

"She was talking to Jeremy, and he said a few things…like where he was born. She got curious and looked up his birthday."

Stan's eyes narrowed. "There could have been a lot of boys born in Colorado on that day and placed for adoption."

"She knows, Stan. When she told me, my reaction was not what she expected, and she realized that I already knew."

They continued walking, slowly. Stan let out a sigh. "I suppose it was bound to happen," he said. "With them being together all the time. Just make sure you don't tell Arlene."

Nate frowned. "I don't think it's a secret that should remain a secret," he said. "At the very least, the adults involved should discuss it."

"Hayley and Arlene?" Stan frowned. "I can't imagine that would go well."

"Maybe not," Nate said, "but the longer it's hidden, the more possibilities of problems."

"I don't want to be involved. Arlene will kill me if she learns I knew something and didn't tell her."

"Yeah," Nate said. "Hayley is pretty mad at me, too."

"Because you knew?"

"And didn't tell her." He sighed. "I was going to come to you again to see if I could convince you to be okay with my revealing it to her. Since you told me in confidence. But before I could do that, she found out and learned that I know. Now she's not speaking to me."

Stan clapped a hand on Nate's back. "Women. They get so emotional."

"Yeah. And so do men." They reached the parking lot and Nate turned toward his truck, then turned back. "Are you going to be okay getting back to your cabin?"

"Yeah. I need the exercise." He put a hand to his heart. "I hope you can make it up to Hayley," he said. "Being old and single isn't a good thing."

"But you have Arlene—"

Stan shook his head. "We haven't made a commitment. Anything could happen."

As the older man turned and started back toward his cabin, Nate couldn't help noticing his slumped shoulders and the slow pace of his walk.

Stan was vital, strong, but he'd been felled by illness. Just as Nate's mother had been.

You never knew what was coming, and life was

short. But if he compared his mother's situation with Stan's, it was Mom who'd done it right.

She'd spent a lifetime caring for others and building a family, and now, in her hour of need, they were all there for her.

Stan, whether through personal issues or bad timing, had never married. He didn't have kids, and while he dated, there was no one here for him for the long term.

Which did he want to be? It was obvious. Nate wanted to be more like his mom. Wanted to build a family around himself.

Unfortunately, he'd managed to nix his one possibility of that.

Moreover, he'd done it because of his own efforts to be perfect. To be the perfect pastor who didn't break a confidence. To be a perfect camp director who worked closely with his co-director.

He wanted to be perfect because his brother hadn't had that option, because Nate was basically living for two.

But by trying to do that, he had messed everything up. The conflict had been impossible, with no solution.

With God all things are possible.

As soon as he thought of that one line of scripture, multiple more came to him. He often counseled people who couldn't see any options ahead, and he almost always saw more than they could see themselves.

It wasn't that he was such a brilliant guy. It was the wisdom of scripture.

Casting all your care upon him; for he careth for you.

In the world ye shall have tribulation: but be of good cheer; I have overcome the world.

He got into his truck, but rather than go straight home, he pulled off on a scenic overlook. He sat in his truck and watched the sun set over the mountains. The highest peaks still had snow on them, in patches, and the sun turned them to rose-gold. A few clouds mingled to the west, making the color even more gorgeous.

"What are You looking for here, Lord?" he asked. "I want to be a good person, and I'm failing miserably."

No direct answer—Nate didn't tend to get those—but he did feel an answering warmth.

Why callest thou me good? There is none good but one, that is, God.

If Jesus had said that even He wasn't good, then what business did Nate have with trying to be so good all the time?

Nate knew that the Lord was trying to tell him something by filling his mind with verses, but for now, he couldn't see what solution there was, if any. Instead, he simply felt a growing sense of peace.

Not that he wouldn't have to do something, work hard to try to fix things with Hayley. Not that he didn't have to give the solution to God.

It was all going to work out, or it wasn't, and only God knew which.

Fourteen

On Monday afternoon, Hayley was in the Bright To-morrows cafeteria kitchen, chopping onions and crying.

After the shocking revelation that Jeremy was her biological son, and that Nate had known it all along, she had fallen apart.

She'd sent an SOS text to Ashley and Emily on Saturday, but they'd both been away for the weekend. They'd both called and knew the basic outline of what had happened. They'd expressed all the sympathy and love in the world, and it helped, but Hayley still hurt.

Jeremy was her *son*. She'd given that precious boy away right after he was born. In her head, she knew it had been for the best, and that she had done the only thing she could do at the time.

Her heart was wrecked, though. She had given him out into the unknown. She'd given up the chance to love him, feed him, watch him take his first steps. She'd made it so he'd be placed with a mom like Arlene, who wasn't a bad person but didn't seem to be warm and easy either.

Now, Hayley had had the chance to get to know and

like him as an individual, to spend time with him and get a little close to him. That was wonderful and terrible at the same time.

Nate had known all about it and hadn't told her.

What did that say about their relationship?

The thoughts had circled in her head all weekend, and she'd cried so much that she'd stayed away from church. Even if she'd been able to get it together to get dressed and attend, she doubted she could sit and listen to Nate sermonizing without calling him out. He talked a good game. But when it came to real-life events, not so much.

She'd worked her weekend shifts but had managed to stay in the background. The counselors must have thought she was sick; they'd stepped up and taken on more responsibility.

But that couldn't continue. Work didn't stop just because her world had fallen apart. Kids still needed to be fed, and that was Hayley's job.

"Hey, girl!" Ashley came through the door to the cafeteria, Emily close behind. "How are you doing?"

"She's crying." Emily hurried to stand beside Hayley, putting an arm around her.

Hayley cleared her throat and gestured with her knife toward the pile of onions. "That's why I'm crying."

"Uh-huh." It was obvious that Emily wasn't convinced. "We're worried about you."

"I didn't think you'd be back until tomorrow." Hayley rinsed her knife and covered the onions with a glass bowl. "Man, those are strong."

"What else needs chopped?" Ashley asked.

Hayley pointed to the stack of tomatoes and peppers. "Those, if you feel like helping. I can mix up the dough while you chop."

Soon her two friends were chopping vegetables while Hayley assembled the rest of the ingredients for their Tex-Mex lasagna. Being with her friends was comforting. At least a little.

"So, explain again what happened," Ashley ordered. "You found out Jeremy is from Colorado and was adopted."

"Yeah, and all of a sudden I looked at him and realized we had the same coloring. Blond hair, grey eyes. And he was the right age. Didn't want to get his hopes up, so I looked up his birthday in our materials and..." She paused to collect herself. "It's the day I gave birth."

"Oh, wow." Emily came over and hugged her from behind. "Do you feel sure he's your baby?"

"Yes," she said. "Because of Nate."

"He confirmed it? How did he know?"

"Some congregation member must have told him about it, although I don't know how anyone would know. It was a mostly closed adoption." She bent to grab some baking pans and slammed them onto the counter. "Who knows? The thing is, he didn't tell *me*."

"That stinks." Ashley finished seeding and chopping the peppers. "Where do you want these?"

"Pop them in this pan. So, yeah, he was a jerk and I'm mad at him," she said, stirring. "Most of all, though, I'm heartbroken. I would never have guessed Jeremy was my biological child." Her throat tightened and it was hard to get more words out. "He's such a great kid. I can't believe I placed him for adoption."

"Hey," Ashley said. "You did the best you could at the time. Making an adoption plan can be the kindest and best thing you can do for a baby, even though it has to hurt."

"It broke my heart. Still does."

The two of them sat and talked with Hayley for another hour. They helped her prep food for the next day, as well, lightening her load. Their presence and reassurance, and lack of judgment, was a comfort. They were good friends.

Suddenly, Nate burst through the door of the kitchen, his shirtsleeves rolled up haphazardly, his hair on end, as if he'd been raking his fingers through it. "Have you seen Jeremy?"

"No." Hayley quelled the rush of contradictory emotions that rose at the sight of him. "Why, what's wrong?"

"What's wrong is that he's missing."

Hayley's stomach dropped. Nate was talking to the others, his mouth saying words, but all she could process was that Jeremy—her son—was in danger.

For the briefest of seconds, Nate's eyes locked with Hayley's, and it was like he could feel everything she was feeling. The worry she'd have about any camper, and the additional trauma of the missing boy being her unacknowledged biological son.

Nate wanted nothing more than to pull Hayley into his arms and comfort her pain and worry away. But there was no time. "We were gathering outside for the flag ceremony," he explained quickly. "We did a head count, and Jeremy wasn't there, so a couple of the boys and Reggie went back to the residence hall. He's not there, and none of his friends know where he is."

Mickey came into the kitchen holding Snowflake's

leash. The dog trotted beside him, but she was looking back and forth, sniffing the ground, panting anxiously.

"It's my fault," the boy said in a choked voice. "I wanted to play with Snowflake, and I dared Jeremy to try to make it until dinner without her. He said he could, and he came over to the dining hall early, and now he's gone."

Hayley's face went white and she looked at Ashley and Emily.

"He came in early?" Ashley asked.

"Do you think he heard us talking?"

About what?

"I saw him running out earlier," Mickey explained. "I thought maybe he forgot something at the dorm. Either that, or he was a wreck without his dog. I went looking for him a little later, because I started feeling bad, but I couldn't find him. It's my fault he ran away!"

Nate put a hand on Mickey's shoulder. "No use assigning blame. Let's put that energy into searching."

"Do the rest of the boys know he's missing?" Ashley looked concerned.

Booker stepped forward. "The boys on our hall do. They're all looking for him."

"I'll go organize them into two or three groups," Ashley said. "That's what we did when Landon went missing. We'll fan out from here, where he was last seen." She put an arm around Hayley and gave her a hug. "Don't worry. We found Landon and we'll find Jeremy."

But Hayley looked more upset than ever, and Nate knew why. Landon had started a fire that had nearly destroyed one of the cabins. He'd been close to being hurt or killed himself.

"You stay with us," Nate said to Booker and Mickey.

"You're Jeremy's closest friends. Where does he go when he needs to get away?"

Booker frowned. "There's a trail that goes over to the ranch next door. He likes to take Snowflake over there to see the horses."

"Mickey, you and I will go there," Emily said, "and we'll take Snowflake along. Maybe Snowflake can find him. Booker, you come, too."

Nate nodded. "Good. Nobody should search alone. Hayley." He looked at her and realized she was shaking and nearly frozen. Even though she was furious with him, he knew he could help her stay calm, as calm as was possible. "We'll do the insides of buildings. Starting with this one. There are all kinds of places to hide."

"Yes. Okay." She looked almost blank with panic.

They searched methodically; the kitchen, the cafeteria and then the classrooms. Most were locked, including the shop classroom where the boys had spent time. They didn't talk, beyond sharing quick instructions and reports.

Where could the boy have gone? Nate knew he'd be found quickly—he couldn't have gone far—but there was no sign, and no phone call from the others to indicate success.

They went outside and down to the dormitory, and checked everywhere they could think of, including the run-down shed where the Margolis boys had been caught smoking before.

Hayley was like a wounded deer. She was searching, hard, but she was so shaken Nate wondered whether she could even think.

Finally, he texted Ashley and Emily, and learned that neither had found anything. Ashley and her squads were still searching, but Emily returned with Mickey, Booker and Snowflake. She shook her head. "We didn't find him."

Emily put her hands on her hips. "I don't know Snowflake and her routines enough to know how to get her to help," she said. "Should we call Jeremy's mom?"

Nate and Hayley locked eyes again. He knew they were both thinking about the volatile woman and her likely reaction.

Overhead, dark clouds were gathering. It looked like they were in for a late-afternoon storm.

Hayley glanced upward and then straightened her shoulders. "She might know how to direct Snowflake. I think we should call her."

"If we call," Nate said, "she'll get hysterical."

"We need Stan," they both said at the same time.

Because in so many ways, they thought alike. Too bad Nate had ruined the possibility of a real lasting connection between them.

"I'll run and get Mr. Stan," Mickey said. "I know where his cabin is."

Meanwhile, the rest of them searched nearby areas, but to no avail, and soon Stan was coming toward them at a too rapid pace. Nate rushed to meet him, followed by Hayley.

Mickey had already explained the situation. Stan, who appeared to have taken it in calmly, now called Arlene.

After he'd gotten out a couple of sentences, they all heard her reaction. Screaming.

Hayley looked gray. She was having a mother's reaction, too.

Stan said calming things and got a conversation going

with Arlene. Minutes later, he ended the phone call. "She says to be playful with Snowflake. Say 'Where's Jeremy?' Give her something of Jeremy's to smell. It's a game they play sometimes."

"I'll get one of his socks so Snowflake can smell it." Mickey ran toward the residence hall.

Emily turned to Nate, Stan and Hayley. "Mickey said Jeremy doesn't much like going into the woods, especially by himself."

Lightning flashed overhead, followed by a boom of thunder. Nate's stomach sank at the thought of the timid boy out in the storm.

Mickey ran back out with a whole handful of dirty socks. He thrust them at Snowflake. She wagged her tail. A few of the campers and a couple of counselors who'd been searching with Ashley milled around, watching.

"Where's Jeremy?" Hayley asked.

"Where is he, girl?" Emily chimed in.

She yapped and looked at them expectantly. "Go," Emily said. "Go find him."

The dog just sat.

"Maybe we should get Lady to help," Emily said doubtfully.

"Let's a few of us walk with Snowflake," Nate said. "We'll take the road, since Mickey says Jeremy doesn't like the woods. Stan, you stay at the school building in case Jeremy comes back."

Drops of cold rain hit them as they searched along the road. Snowflake seemed to get into the spirit of it, running and sniffing. Emily's husband, Dev, brought Lady, and the shaggy service dog lent a new energy to the search.

They divided into two groups and took opposite sides of the road, each group with a dog.

Forty-five minutes later, they had combed the entire area on either side of the school road, to no avail. Rain was falling steadily now, thunder and lightning crashing overhead.

Hayley was shivering, and Nate was cold himself, but there was no going back. If they were cold, how was Jeremy managing alone?

A big car came toward them, headlights on, driving too fast. "Idiot," Dev muttered.

The car screeched to a halt and Arlene got out of the passenger side. A man who wore workman's clothes exited the driver's seat and came around to hold an umbrella over Arlene.

"Have you found him?" Arlene asked, her voice near hysteria.

"Not yet," Nate said.

She glared at him then at Hayley. "I blame the two of you."

Fifteen

Arlene's words stabbed at Hayley with the sharp blade of truth. This *was* her fault. She'd been talking with her friends about being Jeremy's mom, and he must have come in and heard her. Evidently, it wasn't good news to him because he'd run away.

Snowflake trotted up to Arlene and sat before her, seeming to cower. Maybe Hayley was ascribing human feelings to a dog, but Snowflake's ears and tail drooped as if she were ashamed.

Arlene knelt and reached for the dog. "Why didn't you stick with Jeremy, girl?"

The Samoyed lifted her nose and howled.

"It was *my* fault!" Mickey's voice sounded choked. "I made Jeremy give me Snowflake to play with!"

"Then you should be ashamed of yourself," Arlene snapped. "Jeremy needs his dog. No telling where he is, and all alone."

"Hey now." Stan, who'd just joined them on the road, glared at Arlene. His voice sounded like that of the disapproving schoolteacher he so often was. "Blaming a child won't help."

"Her son is missing, Stan," Hayley said. "She can't be expected to be calm." She turned to Arlene. "How can we get Snowflake to help us search for him?"

"The...the game," Arlene said, her voice tight.

"How do you do it?"

Arlene straightened, clapped once and then slumped again. "Jeremy loves the game," she choked out between sobs.

In the midst of her worry, Hayley felt glad to see that Arlene could be warm and emotional. Obviously, she cared deeply for Jeremy. That made up for the abrasive parts of her personality in Hayley's book.

"Can you show us how to play it?" she asked gently.

Arlene stood straight, throwing back her shoulders and sucking in a deep breath. She clapped her hands. "Want to play, do you, girl? Let's find Jeremy! Where's Jeremy? Go get him!"

Snowflake barked once and then took off like a shot, headed for the main road rather than the school. The sun emerged from behind the clouds, revealing drips of water flying up as the dog's big paws hit the puddles on the dirt road.

"We need to follow her," Hayley said.

"But what if..." Nate trailed off.

"Any better ideas?"

"Yes," Nate said. "Some of us need to follow Snowflake, but the boys shouldn't all be leaving camp at once. We could end up with more kids missing."

Quickly, he gathered the counselors and campers who'd been helping with the search and, after a short huddle, they seemed to come up with a plan. Reggie took a group of boys back up the road and another counselor took the other half down a maintenance road.

Hayley, Nate, Arlene and Stan followed Snowflake, hurrying to keep the fluffy white dog in sight. At a bend in the road, the dog gave two sharp barks. Minutes later, they heard a boy's shout.

"Snowflake!"

"Is that—"

"It's Jeremy!"

They all started running, and sure enough, there in the distance, a boy knelt by an ecstatic Snowflake at the side of the road.

Relief washed over Hayley, intense and sweet.

"Jeremy! Get off the road!" Nate's voice was stern and deep and apparently caught Jeremy's attention. The boy moved farther onto the berm, looked at them and then shouted, "Mom!"

Hayley's heart almost stopped. Her son was calling for her.

But of course, he wasn't. He was calling for Arlene, who rushed to him. The two embraced at the side of the road, with Snowflake jumping and bounding around them. Stan, Hayley and Nate hurried up to them.

A truck whooshed by and then a car.

"We need to get off the main road," Nate said. "Come on, everyone. You can talk while we head back up to the school. I'll text the others to let them know Jeremy has been found."

They all headed for the long dirt driveway that led to the school. Arlene had her arm tightly around Jeremy, and Snowflake walked on the boy's other side. The dog seemed to smile with pride.

They were almost halfway up the drive when Jeremy pulled away from Arlene and pointed at Hayley. "Is she really my birth mom?"

Time seemed to stand still.

"What?" Arlene's voice was sharp, shrill. "No, of course not!"

Stan put a hand on her shoulder. "Actually...do you remember the research you had me do?"

She spun on him. "You said you didn't find any answers."

"I didn't want you to know but..." He nodded sideways at Jeremy, as if to remind Arlene of his presence.

Arlene straightened her back and looked directly at Hayley. "Did you have a baby?"

She swallowed. "Yes. Something Jeremy said made me double-check his birth date. It's the same date I gave birth to the baby boy I then placed for adoption."

Stan and Nate walked a little away, giving the three of them privacy. But, thankfully, staying near enough to intervene if anyone—especially Arlene, who was red-faced and shaking—lost it.

Hayley focused on Jeremy. "I was poor and an addict, running with the wrong crowd. I knew I couldn't take care of you well. Placing you for adoption was the hardest thing I ever did."

He knelt down beside Snowflake and wrapped his arms around the dog's neck.

"I've thought about you every day since then." She glanced at Arlene and then knelt so that she was at Jeremy's same level. "I think I did the right thing, even though it was so hard. I can see how much you love your mom, and how much she loves you."

Arlene sank to her knees, as well, seeming oblivious to the mud and dirt defacing her elegant trousers. "I don't know what to say."

Hayley gave her a watery smile and then looked back

at Jeremy. "I hope we can talk more about it once we're all warm and dry and have had some time to think. But it's all up to your mom."

Arlene pressed her lips together.

Nate came over and reached one hand out to Jeremy, the other to Hayley. "Seems like a good time to go back to camp. You missed lunch, but I'm pretty sure there are leftovers."

Stan was helping Arlene to her feet.

As Jeremy walked ahead with Nate, Arlene turned on Hayley. "You haven't handled this revelation professionally," she said. "I'll have something to say about that when I speak with the rest of the board."

Hayley sucked in a breath of mountain air, rich with spicy sage, and blew it out in a sigh. The sun peeked through clouds, casting a golden light on its way behind the mountain. A magpie scolded from the fence beside the road. She wrapped her arms around herself, still cold.

"That's understandable," she said through chattering teeth. "As long as Jeremy is safe, nothing else matters."

Her own efforts to control events and do the right thing had gone way off the rails. Now, it was all in God's hands.

The next morning, Hayley felt like she'd been hit by a truck.

Jeremy had refused to go home with Arlene as she'd asked, insisting he wanted to stay at camp with his new friends.

"How can I let you stay at a camp that lets campers get lost?" Arlene's face had been red, as if she'd been about to cry or shout, at Jeremy, or maybe at everyone.

"I didn't get lost, Mom. I ran away. They can't watch over us all the time."

His calm reasonableness filled Hayley with amazement and love for her child. Apparently, it had convinced Arlene, too, because she'd reluctantly let him stay at camp.

Late last night, Hayley had emailed Arlene to ask for permission to talk to Jeremy about his adoption. Arlene's return note had started out with angry criticism but ended with reluctant permission for Hayley to talk to Jeremy, if he felt up to it.

So, after breakfast, she took the boy aside and shared some ugly truths about herself. No graphic details, but a further explanation of why she'd decided to make an adoption plan for him.

He sat beside her on the bench that overlooked the staff cottages and ball field. He listened to her story and asked a few questions. Mostly, he kept sneaking glances at her face, as if trying to process the idea that she was his mother.

"I loved you too much to try to raise you," she said.

"You're not an addict now," he pointed out, sounding skeptical. "You're in charge of the camp."

"You know what made the difference and helped me change?"

He shook his head.

"I found God," she said. "In fact, it started to happen in the halfway house, with the people who helped me manage my pregnancy and your adoption. They were so kind, and so full of faith. I wanted what they had. It took a while, but I read the Bible a lot and started going to church, and eventually, I dedicated my life to

Christ." She studied Jeremy's face. Was that too abstract for him? Did he believe her?

"I knew God all along," he said matter-of-factly.

She started to put an arm around him and then stopped herself, unsure of what level of physical affection was appropriate between them. "That's just one reason why it's so good you were adopted. I'm glad you grew up in a family of faith. Your mom gave you a wonderful gift."

He nodded. "Mom's high-strung, but she loves me."

The confidence in his voice made Hayley both heartbroken and happy. She swallowed hard. *This* was what she'd wanted for her child: for him to know he was loved. By his family and by God.

He gestured toward the playing field below them. "I gotta go play baseball."

"Go, have fun," she said. "We can talk anytime, as long as it's okay with your mom."

She watched him go, her heart warm and aching. It was all so much. So much more, and so much less, than she wanted.

As he jogged toward the baseball field, Nate came up beside him and they walked together, talking with animation.

Nate.

He'd lied to her by omission, and she was furious at him for that. But he'd been someone to lean on yesterday when the world had seemed to fall apart. Her feelings about him swirled like a kaleidoscope.

He'd texted her this morning, offering to take over director duties for the whole day.

She'd texted back. Thanks.

She was furious at him and yet she needed his help

and kindness. She watched as the two reached the rest of the boys and merged into the group.

Hayley didn't know how long she stood there, staring at the group of boys and at the mountain. Finally, she shook herself out of the fog of emotion and turned back toward the Bright Tomorrows building. She was glad to have a day off from overseeing the camp, but there was always more paperwork to do, more meals to plan and prep.

As she approached the school, a colorful vehicle caught her eye. It was a VW, with the top down and two people inside. They must be tourists. She walked forward to redirect them.

The car pulled up to the side of the road and she recognized the man and woman inside it. Her heart skipped a beat then started pounding hard.

"Mom? Dad?"

Sixteen

What could she do but smile at her parents, hug them awkwardly and bring them into the cafeteria for an early lunch?

As she led the way, as they all made polite chit-chat, Hayley kept stealing glances at them. Her father wore wire-rimmed glasses now, and his hair was gray, but it was still long and pulled back in a ponytail. Her mother's hair had a few strands of gray, too, and she wore it loose and flowing around her shoulders. Both looked healthy, slender, youthful. As befitted a couple of fiftysomethings who'd had few responsibilities their entire lives.

Bitterness warred with a childish desire to please them. "Sit down, and I'll bring out some coffee and snacks."

"We're vegetarians," her mother called after her.

Of course they were. They were sensitive to the plight of farm animals.

Too bad they hadn't been sensitive to the needs of their own child.

She brought out tea and coffeecake and plunked all

of it down in front of them. "How did you find me? Or...
you *are* here to see me, right?"

Her mother's smile wobbled. "Of course we're here
to see you, honey," she said in a husky voice. "We need
to talk to you."

"Okay." That must mean something was wrong. Or
maybe they needed something. Money? She schooled
her face into neutrality. In her lap, her fists clenched
and unclenched.

"We're getting older," her father said, "and...well,
we've been feeling some guilt."

That, she hadn't expected to hear. They couldn't mean
what she thought they meant. Could they?

"Guilt about what?"

"About you."

Finally! She lifted her chin and studied them like
she would have studied a camper apologizing for mis-
behavior. Were they sincere? Could guilt make up for
egregious neglect of duty?

A good Christian should instantly smile and forgive.
But Hayley had longed for their love for way too many
years, had written letters begging them to come and
get her, or at least come and *see* her. She'd watched her
grandmother scrimp and save to get her extra birthday
gifts in an effort to make up for her parents forgetting
to send anything. Almost worse were the times they'd
sent something totally inappropriate: a jolly, toddler-
style princess card when she'd turned fifteen, a tie-
dyed shirt in colors she'd never liked and wouldn't wear.

Though she *had* worn it to bed every night for months.

She looked at their clothes now. Expensive, perfectly
fitted, on-trend hippie clothes in flattering colors. Big
surprise.

Her father was speaking again. "Leaving you with your grandmother was the hardest thing we ever did, but we just weren't equipped to raise a child."

Chills ran up and down Hayley's back. She'd just said almost the exact same thing to Jeremy.

"Leaving you with your grandmother was best," her mother said. "Or at least, we thought so. Were we right?"

Hayley thought of the woman who'd set aside her own retirement plans to raise a difficult granddaughter. Slowly, she nodded. "She was great. To me and for me. I don't know if I was good for her, but yeah, she was great." Her eyes filled with unexpected tears. "I wish she were here."

Her mother let her head drop into her hands.

"That was our biggest mistake," her father said. "Not coming to you when she passed away."

"We didn't know until after the funeral was over," her mother said. "We should have come then."

Hayley bit her lip. "The truth is, I didn't know until after the funeral either. I was occupied with other things." Like figuring out how to manage an unplanned pregnancy and deciding what path to take after that.

Her mother gripped her hand, briefly, and then let it go when Hayley flinched.

"We have no excuse," her father said. "We were terrible parents."

Hayley couldn't disagree.

The door to the cafeteria opened and a group of boys came in. Ready for lunch. A minute later, another group arrived, the baseball players, including Jeremy and Nate.

What kind of a parent had Hayley been to Jeremy? Talk about neglect!

If her parents' mistakes were bad, her own were worse.

And when she compared Nate's faults to her own and to those of her parents, his sank into the realm of "not worth getting mad about." Or certainly, at least, forgivable.

No one deserves forgiveness, but God gives it anyway.

She looked at her parents. "Nobody's perfect," she said. "I understand that better than you think."

"Thank you," her mother said. A tear rolled down her cheek.

Now it was Hayley's turn to pat her mother's hand. She pointed to Jeremy, who was roughhousing with another boy while Snowflake sat, eyes bright, ears upright. "See the kid in the red shirt?"

They both nodded.

"I got pregnant with him when I was seventeen. That's why I didn't know until later that Grandma had died. She'd kicked me out."

"He's our grandson?" her father said, staring at Jeremy.

"I placed him for adoption," Hayley said. "I only met him again this summer."

Her parents looked at each other and then at Jeremy. Her mother put a hand over her mouth. Her father's eyes were shiny.

Around them, the noise of an active group of boys rang out: shouting and horseplay. Happiness.

"He's your grandson," Hayley said slowly, working it out as she spoke, "but you can't meet him now. He's dealing with finding out that I'm his biological mom. We can't add more to his plate."

"Hey!" Jeremy ran over to her and stopped abruptly, a few feet away. "Sorry. I didn't see you were talking to somebody."

"It's okay," Hayley said, and introduced her parents by their first names. "How was batting practice?"

"I hit the ball three times," he said proudly. He stretched his shoulders back and forth.

Hayley glanced at her mother, who glanced back. That was a gesture her father always made.

Both she and her mother teared up.

"C'mon, Jeremy!" another boy called.

He started to run off then turned. "Nice to meet you," he said.

Her father gave a wave. Her mother smiled.

Neither of them seemed to be able to speak, and Hayley wasn't either.

She just pressed her hand to her chest and wished Nate were there beside her.

Saturday was the community open house. Nate wasn't sweating it; it was to be casual, informal, a way to build connections between Bright Tomorrows and the surrounding area. He hoped it would be fun.

The boys all wore their yellow Bright Tomorrows shirts, while the counselors' shirts, and his own, were dark blue with yellow lettering. Clusters of campers worked at various stations. One group had set up three tents and built a campfire, demonstrating their outdoor skills. Another group was doing something with paint at a couple of picnic tables pulled together. Yet another group was gearing up for a tug-of-war. A few of the oldest campers had been designated tour guides and were leading people around the grounds, explaining what they were seeing.

The smell of grilling burgers and hot dogs made Nate's mouth water, and the sound of a small kazoo band made him smile. Reggie had dreamed up kazoo-playing as a rainy-day activity, and the boys who'd taken to it were actually pretty good.

He would have loved to share his enjoyment with Hayley, but that wasn't going to happen. She didn't seem furious anymore, but neither was she the friendly, warm companion he'd come to care for more and more. She was calm, but distant, and seemed to have a lot on her mind. Probably some of it being related to the fact that her parents had come to see her after many years away. And then, of course, there was Jeremy.

He'd tried to talk to her about all of it, but she'd politely dismissed his efforts.

The romance between them was gone. He'd lost his chance.

"Mr. Nate, the popcorn machine isn't working!" Booker was beckoning frantically.

Since they'd borrowed the machine from Nate's church, he knew its idiosyncrasies and was able to quickly fix it.

They had a good turnout, which wasn't surprising. The people of Little Mesa embraced the Bright Tomorrows school and camp and seemed glad for the chance to show support. The boys did skits, including one that involved Jeremy and Snowflake, and it was a huge hit. Stan and Arlene were there, and they clapped as hard as anyone.

So, that was good. Arlene was getting over what she'd

seen and learned. Nate didn't know if she and Hayley had talked or not.

Because Hayley wasn't sharing anything with him.

When there was a lull, he approached Hayley. He hated that she looked guarded. "Just FYI," he said, "I'm going to tell my mom the truth about us. That we're not really dating."

"Good," she said fervently. "Hiding the truth is never a good idea."

"Hayley, I'd love to talk to you about—"

She held up a hand. "I don't want to get into it, okay?"

"Do you want to be there to talk to my mom?"

"Maybe for a little bit." Her guard slipped. "I'm near the edge, to tell you the truth. It's been quite a week."

"Then don't come, it's okay."

"No, I will." She nodded toward the parking lot. "Actually, I think your mom is here now."

"What?" He turned and saw his mother in her wheelchair, with Dad pushing it. She looked pale, which made sense. She hadn't been feeling well and he was surprised that she'd come.

He speed-walked over to her. "Are you sure you're up to this?"

"No, I'm not sure," she said, her voice cross. "But I get tired of being stuck at home. I need to get out and see life and people."

"Of course." He took her hand and walked beside her. He was a little surprised that she was cranky, but only because it was Mom, who was always positive.

Even she was allowed to have a down day, though.

Across the field, he saw Jeremy and Snowflake. They'd stopped beside Hayley, while Arlene looked on with a frown. Hayley seemed to notice because she said something to Jeremy, smiled and turned away.

That was Hayley. Always looking out for others. She didn't want Arlene to get upset.

On impulse, Nate waved to Jeremy and beckoned him over. "Jeremy, this is my mom, Mrs. Fisher. Can she meet Snowflake?"

"Sure!" Jeremy smiled at Mom. "You can pet her if you want."

Mom's face broke into a happy expression. "She's a beauty." She rubbed a hand over Snowflake's head and ears. The dog seemed to sense that she needed cheering up and stood patiently for petting, all the while panting up at her with her trademark smile.

"She knows some tricks," Jeremy said. "Want to see?"

"I sure do," Mom said.

Jeremy snapped his fingers to get Snowflake's attention, and gave a command. Snowflake sat up on her haunches, front paws in the air, and caught a treat Jeremy tossed to her.

Mom clapped delightedly.

A sudden idea came to Nate. Would Mom like an ESA? Or, at any rate, a pet?

While his mother continued to chat with Jeremy and admire Snowflake's tricks, Nate walked over to where Arlene stood surveying the scene with a critical air.

"Question for you," he said. "Does Snowflake have any siblings?"

She frowned over at him. "I would think a camp director would have more to do than chat about pets."

So she was in *that* mood. It made sense, given how recently she'd learned about Hayley. Her whole view of

Jeremy and his presence at the camp must have undergone a radical change.

He gestured toward his mother and Jeremy. "My mom's really enjoying Snowflake, and it occurred to me that she might benefit from an emotional support dog."

"And why would *that* be?"

Nate blew out a breath. "She's...well, she's pretty sick." His throat closed and he had to stop talking.

Arlene glanced at his face, looked over at his mother and Jeremy, and then, awkwardly, patted him on the back. "That must be hard for you," she said. "I can give you the name of the organization where we got Snowflake. They're wonderful."

"Thanks," Nate managed to say.

"Swim races are starting," someone yelled.

Nate had agreed to serve as a judge, so he headed down to the pool to do his duty. Then he got caught up in organizing a tug-of-war between campers and counselors.

An hour later, during a lull in activities, he approached Hayley. She'd been talking to a couple of the boys, and they must have said something funny, because she threw back her head and laughed.

He loved that about her; that she was honest with her emotions and always ready to laugh. Not to mention how beautiful she looked, her hair golden in the sun, her cheeks flushed. His heart pounded, being close to her. If only things had worked between them.

She looked over at him and raised an eyebrow, her smile disappearing.

"I'm going to talk to Mom about us now, before she gets tired and has to leave," he said. "You said you wanted to be there?"

"Sure." She walked beside him in the direction of the picnic table where Mom was sitting with Dad.

"Can we sit for a minute?" he asked his parents.

"Always room for our favorite couple," Dad said heartily.

"We might not be your favorite for long," Hayley said, and looked over at Nate.

He cleared his throat and dove in. "We've been deceiving you about being a couple," he said. "The truth is, we're just friends." As soon as he said that, he looked at Hayley. *Were* they still friends? And could his own feelings really be described as just friendly?

Hayley reached out and took his mother's hand. "I'm so sorry. We wanted to make you happy, so when you assumed we were a couple, we just went with it. That turned into basically lying about our relationship, which was wrong. I just want you to know that I…" She swallowed. "That I love your family and I'm sorry." She got up, gave a little wave and hurried away, her eyes wet with tears.

They all watched her go and then Mom and Dad looked at each other. "Should we tell him?" Dad asked.

"I think so. You see," she said, turning to face Nate, "we've known all along."

"What?" He stared at his mother then at his father.

"We knew you weren't a couple," Dad said.

"From the beginning?"

Mom nodded. "It was just wishful thinking on my part, and I knew it. But then the two of you jumped in to say you actually *were* a couple. I hoped that playacting love would lead to the real thing, because you're perfect for each other."

Nate's head was spinning. "We might have *been* perfect for each other, but I ruined it." He looked up at the mountains surrounding them, his heart full of regret.

"Don't you think," Mom said, "that with God all things are possible?"

Nate blew out a breath and looked from Mom to Dad. "I *should* believe that, but I'm struggling. She's not angry with me anymore, but she's avoiding me, which is almost worse."

"You need to find the right way to spend time with her," Dad pronounced. "Somewhere she can't get away and hide."

Mom looked at Dad, and her face broke out in a huge smile. "I have a great idea," she said.

Seventeen

On Monday after lunch, Hayley was cleaning up the cafeteria when Jeremy burst in. "Will you come down to the waterfall with me and Snowflake?"

Hayley's heart seemed to expand and warm and ache all at the same time. Dozens of times each day, she experienced a little shock, realizing that Jeremy was her son, and she was able to see him and talk to him and share with him a little of the love she'd always held in her heart.

She'd stayed in touch with Arlene by email, and the woman was slowly warming up to the idea of making Jeremy's adoption open, since it had basically already happened.

Arlene and Stan had spent time together at the open house. She seemed to have forgiven Stan for his role in the deception. Just as Nate's mom had instantly forgiven Nate and Hayley for deceiving her.

Their examples, plus a lot of prayer, had led Hayley to mostly forgive Nate for keeping the truth about Jeremy's identity secret from her.

Now, though, she wasn't sure where they stood.

They'd been cordial, if cool, to each other during the week since the truth had come out. They'd worked together efficiently.

But the spark they'd shared had gone way underground. Maybe it had been entirely extinguished, from Nate's side at least.

"Will you come?" Jeremy was still looking at her hopefully.

"Of course." She put away her rag and took off her apron. "I'd be glad to walk down there with you, as long as you let someone know where you're going."

"I did."

"You're sure? We can run over and see your counselor now—"

"No! I told him, and Mr. Nate, too." Jeremy's forehead wrinkled, like he was afraid she didn't want to be with him. It was a feeling Hayley remembered from her own childhood all too well. Being rejected by a parent was a horrible thing.

When, in fact, she treasured every minute she could spend with her amazing son, getting to know him better. "Then let's go!"

Soon they were hiking down a wide, well-used path toward the waterfall. The sky was a spotless blue and a magpie scolded from the branch of a piñon pine. Snowflake trotted alongside, plunging into the bushes a couple of times. Jeremy didn't stop her.

"You realize she's going to need brushing after this," Hayley said.

"That's okay. You can help me." Jeremy smiled at her tentatively. "Want to?"

"We'll see." Hayley was thrilled he wanted to spend more time with her, but she also had to remember that he wasn't truly her child. He was Arlene's. Arlene had watched him take his first steps, and gotten him ready for kindergarten, and encouraged him to learn his manners and be kind to others. "Maybe your mom will want to come up and help you."

He shrugged and nodded. "Probably, she will."

Hayley felt bittersweet happiness, seeing that Jeremy was so confident in his adoptive mother's love.

They threw a stick for Snowflake and stuck their hands into the freezing waterfall. Jeremy used a stick to dig in the sand and shouted over the sound of the water, talking about how he wanted to go back and dig for dinosaur bones soon.

Hayley treasured every second, but all too soon, her duties called. "Come on, kiddo. I need to go back."

He looked at his watch. "Not yet. Free time isn't over."

Even though she adored being with him, she was the adult, and she couldn't let him run the show. "I need to get some things done."

Finally, he agreed, and they hiked back up the hill and through the trees to the school.

And she gasped.

There, in front of the school, was a partially inflated hot-air balloon, a rainbow of bright red, yellow and blue zigzags.

And there was Nate, standing in front of it, beckoning to her.

She pressed her hands to her face as she walked to him. "What's this all about?"

"Happy birthday two days early," he said. He gestured to the crowd of boys on the school's porch.

"Happy birthday, Miss Hayley," they yelled, and broke

into an off-key chorus of "Happy Birthday" accompanied by Reggie's guitar and the kazoo band.

She laughed, and clapped, and thanked them, hugging those who didn't mind it.

Normally, she didn't like a fuss for her birthday. She hadn't planned to tell anyone.

But…what a great treat.

"You thought of this?" she asked Nate amid the boys' talk and noise and the poofs of gas and flame the pilot was using to inflate the balloon.

"I did, with a little help from my mom. She's amazing at doing online research to find out birthdays."

"Thank you. And please thank her for me."

"Time to climb aboard," the pilot called to them.

Nate held out his arm.

She took it and walked with him, overwhelmed.

At the basket, the pilot's helper pointed out the footholds and gestured for someone to bring a step stool. "It's like getting on a horse," she said as she helped Hayley, then Nate, climb in.

There was a quick safety briefing that Hayley had trouble hearing over the noise of the gas bursts. Above them, the balloon was huge, far bigger than she'd expected when seeing balloons in the air.

And then the balloon lifted off, as gently as a soap bubble blown from a child's wand, to the sound of the boys' cheers. The heat from the balloon burners had them shedding their jackets.

It was utterly silent, and beautiful. No wind, because they were a part of the wind, floating on the currents.

Nate stood close as they looked out over the mountains and pointed to landmarks, familiar and unfamiliar.

Inside, beneath her excitement, her heart was practically screaming. Why? Was all of this really for her birthday?

She looked over at Nate, taking in his strong jawline and broad shoulders, his relaxed stance as he leaned on the lip of the basket. Finally, she asked him.

"What made you think of this?"

He smiled at her. "I felt like I needed to apologize for deceiving you, in a big way. And I've heard you say how much you like hot-air balloons."

"I've always loved them," she said. "This was so sweet." And not cheap.

And maybe, not something a "just friends" friend would do.

Her nerves sparked and she skittered away from that thought. "Look," she said, "the church! And you can see the cars on Main Street, like little toys."

He leaned close to look, and she could smell his cologne, could see the slight stubble on his face. He glanced down at her. They were so close. She couldn't stop herself from glancing at his lips, and then she looked away, her face heating.

"I want to talk to you about something." His voice was serious.

Her heart started thumping and fear washed over her.

"I've known you so long, and we've been friends. And I screwed up."

She tried to laugh. "Yeah, you did."

"I'm so sorry, Hayley. I made a big mistake, not finding a way to be open with you. I hurt you and I apologize for that. With all my heart."

"I've already forgiven you." Reading the doubt in his eyes, she squeezed his hand. "Somebody wise once told me that everyone makes mistakes. I guess that's even true for a pastor."

He laughed a little. "It is." His eyes crinkled. "You know how we've faked having a relationship?"

She nodded.

"I want to make it real."

Her heart rate jumped a few more levels. The giant balloon above them, the pilot's discreet presence, the trees and rivers rushing by below…all of it seemed to fall away and there was only Nate's face, his serious eyes.

"What are you talking about when you say you want to make it real?" Sudden insecurity washed over her and she was once again the little girl whose parents claimed to love her but didn't show it in their actions.

He studied her then brushed a hand over her hair. "Things can change in a moment, and life is short." He reached into his pocket, pulled something out and sank to his knees. "Hayley, when I say I want to make it real, what I mean is…will you marry me?"

Nate's head was spinning, and not from the gentle motion of the balloon. It was from his own actions.

What on earth was he doing on his knees?

The floor was hard plywood, its edges bound in leather just as the borders of the basket were. When he looked up, he saw controlled gas flames and the riot of glowing colors that made up the balloon.

But most of all, he saw Hayley's stunned face.

He'd intended to ask her to try dating him. Maybe, if he sensed she was on board, to suggest an exclusive relationship.

He'd had no intention of pulling out the ring in his pocket. Or at least, not much of one. It was way too soon.

When that lost, sad expression had flashed over her face, though, he'd skipped right over the preliminaries. He'd sensed, maybe wrongly, that she needed the re-assurance of knowing the whole scope of his feelings.

But did that mean he had to jump the gun and pro-pose marriage?

He got to his feet and put a hand on her shoulder. "Listen, I'm sorry. That was way too rushed."

She looked shell-shocked.

The balloon floated along, heat from the burners making his already hot face hotter. He looked down at the fields below, trying to find his grounding. But it wasn't there, of course. He let his eyes close for just a moment. Every ounce of the poise he used to lead a con-gregation, every bit of courage he'd summoned while serving overseas, seemed to have deserted him.

I'm messing this up, Lord. Help!

Since Hayley still hadn't said anything, he blundered on. "I just... I have the ring. It's my mom's engagement ring. She wants me to give it to the woman I marry." He held the open box out to her.

Hayley looked at it, eyes wide. "Doesn't she want to wear her ring?"

"It doesn't fit her anymore." His throat tightened on the words as he pictured Mom's thin hands.

Hayley put her hand to her heart, her mouth twist-ing. "Oh no. I'm sorry."

"Don't be. It made her so happy to give it to me. To us." He swallowed hard. "But I get it, it's way too soon. I should just be grateful you'd go on this ride with me and let me apologize."

"Of course," she said faintly.

"Hayley, meeting you was the best day of my life.

And becoming your friend has made these past couple of years happy, in spite of everything my family's been going through."

"I'm glad." Her head tilted and she studied him as she leaned back against the edge of the basket. That was Hayley. She always seemed to *see* him.

Behind her, the scenic mountains flew by, and with them, the time for their ride. He needed to speak his piece.

"I'm a mess," he confessed. "I've been trying to avoid having any happiness my brother couldn't have. But I've realized that's the wrong focus. I want to make you happy, because you deserve it. *That's* what will make me happy."

She made a protesting sound.

"Your smile, and your laugh, and the way we talk together, and how we manage things. Just guessing here, but I think that if we can manage a camp full of at-risk boys together, we'd be great at making a family."

Her eyes widened and she sucked in an audible breath.

He was digging himself in deeper. In addition to proposing, he was talking about starting a family. What was wrong with him?

Yet inside, he knew he wanted to spend the rest of his life with this woman. Wanted to father children with her, to raise a family together. He'd spent so much time praying this past week and God had given him peace about it.

He'd just jumped the gun a little on the timing. Okay, a lot. A woman like Haley needed to be romanced slowly. She was truly worth it. She deserved it.

"I'm in love with you, Hayley. But don't worry. I'm not really proposing."

She blinked and shook her head, rapidly, and then started to laugh. "Are you asking me to marry you or aren't you?"

She was smiling big now, and that made him smile, too. She wasn't the type to hold it against him, the fact that he was incredibly awkward at this. "I would be asking, except it's too soon."

She took his hand. "Nate. Let me talk a minute."

"Of course." He blew out a breath and lifted his warm cheeks to feel the breeze.

"I really care for you, too," she said. "I always have."

His heart stuttered. Was this the beginning of a yes or the beginning of a no?

"In the past, I didn't think I deserved love. But now I'm starting to hope that maybe I do."

"You do. So much."

Their gazes locked.

He had to know. "Will you try a relationship with me?"

She shook her head. "No way."

His heart sank.

"Why would I just *try* a relationship when what I want is to marry you?"

"You want to…" Joy washed over him. "You don't have to…" He stared at her.

She held up a hand. "As long as you're singing my praises, let me sing yours, okay? I love your strength, and your gentleness, and the way you listen. I love watching you with the boys, your patience and your sense of fun. You treat me well." She shrugged. "We're good together, really good. What more could I want?"

What more could *he* want? He leaned forward and kissed her.

Epilogue

One Year Later

"We made it through another summer!" Hayley raised her hands over her head like a cheerleader and then looked around at the assembled guests. "Thank you all so much for what you've done for the Bright Tomorrows camp."

It was the end-of-summer staff celebration, with a few additional guests as well.

Ashley stood beside her. "I'm happy to announce that ten of the boys from this year's camp have put in applications to attend high school here. Combined with the eight from last year, we're on track with our enrolment goals."

A cheer went up and Hayley hugged Ashley. Between the military readiness program that Ashley and Jason had developed, and the success of the summer camps, the academy was thriving. They could all continue their work helping boys who needed a hand up.

It made Hayley happy that Booker, who'd learned to love Colorado, would be attending the academy again this year.

Jeremy would attend for his sophomore year, too, as a day student.

"Eat up, everyone!" Hayley said, gesturing toward the picnic tables laden with food. Although she was certified as a teacher now, and would work here in that capacity come fall, she still loved feeding people. She'd prepared most of the food for this end-of-summer gathering outside the Bright Tomorrows cafeteria.

"I've got to check on the baby," Ashley said, and hurried over to Jason, who was holding little Miranda. At the same table were Emily and Dev and their four kids—Landon and the three siblings they'd adopted.

Hayley surveyed the group to make sure everyone seemed happy and settled. Jeremy was tugging Arlene toward the table next to Emily and Dev and their kids, where Stan already sat. Stan had recovered fully from his heart attack but had decided to take things easy this summer rather than coming back to directing the camp full-time. Now that he and Arlene were married, and he was helping her to raise Jeremy, his life was full. He was great with Jeremy and was a calming force for Arlene, from what Hayley could see.

She was still amazed and grateful that she could be part of Jeremy's life, could see him regularly and watch him grow.

Snowflake was nudging at Titan, Dev's mastiff, but the big dog refused to be baited into playing; instead, he flopped down onto his side next to Dev. Snowflake gave up and went over to Lady, Emily's poodle mix. Emily smiled and let Lady out of the harness, and the two dogs began to chase each other around and around the happy group.

In the parking lot, a colorful VW pulled up next to the other cars, and Hayley's mom and dad got out.

Hayley walked over to greet them. Their relationship wasn't perfect, but her parents were trying, motivated largely by the opportunity to spend time around their grandson. Her father, especially, looked hungrily around until he spotted Jeremy, and then he nudged Hayley's mother and pointed. Jeremy waved to them and then went back to an intent conversation he was having with Emily and Dev's oldest foster son.

Mom and Dad would never have a real grandparenting relationship with Jeremy; it wasn't their right, any more than Hayley could become his full-time mother. But they saw him occasionally and sent him gifts from their travels. Although they did more for Jeremy than they'd ever done for Hayley, she'd released her anger toward them with Nate's help.

Nate. Her husband, the man of her dreams.

She looked around and spotted him. He was sitting at the end of one of the picnic tables with his parents, and she headed over that way. Nate's mother—her mother-in-law, whom she now called Mom—looked flushed and happy. The new treatment had sent her into remission, and although she still used a wheelchair sometimes and had to pace herself, she was an integral part of the family. Hopefully, that would be the case for a few years to come, at least.

As Hayley approached, Nate stood and came to greet her, hugging her and then taking her hand to lead her over to the table. "Come on. Mom says she has a gift for us."

Hayley lifted her eyebrows. "What's the occasion? She already got me a bunch of stuff for my birthday." Indeed, Nate's family seemed intent on showering Hayley with gifts and love, letting her know that she was fully accepted and loved.

Hayley adored them all.

Nate's mother gestured to his father, who pulled out a big brightly wrapped package from under the table. "This is for the two of you," he said. "At least, partly."

"You open it," Nate said, his arm around her.

She kissed her mother-in-law's cheek and then ripped open the package. Nestled in tissue paper was a gorgeous knitted blanket, its mix of pastels suggesting its purpose.

She looked quickly at Nate. "It's a baby blanket," she said, confused. "Did you—"

He lifted his hands, palms out. "I didn't tell them, I promise."

His mother reached out and took Hayley's hand. "I could tell from your glow," she said. "I always know. And I'm absolutely thrilled that you two are expecting."

"Oh, Mom." Tears rose to her eyes and she hugged her mother-in-law and then her father-in-law. "We're thrilled, too." She admired the beautiful blanket, folded it carefully and put it in the box for safekeeping, and then went back to Nate, who wrapped his arms around her. "Are you upset they found out?"

She shook her head. "I could never be upset about that," she said. "And now that the first trimester's safely passed, I guess we can start spreading the news."

"I feel like shouting it from the mountaintops," he said. "I'm the happiest I've ever been, married to you. But I have a feeling our baby will complete the circle."

"Only one?"

"We've talked about that. As many as you want."

Hayley's very soul felt full. She had a wonderful man, a wonderful family, friends, work, and a baby on the way.

"God is so good," she whispered. "So much more than we deserve."

"That's God for you," he said.

She kissed Nate's cheek and sent up a heartfelt prayer of thanks.

* * * * *